CARROLL & GRAF

Lily of the Valley

Lily of the Valley

Honoré de Balzac

translated by

Lucienne Hill

CARROLL & GRAF PUBLISHERS, INC.
NEW YORK

First Carroll & Graf edition 1989
Second edition 1997

Carroll & Graf Publishers, Inc.
19 West 21st Street
New York, NY 10010-6805

Library of Congress Cataloging-in-Publication Data
   Balzac, Honoré de, 1799–1850.
      [Lys dans la vallée. English]
      Lily of the valley / Honoré de Balzac : translated by
   Lucienne Hill. — 2nd ed.
        p.   cm.
     ISBN 0-7867-0471-3
     I. Hill, Lucienne. II. Title.
   PQ2167.L8E5   1997
   843'.7—dc21   97-17484
                                                     CIP

Manufactured in the United States of America

Lily of the Valley

To Madame la Comtesse Natalie de Manerville:

I bow to your wish. It is the privilege of the woman whom we love more than she loves us, to make us forget at every turn the rules of common sense. Rather than see a line appear on your brows, to dispel the expression of displeasure on those mouths which the least refusal saddens, we span miraculous distances, we shed our blood, we spend the future. To-day, you want my past. Here it is. But remember this, Natalie: in obeying you, I have had to ride roughshod over a hitherto inviolate reticence.

Why suspect the deep reveries which seize me, suddenly, when I am at my happiest? Why those pretty flashes of feminine temper at a lover's silence? Could you not play with the contrasts in my nature without enquiring into their causes? Are there, in your heart, secrets which need mine in order to be absolved?

However, Natalie, as you have guessed, it is perhaps better that you should know all. Yes, my life is dominated by a ghost; it takes shape dimly at the slightest word which calls it up; it often flutters uninvited above my head. I have weighty memories shrouded in my soul, like those products of the sea which one glimpses in calm weather and which the stormy waves cast up in fragments on the shore. Although the work ideas require for their expression has curbed those old emotions, which cause me so much pain when they awake too suddenly, should there be in this confession outbursts which might wound you, remember that you threatened me if I did not obey. Do not punish me then, for having done your bidding. I should like my confidence to redouble your affection.

Until to-night.

Félix.

What unknown talent, fed with tears, will some day give us the most moving elegy; the portrayal of torments undergone in silence by souls whose still tender roots meet nothing but hard pebbles in the soil of home; whose first green shoots are torn by hate-filled hands, whose flowers are nipped by frost just as they open? What poet will sing the heartaches of the child whose lips have sucked a bitter breast, whose smiles are driven back by the consuming fire of a stern eye?

A work of fiction which told of these poor souls, oppressed by the very beings placed around them to foster the unfolding of their sensibility, would be the true story of my childhood. Whose vanity could I, a new born babe, possibly wound? What physical or moral disfavour could earn me the coldness of my mother? What was I then—the child of duty? One whose birth is accidental? Or one whose very life is a reproach? Boarded out with a wet nurse in the country, forgotten by my family for three whole years, when I returned to the parental roof I counted for so little that I was an object of compassion to the servants. I do not know what sentiment or happy chance it was that helped me find my feet again after that initial setback. In my case, the child had no inkling and the man is unaware. Far from easing my lot, my brother and my two sisters took a delight in hurting me. The pact by virtue of which children conceal one another's little lapses and which teaches them an early sense of honour, was null and void where I was concerned; nay, I was often punished for my brother's misdemeanours, while powerless to protest against the unfairness of it. Did the fawning instinct, rudimentary in children, prompt them to contribute to the persecutions which afflicted me, in order to secure for themselves the good graces of a mother whom they feared as much as I? Was it a symptom of their tendency to imitate their elders? Was it a need to try their strength, or was it lack of human kindness? Perhaps it was a combination of these factors which deprived me of the sweets of brotherhood.

Already dispossessed of all affection, there was nothing I could love, and nature had made me loving! Does some angel cull the sighs of this perpetually rebuffed sensibility? If in some few souls slighted feelings turn to hate, in mine they drew in upon themselves and hollowed out a bed whence, later on, they gushed forth on to my life. In some natures, habitual trembling slackens the fibres, gives rise to timorousness, and timorousness forces one always to give in. Thence springs a weakness which debases a man and makes him something of a slave. But this continual turmoil trained me to deploy a strength which increased with use and predisposed my soul to spiritual endurance. Forever awaiting some new hurt, as the martyrs of old awaited some fresh blow, my whole being must have expressed a dismal resignation, beneath which the lively grace of childhood was extinguished, an attitude which was mistaken for a sign of mental deficiency and bore out my mother's worst prognostications. The certainty of these injustices gave rise in me to a premature pride, that fruit of reason, which doubtless checked the tendencies toward evil which such an upbringing should have fostered in me. Although virtually forsaken by my mother, I was from time to time the object of her misgivings. She occasionally spoke of my education and expressed a desire to take it in hand. Ghastly shudders ran through me then, at the thought of the anguish which daily contact with her would produce in me. I blessed her neglect of me and considered myself lucky that I could stay in the garden playing with stones, studying insects, gazing at the blueness of the firmament.

Although loneliness was bound to make me prone to day-dreaming, my taste for contemplation sprang from an incident which will illustrate my first misfortunes. I entered so little into the scheme of things that our governess often forgot to send me to bed. One night, quietly curled up under a fig tree, I was watching a star with that strange intensity which seizes children and to which my precocious melancholy lent a kind of soulful awareness. My sisters were shouting and playing; I could hear their distant noise as a background to my thoughts. The noise stopped. Night fell. My mother chanced to notice my absence. Afraid of a scolding, our governess, a terrible Mademoiselle Caroline, justified my mother's suspicions by asserting that I loathed my home; that if she had not kept a close watch on me I should have run away before now; I was not imbecile but sly; of all the children entrusted to her care, she had never met one with a worse disposition. She made a show of looking for me and called my name. I answered. She came to the fig tree where she knew I would be.

"And what are you doing there?" said she.

"Looking at a star."

"You were not looking at a star," said my mother, who was listening from her balcony. "What can a child of your age know about astronomy?"

3

"Oh Madame!" cried Mademoiselle Caroline, "He has turned on the garden tap! The lawn is flooded!"

There was a general commotion. My sisters had turned on the tap for fun, to see the water run; but surprised by the spreading of a jet which had sprayed them from top to toe, they had lost their heads and fled without being able to turn off the tap. Caught and convicted of devising this piece of mischief, called a liar when I affirmed my innocence, I was severely punished. But, dreadful chastisement!—I was derided for my love of the stars and my mother forbade me to stay in the garden in the evening. Tyrannical prohibitions sharpen a desire in children even more than in adults; children have the advantage of thinking of nothing but the thing forbidden, which consequently offers irresistible attractions. So I was often whipped for my star. Having no one to confide in, I told it my sorrows, in that sweet inner prattle with which a child stammers his first thoughts, just as, not long before, he stammered his first words. At the age of twelve, at school, I still gazed at it with inexpressible delight, so deep are the impressions traced on the heart in the morning of life.

Five years older than myself, my brother Charles was as handsome a child as he is a man. He was my father's favourite, my mother's darling, my family's hope; consequently king of the household. Well built and sturdy, he had a tutor. I, undersized and sickly, was sent at the age of five as a day boy to a boarding school in the town, escorted there and back by my father's manservant. I set off with a meagre lunch basket, whereas my schoolfellows brought abundant provisions.

This contrast between my penury and their affluence gave rise to countless miseries. The celebrated "rillettes" and "rillons" of Tours formed the main element of the meal we took in the middle of the day, between breakfast and dinner at home. This dish, so prized by a few gourmets, rarely appears on aristocratic tables in Tours; I had heard of it before being sent to school, but I had never had the joy of seeing that brown concoction spread for me on a slice of buttered bread. Even had there not been a vogue for it at school, my desire for it would have been no less strong, for it had grown into an obsession, comparable to the craving of one of the most elegant Parisian duchesses for the stews prepared

4

by porters' wives—a fancy which, woman that she was, she satisfied.

Children sense envy in a look as easily as your sex read love in it. I became an excellent target for ridicule. My schoolfellows, almost all of whom belonged to the tradesman class, would make a point of showing me their splendid "rillettes" and asking if I knew how they were made, where they could be bought, why I did not have any myself. They licked their lips as they enthused over "rillons", those scraps of pork tossed in their own fat, which look like cooked truffles; they searched my basket, and, finding nothing in it but Olivet cheeses or dried fruit, they would annihilate me with an "Are you hard up, then?" which taught me to measure the difference between my brother and myself.

This contrast between my neglect and the wellbeing of others blighted the roses of my childhood and withered my verdant youth. The first time, fooled by a seemingly generous impulse, that I held out my hand to take the longed-for delicacy, proffered with a hypo-critical air, my tormentor withdrew his slice of bread, to the laughter of his friends, who were forewarned of this manoeuvre.

If the most distinguished minds are prone to vanity, how shall one not absolve the child who cries at seeing himself despised and jeered at? At this game, how many children would have become greedy, cadging, cowardly! To avoid persecution, I used my fists. The courage of despair made me redoubtable, but I was an object of hatred and had no resources against treachery. One evening, on my way home, a rolled handkerchief, filled with stones, hit me in the back. When the manservant, who roundly avenged me, related the incident to my mother, she exclaimed—"That accursed child will bring us nothing but sorrow!"

I sank into an appalling self-distrust on meeting, at school, the same repulsion that I inspired in the family circle. There, as at home, I turned in upon myself. A second snowfall delayed the flowering of the seeds sown in my soul. The boys I saw to be popular were downright scoundrels and my pride took heart at this. I kept myself to myself. So the impossibility of pouring out the feeling which lay heavy on my poor heart continued.

Seeing me perpetually despondent, disliked and alone, the

master confirmed the suspicions which my family had of my evil disposition. As soon as I could read and write, my mother had me dispatched to Pont-le-Voy, a college run by the Oratorians, who took children of my age into a class called the *pas-Latin* class, for schoolboys whose backward intelligence refused to assimilate the Latin Primer. I stayed there eight years, never seeing a soul and leading the life of an untouchable. This is how it came about. I had only three francs a month for my minor pleasures, a sum which barely sufficed for the pens, penknife, paper and ink which we were expected to provide. Therefore, being unable to buy stilts, or skipping ropes or any of the things necessary for a schoolboy's amusements, I was banished from all games; to gain admission to them I should have had to toady to the rich or fawn on the strong boys of my class. The slightest sign of such cravenness, in which children so easily indulge, would set my heart pounding in my chest. I spent my time under a tree, lost in doleful day-dreams; there I read the books with which the librarian issued us each month. How many sorrows lay buried in this monstrous loneliness! Imagine what my tender spirit must have felt at my first prize-giving—when I won the two most coveted prizes: for translation and composition! When I went up to receive them, amid the cheers and fanfares, neither my mother nor my father were there to congratulate me, whereas the hall was filled with the parents of my schoolfellows. Instead of kissing the prize-giver, as was the custom, I buried my head in his breast and burst into tears. That evening, I burnt my laurel wreaths in the stove.

The parents stayed in the town during the week of the exercises which preceded the prize-giving. My schoolfellows would all surge joyfully out in the mornings; whereas I, whose parents lived a few miles away, stayed in class with the "overseas boys", the name given to the pupils whose families were in the Islands or abroad. In the evening, during prayers, the barbarians would boast to us of the good dinners they had enjoyed with their parents. You will always see my unhappiness increase in proportion to the circumference of the social spheres I enter. How many efforts did I not make to rescind the sentence which condemned me to live only within myself! How many hopes, slowly formulated with a thousand leaps of spirit, were dashed in a single day! To persuade my parents to come to the college I would write them heartfelt epistles, fulsomely expressed, no doubt—but ought these letters to have incurred the censure of my mother, who reproved me ironically for my style? Undiscouraged, I would promise to fulfil the conditions which my mother and father set for their coming. I begged the help of my sisters, to whom I wrote on their birthdays and saints' days, with the punctiliousness of all poor neglected children, but with fruitless persistence. As prize-giving day drew near, I redoubled my entreaties, I hinted at probable triumphs. Deceived by my parents' silence, I awaited them with a leaping heart; I announced their coming to my schoolmates; and when, as the families arrived, the footfalls of the old caretaker who called the pupils echoed in the quadrangle, I experienced sickening palpitations. Never once did that old man call my name.

The day that I accused myself of the sin of cursing life, my confessor pointed to Heaven, where flourished the palm promised to the *"beati qui lugent"* of the Saviour; so, at the time of my first communion, I plunged into the mysterious depths of prayer, beguiled by the religious notions whose spiritual fantasies enchant young minds. Quickened by an ardent faith, I prayed to God to renew in my favour the spell-binding miracles of which I read in the Calendar of Martyrs. At five, I flew away in a star; at twelve, I pictured myself asking for Sanctuary. My ecstasy bred in me ineffable dreams which peopled my imagination, enriched my sensibility and strengthened my powers of thought. I have often attributed those sublime visions to angels charged with moulding my soul to divine destinies. They endowed my eyes with the faculty of seeing the inmost spirit of things; they prepared my heart for the magic powers which create the unhappy poet, when he has the fatal gift of comparing what he feels with what he is, the great things desired with the little he obtains; they wrote in my mind a book where I was able to read what I wanted to express. They put on my lips the charcoal of the improvising artist.

My father began to formulate some doubts as to the scope of Oratorian education and took me away from Pont-le-Voy to put me in an institution in Paris, situated in the *Marais* quarter. I was fifteen. On examination of my ability, the boy in the top form at Pont-le-Voy was judged good enough to enter the third grade. The misery I had already experienced at home, at school, at college, I met with again in a different guise during my stay at the *pension Lepître*. My father had given me no money. Once my parents knew that I could be fed, clothed, crammed with Latin and gorged with Greek, all problems were solved. During the course of my college life, I must have known some thousand schoolfellows and not once did I ever meet in any of them the living object of a comparable indifference.

Fanatically loyal to the Bourbons, Monsieur Lepître had had dealings with my father at the time when some devoted Royalists tried to rescue Marie Antoinette from the Temple. They had renewed acquaintance, and M. Lepître consequently thought himself obliged to repair my father's remissness. But the monthly sum he gave me was a poor one. The *pension* was housed in the old *Joyeuse* mansion, where, as in all former aristocratic residences, there was a porter's lodge. During the break which preceded the time when the tutor took us to the *lycée Charlemagne*, my well-to-do schoolmates took luncheon with our porter, a man called Doisy.

Monsieur Lepître was unaware of, or tolerated, the trafficking of Doisy, a veritable old smuggler whom pupils had every interest in cultivating; he was the secret cloak for our lapses, the confidant of our late homecomings, our go-between for the lenders of forbidden books. To breakfast off a cup of white coffee was an aristocratic taste, owing to the exorbitant rise in the price of colonial foodstuffs under Napoleon. If the use of sugar and coffee was a luxury for parents, it denoted among ourselves a sense of superiority, which would have given us our passion for it, had the tendency to imitation, and greed, and the contagiousness of fashion not sufficed. Doisy gave us credit; he assumed we all had sisters or aunts who understood a point of honour among schoolboys and would pay their debts. I long resisted the blandishments of the refreshment bar. If those who condemned me had known the strength of the temptations, the heroic aspirations of my spirit towards stoicism, the contained rages during my long abstinence, they would have dried my tears instead of causing them to flow. But could I, a child, be expected to possess that nobility of soul which scorns the scorn of others?

8

Towards the end of my second year, my father and mother came to Paris. The day of their arrival was announced to me by my brother. He lived in Paris and had not come to visit me once. My sisters were to be in the party too, and we were to see the sights of Paris together. The first day we would dine at the Palais-Royal, so as to be near at hand for the *Théâtre Français*. Despite the rapture aroused by this programme of unhoped-for treats, my joy was damped by the storm wind which so speedily affects those accustomed to misfortune. I had to declare a hundred francs' worth of debts contracted with our Doisy, who threatened to demand the money in person from my parents. I hit on the notion of engaging my brother as agent to Doisy, as spokesman of my repentance, as mediator of my pardon. My father inclined towards leniency. But my mother was pitiless. Her dark blue eyes turned me to stone; she fulminated dire prophecies. "What would I be like in later life if at the age of seventeen I indulged in such escapades? Could I really be her son? Did I want to ruin my family? Was I the only one to be provided for? Did not the career embraced by my brother Charles require a separate allowance, already merited by behaviour which brought glory to his family, whereas I would be its shame? Were my two sisters to marry without dowries? Had I no notion of the value of money and what I was costing? What use were sugar and coffee in a boy's education? Was not such behaviour a training for all the vices?" Marat was an angel beside me. When I had borne the full brunt of this torrent, which swept a thousand terrors into my soul, my brother took me back to my *pension*; I forfeited the dinner at the *Frères-Provençaux* and was deprived of seeing Talma in *Britannicus*. Such was my meeting with my mother after a separation of twelve years.

When I had completed my classical studies, my father left me under the guardianship of M. Lepître; I was to learn transcendental mathematics, do one year's law and begin my higher studies. With a room of my own and freed from the bondage of the classroom, I had high hopes of a truce between penury and me. But, despite my nineteen years, or perhaps because of them, my father continued the arrangement which had sent me, in the past, to school without provisions, to college without minor pleasures, and given me Doisy for a creditor. I had little money at my disposal, and what can a young man do in Paris without money? Besides, my freedom was effectively trammelled. Monsieur Lepître had me escorted to the Law Schools by a tutor who handed me over to the Professor and who later returned to fetch me. A young girl would have been guarded with fewer precautions than my mother's fears inspired for the preservation of my person.

Paris frightened my parents with good reason. Schoolboys are secretly occupied with what also preoccupies young ladies in their boarding schools; do what you will, the latter will always talk about suitors, and the former about women. But in Paris, at the time, talk among schoolmates was dominated by the oriental and sultanesque world of the Palais Royal.

The Palais Royal was an El Dorado of love, where in the evening, gold pieces flowed like water. There, the most virginal of doubts came to an end; there our feverish curiosity was slaked. The Palais Royal and I were two asymptotes drawn towards each other and fated never to meet. This is how fate foiled my designs. My father had introduced me to one of my aunts, who lived in the Ile Saint-Louis. There I had to dine on Thursdays and Sundays, escorted by Madame or Monsieur Lepître, who went out on those days and who fetched me in the evening on their way home. The Marquise de Listomère was a ceremonious *grande dame* who never once had the idea of giving me a cent. As old as God, painted like a miniature, sumptuous in her dress, she lived in her mansion as if Louis XV had never died. She saw no one but old ladies and gentlemen, a company of fossils that gave me the sensation of being in a cemetery. Nobody addressed a word to me and I did not have the courage to speak first. The cold or hostile looks made me feel ashamed of my youth, which seemed to irritate them all.

I staked the success of my escapade on this lack of interest and conceived the idea of slipping away one day, as soon as dinner was over and making with all speed for the Galeries de Bois. Once engaged on a game of whist, my aunt paid no further heed to me and Jean, her manservant, had scant respect for Monsieur Lepître. But that miserable meal would drag miserably on, thanks to the decrepitude of the jaws or the faulty fit of the dentures. At last, one night, between eight and nine o'clock, I got as far as the stairs, palpitating like Bianca Capello on the day of her flight; but when the porter had pulled the cord for me, I saw M. Lepître's cab in the street and the good man asking for me in his wheezy voice. Three times fate stepped between the Hades of the Palais Royal and the Heaven of my youth.

Ashamed of such ignorance at twenty years of age, I resolved one day to face all perils and bring it to an end. But at the very moment that I gave Monsieur Lepître the slip—he was climbing into his carriage, a difficult operation, he was fat as Louis XVIII and clubfooted—who should drive up in a post-chaise but my mother! Her look brought me to a standstill and froze me to the spot like a bird before a snake.

Why did I chance to meet her? The reason is simple. Napoleon was making his last bids to retain power. My father, who foresaw the return of the Bourbons, had come to inform my brother, by then already employed in the imperial diplomatic service. My mother, who had accompanied my father, had undertaken to bring me back to Tours and so preserve me from the dangers which appeared to threaten the capital.

Within a few minutes I was borne away from Paris, just when a stay there threatened to prove fatal to me. The torment of an imagination ceaselessly upset by curbed desires, the strain of an existence saddened by constant privations, had forced me to throw myself into my studies, as men weary of their lot formerly took refuge in a cloister. Studying had become a passion which might well prove fatal to me, incarcerating me as it did at an age when young men should give themselves to the beguiling activities of their verdant natures.

This slight sketch of my early youth was necessary in order to explain the influence it had on my future. Affected by so many morbid elements, I was, at gone twenty, still thin, pale and undersized. My spirit, strong in will, struggled with a body, sickly in appearance, but which, according to the diagnosis of an old doctor in Tours, was undergoing the last melting of an iron constitution. Child in body, and sage in thought, I had read and pondered so much that I knew the heights of life, metaphysically, just when I was about to glimpse its tortuous ravines and sandy plains. By some extraordinary chance, I was still at the blissful stage in life when the first storms toss the soul, when it wakes to the pleasure of the senses, when all is cool and fragrant to it. I was between a puberty prolonged by my labours, and a virility belatedly sprouting its green boughs. No young man was ever better primed than I for feeling and for loving. For a true understanding of my story, cast your mind back to that fair age when the mouth is innocent of lies, when the gaze is clear, though veiled by lids which bashfulness, conflicting with desire, make heavy, when the mind does not bend to the world's Jesuitry, when the heart's cowardice matches in violence the expansiveness of its initial impulse.

I shall not speak of the journey I made from Paris to Tours with my mother. The coldness of her manner paralysed the surge of my affection. As we left each new stage, I promised myself I would speak; but a look, a word scattered the phrases I had carefully prepared for my opening speech. At Orléans, as we were about to retire for the night, my mother chided me for my uncommunicativeness. I threw myself at her feet, embraced her knees, wept copious tears. I opened my heart to her, heavy with affection; I tried to move her by the eloquence of an appeal, hungry for love, which would have stirred the entrails of the proverbial stepmother. My mother retorted that I was play-acting. I lamented her neglect of me; she called me an unnatural son. I felt such a pang of grief that at Blois I ran to the bridge in order to throw myself in the Loire. My suicide was prevented by the height of the parapet.

On arrival, my two sisters, who did not know me, showed more surprise than affection. I was given a room on the third floor. You will understand the extent of my wretchedness when I tell you that my mother left me, a young man of twenty, with no linen other than my miserable boarding-school wardrobe, and with no other clothes than those I had worn in Paris. If I sped from one end of the drawing room to the other to pick up her handkerchief, she gave me no more than the cold "thank you" a woman bestows on her footman. Constrained to study her in order to see if there were in her heart some soft spots where I might plant a few tendrils of affection, I saw a tall woman, dry and slight, selfish and rude, like all the Listomère women, in whom rudeness is included in the dowry. She saw life as a series of duties to fulfil. All the cold women I have met, made, as she did, a religion out of duty. She received our adoration as a priest receives incense at Mass. My elder brother seemed to have absorbed what little maternal feeling she had in her. She stung us perpetually with the pinpricks of a biting irony, the weapon of heartless people, which she used against us, who could not answer back. Despite these thorny barriers, instinctive feelings have so many stubborn roots, the religious terror inspired by a mother of whom it costs too much to despair has such a powerful hold, that our sublimely misdirected love endured until the day when, more advanced in years, we sovereignly judged her. That day begin the reprisals of the children. Their indifference, sprung from the disappointments of the past, swollen by the muddy flotsam they bring back from them, extends right to the grave. This terrible tyranny expelled the wanton thoughts which I, in my madness, had contemplated satisfying in Tours. I flung myself desperately into my father's library, where I set about reading all the books I did not know. My long sessions of work spared me all contact with my mother, but they aggravated my state of mind. At times my sister, the one who married our cousin the Marquis of Listomère, tried to comfort me, without succeeding in soothing the restlessness to which I was a prey. I wanted to die.

Great events, to which I was a stranger, were then in preparation. Having left Bordeaux to join Louis XVIII in Paris, the Duc d'Angoulême received, on his way through each city, orations inspired by the enthusiasm which seized old France on the return of the Bourbons. Touraine agog with excitement for its rightful princes; the city in a ferment; the windows gay with bunting; the inhabitants in their Sunday best; the preparations for festivity and that intoxicating something in the air, made me long to attend the ball given by the prince. When I plucked up courage to voice this desire to my mother, who was not well enough to attend the festiv‑ ities at the time, she flew into a mighty rage. Was I born and bred in darkest Africa to be so ignorant? How could I think that our family would not be represented at this ball? In the absence of my father and brother, was it not for me to go? Had I no mother? Did I imagine she gave no thought to her children's happiness? In one moment, the unnatural son had become somebody of note. I was as dazed by my own importance as by the deluge of ironical reasons with which my mother granted my request. I questioned my sisters

and learnt that my mother, who was fond of such dramatic surprises, had been obliged to take the question of my clothes in hand
herself. Taken unawares by the sudden requirements of their
customers, no tailor in Tours had been able to undertake my out-
fitting. My mother had sent for her daily sewing woman, who, as
is customary in the provinces, could do all manner of needlework.
A cornflower blue dress-coat of sorts was secretly run up for me.
Silk stockings and new pumps were procured without difficulty.
Waistcoats were being worn short. I was able to wear one of my
father's. For the first time in my life I had a ruffled shirt, the frills
of which welled over my chest and wound round in the knot of my
cravat. When I was dressed, I looked so unlike myself that my
sisters' compliments gave me the necessary courage to appear before the assembled notables of Touraine. Arduous undertaking!
Too many were called to that festive gathering for there to have
been many chosen. Thanks to the slightness of my figure, I
threaded my way through a marquee erected in the gardens of the
Papiou mansion and reached a spot near the chair where the prince
sat enthroned.

In a moment I was stifled by the heat; blinded by the lights, the
red hangings, the gilt ornaments, the dresses and the diamonds of
the first public function I had ever attended. I was pushed by a
surging throng of men and women, jostling one another in a cloud
of dust. The spirited brasses and the Bourbonian clash of the
military music were drowned in the shouts of "Long live the
Duc d'Angoulême! Long live the King! Long live the Bourbons!"

This ball was a chaotic riot of enthusiasm, with each man
striving to outdo his neighbour in his ferocious eagerness to greet
the rising sun of the Bourbon dynasty, an example of blatant self-
seeking which left me unmoved, diminished me and drove me
back into myself.

Swept along like a straw in this whirlwind, I had a sudden
childish longing to be the Duc d'Angoulême and to rub shoulders
with the princes now parading before an open-mouthed public.
The foolish yearning of the Touraine-bred lad gave rise to an ambition ennobled which my character and circumstances were later
to ennoble. Who has not envied that adulation, an awe-inspiring

repetition of which was offered me some few months later when the whole of Paris rushed to meet the Emperor on his return from Elba? This sway exercised over the masses, whose lives and feelings flow into a single soul, pledged me, there and then, to glory, that priestess who slaughters the Frenchmen of to-day, as in bygone days the Druidess sacrificed the Gauls. Then, all of a sudden, I met the woman who was to be a constant spur to my ambitions and who was to crown them by throwing me into the very heart of royalty.

Too shy to ask a lady to dance, and afraid in any case lest I should spoil the figures, I naturally became very self-conscious. I was already suffering considerable discomfort, hemmed in as I was by the shuffling crowds around me, when an officer trod on my foot, which was swollen by the tightness of the shoe leather as well as by the heat. This final annoyance took away what little interest I still had in the ball.

It was impossible to leave. I took refuge in a corner at the end of a deserted wall-seat, where I remained, eyes staring vacantly, motionless and sullen. Deceived by my puny appearance, a woman mistook me for a child about to fall asleep while awaiting his mother's good pleasure, and sat down beside me with the grace of a bird alighting on her nest. Immediately, I smelt a woman's fragrance which shone in my soul as oriental poetry was to shine later. I looked at my neighbour and was more dazzled by her than I had been by the ball. If you have really understood my former life, you will divine the feelings which welled up in my heart. My eyes were struck suddenly by shapely white shoulders on which I should have liked to nestle, shoulders faintly tinged with pink, which seemed to blush as if they found themselves unclothed for the first time, modest shoulders that possessed a soul, their satiny skin flashing in the light like silken fabric. These shoulders were divided by a line along which my eyes, bolder than my hands, ran in a wild caress. I half rose, my heart throbbing wildly, in order to see her bodice, and was utterly spellbound by a bosom chastely covered by a wisp of muslin, the globes of which, azure tinted and of a perfect roundness, rested downily in clouds of lace. The tiniest details of her head were fuses which touched off an infinity of delights in me. The gleam of polished hair above a neck velvety as a young girl's, the white lines which the comb had drawn on it and where my fancy ran as if along cool paths—all this caused me to lose my head.

After making sure that nobody could see me, I plunged into that back like a child throwing itself on to its mother's bosom, and, burying my head in those shoulders, I covered them with kisses. The woman gave a sharp cry, which the music rendered inaudible; she turned, saw me and said "Monsieur!" Ah!—had she said "My little man, and what are you doing, pray?" I think I might have killed her. But at that "Monsieur!" hot tears sprang to my eyes. I was turned to stone by a look quickened by saintly anger, by a sublime head crowned with a diadem of ash-blonde hair. The crimson flush of outraged modesty flashed across her face, already half disarmed by the forgiveness of a woman who understands a fit of frenzy when she is the object of it, and who senses infinite adoration in repentant tears. She moved away with the gait of a queen.

It was then that I felt the absurdity of my position: only then did I realise that I was dressed up like an organ-grinder's monkey. Shame filled me. I stood there, dazed, savouring the apple I had just stolen, the warmth of that blood which I had breathed still on my lips, my eyes following this goddess descended from the skies. Gripped by the first carnal aspect of the heart's great fever, I wandered through the now deserted ballroom, unable to find my unknown beauty. I returned home to bed, a changed man.

A new soul, a soul with multicoloured wings, had burst from its cocoon. Fallen from the vast blue expanses where I admired it, my beloved star had turned itself into a woman, while keeping its lustre, its coolness and its flashing light. All of a sudden, I was in love. Is there anything more strange that this first inrush of man's most powerful emotion? I had met a few pretty women in my aunt's drawing room, yet none of them had caused the slightest stir in me. Is there then, an hour, a conjunction of stars, a combination of related circumstances, one woman out of all others, to determine an exclusive passion, at an age when passion embraces the entire sex? At the thought that my queen-elect lived in Touraine I breathed the air with delight, I saw in the blueness of the sky a colour I have seen nowhere else.

Mentally enraptured though I may have been, I looked seriously ill and my mother began to be alarmed, and even a little remorseful. Like an animal when it feels the approach of pain, I would slink away into a corner of the garden, to dream of the kiss I had stolen.

Some days after this memorable ball, my mother attributed my neglect of my work, my indifference to her crushing looks and ironical sallies and my generally sombre behaviour, to the disturbances natural to all young men of my age.

The country, that eternal remedy for ailments of which medicine knows nothing, was looked upon as the best way of lifting me out of my apathy. My mother decided that I should go to spend a few days at Frapesle, a château situated on the Indre, between Montbazon and Azay·le-Rideau, with one of her friends, to whom she no doubt gave secret instructions. The day that I was thus given my freedom, I had swum so deep into the ocean of love that I had crossed it. I did not know the name of my unknown lady. How could I describe her? Where was I to find her? In any case, to whom could I speak of her? Natural shyness enhanced the nameless fears which seize young hearts at the outset of love and made me begin with the melancholy which normally brings hopeless passions to an end. I asked for nothing better than to roam freely through the fields. With that childlike courage which knows no doubts and which contains an indefinable element of chivalry, I resolved to search the country houses of Touraine, travelling on foot and exclaiming at the sight of each fair turret—"It is here!"

So, one Thursday morning, I left Tours by the Saint-Eloi gate, crossed the Saint-Sauveur bridges, arrived at Poncher, looking up at every house, and reached the road to Chinon. For the first time in my life I could stop under a tree, walk fast or slowly as the fancy took me, without anyone asking any questions. For a poor creature crushed by the diverse tyrannies which afflict more or less all young people, the first use of free will, exercised even on trifles, gave my soul an indefinable sensation of release.

Many reasons combined to make that day a holiday of enchantments. During my childhood, my walks had never taken me more than a mile out of the town. Neither my excursions to the neighbouring countryside of Pont-le-Voy, nor those I made from Paris, had

given me more than a glimpse of the beauties of nature. Nevertheless, there remained, from my first childhood memories, the feeling
of beauty which breathes in those parts of the countryside near
Tours that I knew well. Although completely new to the poetry of
place, I was unconsciously demanding, just as those who, without
any practical knowledge of an art, imagine, first and foremost, its
ideal. To reach the castle of Frapesle, visitors on horseback or on
foot take a short cut through the so-called *landes de Charlemagne*,
fallow lands situated at the summit of the plateau which separates
the basin of the river Cher from that of the Indre. These flat sandy
moors, which depress one for a mile or so, end in a small wood
which joins the road to Saché, the name of the parish of which
Frapesle forms part. This road, which comes out on to the main
Chinon highway well beyond Ballan, skirts a rolling plain, without
any noticeable features, as far as the small village of D'Artanne.
There a valley is revealed, beginning at Montbazon and ending at
the Loire, which seems to leap under the castles set on these
double-crested hills; a magnificent emerald goblet at the bottom of
which the Indre winds snake-like on its way. At this sight, I was
seized with voluptuous astonishment all the stronger for the tedium
of the *landes* and the fatigue of the journey.

"If this woman, flower of her sex, lives somewhere in this world,
this is the place."

At this thought, I leaned against a walnut tree, beneath which,
ever since that day, I rest each time I come back to my beloved
valley. Under that tree, the confidant of my thoughts, I question
myself on the changes that have taken place in me since the last
time I saw it. She lived there. My heart had not misled me; the
first castle I saw on the sloping stretch of moorland was her dwell-
ing place. When I sat down under my walnut tree, the midday sun
was sparkling on the tiles of her roof and the panes of her windows.
Her muslin dress produced the white dot which I noticed under a
peach tree, among her vines. She was, as you already know, though
you know nothing yet, the lily of this valley, where she grew for
Heaven, filling it with the perfume of her virtues. Boundless love,
without other nourishment than an object, scarce perceived, of
which my soul was full, found expression, in my fancy, in that long
ribbon of water streaming in the sunlight between two green

banks; in those rows of poplars adorning with their quivering lace this vale of love; in the oak woods thrusting between the vineyards upon slopes which the river rounds in ever varying curves, and in those blurred horizons that merged in the far distance. If you want to see nature fair and virginal as a bride, go there on a day in spring; if you want balm for the heart's aching wounds, come back there in the last days of autumn. In the springtime, love beats its wings in the open sky; in the autumn, the mind turns to those who are no more. The ailing lung breathes a beneficient freshness there. The gaze rests on golden tufts which convey their peaceful sweetness to the soul. At that particular moment, the mills situated on the waterfalls of the Indre gave a voice to that quivering valley, the poplars swung to and fro, laughing, the sky was cloudless, the birds sang, the cicadas croaked, and all was melody. Never ask again why I love Touraine. I love it, not as one loves one's cradle, nor an oasis in the desert; I love it as an artist loves art; I love it less than I love you; but without Touraine, it is possible that I might not go on living. Without knowing why, my eyes kept on turning to the white dot, to the woman who shone in this vast garden just as, in the midst of green hedgerows, the white bell of the convolvulus, withering at a touch, might strike the eye.

Moved to my very soul, I went down into that basin, and soon saw a village which in my overflowing lyricism seemed to me quite matchless. Imagine three watermills, set among gracefully chiselled islets crowned with a few clumps of trees, amid a water-meadow— what other name can one give to that aquatic vegetation, so hardy and so bright, which carpets the river, undulates with it, yields to its whims and bends to the storm waves lashed by the millwheels? Here and there mounds of gravel rise, on which the water breaks, forming fringes which glisten in the sun. Amaryllis, reeds, yellow pond lilies and phlox adorn the banks with their tapestried magnificence. A rickety bridge, composed of rotten beams; its piles covered with flowers; its handrails, encrusted with hardy weeds and velvety mosses, leaning outwards over the river; some old boats; a few fishing nets; the toneless chant of a shepherd; the ducks cruising between the islets or preening on the "jar", the coarse sand carried by the Loire; the millhands, cap over one ear, loading their mules: each of these details made this scene into one of astonishing artlessness. Imagine, beyond the bridge, two or three farms, a dovecote, turtledoves, some thirty tumbledown cottages separated by gardens and hedges of honeysuckle, jasmin and clematis; then a flower-covered dung heap before every door, hens and cockerels over the paths, and you have Pont-de-Ruan. The village is topped by an old church, full of character, a church of the time of the Crusades, such as painters seek for their canvases. Frame the whole with ancient walnut trees and young poplars with pale golden leaves; set graceful workshops in the midst of the long meadows where the eye loses itself beneath a warm and hazy sky, and you will have an idea of one of the thousand viewpoints of this lovely place.

I followed the Saché road along the left side of the river, looking at the contours of the hills which crown the opposite bank. Then, at last, I reached an estate, adorned with century-old trees, which told me I was at the castle of Frapesle. I arrived just as the bell was ringing for luncheon. After the meal, my host, never dreaming that I had come from Tours on foot, showed me over his land, where I saw the valley in all its forms; here, a glimpse, there in its entirety. Often, my eyes were drawn to the horizon by the fine golden blade of the Loire where, outlined against the sky, the sails made fantastic shapes which sped before the driving wind. Climbing a ridge, I gazed for the first time on the castle of Azay, faceted diamond set in the Indre, mounted on piles masked by flowers. Then I saw, in a hollow, the romantic masses of the castle of Saché, melancholy residence, full of harmony, too deep for superficial folk, but dear to poets whose souls have felt the touch of pain. Later, too, I loved the silence of it, its great hoary trees and that faint air of mystery wafting in its lonely vale. But each time I saw, on the slopes of the neighbouring hillside, the enchanting little castle singled out by my first glance, my gaze lingered there with pleasure.

"Aha!" said my host, reading in my eyes one of those sparkling desires so artlessly expressed at my age, "you scent a pretty woman as a dog scents game."

I did not care for this last word, but I asked the name of the house and of its owner.

"That is Clochegourde," he said, "a charming house belonging to the Comte de Mortsauf, last surviving member of a family, historic in Touraine, whose fortunes date from Louis XI's time, and whose name records the adventure to which he owes both his coat of arms and his celebrity. He is descended from a man who survived the gallows. The Count came to settle in this estate on his return from exile. The property belongs to his wife, a Mademoiselle de Lenoncourt of the house of Lenoncourt-Givry, which is about to die out. Madame de Mortsauf is an only daughter. The meagre fortune of this family contrasts so singularly with the illustriousness of its name that out of pride, or necessity perhaps, they never leave Clochegourde and receive nobody. Until now, their loyalty to the Bourbons could account for their isolation. But I doubt whether the King's return will change their way of life. When I took up residence here, last year, I paid them a courtesy call; they returned it and invited us to dinner. The winter kept us apart for several months. Then political events delayed my return —I have only been back at Frapesle for a very short time. Madame de Mortsauf is a woman who could take pride of place in any gathering."

"Does she go often to Tours?"

"Never. But," he said, correcting himself, "she did go recently, during the visit of the Duc d'Angoulême, who showed himself most gracious to Monsieur de Mortsauf."

"It is she!" I cried.

"Who is *she?*"

"A woman with lovely shoulders."

"You will meet many women in Touraine with lovely shoulders," he said laughing. "But if you are not tired, we can cross the river and go up to Clochegourde, where you can set to work identifying those shoulders of yours."

I accepted, not without blushing with shame and delight. Towards four o'clock, we arrived at the little castle which my eyes had been caressing for so long. This abode, so effective in the landscape, is in reality a modest one. It has five windows in the front. The ones flanking the south elevation project slightly, an architectural device which lends a certain air of grace to the building. The centre window serves as a door. Through it, a double flight of steps leads out on to terraced gardens, which end in a strip of meadow running along the Indre. Although a public footpath separates this meadow from the last terrace, which is shaded by a lane of acacias and lacquer trees, it seems to form part of the gardens, for the path is sunken, banked on one side by the terrace and on the other by a Norman hedge. The graded slopes set enough distance between the house and the river to obviate the drawbacks of being so near the water, without detracting from the pleasantness of it. Under the house are coach-houses, stables, store rooms and kitchens, of which the various entrances form arcades. The roof is gracefully turned at the corners, decorated with gables, with sculptured cross-pieces and leaded clusters on their points. The roofing, doubtless neglected during the Revolution, is coated with that particular kind of rust produced by the flat, reddish moss which grows on houses exposed to the southern sun. The french window is surmounted by a bell tower, where the escutcheon of the Blamont-Chauvry family is carved. The device, "Look ye all, let no man touch", struck me vividly. The supports, a griffon and a dragon with jaws chained in gold, made an attractive sculptural effect. The Revolution had damaged the ducal crown and the crest, which consists of a vert palm tree, with gold fruit. Sénart, secretary of the Committee of Public Safety, was bailiff of Saché before 1781, which explains these depredations.

Seen from the valley, the ground floor seems to be on the first, but on the courtyard side, it gives on to a wide sanded driveway, flanked by a lawn ornamented by several urns of flowers. To left and right, vineyards, orchards and several plots of arable land planted with walnut trees form a steep descent, surrounding the house with a wall of foliage and running down to the banks of the Indre, which are lined at this point with clumps of trees, whose green hues Nature itself has tinted. I climbed the path that skirts Clochegourde, gazing with admiration at its well proportioned features and breathing an air laden with happiness. Has man's spiritual nature, like his physical nature, its electric communications and its swift changes of temperature? My heart began to beat at the approach of the unknown events which were to alter it for always, just as animals become playful at the expectation of fine weather. That day, so significant a one in my life, lacked none of the circumstances that could lend it solemnity. Nature had put on its finery like a woman going to meet her love. My soul heard its voice for the first time, my admiring eyes beheld it, as fruitful, as varied, as my fancy had seen it in my dreams at school, those dreams about which I have said but a few words, inadequate to explain their influence, for they might be said to have been an Apocalypse, in which my life was figuratively foretold. Each event, happy or unhappy, is connected to them by strange images, links visible only to the eyes of the soul.

We crossed a first courtyard surrounded by farm buildings—a barn, a wine-press, stables and cowsheds. Alerted by the watchdogs' barking, a servant came to meet us and told us that Monsieur le Comte had left for Azay early in the morning. He was expected back soon and Madame la Comtesse was at home. My host looked at me. I trembled lest he should be unwilling to see Madame de Mortsauf in her husband's absence, but he told the man to announce us. Impelled by a childish avidity, I dashed into the long anteroom which runs through the house.

"Come in, sirs," said a golden voice.

Although Madame de Mortsauf had uttered but one word at the ball, I knew her voice at once, and it entered my soul and filled it as a ray of sunlight fills and gilds a prisoner's cell. At the thought that she might remember my face, I wanted to run away; it was too late, she appeared in the doorway. Our eyes met. I do not know which of us two blushed the deeper. Struck speechless with surprise, she returned to her tapestry loom and sat down, after the servant had brought forward two armchairs. She finished drawing her needle through her work, to give some excuse for her silence, counted several stitches and then lifted her head, gently and proudly at the same time, and asked Monsieur de Chessel to what happy circumstance she owed his visit. Although curious to know the truth about my sudden appearance there, she looked at neither of us. Her eyes were fixed on the river. But, from the way in which she listened, you would have said that, like the blind, she could sense the turmoil of the heart in the faintest inflexions of the spoken word. And this was indeed so. Monsieur de Chessel told her my name and history. I had been, he said, some months in Tours, where my parents had brought me back to live when the hostilities had threatened Paris. Child of Touraine to whom Touraine was unknown, the young man, weakened by immoderate

23

labours, whom she saw before her, had been sent to Frapesle to enjoy himself. Monsieur de Chessel explained that he had shown me over his land, which I was visiting for the first time. It was not until we reached the foot of the hill that I had told him of my walk from Tours to Frapesle, and fearing for my already delicate state of health, he had taken the liberty of calling at Clochegourde, hoping that she might allow me to rest there. Monsieur de Chessel was telling the truth, but a fortunate coincidence seems so very contrived that Madame de Mortsauf remained slightly aloof. She gave me a cold, stern look, which made me drop my eyes, partly out of some vague feeling of humiliation and also to hide the tears which hung on my lashes. The stately chatelaine saw the sweat on my brow. Perhaps she also sensed the tears, for she asked me if there was anything I needed, with a comforting kindness which gave me back my tongue. I was blushing like a guilty girl. In a voice quavering like an old man's, I thanked her and declined the offer.

"All I ask," I said, raising my eyes and meeting hers for a brief second, "is that you do not send me away. I am so numb with fatigue that I could not walk."

"Why do you doubt the hospitality of our fair county?" said she. "Perhaps you will grant us the pleasure of dining at Clochegourde?" she added, turning to her neighbour.

I threw my mentor a look so pregnant with supplication, that he took steps to accept the invitation, the form of which required a refusal. If knowledge of the world allowed Monsieur de Chessel to sense these fine distinctions, a young man without experience has so firm a belief in the union of mind and utterance in a beautiful woman, that I was most astonished when, on our way home later that evening, my host told me that he had stayed because I so obviously longed to do so. "But," said he, "if you do not mend matters, I may not be on speaking terms with my neighbours."

This phrase, "If you do not mend matters", immediately set me dreaming. If Madame de Mortsauf liked me, she could not bear a grudge against the person who had brought me to her house. Monsieur de Chessel must therefore suppose that I had the power to interest her—and was that not tantamount to giving me that power? This explanation buoyed up my hopes at a time when I was sorely in need of encouragement.

"I am afraid that would be difficult," he said, "Madame de Chessel is expecting us."

"She has you every day," returned the Countess. "We can send word to her. Is she on her own?"

"Monsieur l'abbé de Quélus is with her."

"Good," said she, rising to ring the bell, "you will dine with us then."

This time, Monsieur de Chessel took her to be sincere, and glanced at me in mute congratulation. Now that I was sure of spending an entire evening under this roof, an eternity of time seemed to stretch ahead of me. For many unhappy people, the word "to-morrow" has no meaning, and I was, at the time, one of those who have no faith in the morrow. When I had a few hours to myself, I crammed into them a whole lifetime of delights. Madame de Mortsauf embarked on a conversation about the neighbourhood, the crops, the vines; topics of which I knew nothing. In a hostess, such behaviour is a sign of bad manners, or contempt for the person whom she thus excludes from the discussion, but with the Countess it was embarrassment. If, at first, I thought she chose to treat me as a child; if I envied the privilege of men of thirty which allowed Monsieur de Chessel to converse with his fair neighbour on topics of which I understood nothing; if I was vexed at the thought that all was going his way, a few months hence I was to find out how meaningful is a woman's silence and how many thoughts lie hidden beneath a casual conversation. First I tried to make myself at ease in my armchair; then I began to be aware of the advantages of my position and abandoned myself to the spell of the Countess' voice. The life's breath of her soul was revealed in the folds of her syllables, as sound is divided by the keys of a flute; it expired undulatingly on the ear, whence it set in motion the action of the blood. Her way of pronouncing words ending in "i" put one in mind of a bird's singing. The "ch" sound, as uttered by her, was a caress and the way in which she attacked the "t's" challenged the despotism of the heart. Without knowing it, she extended the meanings of words and lured your soul into a superhuman world. How often did I prolong a discussion, when I could have ended it! How many times did I not incur an undeserved reproof, merely in order to

25

listen to those vocal harmonies; to breathe the air that issued from her lips, laden with her soul; to embrace this spoken light with the same ardour with which I would have clasped the Countess to my bosom! What joyful swallow's song when she could laugh! But, oh!—how like a swan calling to its fellows, was her voice when she spoke of her sorrows!

The Countess' inattention allowed me to examine her. My gaze drank its fill as it swept over the lovely speaker, clasping her waist, kissing her feet, playing among the tendrils of her hair. I was, notwithstanding, in the throes of a terror which will be understood by any who have experienced the boundless joy of a true passion. I feared lest she might catch me with my eyes riveted to the spot on her shoulders which I had kissed so ardently. The fear sharpened the temptation and I succumbed to it. I gazed at them, my eyes ripped away the material, I saw again the freckle which marked the rise of the pretty line that divided her back in two, fly lost in milk which since that ball had blazed at night in that blackness where streams the slumber of young men whose fancy is aflame, whose lives are chaste.

I can give you a rough sketch of the main features which would have made the countess a focus for all eyes in any company; but the finest drawing, the warmest colour would convey nothing of her real self. Her face was one of those whose likeness calls for that nonexistent artist whose hand can paint the glow of inner fires and capture that luminous aura which science denies and which speech cannot render, but which a lover's eyes can see. Her fine, ash-blonde hair often gave her pain, due no doubt to the sudden rush of blood to the scalp. Her rounded brow, prominent like the Gioconda's, seemed full of unvoiced thoughts, unexpressed feelings, flowers drowned in bitter waters. Her greenish eyes, dotted with brown flecks, were always pale, but, if it were a question of her children, if some of those swift spurts of joy or sorrow, rare in resigned women, escaped her, her eyes would throw out a faint gleam which seemed to take fire from the mainspring of life itself; a flash which had drawn tears from me when she covered me with her fearsome disdain and which was enough to make the boldest eyelids droop. A Greek nose, as Phidias would have moulded it, and joined by a double arch to elegantly curving lips, spiritualised her oval face. Her complexion, comparable in texture to white camellias, warmed on the cheeks to a faint, rosy blush. Her plumpness spoilt neither the grace of her figure nor the roundness necessary for her bosom, though full, to remain lovely. You will immediately understand this kind of perfection when I tell you that, at the junction with the upper arm, the dazzling treasures which had fascinated me seemed to form no crease. The base of her head showed none of those hollows which make some women's necks look like the trunks of trees; her muscles traced no cords on it and everywhere the lines followed sinuous curves which were the despair of eye and brush alike. A wayward down ran along her cheeks and down the flat planes of her neck, trapping the light which lay silkily along it. Her ears, small and well shaped, were, depending on her expression, those of a mother or a slave.

Later, when I dwelt in her heart, she used to say "Here comes Monsieur de Mortsauf", and she was right, when I had not yet heard a sound, I whose sense of hearing is remarkably acute.

Her arms were lovely, her hands, with their upturning fingers, were long, and as in the statues of antiquity, her nails were overlapped by fine ribs of skin. It would displease you if I gave flat waists the advantage over rounded waists, were you not an exception. The rounded waist is a sign of strength, but women so built are imperious, wilful, and more sensual than tender. Conversely, flat-waisted women are devoted, eminently sensitive and inclined to melancholy. They are more womanly than the others. The flat waist is soft and yielding, the rounded is inflexible and jealous. You know now how she was built. She had a gentlewoman's foot, a foot which walks little, soon tires and delights the eye when it peeps below the skirt.

Although she was the mother of two children, I never met anyone of her sex with more of the young girl about her. Her manner breathed a lissomness, coupled with a faint air of the remote and of thoughtfulness, which drew one back to her, as the painter leads one back to the face where his genius has conveyed a world of emotion. Her visible qualities cannot indeed be expressed other than by comparison. Think of the wild, chaste scent of that heather we picked on our way back from the villa Diodati, that flower whose black and rose you so admired, and you will guess how elegant this woman could be, far from the world, how natural in her expressions, how cultivated in the things she made her own: both black and rose. Her body had the verdant quality we admire in newly opened leaves; her mind the deep conciseness of the savage; she was child in feeling, grave through suffering, both chatelaine and maiden. She was pleasing without artifice, in her very way of rising or of sitting down, of throwing in a word or of keeping her own counsel. Habitually reserved, alert as the sentinel on whom the safety of all depends and who keeps a wary eye upon misfortune, she would break sometimes into the kind of smile which gave her away as a person, born to laughter, but swamped beneath the self control demanded by the life she led. Her natural femininity had become mystery; she made men dream instead of inspiring the gallant attentions that women seek for, and gave one occasional bright glimpses of her real, flame-like self, her first azure dreams, the way one sees the sky through gaps in the clouds. This involuntary self-revelation gave pause to those in whom an inner tear was not dried by the flame of desire. The rareness of her movements, and especially of her looks (apart from her children she looked at nobody) lent an incredible solemnity to whatever she did or said, whenever she did or said something with that air which women know how to assume when they compromise their dignity by an avowal.

That day, Madame de Mortsauf was wearing a finely striped pink dress, a wide-hemmed collar, a black belt and slippers to match. Her hair, wound simply round her head, was held in place by a tortoiseshell comb. Such is the imperfect sketch I promised you. But the constant emanation of her spirit to her loved ones, that nourishing essence poured out in waves as the sun emits its light; her inner self, her attitude in the serene hours, her resignation in the hours of stress, all those vicissitudes of life when the character reveals itself, depend, like sky-effects, on untoward and fleeting circumstances linked only by the background against which they are set. Their description will necessarily be interwoven with the events of this story, a veritable domestic epic, as great in the eyes of the sage as are tragedies to the crowd and one which will hold your interest not only for the part I myself played in it, but for its similarity with a great many feminine destinies.

Everything at Clochegourde bore the stamp of a truly English cleanliness. The drawing-room where the Countess sat was entirely panelled, and painted in two shades of grey. The chimney breast had, for ornament, a clock set in a block of mahogany surmounted by a goblet, and two tall vases of white porcelain laced with gold, filled with spreading tufts of Cape leather. A lamp stood on the console table. There was a backgammon table facing the fireplace. Two wide cotton loops held the white, unfringed cambric curtains. Grey slip covers, trimmed with green braid, covered the chairs, and the tapestry stretched on the Countess' loom explained why these pieces of furniture were thus screened from view. It was of a simplicity bordering on grandeur. No apartment I have seen since created such fruitful impressions as those which crowded in upon me in that Clochegourde drawing-room, calm and with-drawn like the Countess' own life, where one could sense the almost monastic regularity of her activities. The greater part of my ideas, even the most audacious in the spheres of politics and science, were born there, as scents emanate from flowers; there flourished the unseen plant which shed its fertile dust over my spirit, there shone the solar warmth which developed my good qualities and dried up my bad.

From the window the eye took in the sweep of the valley from the hill where spreads Pont de Ruan, over to the castle of Azay, following the curves of the opposite slope, which are broken by the towers of Frapesle, then to the church, the town and the old manor house of Saché, whose masses dominate the meadowland. In harmony with an existence untroubled by any excitements other than those incidental to family life, the place imparted its serenity to the soul. Had I met her for the first time between the Count and her two children, instead of coming upon her resplendent in her ball dress, I should never have snatched that vertiginous kiss, which I regretted now, fearful lest it might destroy the future of my love. No, in the black moods induced by my unhappiness, I would have knelt and kissed her slippers, left on them a tear or two and thrown myself into the Indre.

But having brushed against the jasmine freshness of her skin and drunk the milk of that brimming cup of love, the taste and hope of human bliss were in me now. I wanted to live and await the hour of delight, as the savage lies in wait for the hour of vengeance. I wanted to hang from the trees, creep through the vines, crouch in the Indre; I wanted the silence of the night, the lassitude of life, the heat of the sun for my accomplices, in order to finish the delicious apple into which I had already bitten. Had she asked me for the Singing Flower, or the treasures buried by the companions of Morgan the Pirate, I would have brought her them in order to obtain the certain treasure and the Silent Flower for which I longed!

This dream into which the lengthy contemplation of my idol had plunged me was brought to a sudden end by the entry of a servant, who said something to her. I heard her mention the Count. Only then did it cross my mind that a woman belonged by rights to her husband. My head reeled at the thought. Then I felt a dark and violent curiosity to see the possessor of this treasure. Two emotions were uppermost in me, hatred and fear: a hatred which measured all obstacles and shrank from none; a fear, vague but real, of the possible combat, of its outcome and, most of all of HER. In the throes of inexpressible presentiments, I dreaded those dishonouring handshakes, I feared already those elastic difficulties against which the toughest wills pit their strength and are blunted. I feared that massive inertia which nowadays robs social life of the clear-cut solutions which passionate spirits seek for.

"Here comes Monsieur de Mortsauf," she said.

I sprang up like a frightened horse. This gesture escaped neither the Countess nor Monsieur de Chessel, but it incurred no unspoken reproof, for at that moment a little girl, whom I guessed to be about six years old, came into the room.

"My father is back," said the child.

"Well, Madeleine?" said her mother. The child took Monsieur de Chessel's proferred hand, dropped me an astonished little curtsey and looked at me very attentively.

"Are you pleased about her health?" Monsieur de Chessel asked the Countess.

"She is better," she replied, stroking the dark head already buried in her lap.

An enquiry from Monsieur de Chessel told me that Madeleine was nine years old. I showed some surprise at my miscalculation and my reaction brought clouds to the mother's brow. My sponsor threw me one of those meaningful looks by which men of the world give us a second education. There, no doubt, lay a maternal wound whose covering had to be respected. A sickly child, with pale eyes and skin as white as faintly glowing porcelain, Madeleine would probably not have survived in the atmosphere of a city. The country air, the attentions of her mother, who seemed to brood protectively over her, sustained the life in that frail body, as a rare plant grows under glass despite the rigours of a foreign climate. Although she bore no bodily resemblance to her mother, she appeared to have her spirit and that spirit was her mainstay. Her sparse black hair, her hollow eyes, sunken cheeks, thin arms and narrow chest proclaimed a struggle between life and death, an unremitting duel in which the Countess, so far, held the upper hand. She did her best to be sprightly, no doubt so as not to grieve her mother; for, at certain moments, when she forgot herself, she looked like a weeping willow. She put one in mind of a little gypsy girl, who had begged her way from her native land, hungry, exhausted, but bravely arrayed in her finery for her public.

"Why, what have you done with Jacques?" asked the Countess, kissing her on the white parting which divided her hair into two bands as black as raven's wings.

"He's coming with my father."

At that moment, the Count came in, leading his son by the hand. Jacques, the living image of his sister, showed the same symptoms of ill health. At sight of these two frail children beside so magnificently beautiful a mother, it was impossible not to guess the source of the sorrow which softened the Countess' temples and caused her to leave unspoken one of those thoughts which one confides only to God, but which leave terrible marks of pain upon the brow.

As he greeted me, Monsieur de Mortsauf threw me a look, not appraising so much as awkwardly anxious, the glance of a man whose distrust springs from his lack of experience in analysing character. After she had introduced me and explained the reason for our visit, his wife gave him her place and left us. The children, whose eyes held their mother's as if they drew their light from them, wanted to go with her, but she said "Stay where you are,

31

darlings", and put her finger to her lips. They obeyed, but their eyes clouded. Ah, to hear oneself addressed by that word "darling", what tasks would one not have undertaken! Like the children, I felt less warm when she had left us.

At mention of my name, the Count's attitude towards me changed. From cold and supercilious, it became, if not cordial, at least politely attentive. In the old days, my father's devotion to our masters had led him to play an important if obscure role, and one which though dangerous, might well have accomplished valuable things. When all was brought to naught by Napoleon's rise to the head of affairs, he had, like many secret conspirators, taken refuge in the sweets of provincial and private life, accepting accusations as harsh as they were undeserved, the inevitable reward of gamblers who stake their all and succumb after serving as pivot to the political machine. Knowing nothing of the antecedents, prospects, or financial position of my family, I was unaware of the details of that lost cause, which the Comte de Mortsauf now called to mind. However, if the oldness of my name, a man's most precious virtue in his eyes, warranted this welcome, I only learnt the real reason for it later. For the moment, this sudden transition put me at my ease. When the two children saw that the conversation was once more under way, Madeleine freed her head from her father's hands, eyed the open door and slid out like an eel, followed by Jacques. They went to join their mother, for I could hear their voices in the distance, like the buzzing of bees around the beloved hive.

I studied the Count and tried to form some assessment of his character, but I was sufficiently arrested by one or two of his main features, to confine myself to a superficial study of his physical appearance. Though only forty-five years of age, he looked nearly sixty, so rapidly had he aged in the great shipwreck which brought the eighteenth century to a close. The monkish crescent of hair which encircled the back of his bald head ended at the ears, caressing his temples with tufts of grey peppered with black. His face looked vaguely like that of a white wolf with blood on its snout, for his nose was swollen like a man's whose stomach has been weakened and whose blood thinned by past illnesses. His flat brow, too wide for his pointed face, and furrowed by horizontal lines, bore witness to the habits of an outdoor life rather than the strain of mental activity, the weight of constant ill fortune rather than the efforts made to overcome it. His cheekbones, prominent and brown amid the pasty tones of his complexion, betokened a frame strong enough to assure him a long life. His eyes, clear, yellow and hard, fell on one like a ray of winter sunlight, bright without warmth, anxious without thought, wary without reason. His mouth was violent and imperious, his chin long and straight. Thin and tall, his bearing was that of the nobleman reclining on conventional values, who knows himself to be above others by right and beneath them in point of fact.

The informality of country life had led him to neglect his appearance. His dress was that of the country dweller whom neither neighbour nor peasant now respects for anything but his landed wealth. His tanned, nervous hands betrayed the fact that he never wore gloves save for riding or going to Mass on Sundays. His footwear was coarse. Although ten years of exile and ten more of farming had left their mark on his physique, some vestiges of his noble birth remained. The most fanatical liberal, a term not yet coined then, could not have failed to recognise in him the chivalrous loyalty and the unshakable convictions of a lifelong subscriber to the *Quotidienne*.* He would have admired the religious man, fervently devoted to his cause, outspoken in his political antipathies; incapable of personally serving his party, eminently capable of ruining it and totally ignorant of the present state of affairs in France. The Count was in fact, one of those upright men who bend the neck to nothing and stubbornly bar the way to everything; fit enough for dying, sword in hand, at the post to which they are assigned, but mean enough to give their lives sooner than part with their gold.

During dinner, I noticed, in the sinking of his withered cheeks and in certain furtive glances at his children, the faint ripple of unwelcome thoughts which broke on the surface of his face. At sight of him, could one not understand how he felt? How could one not accuse him of transmitting to his children those bodies from which the breath of life was lacking? If he condemned himself, he denied others the right of judging him. Bitter as a

* A royalist newspaper. (*Translator's note.*)

power that knows itself to be at fault, but lacking the necessary charm or greatness to compensate the sum of pain he had thrown into the scales, his inner life no doubt provided the bitterness which his sharp features and perpetually anxious eyes betrayed. When his wife came back, with the two children clinging to her skirts, I sensed some secret misfortune, just as, walking on the roof of a cellar, the feet can in some way gauge its depth. As I saw those four people together, as my eyes went from one to the other, studying their bearing and the expression on their faces, thoughts drenched with melancholy fell on my heart, as fine grey rain veils a lovely landscape after a fine sunrise. When the subject under discussion was exhausted, the Count again brought me into the forefront of the conversation, to Monsieur de Chessel's disadvantage, by informing his wife of several circumstances concerning my family, with which I was unfamiliar. He asked me my age. When I told him, the Countess returned my own gesture of surprise with regard to her daughter. I think she had put my age at fourteen. This, I learnt later, was the second link which bound her to me so strongly. I read her mind. Her maternal instinct gave a leap, lit by a belated ray of sunshine cast by hope. Seeing me at past twenty so frail and sickly and yet so highly strung, some voice inside her may have cried "They will live!" She looked at me with curiosity and I felt that at that moment, much ice was broken between us two. She seemed to have a hundred questions for me and she withheld them all.

"If studying has made you ill," she said, "the air of our valley will make you well again."

"Modern education is fatal to children," said the Count. "We cram them with mathematics, we half kill them with science, and we wear them out before their time. You must rest while you are here," he said to me. "You are crushed under the avalanche of ideas that has rolled over you. What sort of century are we preparing for ourselves, with education available as it is to all, if we do not avert the evil and hand public instruction back to the religious bodies?"

These words were a true foretaste of the remark he made one day at the elections, when he refused to vote for a man whose talents might well have served the royalist cause. "I shall always," he told the vote collector, "be chary of a clever man."

He suggested showing us round his gardens and rose to his feet.

"Sir ..." said the Countess.

"Well, my dear?" answered he, turning with a haughty abruptness which showed how much he longed to be absolute master in his own house, and how little he really was by now.

"Monsieur came from Tours on foot. Monsieur de Chessel did not know this and has already taken him on a tour of Frapesle."

"That was unwise of you," he said to me, "although, at your age ..." He nodded his head regretfully.

The conversation was resumed. It did not take me long to discover how intractable was his royalism and how carefully one had to tread to avoid collisions in his waters. The manservant, who had speedily donned his livery, announced dinner. Monsieur de Chessel gave his arm to Madame de Mortsauf, the Count gaily seized mine and we went through to the dining room, which, in the layout of the ground floor, formed the counterpart of the drawing-room.

Paved with white tiles made in Touraine and panelled to shoulder level, the dining room was hung with varnished wallpaper figuring large framed panels of fruit and flowers. The window curtains were of cambric trimmed with red braid, the sideboards were old Boule pieces and the chairs, covered in hand-worked tapestry, were of carved oak.

The table, abundantly laid, offered nothing especially luxurious: unmatched family silverware, Saxon porcelain which had not yet come back into fashion, octagonal water jugs, knives with agate handles, and, under the bottles, Chinese lacquer mats; but there were flowers set in enamelled urns, their dogstooth edging picked out in gold. I liked these old things. I thought the festive wallpaper with its floral borders superb. The contentment which swelled all my sails prevented me from seeing the inextricable difficulties set between herself and me by the ordered solitude of country life. I was near her, on her right hand and I was filling her glass. Yes, undreamed of bliss!—I was brushing against her dress, eating her bread. After three short hours, my life was mingling with hers! We

35

were linked by that terrible kiss, a sort of secret which aroused in us a mutual shame. I was gloriously craven. I went out of my way to make myself agreeable to the Count, who lent himself to all my sycophantic flattery. I would have patted the dog, I would have pandered to the children's slightest whim, brought them hoops and agate marbles, played bears with them. Love, like genius, has its intuitions, and I sensed dimly that temper, sulks and hostility would ruin all I hoped for. Dinner ran its course, full of inner joys for me. At the thought that I was in her house, I could think neither of her undeniable aloofness, nor of the indifference behind the Count's politeness. Love, like life, has a period of puberty, during which it is self-sufficient. I gave several awkward replies, in keeping with the secret tumults of passion, but which no one could suspect, not even *she*, who knew nothing of love. The rest of the time was like a dream. This fine dream only ceased when, in the warm, scented moonlit night, I crossed the Indre, among the fanciful white shapes which adorned the meadows, banks and hills; as I listened to the clear song, the single, melancholy-laden note, uttered at regular intervals by a tree frog, whose scientific name I do not know, but which, since that solemn day, I never hear without infinite delight. I became aware, a little late, there as elsewhere, of the marble-like insensitivity against which my feelings had hitherto been blunted; I wondered whether this would always be so; I believed myself to be under a fatal star and the baleful events of the past warred with the purely personal pleasures I had tasted. Before reaching Frapesle, I looked back at Clochegourde and noticed, below it, a boat, known in Touraine as a *toue*, moored to an ash and rocking in the water. This boat belonged to Monsieur de Mortsauf, who used it for fishing.

"Well," said Monsieur de Chessel, when we were safely out of earshot, "no need to ask if you found your lovely shoulders. I must congratulate you on the reception given you by Monsieur de Mortsauf! By Hades, you found your way into the bosom of the family at first go!"

This remark, coupled with the one I have already mentioned, cheered my downcast heart. I had not said a word since Clochegourde and Monsieur de Chessel ascribed my silence to my happiness.

"I beg your pardon?" I replied with a touch of irony which could equally well appear to spring from contained passion.

"He never received anyone half so cordially."

"I confess I am amazed at this reception myself," said I, sensing the bitterness revealed by this last remark. Although I was too unversed in worldly matters to understand the cause of the sentiment experienced by Monsieur de Chessel, I was nevertheless struck by the expression with which he betrayed it. My host was unfortunate enough to be called Durand and absurd enough to disclaim his father's name, that of an illustrious manufacturer who had made an immense fortune during the Revolution. His wife was the sole heiress of the de Chessels, an old parliamentary family, burghers in Henry IV's time, like the majority of Parisian magistrates. Monsieur de Chessel, ambitious social climber that he was, decided to kill the Durand of his origins in order to achieve the future of his dreams. First he styled himself Durand de Chessel, then D. de Chessel. This made him into Monsieur de Chessel. At the Restoration he established a claim to the title of Count, by virtue of letters patent granted by Louis XVIII. His children will reap the fruits of his courage without knowing the size of it. Social upstarts are like monkeys, whose cleverness they share. One views them from above and admires their agility on the way up, but once they reach the summit, one sees only their less edifying aspects. The underside of my host was built up of pettiness enlarged by envy. He and the peerage are up till now at irreconcilable tangents. To have pretensions and to make them good is the impertinence of strength. But to fall short of one's self-confessed pretensions constitutes a perpetual absurdity which small minds thrive upon. Monsieur de Chessel lacked the strong man's ability to follow a straight course. Twice a deputy, twice unreturned at the elections, yesterday director-general, to-day nothing, not even *préfet*, both his successes and his failures spoiled his character and gave him the asperity of the thwarted social climber.

Gentleman, man of lively mind and capable of great things though he is, possibly envy, consuming passion in Touraine, where the natives devote their energies to coveting everything, was detrimental to him in those exalted circles which do not open readily to faces that stiffen at the success of others, to curling lips averse to compliment and swift to epigram. By wanting less, he might perhaps have obtained more. But, unfortunately for him, he was sufficiently superior to insist on walking upright. At this particular moment, Monsieur de Chessel was at the dawn of his ambition; royalism smiled upon him. Perhaps he did put on airs, but he was irreproachable with me. Besides, I liked him for a very simple reason. In his house, I found peace for the first time. The interest he showed in me, slight though it perhaps was, seemed to the unhappy, rejected child I had always been, a replica of paternal love. His attentive hospitality contrasted so strongly with the indifference which had hitherto been my lot, that I showed a childlike devotion at living without chains and almost cherished. Then again, the lords of Frapesle are so closely intermingled with the dawning of my happiness that I confuse them in thought with the memories on which I love to dwell. Later—in the business of the letters patent to be exact—I had the pleasure of rendering my host one or two services. Monsieur de Chessel enjoyed his wealth with an ostentation which offended some of his neighbours. He could afford to renew his fine horses and his elegant carriages; his wife dressed with studied elegance; he entertained on a grand scale; his household staff was larger than the custom of the neighbourhood required; he aped the princeling.

The Frapesle estates are immense. Beside his neighbour, and before all this luxury, the Comte de Mortsauf, reduced to the family cabriolet (which in Touraine comes midway between the stage cart and the post-chaise), obliged by his modest income to exploit the resources of Clochegourde, was consequently a provincial, until the day when royal favour restored to his family a glory possibly beyond his fondest dreams. His welcome to the younger son of a ruined house, whose family crest dates from the time of the Crusades, served to humble the wealth and reduce the woods, fields and pastures of his neighbour, who was not of noble birth. Monsieur de Chessel had been quick to divine the Count's intention. Their relations had always been courteous, but without any of that daily interchange, that pleasant intimacy which should have grown up between Clochegourde and Frapesle, two estates separated by the Indre, from which the respective ladies of the house could wave to each other from their windows.

Jealousy was not the only reason for the solitude in which the Comte de Mortsauf lived. His early education was that of most children of noble families, an incomplete and superficial schooling supplemented by a training in the ways of society and court custom and the discharge of the great offices of the Crown or other eminent positions. Monsieur de Mortsauf had left the country just when his second education was beginning. He was to feel the lack of it. He was among those who were confident of the speedy restoration of the monarchy in France. Owing to this conviction, his exile had been spent in the most deplorable idleness. When Condé's army, in which his valour set him in the ranks of the most loyal, was disbanded, he expected to be recalled before very long to the White Banner and did not attempt, as did some *émigrés*, to create an industrious new life for himself. Then again, he may have lacked the strength to relinquish his name in order to earn his living in the sweat of despised toil. His hopes always pinned to the morrow, and perhaps honour too, prevented him from entering the service of a foreign power. Physical suffering undermined his courage. Long journeys undertaken on foot without sufficient food, on hopes perpetually dashed, impaired his health and discouraged his spirit. By degrees, his destitution became acute. If for many men poverty acts as a tonic, there are others to whom it is a dissolvent and the Count was one of them. At the thought of this poor nobleman of Touraine, wandering and sleeping on the roads of Hungary, sharing a haunch of mutton with Prince Esterhazy's shepherds, from whom the traveller begged the bread which the nobleman would not have accepted from the master, and which he refused many a time from the hands of the enemies of France, I have never felt malice in my heart towards *émigrés*, even when I have seen them ridiculous in their triumph. Monsieur de Mortsauf's white hairs told me of appalling hardships and I have too much sympathy for exiles to be able to condemn them.

The gaiety native to France and to Touraine had withered in the Count. He grew morose, fell ill and was cared for, out of charity, in some German hospital. He was suffering from an inflammation of the mesentery, a condition often fatal, but which, when cured produces frequent changes of mood and nearly always causes hypochondria. His loves, buried deep in his soul and which

I alone ever uncovered, were affairs of low degree which not only harmed him at the time but also left their marks on him. After twelve years of hardship, he turned his eyes towards France, to which Napoleon's decree allowed him to return. When, on crossing the Rhine, the ailing, footsore wanderer caught sight of the Strasbourg bell tower one fine evening, his knees gave way under him. "I cried 'France! France! France at last!' " he told me, "the way a child cries 'Mother!' when he has been hurt."

Born into riches, he was now poor; born to command a regiment or rule the state, he found himself without authority or prospects; born strong and healthy, he was returning, broken in health and quite worn out. Without training, in the middle of a country where men had of necessity learnt to make their way without influence, he found himself destitute, stripped even of his physical and moral strength. His lack of fortune made his name a burden. His unshakable opinions, his antecedents in Condé's army, his sorrows, his memories and his lost health bred in him a sensitivity that could expect scant mercy in France, the land of mockery. Half dead, he reached the province of Maine, where, by some oversight, due perhaps to the civil war, the revolutionary government had left one of his farms unsold, a property of considerable size, which his tenant was keeping for him by passing himself off as its owner. When the Lenoncourt family, who lived at Givry, a castle situated near this farm, heard of the Comte de Mortsauf's arrival, the Duc de Lenoncourt invited him to stay at Givry for the time needed to furnish himself with a place to live. The Lenoncourt family acted with noble generosity towards the Count, who stayed with them for several months, recuperating and doing his best, during that first halt, to hide his suffering. The Lenoncourts had lost their vast estates. Monsieur de Mortsauf's name made him a suitable match for their daughter. Far from raising any objection to marriage with a sick, prematurely aged man of thirty-five, Mademoiselle de Lenoncourt seemed glad of it. Marriage enabled her to live with her aunt, the Duchesse de Verneuil, sister to the Prince de Blamont-Chauvry, and adopted mother to her.

An intimate friend of the Duchesse de Bourbon, Madame de Verneuil was a member of a religious society, whose presiding spirit was Monsieur de Saint-Martin, born in Touraine and known as The Unknown Philosopher. His disciples practised the virtues prompted by the high speculations of mystical illuminism. This doctrine offers the key to the divine worlds; interprets life as a series of transformations through which man makes his way towards sublime destinies; frees duty of its legal degradation; applies to the labours of living the unfailing gentleness of the Quaker and commands contempt for one's personal suffering. It is stoicism with a future. Active prayer and pure love are the basic elements of this faith, which departs from Roman Catholicism to enter into the Christianity of the primitive church. Mademoiselle de Lenoncourt, however, remained in the bosom of the Apostolic Church, to which her aunt was equally faithful. Sorely tried by the revolutionary troubles, the Duchesse de Verneuil had adopted, in the last days of her life, a strain of impassioned piety which filled the soul of her beloved child with "the light of Heavenly love and the oil of inner joy", to quote Saint-Martin. The Countess several times received this man of peace and virtuous learning at Clochegourde, after the death of her aunt, to whose house he often came. Saint-Martin supervised, from Clochegourde, the printing of his last books at Letourmy's in Tours. Prompted by the wisdom of an old woman who has explored the stormy straits of life, Madame de Verneuil gave the young bride Clochegourde for her to make her home there. With the grace of the old, which is always faultless when they are gracious, the duchess made over everything to her niece, contenting herself with a room above the one she had previously occupied, which the Countess now took over. Her sudden death cast mourning veils on the joys of that union and left an indelible sadness on Clochegourde, as it did on the bride's superstitious soul. The first days of her establishment in Touraine were the only, I will not say happy, but carefree days of her whole life.

After the vicissitudes of his sojourn abroad, Monsieur de Mortsauf, glad of this glimpse into a favourable future, underwent what one might call a spiritual convalescence. He breathed, in that valley, the heady perfumes of full-flowering hope. Obliged to turn his mind to money, he threw himself into the preparations for his agricultural enterprise, and was at first comparatively happy. But the birth of Jacques marked a sudden blow which ruined the present and the future; the doctor predicted an early death for the newborn. The Count carefully kept this verdict from the mother. He proceeded to take other advice and received hopeless answers which the birth of Madeleine confirmed. These two events and a sort of inner certainty as to the fatal verdict, increased the *émigré's* tendency to ill health. His name forever extinct; by his side a young woman, pure, blameless and unhappy, condemned to the anguish of motherhood without any of its joys; that humus of his past, from which sprouted new sufferings, fell upon his heart and completed his destruction. The Countess deduced the past from the present and read into the future. Nothing is harder than to make a man happy who feels conscious of his guilt, yet this, a task worthy of an angel, the Countess undertook. She became a stoic overnight. She descended into the abyss, whence she could still see the sky, and pledged herself, for the sake of one man, to the vocation which the Sister of Charity embraces for the sake of all; and in order to reconcile him to his own nature, she forgave him what he could not forgive himself. The Count grew mean; she accepted the privations he imposed. He had a fear of being deceived, as have all those whose scant knowledge of the world has left them only with disgust for it; she accepted solitude and bowed without a murmur to his suspicions. She used her woman's wiles to make him want what was right and good; he thus fancied that he had ideas of his own and tasted in his own house the delights of superiority which he would have had nowhere else. Then, having travelled a little further on the matrimonial road, she resolved never to leave Clochegourde, recognising, in the Count, an hysterical soul whose aberrations might, in a land of backbiting and gossip, be detrimental to her children. No one, moreover, had any inkling of Monsieur de Mortsauf's real inadequacy, for she draped his ruins with a heavy cloak of ivy. The Count's erratic and discontented nature met therefore, in his wife's, a soft and easy soil where he could lie in comfort and feel his secret griefs soothed by a cool balm.

This account is the simplest rendering of the discourses torn from Monsieur de Chessel by his secret resentment. His knowledge of the world had allowed him to glimpse some of the mysteries buried at Clochegourde. But if, by her sublime attitude, Madame de Mortsauf deceived the world, she could not fool love's intelligent senses. When I found myself in my little room, a presentiment of the truth made me leap up in my bed. I could not bear to be at Frapesle when I could see the windows of her room. I dressed, crept downstairs and left the house by a door in a tower where there was a spiral staircase. The cold night air restored my equanimity. I crossed the Indre by the red mill bridge and reached the blessed little boat moored opposite Clochegourde. A light shone in the last window on the Azay side. I knew once again my old contemplations—peaceful now, though mingled with the trilling song of the minstrel of amorous nights and the single note of the river nightingale. Thoughts arose and glided through my mind like ghosts, removing the veils which had hitherto hidden my fine future from sight. Soul and senses both were spellbound. How violently did my desires soar up to her! How many times did I say, like a madman his refrain, "Will she be mine?" If, in the last few days, my world had grown larger, in a single night it found a centre. On her were pinned all my ambitions and desires; I wanted to be everything to her, and so mend and fill her lacerated heart. Lovely was the night I spent under her windows, amid the murmur of the waters trickling through the mill sluices, punctuated by the hours ringing from the Saché tower. During that night, bathed in light, where that starry flower lit up my life, I pledged my soul to her with the faith of the poor Castilian Knight whom we laugh at in Cervantes, and with which our love begins. At the first glow in the sky, at the first bird call, I fled to the Frapesle grounds. No countryman saw me; nobody had any inkling of my escapade and I slept until the bell rang for luncheon. Despite the heat, after the meal I went down into the meadow, ostensibly to have another look at the Indre and its islets, the valley and its slopes, of which I appeared to be a passionate devotee. But with feet which rivalled the speed of a runaway horse I found my boat, my willows and my Clochegourde again. All was silent and a-quiver as is the countryside at noon. The still foliage was sharply outlined against the blue background of the sky; the insects which draw life from the light, dragon flies and blister flies, flew to their reeds and ash trees; the herds browsed in the shade, the red soil of the vines burned and the grass snakes slithered along the banks.

What a change in this landscape, so fresh and trim before my sleep! Abruptly, I leapt out of the boat and went back up the path intending to walk round Clochegourde, whence I thought I had seen the Count emerge. I was not wrong. He was walking along a hedge, doubtless making for a gate leading on to the path to Azay which runs by the river. "How are you this morning, Monsieur le Comte?" He looked at me happily. He did not often hear himself so addressed. "Very well," he said. "But you must be fond of the country to wander about in this heat."

"I was sent here to live in the fresh air, was I not?"

"Would you care to come and see my rye cut, then?"

"Gladly," said I. "I am unbelievably ignorant, I must confess. I cannot tell wheat from rye, nor an aspen from a poplar. I know nothing about crops nor the different ways of cultivating land."

"Come with me then," said he, gaily, retracing his steps. "Go through the little gate at the top." He walked back along the hedge on the inside and I on the outside.

"You will learn nothing with Monsieur de Chessel," he said. "He is much too grand to bother with anything more than his bailiff's account book."

So he showed me his farmyards and outbuildings, the flower gardens, orchards and kitchen gardens. Finally, he led the way to that long avenue of acacias and trees of heaven, bordered by the river, where, at the far end, sitting on a bench, I caught sight of Madame de Mortsauf, busy with her two children. A woman looks lovely indeed under those thin, quivering, delicately outlined leaves. Surprised perhaps by my artless haste, she made no move, knowing that we would come to her. The Count made me admire the view of the valley, which presents, at that point, a quite different aspect from those it had displayed at the varying altitudes along which we had come. Here, you would have thought yourself in a small corner of Switzerland. The pasture-land furrowed by the streams which tumble into the Indre is revealed in its entire length and fades away into the misty distances. Looking towards Mont-bazon, a vast green expanse opens to the view, blocked in every other direction by hills, clumps of trees and rocks. We quickened our pace and went to greet Madame de Mortsauf. All of a sudden, she dropped the book from which Madeleine was reading and took Jacques, who was in the throes of a coughing fit, on to her knee.

"What's the matter with him?" cried the Count, turning white.

"He has a sore throat," answered his mother, who seemed not to have seen me. "It's nothing serious."

She was holding his head and his back and from her eyes came two beams of light which poured life into the poor weak creature.

"You are unbelievably rash," said the Count harshly. "You expose him to the cold river air and you let him sit on a stone seat!"

"But father, the bench is burning hot!" cried Madelaine.

"They were stifling up there," said the Countess.

"Women must always have the last word!" said he, giving me a look.

To avoid showing approval or disapproval I turned my gaze on Jacques, who complained that his throat hurt. His mother took him away. but before she left us, she was able to overhear her husband say, "When one brings such unhealthy children into the world, one should know how to look after them."

The words were profoundly unfair, but his vanity urged him to justify himself at his wife's expense. The Countess flew up the steps and along the terraces. I saw her vanish through the French window. Monsieur de Mortsauf had sat down on the bench, head bowed, sunk in thought. My position was growing intolerable; he neither spoke nor looked at me. Farewell to that walk, during which I had planned to establish myself so well in his good graces! I cannot remember spending a more horrible fifteen minutes in my life. I poured with sweat as I said to myself "Shall I go? Shall I stay?" What sad thoughts must have arisen in him to make him forget to go and see how Jacques was! He rose abruptly and came and stood beside me. We turned to look at the laughing valley.

"We will postpone our walk until another day, Monsieur le Comte," I said gently.

"Let us go," he replied. "I am unfortunately used to seeing sudden attacks of this sort, I who would gladly give my life to save that child's."

"Jacques is better, my dear. He is sleeping," said the golden voice. Madame de Mortsauf appeared suddenly at the end of the avenue. She came up to us, with no bitterness, no rancour, and returned my greeting.

45

"I am glad to see," she said, "that you appear to like Cloche-gourde."

"My dear, would you like me to ride over and fetch Doctor Deslandes?" he said, showing his desire to be forgiven for his unjustness.

"Do not torment yourself," she said. "Jacques did not sleep last night, that's all. The child is very highly strung. He had a bad dream and I spent the night telling him stories to send him to sleep again. The cough is a purely nervous one. I soothed it with a gum pastille, and he has dropped off to sleep."

"Poor thing," he said, taking her hand in both of his and giving her a melting look, "I had no idea."

"Why should I worry you over nothing at all? Go and see to your rye. You know, if you are not there, the farmers will let the gleaners into the field before the sheaves have been removed."

"I am about to have my first lesson in agriculture, Madame," said I.

"You are in good hands," she replied, indicating the Count, whose mouth pursed into a gratified smirk.

Not until two months later did I learn that she had spent that night in appalling anxiety, fearing that her son had croup. And there had I been, in the boat, lulled by soft thoughts of love, fondly imagining that from her window she would see me worshipping the light of the candle which, at that moment, was lighting up the furrows of her mortally anxious brow.

Croup was raging in Tours and was taking a fearful toll there. When we reached the door, the Count said in a shaky voice:

"Madame de Mortsauf is an angel!" The words made me reel. I still only knew this family slightly, and the remorse, so natural to a young heart in similar circumstances, cried out in me: "By what right would you disturb this deep tranquillity?"

Glad to have as a listener a young man over whom he could score easy victories, the Count spoke to me of what the return of the Bourbons would mean for the future of France. We had a rambling conversation, in which I heard some truly childish nonsense which surprised me strangely. He was ignorant of mathematically self-evident facts; he was afraid of educated people; superiority of talent he denied. He cared nothing, and perhaps rightly, for progress. In short, I recognised in him a great quantity of sore spots which obliged one to tread so gingerly in order not to hurt his feelings that a sustained conversation became a mental feat. When I had, so to speak, put my finger on his shortcomings, I adapted myself to them with as much pliability as the Countess employed in caressing them. At some other period in my life I would undoubtedly have offended him. But, timid as a child, thinking I knew nothing, or that grown men knew it all, I was open-mouthed at the wonders achieved at Clochegourde by this patient agriculturist. I listened admiringly to his plans. Finally—a piece of unconscious flattery which earned me the old nobleman's good-will—I expressed my envy of this lovely estate, its position, the earthly paradise it was, setting it high above Frapesle. "Frapesle," I told him, "is a massive silver service, but Clochegourde is a casket of precious stones," a phrase that he often quoted later, with acknowledgements to the author.

"Well," he said, "before we came here, it was a wilderness."

I was all ears when he spoke of his nurseries and seed-beds. New to the labours of the country, I showered him with questions on the price of things and on methods of cultivation and he seemed happy at having to teach me so many details.

"Why, what do they teach you, then?" he asked me in astonishment.

That very first day, the Count said to his wife when he came in, "Monsieur Felix is a charming young man."

That evening, I wrote to my mother asking her to send me some clothes and linen and telling her that I should be staying on at Frapesle. Ignorant of the great revolution which was then taking place and not grasping the influence it was to wield on my future, I fully expected to return to Paris to finish my law studies, and the Law School did not reopen until the beginning of November. I had, therefore, two and a half months ahead of me.

During the early days of my stay, I tried to form a close association with the Count and it proved to be a period of cruel impressions. I discovered in this man an irascibility without cause and a promptness to action in hopeless situations which frightened me. One met in him sudden returns of the nobleman who had been so brave in Condé's army, a few parabolic flashes of the kind of will which can, on the dark day of crisis, blow a hole in a nation's politics in the manner of a bomb and which, by the accidents of integrity or courage, turn a man condemned to live in his country residence into a d'Elbée, a Bonchamp, a Charette.* At certain suppositions his nose contracted, his brow cleared and his eyes flashed with a fire straightway quenched. I was often afraid that if he surprised the language of my eyes Monsieur de Mortsauf would kill me on the spot. At that time, I was affectionate to the exclusion of all else. The will which alters men so strangely was only then beginning to sprout in me. My excessive desires had given me those swift spasms of feeling which resemble the sudden jolts of fear. It was not the fight that made me tremble, but I did not want to lose my life without having tasted the happiness of requited love. The obstacles and my desires grew along two parallel lines. How was I to speak of my feelings? I was in the grip of distressing perplexities. I awaited a chance occasion; I watched; I made friends with the children, whose love I won; I strove to identify myself with the things of the household.

Imperceptibly, the Count grew less reserved with me. Thus I got to know his sudden changes of mood, his deep, unaccountable bouts of sadness, his bursts of temper, his bitter, cutting complaints, his hate-filled coldness, his spasms of madness instantly checked, the whimpering child in him, the man crying out in his despair, the unexpected bouts of rage. Man's moral differs from his physical nature in that nothing in it is absolute: the intensity of the effects depends on the individual character or on the ideas which we group around a fact. My continued presence at Clochegourde, the future of my life, depended on this temperamental will. I would be at a loss to tell you the anguish that weighed on my soul, as quick, at that time, to open as to contract, when, on entering the house, I would say to myself "How will he receive me?" What anxiety would crush my heart when all of a sudden a storm gathered on that hoary brow! It was a perpetual *qui-vive*. I fell, then, under this man's despotic sway.

My sufferings made me guess those of Madame de Mortsauf. We began to exchange understanding glances; my tears flowed sometimes when she withheld hers. The Countess and I put each other

* All three were famous Royalist leaders in the Vendée. (*Translator's note.*)

48

to the test through pain. How many discoveries did I not make during those first forty days, days full of genuine bitterness, of unspoken joys, of hopes now engulfed, now floating on the surface! One evening I came upon her, in religious contemplation before a sunset which tipped the hilltops with so voluptuous a red, as it revealed the valley like a bed below them, that it was impossible not to hear the voice of that eternal Song of Songs, with which Nature invites her creatures to love. Was the young girl taking back illusions long since flown? Was the woman suffering from some secret comparison? I thought to detect in her attitude an abandon favourable to an initial declaration and I said "Some days are difficult!"

"You have read my thoughts," said she, "but how?"

"We touch each other on so many points!" I replied. "Do we not belong to that little band of creatures, privileged in pain and pleasure, whose sensitive qualities vibrate in unison and produce great inner reverberations; whose highly strung natures are in constant harmony with the principle of things? Place them in a setting where all is discord and these people suffer horribly, just as their pleasure rises to exaltation when they meet the ideas, sensations or beings with whom they are in sympathy. But there is, for us, a third state, the misfortunes of which are known only to souls afflicted with the same malady and in whom fraternal understanding finds a meeting-ground. It can happen that nothing external makes its mark on us, either for good or ill. An expressive organ, endowed with movement, works within us then, in the void, warms to unfocused passion, emits sounds without producing a melody, gives out accents which lose themselves in silence; a sort of terrible contradiction in a soul which rebels against the uselessness of the void; heartbreaking games in which our entire strength leaks away without nourishment, like blood from an unknown wound. Feeling flows in torrents, resulting in dreadful fits of weakness and unspeakable bouts of melancholy, for which the confessional has no ears. Have I not expressed our mutual heartaches?"

She gave a start and without taking her eyes off the sunset she replied, "How, young as you are, can you know these things?"

"Ah," I replied, in a voice charged with emotion, "my childhood was like one long illness."

49

"I hear Madeleine coughing," she said and hurried away.

The Countess took no exception to my assiduous visits to her house, for two reasons. Firstly, she was as pure as a child and her thoughts never strayed from the straight path. Then again, I amused the Count, I was food for this clawless and maneless lion. I had finally managed to find a reason for coming which seemed plausible to all of us. I did not know how to play back-gammon. Monsieur de Mortsauf offered to teach me and I accepted. At the moment that we made the arrangement, the Countess could not help throwing me a compassionate glance, which said "Why you are jumping straight into the lion's mouth!" Though I may not at first have understood, I knew by the third day to what I had committed myself. My untiring patience, that fruit of my childhood, ripened during this period of trial. It was a source of joy to the Count to indulge in cruel jibes whenever I failed to put into practice the method or rule he had explained to me. If I stopped to think, he complained of the boredom of a slow game; if I played fast, he grew irate at being hurried; if I forgot to score, he would say, while taking advantage of my error, that I was in too much of a hurry. It was a donnish tyranny, a despotism of the rod of which I can only give you some idea by comparing myself to Epictetus under the yoke of a spiteful child. When we played for money, his constant gains caused him a shaming, petty glee. A word from his wife consoled me for it all and straightway restored his sense of politeness and good form.

Before long I fell into the hot coals of an unforeseen torment. At this activity, my money melted away. Although the Count always remained between his wife and me until I left them, which was sometimes very late, I was always hopeful of finding a moment when I could steal into her heart; but to win this hour, awaited with the painful patience of the hunter, was I not obliged to continue with these plaguing games, where my soul was perpetually anguished and which ran away with all my money! How many times, already, had we not stood in silence, absorbedly watching an effect of sunlight on the meadows, or banked clouds in a grey sky, the misty hills or the moon quivering in the pebbles of the river, saying no more than:

"How beautiful the night is!"

"The night is a woman, Madame."

"How quiet it is!"

"Yes, one could never be completely unhappy here."

At this reply, she would go back to her tapestry. I had at last heard in her the deep heart-stirrings caused by an affection clamouring for its place. Without money, it was goodbye to those evenings. I had written to my mother asking her to send me some; my mother scolded me and did not give me any for a week. Whom in the world could I ask? And it was a matter of life and death! So, once again, I encountered, at the heart of my first great happiness, the suffering which had everywhere assailed me; save that in Paris, at college, at boarding school, I had escaped them through thoughtful self-denial. My unhappiness had been a negative one. At Frapesle it became positive. I knew now the temptings of theft, the imagined crimes, the terrible rages which furrow the soul and which we must smother under pain of forfeiting our self-esteem. The memory of the cruel meditations, the agonies of mind imposed on me by my mother's parsimoniousness, have inspired in me that blessed indulgence towards the young common to those who, without flinching, have travelled to the edge of the abyss, in order as it were, to gauge its depth. Although my probity, bred of cold sweats, gained strength at those moments when life opens and lets us glimpse the arid gravel of its bed, yet each time that mankind's terrible justice has drawn its blade across the neck of a man, I have said to myself, "The penal code was made by men who never knew misfortune."

In this extremity, I discovered, in Monsieur de Chessel's library, the book of rules of backgammon and I studied it. My host was kind enough to give me a few lessons; less harshly driven, I was able to improve my game and to apply the rules and calculations, which I proceeded to learn by heart. In a very few days I was in a fit state to beat my master; but when I won, his mood became execrable. His eyes flashed like a tiger's, his face stiffened, his eyebrows worked as I never saw anyone's do before or since. His complaining was that of a spoilt child. Sometimes he would fling away the dice, fly into a rage, stamp his feet, bite his dice shaker and hurl abuse at me. These outbursts soon ceased. When I had learnt to play the better of the two, I conducted the battle as I pleased. I saw to it that at the end of the game we were more or less even, by letting him win for the first half and righting the balance during the second. The end of the world would have surprised the Count less than the superiority of his pupil; but he never acknowledged it. The unvarying outcome of our games was new food for his mind to seize on.

"No doubt about it," he would say, "my poor wits are growing tired. You always win towards the end of the evening, because by then I have lost my resources."

The Countess, who knew the game, noticed my tactics the very first time and sensed in them an immense token of devotion. These details can only be appreciated by those who are familiar with the horrible difficulties of backgammon. What worlds were spoken by my little gesture! But love, like Bossuet's God, sets the poor man's glass of water, the strivings of the soldier who dies unknown, above the richest victories. The Countess threw me one of those unspoken "thank you's" so shattering to a young heart: she granted me the glance which she reserved for her children!

Since that beatific evening, she always looked at me when she spoke to me. I would be at a loss to explain in what state I was when I left. My soul had absorbed my body. I was light as air, I did not walk, I flew. I could feel that look inside me, it had flooded me with light, just as her "Goodbye, sir" had made my soul ring with the harmonies contained in the "*O filii O filiae*" of the Easter resurrection. I was being born to a new life. So I meant something to her! I fell asleep in swaddling clothes of purple. Flames sped before my closed eyes and chased each other in the darkness like those pretty tongues of flame that lick across the ashes of burnt paper. In my dreams, her voice became something strangely tangible, an atmosphere which enveloped me in fragrances and light, a melody that caressed my mind. The next day, her greeting expressed the plenitude of feelings freely given and I was initiated there and then into the secrets of her voice. That day was to be one of the most significant of my whole life.

After dinner we went for a walk over the hills and along a heath, a patch of land where nothing could grow. The ground was stony and parched and bare of topsoil: there were, however, a few oaks and bushes, but, instead of grasses there stretched a carpet of tawny, crinkly moss, fired by the rays of the setting sun and slippery underfoot. I held Madeleine's hand to steady her and Madame de Mortsauf gave Jacques her arm. The Count, who was walking ahead, turned, struck the ground with his stick and said to me in a frightful tone of voice, "There is my life for you! Before I met you, of course," he corrected himself with an apologetic look at his wife. Belated amends, the Countess had turned pale. Where is the woman who would not have reeled as she did under such a blow?

"What delicious scents there are here" I exclaimed. "And how beautiful the light is! I wish this heath were mine. I might find treasures here if I explored it. But its most certain wealth would be its proximity to you. Who would not pay dearly for a view so harmonious to the eye? And that winding river where the soul bathes among the alder and the ash! You see how tastes vary? For you this stretch of land is a heath, for me it is a paradise."

"Idyllic nonsense!" said he sourly. "There is no life here for a man who bears your name." Then he changed the subject and said, "Do you hear the bells of Azay? I swear I can hear the bells ringing."

Madame de Mortsauf gave me a frightened look. Madeleine's hand tightened in mine.

"Shall we go back and play a game of backgammon?" I asked. "The click of the dice will drown the sound of the bells."

We went back to Clochegourde, talking desultorily on the way. The Count complained of sharp pains without, however, being any more explicit. When we were in the drawing-room, there arose an indefinable sensation of uncertainty amongst the three of us. The Count was sunk in an armchair, deep in a brown study respected by his wife, who knew the symptoms of the illness and could foresee its attacks. I imitated her silence. If she did not ask me to leave, it was perhaps because she thought that a game of backgammon would cheer the Count and dispel that fatal irritability the outbursts of which were killing her. Nothing was ever harder than to get the Count to play that game of backgammon, a thing he was always dying to do. Like a kept woman he wanted to be begged, coerced, so as not to look as though he were under any obligation, perhaps for the very reason that this was indeed the case.

53

If, in the course of an interesting conversation, I forgot for a moment to bow and scrape to him, he became sullen, harsh and wounding and would show his irritation at the conversation and contradict all that was being said. Alerted by his ill humour, I would suggest a game. He would then make a show of reluctance. In the first place, he would say, it was too late, and besides I wasn't interested. Then followed a series of affected, unreasoning objections as in the case with women, who leave you, in the end, wondering what it is they really do want. I would crawl to him, beg him to help me keep my hand in at a game which was so easily forgotten through lack of practice. This time, it took a wild gaiety on my part to persuade him to play. He complained of giddy spells which would prevent him from working out his moves; he had iron bands round his skull; there was a singing in his ears; he was choking. He fought for breath and heaved enormous sighs. At last, he consented to sit at the card table. Madame de Mortsauf left us to put her children to bed and hold the household prayers. All went well during her absence. I played so that Monsieur de Mortsauf should win and his delight abruptly cleared his brow. The sudden transition from a sadness which tore from him dire prophecies about himself to this inebriated joy, this mad, almost motiveless laughter, disquieted me and sent chill shivers down my spine.

I had never seen him in so frankly obvious a fit. Our close acquaintance had borne fruit. He could be himself with me now. Every day he tried to envelop me in his tyranny and to make certain of new food for his ill-humour, for it would really seem that mental illnesses are creatures with their own appetites and instincts, who want to increase the extent of their sway, just as a landowner wants to add to his acres. The Countess came in and moved nearer to the card table to get a better light for her tapestry work, but she sat down to her loom with ill-disguised apprehension. A fateful move, which I could not forestall, altered the Count's expression. It turned from gay to sombre; from crimson it grew yellow. His eyes flickered.

Then came one last disaster which I could neither foresee nor repair. Monsieur de Mortsauf threw a devastating die which sealed his downfall. He leapt to his feet, threw the board on to me, the lamp on to the floor, banged the table with his fist and jumped around the room—he can hardly be said to have walked. The torrent of insults, imprecations, apostrophes and incoherent phrases which issued from his lips put one in mind of some medieval victim of possession. You can imagine my state of mind!

"Go into the garden," she said, pressing my hand.

I left the room without the Count noticing my disappearance. From the terrace, to which I slowly made my way, I could hear the moans and sudden shouts that issued from his room, which adjoined the dining room. Through the storm, I heard, too, the angel's voice rising intermittently, like the song of the nightingale when the rain is about to cease.

I wandered under the acacias on the finest night of the dying month of August, waiting for the Countess to join me. She would come; her gesture had promised it.

For some days now, an explanation had been hovering between us and it seemed bound to break out at the first word which released the swollen stream in our two hearts. What secret shame was it that delayed the hour of our perfect understanding? Perhaps she cared as much as I for that spasm, so like the emotions of fear, which bruises the sensibility in those moments when one holds back the brimming swell of life in one, when, loth to unveil one's inmost self, one obeys that modesty that stirs in maidens before they show themselves to the bridegroom they love. We had ourselves increased, by our accumulated thoughts, that first exchange of confidence, grown necessary now. An hour went by. I was seated on the brick balustrade, when the echo of her step and the rustle of her fluttering dress quickened the calm night air. The heart is unequal to sensations such as these.

"Monsieur de Mortsauf is asleep now," she said. "When he is like this, I give him a cup of water with a few poppy heads infused in it. The attacks are far enough apart for this simple remedy to retain its efficacy. Monsieur," she said, changing her tone and adopting her most persuasive accents, "by a regrettable mischance, certain secrets, up till now carefully guarded, are now in your possession. Promise me that you will bury the memory of that scene in your heart. Do it for my sake, I beg of you. I am not asking you for any solemn promise. Say 'Yes', as a man of honour, and I shall be satisfied."

"Need I even pronounce that 'yes'?" said I. "Is there no understanding between us at all?"

"Do not think too badly of Monsieur de Mortsauf, when you see the effects of years of suffering undergone during his exile," said she. "To-morrow he will have no idea at all of the things he said and you will find him affectionate and irreproachable."

"Stop trying to justify the Count, Madame," said I. "I will do anything you ask of me. I would jump into the Indre forthwith if by so doing I could restore Monsieur de Mortsauf to health and you to happiness. The only thing I cannot reshape is my opinion; nothing is more strongly welded in me. I would give you my life, but I cannot give you my conscience. I can refuse to listen to it, but can I still its voice? Now, in my opinion Monsieur de Mortsauf is—"

"I know what you want to say," she broke in, with untoward abruptness. "You are right. The Count is as excitable as a capricious girl," she added, softening the notion of madness by softening the word, "but he is only like this occasionally, once a year at the most, during the very hot season. Oh, the harm that emigration has caused! How many fine lives wasted! He would have been a great soldier, I am sure of it, the glory of his country."

"I know," said I, interrupting in my turn, and giving her to understand that it was pointless to deceive me.

She stopped, laid her hand on my brow and said "Who was it then, who brought you into our home like this? Does God mean to send me a helping hand, a strong friendship to lean upon?" she added, pressing her hand firmly upon mine, "for you are generous and kind ..."

She raised her eyes to Heaven as if to invoke a visible witness to confirm her secret hopes and then turned them to me again. Electrified by this gaze, that threw a soul into my own, I made a remark, which could, by worldly standards, fairly be deemed tactless; but, with certain souls, is this not, often, a headlong impulse towards danger, a desire to parry a blow, a fear of the expected disaster, or more often still, is it not an abrupt question put to a human heart, a blow struck in hope of an answering echo? Several

56

thoughts arose like gleams of light in me and prompted me to wash away the stain on my sincerity, now that I foresaw a complete initiation.

"Before we go any further," I said, in a voice made jerky by the heartbeats easily audible in the deep silence that surrounded us, "will you allow me to purify a memory of the past?"

"Be quiet," she said quickly, laying a finger on my lips and withdrawing it immediately. She looked at me proudly, like a woman too highly placed for insult to attain her and said in a troubled voice, "I know what it is you want to speak of. You are referring to the first, last and only outrage I have ever known! Never speak of that ball again. The Christian may have forgiven you, but the woman suffers from it still."

"Do not be more implacable than God," said I, holding in my lashes the tears that sprang to my eyes.

"I must be more severe, for I am the weaker," she replied.

"But," I went on, with a kind of childish rebelliousness, "listen to me, were it but for the first, last and only time in your life."

"Very well," said she, "say what you have to say. Otherwise you will think I am afraid to hear it."

And so, sensing that this moment was a unique one in our lives, I told her, in that tone of voice which commands attention, that I had been indifferent to all the women at the ball, as well as to all those I had seen until that day. But that on seeing her, I whose life was so studious, whose soul was the opposite of bold, I had been seized by a sort of frenzy which only those who had never known it could condemn; that never was man's heart so truly filled with that desire which no living creature can resist and which can make one triumph over all things, even death ...

"And contempt too?" she said, cutting me short.

"Did you despise me, then?" I asked.

"Let us not talk of these things any more," said she.

"We must!" I replied, with the exultation caused by a superhuman pain. "This concerns all of myself, my life of which you know nothing, a secret which you must be told; otherwise I will die of despair! And does it not concern you too, you who, without knowing it, have been the Lady in whose hands gleams the crown promised to the victor of the tournament?"

I told her of my childhood and early youth, not as I told it to you, from the vantage point of distance, but in the burning words of the young man whose wounds are still raw. My voice rang like a woodcutter's axe in a forest. Before it, with a mighty noise, fell the dead years, the long sufferings which had left them bristling with leafless branches. I painted for her, in fevered words, a host of terrible details which I spared you. I displayed the treasure of my shining vows, the virgin gold of my desires, a whole burning heart preserved beneath the alpine ice piled high by a perpetual winter.

Bowed beneath the weight of my woes, retold with Isaiah's burning coals, I awaited for a word from the woman who stood listening with bent head. She lit up the darkness with a look, she brought the divine and earthly worlds to life with a single phrase.

"We had the same childhood!" she said, showing me a face where shone a martyr's crown.

After a pause, in which our souls wedded in the same consoling thought of "So I was not the only one who suffered", the Countess told me, in the voice she reserved for her precious little ones, how she had made the mistake of being a girl in a family whose sons had died. She explained the differences between the sufferings of a girl forever tied to the maternal apron strings and those of a child flung into the world of college life. My loneliness had been a paradise beside the millstone under which her spirit was continually bruised, until the day when her dear, good aunt, her true mother, had come to the rescue and snatched her from this torment, whose reawakening pangs she related to me now. There were the gratuitous pinpricks, unbearable to those highly strung natures, who do not flinch before a dagger thrust, and die beneath the sword of Damocles; now an open-hearted impulse checked by an icy look, now a kiss coldly received, or a silence by turns commanded or reproved; swallowed tears which lay heavy on her heart; and then the hundred and one tyrannies of convent life—a harshness screened from outside eyes by the outward show of a maternity gloriously vowed to God. She was a source of vanity to her mother, who praised her in public; but she paid dearly the next day for the flattery essential to her schoolmistress' gratification. When, through sustained obedience and sweetness, she thought she had won her mother's love and opened her heart to her, the tyrant would rise uppermost again, armed with these confidences. A spy could not have been baser nor more treacherous. All her holidays, all her girlish pleasures had been dearly sold to her, for she was scolded afterwards for her enjoyment as for a misdeed. Never was her noble education given her with love, but with a hurtful irony. She felt no resentment against her mother, she only blamed herself for feeling less love for her than terror. Perhaps, thought this angel, such severity was necessary; had it not prepared her for her present life? As I listened, it seemed to me that Job's harp, from which I had drawn savage chords, handled now with Christian fingers, was responding with the melodious litanies of the Virgin at the foot of the Cross.

"We lived in the same sphere before meeting here. You came from the Orient and I from the West."

She shook her head in a gesture of despair.

"Yours is the Orient," said she, "the Occident for me. You will live happy. I shall die of pain. A man shapes his own circumstances. Mine are forever fixed. No power can break the heavy chain to which a woman is held by a gold ring, that symbol of wifely purity."

Then, sensing that we were twins from the same breast, it did not cross her mind that there could be half-confidences between brothers who had drunk from the same springs and, with the sigh natural to pure hearts at the moment when they open, she told me of the early days of her marriage, her first disappointments, the whole springtide of misfortune. Like me, she had known the little incidents, so great to those souls whose limpid substance is shaken through and through at the least shock, just as a stone thrown into a lake disturbs both its surface and its depths. When she married, she had her savings, that little store of gold which represents the happy hours, the hundred and one whims of youth. On one needy day, she had generously parted with it, without mentioning that they were memories and not gold coins. Her husband never so much as mentioned it again; he did not even realise that he was in her debt. In exchange for this treasure, sunk in the still waters of oblivion, she was never given that soft look which cancels every debt and which is, for generous souls, the eternal gem whose fires shine on the difficult days. How fast pain had succeeded pain! Monsier de Mortsauf would forget to give her the housekeeping money. He woke as if from a dream when, overcoming all her feminine reticence, she would ask him for some, and not once had he spared her those cruel pangs of distress. What terror gripped her heart when this ruined man's morbid nature first revealed itself! His first outburst of insane rage had quite crushed her. How many bitter heartsearchings had she not known before she came to regard her husband, that impressive figure who dominates a woman's life, as a nonentity! What terrible calamities followed the birth of those two children! How her heart must have turned over at the sight of those two stillborn babes, and what courage it took to say to herself, "I shall breathe life into them! I shall give birth to them anew each day!" And then, think of the despair of feeling a barrier in the heart and hand whence a woman normally draws her succour! She had seen that vast expanse of woe spreading its thorny savannas at each new setback overcome. As each rock was climbed, she had viewed new wastes to cross, before the day came when she was fully versed in her husband's nature, and the planning of her children's lives and the place where she was going to have to live; before the day when, like the child torn by Napoleon from the tender care of home, she trained her feet to trudge through snow and mud, inured her brow to cannon-fire and her whole person to the passive obedience of the soldier. The things which I am now condensing for you, she told me in all their murky length, with their cortège of painful episodes, lost matrimonial battles and fruitless effort.

"You would need to stay here several months," she concluded, "in order to realise the amount of trouble that the improvements to Clochegourde are costing me, the amount of exhausting wheedling it takes to make him want the thing which will be to his best advantage. If you knew the childish spite that comes over him when something done on my advice does not immediately succeed! And how gleefully he claims the credit for anything that turns out well! Oh, the patience it takes to hear nothing but complaints when I strain every nerve to keep his hours free from weeds, to sweeten the air he breathes, to sand and plant with flowers the paths he has strewn with stones! The terrible refrain of 'I am going to die! Life is too hard for me!' is my reward. In the happy event of his having visitors all is forgotten and he is gracious and polite. Why can he not be like that with his family? I am at a loss to explain this want of loyalty in a man who can on occasions be so chivalrous. He is capable of riding secretly to Paris at full gallop to buy me a necklace, as he did recently for the Tours ball. Mean for his household, he would be lavish with me, if I wanted. It should be the reverse. There is nothing I need, and his household expenses are heavy. In my desire to make life happy for him, and heedless of the fact that I would one day be a mother, I may have encouraged him to use me as his habitual whipping boy, I who with a little cajolery could lead him like a child, if I could lower myself to play a rôle which seems to me an infamous one. But, in the interests of the household, I must be as severe and calm as the statue of Justice. Yet I, too, have a tender, openhearted nature!"

"Why," said I, "do you not use this influence you have to master him and rule him?"

"If I had only myself to consider, I could neither overcome his mulish silence, pitted as it is for hours on end against reasonable arguments, nor answer criticisms that are quite without logic, reasoning that is positively childish. I have no courage against children or the weak. They can strike at me and I shall not resist. I might perhaps meet force with force but I am nerveless against those whom I feel sorry for. If I had to force Madeleine to do something which could save her life, I would die with her. Pity slackens my heartstrings and softens all my nerves. Besides, the violent shocks of these ten years have left me crushed. Now my sensibility, so often attacked, is sometimes without substance; nothing revives it. The energy which used to help me ride the storm fails me now sometimes. Yes, at times, I am beaten. Without the rest and the sea bathing which could infuse new life into me, I shall die. Monsieur de Mortsauf will have killed me and he will die of my death."

"Why do you not leave Clochegourde for a few months? Why not go with your children to the seaside?"

"To begin with, Monsieur de Mortsauf would be lost if I went away. Although he refuses to believe the truth about himself, he is nevertheless aware of it. There are two people in him, the man and the invalid, two differing natures whose contradictions explain many a curious aberration! And he would have good reason to quake. Everything would go wrong here. You see me, perhaps, as a mother busy protecting her children against the menace that looms over them—a crushing task, increased by the attentions demanded by Monsieur de Mortsauf, who is forever asking 'Where is Madame?' That is nothing. I am also Jacques' tutor, and Madeleine's governess. That too is nothing! I am the bailiff and the steward. One day you will know the implications of what I am telling you when you find out that the exploitation of an estate is the most exhausting of activities. We have few revenues in actual money. Our farms are cultivated on the 'half-and-half', a system which demands continuous supervision. One must do one's own selling of grain, livestock and crops of all kinds. We are in competition with our farmers, who strike their own bargains in the tavern with the buyers and who fix the prices after selling their produce first.

"It would bore you if I explained the thousand and one difficulties of our agriculture. With the best will in the world I cannot be always on the watch to see that our tenants do not fertilize their land with our manure. I cannot go and see if our bailiffs are not making private agreements with them when the time comes for the division of the crops, nor can I know the favourable time to sell. Now, if you stop to consider how bad Monsieur de Mortsauf's memory is, and how much trouble you have seen me take to force him to see to his affairs, you will understand the weight of my burden and how impossible it is for me to set it down, even for a second. If I went away we should be ruined. No one would pay any attention to him. His orders contradict each other half the time. Besides, nobody likes him; he carps too much, he is too autocratic. Then again, like all weak people, he listens too readily to his inferiors to inspire the affection which binds households together. If I went away, no servant would stay here a week. Can't you see that I am tied to Clochegourde just as those clusters of lead are to our roof? I have kept nothing back from you, sir. Not a soul in the county has any inkling of the secrets of Clochegourde and now you know them. Say nothing about it but what is kind and obliging and you will earn my esteem—my gratitude," she added, in a gentler tone. "On those conditions, you may always come back to Clochegourde. You will find friendly hearts there."

"Why," said I, "*I* have never suffered! You alone—"

"No," said she, with that fleeting smile, common to resigned women, which would cut through granite, "do not be too taken aback by these confidences. They show you life as it is, not as your imagination led you to hope it might be. We all of us have our virtues and our faults. Had I married some spendthrift, he would have ruined me. Had I been given to some passionate, pleasure-loving young man, he would have made easy conquests, I might not have known how to keep him, he would have left me and I should have died of jealousy. I am a jealous woman!" she said, with a new note of excitement in her voice that resembled the last clap of thunder in a dying storm. "Monsieur de Mortsauf loves me as much as he can love. All the affection that his heart can hold he pours at my feet, as Magdalen poured the remains of her unguents on the feet of the Saviour. Believe me! A lifetime of love is the fatal exception to terrestial law. Every flower dies, great joys have a sour tomorrow, if they have a morrow. Real life is a life of anguish. Its image is in that nettle, growing at the foot of this terrace, which without sunlight, remains green on the stem. Here, as in Northern countries, there are smiles in Heaven, rare, to be sure, but which repay one for many cares. And are not women who are purely mothers more strongly bound to their loved ones by sacrifice than pleasure? Here, I draw down on myself the storms which I see about to break over the servants or my children and I experience, as I avert them, some nameless feeling which gives me a secret strength. Yesterday's resignation has always paved the way for the morrow's. Besides, God does not leave me without hope. My children's health made me despair at first, but now, the longer they live, the healthier they are. After all, our home has grown finer, the family fortunes are building up again. Who knows if Monsieur de Mortsauf's old age will not be a happy one because of me? The human being who appears before the Supreme Judge, with a green palm in his hand, leading back to Him, comforted, those who railed against life, believe me, that human soul will have converted his sorrows into bliss. If my suffering serves to create the happiness of my family, is it truly suffering?"

"Yes," I replied, "but it was necessary, just as mine is, to make me value the savour of the fruit that has ripened among our rocks. Now perhaps we will taste it together, look with wonder at its prodigies—those torrents of affection with which it bathes the soul, that sap which revives the yellowing leaf. Life is no burden then, it is no longer ours. Dear God! Can you not hear me? See by what highways we have travelled towards each other," I went on, employing the mystical language to which our religious education had accustomed us. "See the magnet that has led us, over the ocean of bitter waters, towards the freshwater spring that flows at the foot of the hills, over a glittering bed of sand, between two green and flower-strewn banks. Have we not, like the Magi, followed the same star? And here we stand, before the crib, where wakes a divine child who will shoot his darts at the leafless trees and revive our world with his glad cries, who, by ceaseless delights, will lend a zest to living, will give the nights back their slumber and the days their joy. Who is it, tell me, who year by year, forged new bonds between us two? Are we not more than brother and sister? Never cast asunder what Heaven has joined together. Those sufferings you speak of were the seed scattered in handfuls by the sower to ripen the harvest already gilded by the sun's finest rays. See! See! Shall we not go forth together hand in hand, to gather it, ear by ear? What strength there is in me, that I should dare to speak to you like this! Oh, answer me, or I'll not go back across the Indre!"

"You have spared me the word 'love'," she interrupted sternly, "but you have spoken of a sentiment of which I know nothing and which is forbidden me. You are a child, I shall forgive you once again, but for the last time. Remember this, sir, my heart is as it were intoxicated with maternity. I love Monsieur de Mortsauf, not out of social duty, nor for the eternal blessedness I might hope to win thereby, but with an irresistible emotion which binds him to all the fibres of my heart. Was I forced into marriage with him? I took the step through my inborn sympathy for the victims of misfortune. Is it not a woman's task to repair the evils of the time, to comfort those who ran to fill the breach and came back wounded? How can I put it? I felt a kind of selfish satisfaction to see that you entertained him. Is not that purely maternal? Has not my confession sufficiently shown you that I have *three* children whom I must never fail, on whom I must pour a rain of healing dew and the warming rays of a spirit, not one particle of which must ever show a stain? Do not turn a mother's milk to gall! Although I am invulnerable as a wife, do not talk like this to me again. If you do not respect this very simple injunction, I warn you, this house will be forever closed to you. I imagined there could be such a thing as pure friendship, voluntary fraternity—more reliable than the brotherly love imposed upon true siblings. How wrong I was! I wanted a friend who was not a judge, one who would listen to me in those moments of weakness when a voice that scolds is a voice that kills—a blest friend with whom I would have nothing to fear. Youth is noble, truthful, capable of sacrifice, disinterested. Seeing your persistence, I believed, I confess, in some Heavenly design. I imagined I would have a soul who would be mine alone, the way a priest belongs to all; a heart where I could pour my woes when they brim over, cry out when my cries, too strong to resist, would choke me if I continued to swallow them. So my life, so precious to those children, could have endured until the day when Jacques became a man. But is that not too selfish of me? Can there be a second Petrarch's Laura? I was wrong, God does not will it so. I must die at my post, like the friendless soldier. My father confessor is austere and harsh and ... my aunt is no more."

Two great tears, lit by a moonbeam, came welling out of her eyes and rolled down her cheeks. I held out my hand to catch them as they fell and drank them with a pious avidity that her words had inflamed, words already signed by ten years of secret tears, spent sensibility, unremitting care, constant fears and the most exalted heroism of which your sex is capable! She looked at me in a gently stupefied way.

"Here," said I, "is the first, the blessed communion of love. I have just shared in your pain and united with your soul as we unite in Christ when we drink His divine substance. To love without hope is still a kind of happiness. Ah, what woman on this earth could give me a joy as great as that of having inspired those tears? I accept this pact, which must result in suffering for me. I am yours, unreservedly, and I shall be whatever you want me to be."

She stopped me with a gesture and said in her low voice, "I

65

consent to this pact, if you will agree never to press upon the ties that bind us two."

"Yes," said I, "but the less you grant me, the more certain shall I be of possessing."

"Your first thought is one of reservation," she replied, in a tone of melancholy doubt.

"No, one of pure joy. Listen to me. I should like to call you by a name that belonged to no one else, like the sentiment which we are pledging to each other."

"You are asking a great deal," said she, "but I am less small-minded than you think. Monsieur de Mortsauf calls me Blanche. One person in the world, the one I loved the most, my adored aunt, called me Henriette. So I shall be Henriette again for you."

I took her hand and kissed it. She surrendered it with that trust which sets a woman so far above a man, a trust that wrings our hearts.

"Is it not a mistake, my dear," said she, "to jump, at the first leap, right to the end of the course? You have, with your first breath, drained a goblet offered you with candour. But a true sentiment cannot be divided. It must be entire or it does not exist. Monsieur de Mortsauf," she went on, after a moment's silence, "is above all loyal and proud. You may perhaps be tempted, for my sake, to forget the things he said. If he does not remember, I shall remind him of them to-morrow. Stay away from Clochegourde for a short while. He will think all the more of you. Next Sunday, after Church, he will go to you himself. I know him, he will apologise and he will like you for having treated him as a man responsible for his own words and actions."

"Five days without seeing you, without hearing your voice!"

"Never put such warmth into the things you say to me," she said.

We walked twice round the terrace in silence. Then, in a tone of command which was proof to me that she was taking possession of my soul, she said, "It is late. We must part now."

I made to kiss her hand. She hesitated, surrendered it and said imploringly, "Take it only when I give it to you. Leave me my free will. Otherwise, I shall be a thing belonging to you and that must not be."

"Goodbye," I said.

I left by the little gate down below, which she opened for me. She made to shut it but opened it again, offered me her hand and said "You have been very kind this evening. You have brought comfort to my entire future. Take it, my friend, take it!"

I kissed her hand several times and when I raised my eyes, I saw tears in hers. She walked back on to the terrace and stood looking at me for a while longer across the meadow. When I was on the path to Frapesle, I could still see her white dress, lit up by the moon. Then, a few seconds later, a light appeared in her room.

"O my Henriette," I murmured, "I give you the purest love that ever shone upon this earth."

I reached Frapesle, looking over my shoulder at each step I took. I felt an indescribable contentment inside of me. A brilliant career was opening at last to the devotion that swells every youthful heart, and which had been for so long an inert force in me. Like the priest, who, with a single step, goes forward into a new life, I was consecrated, promised. A simple "Yes, Madame" had committed me to keeping an irresistible love locked in my heart, had bound me never to take advantage of friendship in order to entice this woman by small degrees, into the path of love. All the noble sentiments thus roused made their confused voices heard in me. Before entering the narrow confines of a room, I wanted to enjoy the voluptuous, star-studded blueness of the sky, to hear again within me the song of the wounded ring-dove, the artless tones of that trustful confidence, gather in the surrounding air the emanations of that spirit which were all destined for me. How great this woman seemed to me, with her deep forgetfulness of self, her religious dedication to wounded, weak or suffering creatures, her devotion, quite free of legal bonds! There she was, serene on her stake of saint and martyr. I was gazing with admiration on her face as it appeared to me in the surrounding darkness, when all of a sudden I thought to divine a mysterious significance in her words, which rendered her utterly sublime to me. Perhaps she wanted me to be to her what she was to her own little world; perhaps she wanted to draw her comfort and her strength from me, put me by so doing in her sphere, on her own level or above it. So the stars, say some bold builders of new worlds, impart to each other their own movement and light. The thought of this lifted me suddenly to ethereal heights. I found myself, suddenly, up in the sky of my old daydreams and I explained the heartaches of my childhood in terms of the immense happiness that now flowed over me.

Geniuses snuffed by tears, misunderstood hearts, saintly unknown Clarissa Harlowes, repudiated children, outlawed innocents, all of you who entered life by way of its deserts, you who found cold faces, blocked ears and closed hearts on every side, never bemoan your lot! You alone can know the boundlessness of joy when a heart opens for you, an ear listens, a look answers you. A single day can obliterate the bad days. The pain, the ruminations, the despair, the bouts of melancholy spent but not forgotten are so many ties which link soul to confiding soul. Her beauty increased by our repressed desires, a woman inherits then the sighs and the lost loves, she gives us back tenfold all our betrayed affections, she explains past sorrows as the pledge required by Fate for the eternal felicity it bestows on the day of the betrothal of the soul. Angels' lips alone can say the new name which should be given to this blest love, just as you alone, dear martyrs, will know what Madame de Mortsauf had suddenly become for me in my poverty and loneliness.

This scene had taken place on a Tuesday. I waited until the Sunday without crossing the Indre during my walks. In these five days, great events happened at Clochegourde. The Count received the rank of Camp Marshal, the Cross of Saint-Louis and a pension of four thousand francs. The Duc de Lenoncourt Givry, elected peer of France, recovered two forests and resumed his service at the Court, and his wife came into possession of those of her unsold estates which had formed part of the Imperial Crown lands. The Comtesse de Mortsauf thus became one of the richest heiresses in the province of Maine. Her mother had brought her a hundred thousand francs saved on the revenues of Givry, the balance of her dowry, which had never been paid and to which the Count, despite his financial difficulties, had never referred. In his dealing with the outside world, this man's conduct bore witness to the most proud disinterestedness. By adding this sum to his savings, the Count would now be able to buy two neighbouring estates, an investment worth an income of about nine thousand *livres*. As his son was to succeed to his grandfather's peerage, he suddenly hit on the notion of establishing an estate, consisting of the landed wealth of the two families, to be held in trust until the boy's majority, without in any way harming Madeleine's prospects, who would, thanks to the Duc de Lenoncourt's influence, make a very handsome marriage. These felicitous arrangements poured a little balm on the *émigré's* wounds. The Duchesse de Lenoncourt's visit to Clochegourde was an event in the neighbourhood. I reflected, with distress, that this woman was a great lady and I noticed then in her daughter the spirit of caste which the nobility of her sentiments hid from my view. What was I, poor as I was, with no other future than my courage and my native faculties? To the consequences of the Restoration, for myself or for others, I did not give a thought.

On the Sunday, from the side chapel where I sat with Monsieur and Madame de Chessel and the Abbé de Quélus, I threw avid glances at the chapel opposite, where sat the Duchess, her daughter, the Count and the children. The straw hat which hid my idol from me did not so much as quiver and this obliviousness of me seemed to bind me to her more strongly than the whole of the past. The noble Henriette de Lenoncourt, now my dear Henriette, whose life I wished to strew with flowers, was fervently praying; faith lent a certain air of prostrate, submerged humility, something of the pose of a religious statue to her attitude, that touched me to the heart.

According to the custom in village parishes, vespers were sung some while after Mass. On coming out of church, Madame de Chessel naturally invited her neighbours to spend the two hour wait at Frapesle, instead of making the double journey over the Indre and across the meadow in the midday heat. The offer was accepted. Monsieur de Chessel gave the Duchess his arm, and Madame de Chessel took the Count's. I offered mine to the Countess, and I felt, for the first time, that cool, lovely arm along my side. On the way back to Frapesle, walking through the Saché woods, where the light, filtering through the leaves, shed brightly-coloured patches, like painted silks, on to the sandy path, the thoughts and the sensations of pride that rose in me set my heart beating wildly.

"What is the matter?" she asked, after a few steps taken in a silence which I dared not break. "Your heart is beating far too fast ..."

"I have heard of your good fortune," said I, "and like all those who care for someone, I am faintly apprehensive. Will your high status not be detrimental to your friends?"

"I?" said she. "Nonsense! Another remark of that sort and I should, not despise you, but put you out of my mind for ever."

I looked at her, seized with a feverish elation which must have been infectious.

"We stand to gain from laws which we have neither solicited nor brought about. But we shall neither beg nor grasp for favours. Besides," she went on, "you know very well that neither Monsieur de Mortsauf nor I can leave Clochegourde. On my advice, he has refused the command in the *Maison Rouge* to which he was entitled. My father has his position at Court, that is enough for us! Our enforced modesty," she added, with a bitter smile, "has already served our child well. The king, in whose personal service my father is, has very graciously said that he would transfer the favour we have declined to Jacques. Jacques' education, to which thought must be given, is now the subject of serious discussion. He will represent two houses, the Lenoncourts and the Mortsaufs. Any ambition I have is for him, so my anxieties are consequently increased now. Jacques must not only survive, he must become worthy of his name, two obligations that run counter to each other. I have, until now, been able to meet the needs of his education by suiting the work to his strength. But where am I to find a suitable tutor for him? Then again, where is the friend who will keep him safe in that horrible city of Paris, where everything is a trap for the spirit and a danger to the body? My dear," she said in a voice touched with emotion, "judging from your brow and eyes, how can one help but sense in you one of those birds destined to dwell in high places? Carve out your own career and, one day, be the guardian of our beloved child. Go to Paris; if your father and brother do not give you their support, our family, especially my mother, who has a flair for business, is sure to be most useful to you. Take advantage of our influence; you will lack neither the backing nor the assistance for any career you may choose. So put all your excess energies into some noble ambition."

"I know what you mean," I broke in, "my ambition shall be my mistress. No, I do not need that in order to be wholly yours; I do not want to be rewarded for my good behaviour here by favours over there. I shall go there and I shall make my way alone, by my own efforts. I would accept everything from you. From others I want nothing."

"What nonsense!" she murmured, with an ill-disguised smile of satisfaction.

"Besides," said I, "I have made my vows. On thinking over the situation as it concerns us, I have resolved to bind myself to you with ties that can never be broken."

She trembled slightly, stopped and looked at me.

"What do you mean?" she said, letting the two couples in front go on ahead, but keeping the children by her.

"Well now," I replied, "tell me frankly how you wish me to love you."

"Love me as my aunt loved me, whose rights I gave you when I let you call me by the name she chose for herself among my other names."

"I shall love without hope then, and with complete devotion. I shall do for you what man does for God. Is that not what you demanded of me? I shall enter a seminary, I shall emerge a priest and I shall bring up Jacques. Your son will be my second self; political concepts, ideas, energy, patience, I shall give him everything. So I shall still be near to you and my love, set in religion as a silver image is in crystal, will not be suspect. You need fear none of those immoderate ardours which take possession of a man and which overcame me once before. I shall be consumed in the fire and I will love you with a purified love."

She turned pale and said in urgent tones, "Felix, do not bind yourself to something which will one day stand in the way of your happiness. I should die of grief if I were the cause of such deliberate suicide. Child that you are, can hopeless love be a vocation? Wait and see what trials life holds for you before you pass judgement upon life. I want you—I order you to do so. Do not marry, whether it be a woman or the Church, I forbid it. Keep your freedom. You are twenty-one. You scarcely know what the future holds for you. Dear Heaven, can I have misjudged you? I would have thought that two months was time enough for knowing certain souls."

"What hope is there for you?" I cried, my eyes flashing.

"My dear, accept my help, better yourself, make your fortune and you will know what hopes I cherish. Either way," she added, as if giving away a secret, "always keep as tight a hold on Madeleine's hand as you are doing now."

She had whispered these words in my ear, words which proved how much thought she was giving to my future.

"Madeleine?" said I. "Never!"

These two words plunged us back into a silence full of troubled thoughts. We were in the throes of those violent upheavals that streak across the soul and leave indelible imprints upon them. We were within sight of a wooden gate leading into the grounds of Frapesle, the two derelict posts of which, overgrown with moss and creepers, briars and weeds, I still see in my mind's eye. Suddenly a thought flashed like a dart across my brain, the thought of the Count's death and I said "I know what you mean!"

"I am glad," she replied, in a tone of voice which made it clear to me that I was imputing to her a thought which would never enter her head. Her purity drew from me a tear of admiration which the selfishness of passion turned bitter indeed. Turning my attention back on to myself, I reflected that she did not love me enough to wish for her freedom. So long as love shrinks from a crime we feel that it has limits and love should be limitless. A sickening spasm contracted my heart. "She does not love me" I thought to myself. To prevent her reading my thoughts I kissed Madeleine's hair.

"I am afraid of your mother," I said to the Countess, in order to resume the conversation.

"So am I," she replied, with a wholly childlike gesture. "But always remember to call her Madame la Duchesse and to address her in the third person. The modern generation has lost the habit of these polite forms of speech. Please do so, for my sake. Besides, it is such a mark of good taste to respect women, whatever their age, and to acknowledge social distinctions without questioning them! Is not the honour you pay to established superiority a guarantee of the honour due to you? All is interdependent in society. The Cardinal de la Rovere and Raphael d'Urbino were once two equally revered powers. You have sucked the milk of revolution in your schools, and your political ideas may be redolent of it. But you will learn, as you grow older, how powerless vague principles of liberty are to bring about the happiness of peoples. Before I consider, in my capacity as a de Lenoncourt, what aristocracy is or ought to be, my countrywoman's good sense tells me that society can only be based on hierarchy. You are at a stage in life when you must choose wisely. Stand by your own party. Especially," she added, laughing, "when it is victorious."

I was vividly struck by these words, where political insight lay hidden beneath an affectionate warmth, a combination which gives women such vast power over a man. They all know how to lend the outward cloak of sentiment to the most perspicacious reasoning. It was as if Henriette, in her desire to justify the Count's behaviour, had foreseen the comments which must spring to my mind, on seeing sycophancy at work for the first time; for Monsieur de Mortsauf, king of his castle, crowned by his historic halo, had assumed heroic proportions in my eyes and I was, I confess, strangely surprised to see the distance he set between himself and the Duchess. His manner was, to say the least, obsequious. The slave has his vanity; he will obey none but the greatest despots. I felt almost humiliated to see the self-abasement of the man who made me tremble and who lay like a great shadow over my love. This inward reaction gave me an insight into the torment of those women whose generous spirits are chained to a man whose petty cowardice they daily screen from view. Respect is a barrier which protects both great and lowly; each can, from his own side of it, look the other in the face. I was respectful to the Duchess because of my youth; but where others saw a duchess, I saw the mother of my Henriette and I put a sort of veneration into my attentions. We entered the main courtyard of Frapesle, where we found the assembled company. The Comte de Mortsauf introduced me most graciously to the Duchess, who examined me with a cold and distant air. Madame de Lenoncourt was then a woman of fifty-six years old, perfectly preserved and with an elaborately formal manner. When I saw her hard blue eyes, her lined temples, her thin, ascetic face, straight imposing figure and infrequent

73

movements, and the tawny whiteness of her skin, which reappeared so dazzlingly in her daughter, I recognized the cold breed from which my mother sprang, as quickly as a mineralogist recognizes Swedish iron. Her way of speaking was that of the old Court. She pronounced *oit* as *ait* and said *frait* for *froid* and *porteux* instead of *porteurs*. I was neither fawning nor over formal. I behaved so well that later, on our way to vespers, the Countess whispered "You were perfect!"

The Count came over to me, took my hand and said, "We are still friends, aren't we, Felix? You'll forgive your old companion if he was a little hasty, won't you? We shall probably be staying here for dinner and we shall invite you for Thursday, the day before the Duchess leaves. I am going to Tours to conclude some business. Do not neglect Clochegourde. My mother-in-law is a woman whose acquaintance I do urge you to cultivate. Her drawing room will soon set the tone in the Faubourg St Germain. She has the traditions of high society, possesses vast knowledge and knows the coat of arms of the highest and lowest nobleman in Europe."

The Count's good taste, or perhaps the advice of his household genius showed itself in the new circumstances in which the triumph of his cause had placed him. He was neither arrogant nor woundingly polite. He showed no trace of pomposity and the Duchess was quite unpatronising. Monsieur and Madame de Chessel gratefully accepted the invitation to dinner the following Thursday. I made a good impression on the Duchess and from the way she looked at me, I could see that she was examining a young man of whom her daughter had previously spoken. On the way back from vespers, she questioned me about my family and asked if the Vandenesse already engaged in the diplomatic service was any relation.

"He is my brother," I replied.

She then became almost warm. She told me that my great aunt, the old Marquise de Listomère, was a Grandlieu. Her manner was as courteous as Monsieur de Mortsauf's had been the day he saw me for the first time. Her eyes lost that haughty look with which the princes of the earth make you measure the distance between yourself and them.

I knew next to nothing about my family. The Duchess informed me that my great uncle, an old abbé whose name I did not even know, was a member of the Privy Council; my brother had been appointed to a higher post; finally, by a clause in the Charter of which I as yet knew nothing, my father became once again Marquis de Vandenesse.

"I am but one thing, the serf of Clochegourde," I whispered to the Countess.

The Restoration was waving its magic wand with a speed which stupefied those who had grown up under the Imperial régime. This Revolution meant nothing at all to me. Madame de Mortsauf's slightest word, her simplest gesture were the only events to which I attached any importance. I had no idea what the Privy Council was; I knew nothing of politics nor worldly matters. I had no other ambition than to love Henriette better than Petrarch had loved Laura. This lack of interest caused the Duchess to take me for a child. There were a great many guests at Frapesle. We sat down thirty to dinner. What heady bliss for a young man to see that the woman he loves is the loveliest of all, to watch her become the focus of impassioned looks and to know that he alone receives the chaste glow of her downcast eyes; to be familiar enough with all the intonations of her voice to discover, in her speech, outwardly light or ironic, the evidence of constant thought, even when one feels, deep inside one, a gnawing resentment against the distractions of the world.

The Count, happy at the attentions that were being paid him, was almost youthful; his wife had high hopes of some resultant change of mood. I joked with Madeleine, who, like all children whose bodies wilt beneath the soul's embrace, would come out with some astonishing remarks, full of an ironic wit quite free from malice, but which held no one sacred. It was a lovely day. A word, a hope born of the morning had made Nature luminous and, seeing me so gay, Henriette was gay too.

This patch of happiness across her grey and cloudy life had seemed very sweet to her, she told me the next morning. The following day I naturally spent at Clochegourde. I had been banished for five days; I was athirst for my life. The Count had left at six o'clock in the morning to draw up his contracts of possession at Tours.

A serious subject of discord had arisen between mother and daughter. The Duchess wanted the Countess to go with her to Paris, where she would obtain a post for her at Court and where the Count, by reconsidering his decision, could hold high office. Henriette, who passed for a happy woman, was loth to disclose to anyone, not even a mother's heart, how appallingly unhappy she was, or to betray her husband's inadequacy. So that her mother should not fathom the secret of her married life, she had sent Monsieur de Mortsauf to Tours, where he was to battle with his lawyers. No one but myself, as she had told me, knew the secrets of Clochegourde. Knowing from experience how the clean air and blue sky of the valley soothed the irritations of the mind and the bitter pain of illness and what an effect life at Clochegourde had on her children's health, she gave reasons for her repeated refusals, countered in turn by the Duchess, an overwhelming woman, who was less distressed than humiliated by her daughter's regrettable marriage. Fearful discovery, Henriette noticed that her mother showed scant concern for Jacques and Madeleine! Like all mothers accustomed to prolonging on the married woman the tyranny they wielded on the unwed girl, the Duchess would not take no for an answer. She affected, now a specious friendliness, so as to wrest her daughter's consent to her views, now a thin-lipped coldness, in an attempt to obtain by intimidation what sweetness could not win her. Then, seeing that her efforts were useless, she displayed the same sarcastic strain I had observed in my own mother. In ten days, Henriette knew all the agonising distress young women undergo in the struggle essential to the assertion of their independence. You, who in your good fortune, have the best of mothers, could never understand these things. To form some idea of the struggle between a dry, cold, calculating and ambitious woman and a daughter, so full of that fresh and unctuous goodness that never runs dry, you would have to imagine a lily, to which my heart has constantly compared her, crushed in the wheels of a machine of polished steel.

That mother had never had anything in common with her daughter. She was incapable of sensing any of the real difficulties which prevented her from enjoying the benefits of the Restoration and which obliged her to go on leading her isolated existence. She concluded that there must be some little romance between her daughter and myself. This word, which she used to voice her suspicions, opened a gulf between the two women which nothing henceforward could ever bridge. Although families carefully cover over all these intolerable rifts, look a little closer. You will find in nearly all of them deep, incurable wounds which diminish the natural sentiments. There may be true and moving love, which mutual accord of kindred natures renders eternal and which gives to death a recoil whose dark bruises are ineffaceable; or there are latent hatreds which slowly freeze the heart and dry the tears on the day of eternal farewell. Tormented in the past, tormented now, struck at by all, even by her two ailing cherubs, who were responsible neither for the ills they suffered nor for those they caused, how could that poor soul help but love the one person who never raised his hand against her, whose one aim was to surround her with a triple hedge of thorns, to shield her from all storms, all contact and all hurt?

Although this battle of wills distressed me, there were times when I welcomed it and felt that she was taking refuge in my heart, for Henriette would confide her latest sorrows to me. It was then that I appreciated to the full her calmness in the face of pain and the vital reserves of patience she had at her command. Every day I learnt more fully the meaning of the words "love me as my aunt loved me".

"Have you no ambition, then?" the Duchess asked me sharply, when we were at dinner.

"Madame," I answered, giving her a serious look, "I feel I have the strength in me to conquer the whole world, but I am only twenty-one and I am alone in life."

She threw her daughter a questioning look; clearly she thought that, in order to keep me by her side, the Countess was stifling all ambition in me.

The Duchess de Lenoncourt's stay at Clochegourde was a period of perpetual uneasiness. The Countess urged me to watch my behaviour; she would stiffen with alarm at a softly spoken word and to please her, I had to don the heavy harness of dissimulation.

The great Thursday came. It was a day of tedious ceremony, one of those hated by lovers used to the beguilements of daily informality, accustomed to seeing their chair in its right place and the mistress of the house with ears for none but them. Love shrinks from everything extraneous to itself. The Duchess departed to enjoy the pomp of Court and everything went back to normal at Clochegourde.

My short-lived quarrel with the Count had the result of bringing me even closer to him than before. I could go there at any time without arousing the least suspicion and the circumstances of my past encouraged me to spread like a climbing plant, in that fair spirit where the enthralling world of shared sentiments was opening its doors to me. Hour by hour, moment by moment, our fraternal marriage, based on trust, took firmer shape. We were each settling into our respective rôles; the Countess swathed me, nurselike, in the protective white draperies of a wholly maternal love; whereas my love, seraphic in her presence, became, when I was away from her, biting and parched as red-hot iron. I loved her with a twofold love which by turns loosed the thousand arrows of desire and lost them in the sky, where they melted in an impassable ether. If you ask me why, young and full of urgent longings as I was, I clung to the self-deceptions of platonic love, I will confess that I was not yet man enough to torment this woman, forever fearful as she was of some disaster to her children; forever expecting some outburst, some stormy change of temper in her husband; attacked by him when she was not afflicted by Jacques' or Madeleine's ill health; seated at one or the other's bedside whenever her husband, his temper soothed, allowed her to take a little rest.

The sound of an overloud word shook her to the roots of her being; the slightest sign of desire made her shrink. For her one had to be veiled love, strength fused with tenderness, everything in short, that she was for others. Then again—need I tell you this, you who are so much a woman?—this situation brought with it spells of enchanting langour, moments of divine sweetness and the contentment which springs from silent sacrifice. Her conscience was contagious, her devotion, unrewarded on this earth, beguiled one by its persistence. That vital, secret piety, which acted as a link for all her other virtues, made itself felt round about her like spiritual incense. Besides, I was young! Young enough to pour all of myself into the kiss that she allowed me, so rarely, to place upon her hand, of which she would only grant me the back and never the palm—the point perhaps, where for her sensual pleasure began. Though never did two souls embrace with greater ardour, never was the body more fearlessly and victoriously tamed.

Later, I came to recognise the cause of this full happiness. At that age, no other interest diverted my heart, no ambition cut across this torrential emotion that swept away all that stood in its path. Later, yes, we love the woman in a woman, whereas, in the first beloved we love everything; her house is our house, her interests are our interests, her unhappiness is our greatest woe. We love her clothes and her furniture: we are more grieved to see her cornfields flattened than our money lost; we are ready to scold the visitor who disturbs the curios on our overmantel. This blest love makes us live through another life, whereas, later, alas, we draw another life into ourselves, and ask a woman to enrich by her youthful emotions our own impoverished faculties.

I was soon part of the household, and I experienced for the first time that infinite sweetness which is to the tormented soul what a bath is to the weary body. The spirit is then refreshed on all its surfaces, caressed in its deepest folds. You could not know what I mean, you are a woman and I speak here of a happiness which you bestow without ever receiving a similar one in return. Only a man can know the rare delight of being, in the heart of a strange household, the mistress' favoured one, the secret hub of her affections. The dogs no longer bark at you. The servants, like the dogs, recognise the unseen talisman you carry; the children, who never dissemble, who know that their portion will never grow less and that you are beneficial to the light of their young lives—these children have a sixth sense; they purr like cats over you, they exercise that good-natured tyranny which they reserve for those they worship and who worship them. They are inspired in their discretion, innocent in their complicity; they come to you on tiptoe, smile and creep noiselessly away again. For you all is eagerness to please, all things love you and smile upon you. True passion, it would seem, is like a lovely flower that gives all the more pleasure to the eye, the more barren the soil that has produced it.

But if I enjoyed the sweet rewards of this adoption into a family where I found parents after my own heart, I also shared its burdens. Until now, Monsieur de Mortsauf had put up some sort of front with me. I had seen only the broad outlines of his faults. I was soon to know the full extent of their application and to see how nobly charitable the Countess had been in the description of her daily battles. I now got to know every angle of that intolerable character; I heard the incessant recriminations over nothing, the whining over ailments of which no outward signs existed; that innate discontent which blighted his life and that perpetual need to act the tyrant which would have claimed a yearly toll of victims if it could. When we went for our evening strolls, it was he who led the way; but no matter what direction we took, the walks always bored him. Back at home, he shifted on to others the burden of his lassitude; it was all his wife's fault for dragging him against his will where she herself wanted to go. Forgetting that he had himself chosen the itinerary, he complained that he was ruled by her in the minutest details of daily life; that he could not call a single wish or thought his own; that he was a nobody in his own house. If his unkindness met with a patient silence, he would sense that there was a limit to his power and begin to lose his temper. He would ask acidly if religion did not order wives to please their husbands and if it was seemly to despise the father of one's children. He always succeeded in the end in touching some vulnerable chord in his wife, and when he had struck it and heard it ring, this pointless bullying seemed to give him a particular delight. Sometimes he affected a sullen silence, a morbid despondency which would suddenly alarm his wife, from whom he would then receive touching attentions. Like those spoilt children who use their power without giving a thought to a mother's apprehensions he let himself be coddled like Jacques and Madeleine, of whom he was jealous. I discovered, finally, that in matters both great and small, the Count behaved towards his servants, his children and his wife, the way he did towards me when we played backgammon. The day I grasped these difficulties root and branch and saw how, creeper-like, they constricted the breath and the free movement of this family, hampered with a myriad fine, entangling threads the running of the household and delayed, by their complication of the most necessary steps, the increase of the family fortunes, I felt a sudden panic tinged with admiration, which overpowered my love and sent it deeper into my heart. Dear God, what did I matter? The tears I had drunk induced in me a sort of sublime intoxication and I found happiness in shouldering this woman's burdens. I had, up till now, bowed to the Count's tyranny the way a smuggler pays his fines. Henceforward, I purposely laid myself open to the tyrant's blows, so as to be as near as possible to Henriette. The Countess sensed my intention, let me take a place by her side and gave me for reward the permission to share her pain, as in Roman times, the repentant apostate, anxious to go up to Heaven in company with his brothers, obtained the redeeming grace of dying in the arena.

"Had it not been for you, I was about to succumb to this existence," Henriette told me one evening when the Count had been, like the flies on a very hot day, sharper, more stinging and more changeable than usual. The Count had gone to bed. We stayed, Henriette and I, under our acacias for a part of the evening. The children were playing around us, bathed in the rays of the setting sun. Our remarks, infrequent and purely exclamatory, revealed the harmony of the thoughts to which we turned for rest after our mutual sufferings. When words failed us, the silence lent its faithful aid and our spirits entered, as it were, unhindered into each other, without the invitation of a kiss; savouring together the charms of a pensive torpor, they drifted into the same rippling daydream, plunged side by side into the river and emerged refreshed like two nymphs united as closely as jealousy could wish yet with no earthly bond. We would sink into a bottomless abyss, surface again, empty-handed and ask each other with a look "Will we have a single day, among so many days, to call our own?" When the god of pleasure picks for our delight some of those blossoms born without a root, why does the flesh murmur? Despite the heady poetry of evening, which lent to the bricks of the balustrade those orange tints, so soothing and so pure; despite the awesome atmosphere which sent the muted voices of the two children winging on the wind and which left us at peace, desire streaked through my veins like a kindling bonfire. After three months I was growing dissatisfied with the share allotted to me. Gently I stroked Henriette's hand, in an attempt to transfer the wealth of sensuous delight that set my

whole being aglow. Henriette changed back to Madame de Mortsauf and withdrew her hand; a few tears rolled into my eyes, she
saw them and gave me a warm look as she bore my hand to her lips.

"Remember," she said, "that this costs me many tears! Friendship that makes such great demands is dangerous indeed."

I burst into a torrent of reproaches, I spoke of my unhappiness
and how very little relief I asked for in order to endure it. I dared
to tell her that at my age, if the senses were all spirit, the spirit too
had a sex, and that I would know how to die, but not how to die
with closed lips. She silenced me with her proud glance, in which
I thought I read the Indian Chief's mute retort "And I, is mine a
bed of roses?" Then again, I may have been wrong. Ever since that
day, outside the Frapesle gates, when I had mistakenly imputed to
her a thought that based our happiness upon another's grave, I
shrank from tainting her soul with wishes that bore the imprints of
brute passion. She began to speak and with honeyed mouth told
me she could not be everything to me and that I ought to know
that. I realised, as she spoke, that if I did not obey her, I would dig
a deep chasm between us two. I bowed my head. She had, she
went on, the religious conviction that she might love a brother
without offending God or man. There was a certain sweetness, she
said, in making this creed into a real image of that Divine Love,
which is, according to her dear Saint-Martin, the life's-breath of
the world. If I could not be something in the nature of her old
confessor, less than a lover, though more than a brother, then we
must not continue to see each other. She would know how to die,
taking up to God this extra burden of sharp sorrow, borne not
without tears and inner anguish.

"I gave more than I should," she concluded, "so as to have
nothing left to take, and I am already punished for it."

I had to soothe her, promise that I would never cause her a
moment's pain and that I would love her, with my twenty-odd
years, as old men love their youngest born.

The next day I came early. She had no flowers for the vases in
her grey drawing-room. I sped into the fields and vineyards in
search of blooms with which to make up two bouquets for her and
as I picked them, one by one, cutting them near the root, admiring
them, I reflected that their leaves and colouring had a harmony,

a poetry which found its way into the understanding by charming the eye, just as musical phrases arouse a thousand memories in the hearts of those who love and are beloved. If colour is organic light, must it not have a meaning in the same way that organised vibrations of the air have theirs?

With the help of Jacques and Madeleine, happy, all three of us, to be planning a secret surprise for our darling, I set to work, at the bottom of the flight of steps where we set up the headquarters for our flowers, to arrange two bouquets, by means of which I attempted to convey a feeling. Imagine a stream of flowers bubbling frothily out of two vases, falling in fringed waves, and from it, in the form of silver cupped lilies and white roses, my heart's wishes soaring. On this cool background shone cornflowers, myosotis, borage, all those blue flowers whose tints, borrowed from the sky, blend so well with white. Are there not two forms of innocence, one that knows nothing and one that knows it all—the child's mind and the martyr's? Love has its coat of arms and the Countess deciphered it. She gave me one of those incisive glances that resemble the cry of a sick man when his wound is touched. She was both shamefaced and delighted. Oh, the reward in that look! And how inspiring it was to make her happy and refresh her heart!

And so I adapted Père Castel's theory to love's advantage and rediscovered, for her, an art lost to Europe, where the flowers of the writing desk have replaced the pages written, in the Orient, with perfume-laden colour. What enchantment there is in expressing one's sensations by means of these daughters of the Sun, sisters of those flowers that open beneath the warming rays of love! I was soon on good terms with the rural flora, just as a man I met later at Grandlieu had a secret understanding with his bees.

Twice a week, for the rest of my stay at Frapesle, I repeated the lengthy labours of this poetic creation, for which were needed all the varieties of greenery. Of these plants I made a thorough study, less as a botanist than as a poet, examining them for their spirit rather than their form. To reach the place where a certain flower grew, I often covered enormous distances, to the edge of lakes, into valleys, up on to high rocks and into open heathland, finding a prized sprig of heartsease deep in a wood or hidden among bracken. I found, during these trips, my own initiation into pleasures unknown to the scholar in his world of thought, to the farmer busy with his marketable produce, to the artisan glued to the city, or to the tradesman chained to his counter, pleasures known to a few foresters, a few woodsmen, a few dreamers. There are to be found, in nature, effects of limitless significance, which rise to the level of the greatest moral concepts. A clump of heather in bloom, perhaps, covered in diamonds of dew with sunlight dancing on them—an immense wonder, adorned for the single glance of a chance wayfarer. Or a patch of woodland, ringed with crumbling rocks, streaked with sand, clad in moss and decked with junipers, which makes you catch your breath at the savage, jarring, fearfulness of it, as the shriek of the osprey breaks the silence. Or else a torrid stretch of wasteland, bare of vegetation, stony, steep-sided, with a skyline reminiscent of the desert, where I met a sublime and solitary flower, a pulsatilla, with violet silk panoply outspread for its gilt stamens; touching image of my white idol, all alone in her valley! Or again, great pools of water on which nature straightway flings green stains, half animal, half vegetable, which stir to life in a few days, with plants and insects floating there like a world suspended in the ether. Or else a cottage, with its cabbage-filled garden, its vine and its palings, blanced upon a swamp and framed by a few meagre fields of rye, prototype of so many humble existences! Or a long path in the forest, similar to the nave of some cathedral, with trees for pillars, their branches meeting to form the spines of the vaulting overhead and where, at the far end, a clearing, with patches of light interspersed with shadows or tinged with the red hues of the setting sun, appears through the leaves, displaying the stained glass windows of a choir full of singing birds. Then, outside those cool, leafy woods a stretch of chalky fallowland, where, over hot, crackling mosses grass snakes slither homeward, replete, their slender, elegant heads held high. Fling over these scenes, now torrents of sunshine streaming down like nourishing waves, now grey banks of clouds aligned like furrows on an old man's brow, now the cold tones of a sky weakly tinged with orange and streaked with pale blue bands. Then listen: you will hear indefinable harmonies in the midst of a confounding silence. During the months of September and October, I never put together a single bunch of flowers which cost me less than three hours of searching, so long did I stand and wonder, with the poet's sweet abandon, at these fleeting allegories, where for me were painted the most contrasting phases of human existence, majestic spectacles where now my memory dips. Often, to-day, I blend with these great scenes the memory of the spirit who shed her fragrance over nature. Once again I wander with the sovereign lady whose white dress rippled through the coppices, floated over the lawns, the thought of whom rose like a promised fruit from every calyx full of amorous stamens.

No declaration, no proof of insane passion was more violently contagious than those symphonies of flowers, where my thwarted desire made me deploy the efforts Beethoven expressed with his notes; deep inroads into himself, prodigious leaps toward the sky. Madame de Mortsauf was no longer anyone but Henriette at sight of them. She came back to them again and again, drew sustenance from them, and she culled all the thoughts I had put into them, when, as I handed them to her, she lifted her head from her tapestry and said "Heavens, how beautiful they are!"

You will understand this delightful correspondence if I describe the details of one of these bouquets, just as from a fragment of poetry you would understand Saadi. Have you ever smelt, in the meadows, in the month of May, that fragrance which communicates to all living things the heady joy of fecundation, which prompts you, when in a boat, to dip your hands into the water, to surrender your hair to the wind, and which makes your thoughts verdant again like the sprouting woodland green? A small plant, the sweet scented vernal grass, is one of the most powerful elements of this veiled harmony. No one can keep it with impunity upon his person. Put its gleaming blades, finely striped like a dress of white and green, among a bunch of flowers and inexhaustible exhalations will stir the budding roses which modesty has kept crushed deep in your heart. Around the flaring neck of the porcelain, picture a deep border entirely composed of the white tufts peculiar to the blossom of the vine in Touraine; vague image of those forms I so desired, undulating like those of a submissive slave girl. From this bed rise the spiralling, white-belled convolvulus, the thread-like leaves of the pink rest-harrow, interspersed with a few ferns and oak shoots with lustrous, magnificently coloured leaves. All of these lean forward, humbly bowed like weeping willows, shy and suppliant as prayers. Above them, see the unfurled, perpetually quivering fibrils of the purple quaking-grass, its anthers tumbling in clouds of palest yellow; the snowy pyramids of the meadow-grass, the green-hair of the sterile bromus, the frayed plumes of those agrostes known as wind-spikes, hopes shot with violet that crown a man's first dreams, outlined against a background of grey flax, its flowering blades radiant with light. Then, higher up, a few Bengal roses, strewn among the dancing laces of the daucus, the plumes of the cottongrass, the marabou feathers of the meadow-sweet, the umbels of the wild chervil, the flaxen hair of the clematis in fruit, the winsome crosses of the milk-white crosswort, the corymbs of the yarrow, the diffuse stems of the fumitory with its pink and black flowers, the tendrils of the vine, the winding strands of the honeysuckle: in short, all that is most windswept, most ragged, in these artless creatures—triple-darted flames, jagged spear-shaped leaves, stems writhing like the desires tangled deep in the soul.

From the heart of this brimming torrent of love, there springs a magnificent double corn poppy, with its escort of bursting buds, spreading its sparks of fire over the starry jasmine and dominating the incessant rain of pollen, lovely cloud fluttering in the air and reflecting the light of day in its myriad gleaming particles. What woman, intoxicated by the fragrant love-philtre lurking in the vernal grass, would not understand this profusion of submissive thoughts, this white tenderness quivering with untamed movements and the red desire of love demanding a happiness denied, in the battles a thousand times repeated, of contained, tireless and eternal passion? Set this unspoken tribute in the light of a casement window and display its fresh details, its delicate antitheses, its arabesques, so that the sovereign lady, deeply stirred, may see a flower, more full blown than its neighbours, on which hangs a tear, and her defences will be frail indeed: only an angel or the voice of her child will stay her on the edge of the abyss. What does one give to God? Scents, light and song, the most purified expressions of our nature. Well now, was not all that one offers up to God offered to Love in that poem of luminous flowers, that hummed its ceaseless melodies to the heart, caressing hidden amorous longings, unspoken hopes, illusions which leap into flame and die out like gossamer on a hot night?

These neutral pleasures were of great help to us in outwitting the natural instincts, exacerbated by long contemplation of the beloved, those looks which rise to the pitch of ecstasy as they send their shafts of light deep into the forms they penetrate.

For me—I cannot speak for her, I dare not speak for her—it was like those fissures through which spurt the waters held in by an invincible dam, outlets which often prevent disaster by bowing to necessity.

Abstinence can have peaks of mortal exhaustion which are averted by a few crumbs falling one by one from that sky, which from Dan to the Sahara, gives manna to the traveller. Yet, I have often come upon Henriette before those bouquets, her arms hanging loosely by her side, sunk in those stormy daydreams during which thoughts swell the breast, animate the brow, come in waves, rise foaming, loom threateningly and leave behind them an enervating lassitude. Never since have I made a bouquet for anyone! When we had moulded this language to our own use, we experienced a satisfaction similar to that of the slave who deceives his master.

During the rest of this month, when I ran up through the gardens, I sometimes saw her face pressed to the window-panes, but when I came into the drawing-room, I would find her at her tapestry. Sometimes, if I did not arrive at the appointed hour, a time agreed on without our ever having mentioned it, her white form would be wandering on the terrace and when I chanced upon her she would say "I came to meet you. Must one not make a little fuss over the last born child?"

The cruel games of trictrac between the Count and myself had been interrupted. His latest acquisitions obliged him to make a mass of errands, reconnoitring, verifying, demarcating and surveying. He was busy giving orders and supervising agricultural tasks which required the master's eye, and which were decided between himself and his wife. The Countess and I often went to join him in the new estates with her two children, who chased insects, stag beetles and tailor birds on the way and picked their posies too, or, to be precise, their bunches of flowers. To stroll with the woman one loves, to give her one's arm, to choose her paths for her!—these limitless joys are enough for one lifetime. Conversation is so trusting then! We went alone, we came back with the "general", our gently mocking nickname for the Count when he was in a good mood. These two ways of making the trip gave subtle modifications to our pleasure, by contrasts of which the secret is known only to hearts uneasy in their union.

On the way back, the same joys, a look, a handclasp were mingled with anxiety. Speech, so free on the way out, took on a mysterious significance on the return journey, whenever one of us, after a certain pause, produced an answer to some insidious question, or when a discussion, already begun, continued under those enigmatic forms to which our language lends itself so well and which women so ingeniously create. Who has not tasted the pleasure of understanding each other thus, meeting as it were in an unknown sphere where kindred spirits draw away from the crowd and unite, escaping the vulgar laws? One day, I had a wild hope, (too soon dispelled) when, in answer to a question of the Count's, who wanted to know what we were talking about, Henriette made a remark which had a double meaning and which vastly amused him. This harmless piece of raillery made Madeleine laugh, at which her mother flushed and informed me, with a stern look, that she intended to remain a blameless wife and could withdraw her soul just as she had formerly withdrawn her hand. But this purely spiritual union has so much appeal that the next day we began again.

The hours, the days, the weeks sped by like this, full of renewed felicities. We came to the time of the grape harvest, the occasion in Touraine for veritable celebrations. Towards the end of September, the sun, less hot than during the grain harvest, allows one to stay out in the fields without fear of sunburn or fatigue. It is easier to pick grapes than to cut wheat. All the fruit is ripe. The harvest is in, bread becomes cheaper and this abundance brings general good cheer. Fears for the results of agricultural toil, which swallows up as much money as sweat, vanish before the full barn and the vats soon to be filled. The grape gathering is like the gay dessert after the harvest banquet; the heavens always smile upon it in Touraine, where the autumns are magnificent. In this hospitable region the grape pickers are fed at the big house. These being the only meals when these poor folk have, every year, substantial and well-cooked victuals, they are as attached to them as children in patriarchal families are to birthday celebrations. Then, too, they flock in droves to the houses where the masters treat them without parsimony. The house is therefore crammed with people and provisions. The pressrooms are constantly opened. It is as if everything were brought to life by this flurry of coopers, and carts packed with laughing girls, and folk who, earning, as they do, better wages than at any other time of year, burst into song at the slightest provocation. Besides—another source of pleasure—social barriers are dropped; women, children, masters and servants, all share in the blest grape gathering. These diverse circumstances explain the hilarity handed down through the ages, that develops in these last fine days of the year, the memory of which inspired Rabelais to the bacchic form of his great work.

Jacques and Madeleine, always ailing as they were, had never been to the grape harvest before. Nor had I, and they took a child-like joy in seeing their excitement shared, for their mother had promised to accompany us. We had been to Villaines, where the local baskets are made, and ordered ourselves some exceedingly pretty ones. The four of us were to pick grapes in one or two lanes reserved for our scissors; but it was agreed that we could not eat too much fruit. To eat the big *co* of Touraine in the vineyard itself was a source of such delight that we scorned the finest grapes at table. Jacques made me swear not to go and see the grape harvest anywhere else and to keep myself for the Clochegourde vineyards. Never were those two little children, usually so wan and sickly, fresher, rosier, nor more active and tireless than they were that morning. They babbled for the sake of babbling; they trotted back and forth for no apparent reason, but, like other children, they seemed to have too much life in them to shake off. Monsieur and Madame de Mortsauf had never seen them like this. With them I was a child again, more of a child than they perhaps, for I hoped for my harvest too. We went, in the finest conceivable weather, to the vineyards and stayed there half a day. How we bickered as to who should find the finest bunches and who would be quickest at filling his basket! There was an endless coming and going from the vines to the mother; not a bunch was picked that was not shown to her. She broke into the rich laughter of her girlhood when, following her daughter with my basket I said, like Madeleine, "And what about mine, mamma?" "Dear child," she replied. "Don't get too hot!" Then, passing her hand over my neck and through my hair, she gave me a little tap on the cheek and added "You're bathed in perspiration!"

That was the only time I ever heard that vocal caress, the intimate "*tu*" of lovers. I looked at the pretty hedgerows covered with red fruit, haws, and blackberries; I listened to the children's cries; I gazed at the flock of fruit pickers, the wagon heaped with barrels and the men with their loaded baskets. Ah, how I etched it all on my memory, even to the young almond tree beneath which she stood, cool, rosy-cheeked and laughing, under her open sunshade! Then I set to work picking the heavy bunches, filling my basket, emptying it into the harvest barrel with a silent, sustained bodily concentration, a slow and measured tread which left my spirit free. I tasted the ineffable pleasure of outdoor toil which carries life along with it while checking the course of passion, so near, but for this mechanical motion, to setting everything ablaze. I found out how much wisdom is contained in steady labour and grasped the meaning of the monastic rule.

For the first time for many a day, the Count was neither sullen nor cruel. His son in such good health, the future Duc de Lenoncourt-Mortsauf, white and rosy and smeared with grape juice, gladdened his heart. This being the last day of the grape gathering, the "general" promised there would be dancing in the evening outside Clochegourde in honour of the returned Bourbons; the holiday was thus complete for everyone. On the way home, the Countess took my arm; she leaned against me and I felt the full weight of her heart against my own, the gesture of a mother wishing to communicate her joy, as she whispered "You bring us luck!"

Indeed, for me, who knew her sleepless nights, her apprehensions and the times in the past when, although sustained by the hand of God, everything was wearisome and arid, this phrase, enhanced by that rich voice of hers, bred in me delights which no woman on earth could ever give me again.

"The wretched sameness of my days is broken, life grows lovely and full of hope," she said after a pause.

"Oh, do not leave me! Never betray my innocent illusions! Be like every eldest son, the younger ones' good angel."

There is nothing foolishly romantic in all this, Natalie. In order to know the boundless depth of some feelings, one must, in one's youth, have cast one's sounding line into the great lakes beside which one has lived. If for many people the passions have been torrents of lava flowing between dried up banks, are there not souls in whom passion, hemmed in by insurmountable obstacles, has filled the volcanic crater with pure water?

We had another holiday similar to this one. Madame de Mortsauf wanted to train her children in the facts of living and make them aware of the painful labours whereby money is earned. She had therefore arranged for them a source of income dependent on the hazards of agriculture. To Jacques belonged the produce of the walnut trees, to Madeleine that of the chestnuts. Some days later, we had the walnut and chestnut harvest. To thrash Madeleine's chestnut trees, to hear the fruit fall, as their husks sent them bouncing on the dry, smooth velvet of the barren ground where the chestnut thrives; to see the gravity with which the little girl examined the piles and estimated their worth, a sum which represented unstinted pleasures for her; the congratulations of Manette, the housekeeper, who alone could replace the Countess where the children were concerned; the lesson afforded by the spectacle of how much effort is required to ensure the smallest gains, so often endangered as they are by the vicissitudes of climate, all this created a scene where the happy innocence of childhood, set against the sombre tints of autumn, showed in all its charm.

Madeleine had her own loft, and sharing in her joy, I demanded to witness the storing of her brown treasure. Why, my heart still gives a leap when I recall the thud as each basketful of chestnuts rolled on to the yellowish flock, mixed with earth, which covered the floor. The Count bought some for the household needs; the tenant farmers, the servants, everyone around Clochegourde found buyers for the "Little Sweeting", an endearment which the local country folk freely bestow, even on strangers, but which seemed specially coined for Madeleine.

Jacques had less luck for his walnut gathering; it rained for several days. But I consoled him with the advice that he should keep his nuts and sell them a little later. Monsieur de Chessel had informed me that the walnut crop was bad in the Brehémont, Amboise and Vouvray districts. Walnut oil is extensively used in Touraine. Jacques should make at least forty *sous* from each tree. He had two hundred of them; the sum was therefore considerable! He wanted to buy himself some accoutrements for horse-riding. This wish gave rise to an open discussion, in which his father gave him a lecture on the instability of prices, and the necessity of building up reserves for years when the walnut yield was poor, in order to secure an average income. I sensed the Countess's soul in her silence; she was overjoyed to see Jacques listening to his father and the father winning back a little of the paternal sacredness which he lacked, thanks to the sublime falsehood for which she had paved the way. Did I not tell you when I described this woman, that earthly language would be powerless to render her features and her genius? When this sort of scene takes place, the soul savours its delights without analysing them, but how vigorously they stand out later against the murky background of a troubled life! Like diamonds, they shine in a setting of alloyed thoughts and regrets fused in the memory of vanished bliss. Why do the names of those two recently purchased estates to which Monsieur and Madame de Mortsauf devoted so much attention, La Cassine and La Rhé-torière, move me more than the loveliest names of Greece or of the Holy Land? "He who loves, declares his love!" cried La Fontaine. These names possess the talisman-like virtues of the constellated words used in evocations, they explain magic to me, they awaken slumbering figures which arise forthwith and speak to me, they set me in that happy valley, they create landscapes and a sky. But have not evocations always happened in the regions of the spirit world? Do not be surprised then, at my entertaining you with such familiar scenes as these. The tiniest details of this simple, almost commonplace existence were so many links, outwardly weak, by which I bound myself so closely to the Countess.

Her children's financial future caused Madame de Mortsauf as much grief as did their frail health. I soon recognised the truth of what she had told me regarding her secret rôle in the household affairs, into which I was gradually initiated as I learnt those details about the neighbourhood which the man of state is required to know. After ten years of hard work, the Countess had changed the system of cultivation on her land. She had "turned it into fours", an expression used in that part of the country to explain the results of the new method of crop rotation, whereby farmers only sow wheat every fourth year, and ensure, by so doing, that the land yields a crop of one sort or another, every year. To overcome the opposition of the peasants, she had had to curtail leases, divide her estates into four large holdings and run them on "cheptel by moity" lines, a system of land-tenure particular to Touraine and the surrounding regions. The owner-landlord provides a farmhouse, outbuildings and seed to tenant-farmers of goodwill, with whom they share the costs of cultivation and the produce. This sharing out is supervised by a *metivier*, the man whose duty it is to take the half share due to the landlord. It is a costly system, complicated by a method of book-keeping which varies from one moment to the next according to the nature of the shares.

The Countess had made Monsieur de Mortsauf cultivate a fifth farm, consisting of reserved fields situated around Clochegourde, partly to give him something to do, and partly to provide her tenant farmers with a practical demonstration of the excellence of the new methods. Past mistress at farm-planning, she had, slowly and with her womanly persistence, made her tenants reorganise two of her holdings on the model of the farms of Artois and Flanders. It is easy to divine her intention. After the expiry of the "half-share" leases, the Countess intended to make two fine farms out of her four holdings and rent them for money to active and intelligent tenants so as to simplify the Clochegourde revenues. Afraid that she might die before he did, she was striving to leave the Count with rents that could be easily collected, and her children with property which no amount of incompetence could jeopardise. Now, fruit trees planted ten years before were in full yield. The hedges which guaranteed the estates against all future dispute were fully grown. The poplars and the elms had reached a good height. With its new acquisitions, and by the general introduction of the new system of cultivation, the Clochegourde estate, divided into four large farms, of which two were yet to be built, was likely to bring in an income of sixteen thousand francs in crowns, that is,

four thousand francs for each farm; without counting the vineyards, the two hundred acres of adjoining woodland, or the model
farm. The cart-tracks of these four farms could all end in a big
driveway which would lead direct from Clochegourde to join the
main Chinon road. The distance between this avenue and Tours
being no more than five leagues, there was sure to be no lack of
farmers on it, particularly now when everyone was talking about
the improvements made by the Count, how successful they had
been and how his land had improved. In each of the two estates
purchased, she wanted to sink some fifteen thousand francs for
converting the two manor houses there into large farmhouses, and
so get a better rent for them, after the land had been under cultivation for a year or two.

For this purpose, she sent as bailiff there a certain Martineau,
the best and most honest of her overseers, who was soon to find
himself out of a job, for the leases of her four large holdings were
now up and the time had come for turning them into two large
farms and renting them on a financial basis. These ideas, essentially
simple enough, but complicated by the necessary outlay of thirty
thousand francs, were just now the subject of lengthy arguments
between herself and the Count, appalling quarrels which only the
interests of her two children gave her strength to meet. The
thought, "What would happen if I died to-morrow?" gave her
palpitations. Only quiet and gentle souls, in whom anger is impossible, and who wish to impart their own inner peace to those
around them, can know how much strength is required for such
battles, what heavy waves of blood rush to the heart before embarking on the fight, what lassitude floods the spirit, when, after
so much striving, nothing has been won. Just when her children
were healthier, plumper, more lively, (for the fruit season had had
its effect on them), just when she followed them with moist eyes
as they played, experiencing a contentment which renewed her
strength and refreshed her heart, the poor woman was undergoing
the carping insults, the stinging attacks of a bitter opposition. The
Count, afraid of these changes, denied their advantages and the
possibility of putting them into effect, with stolid obstinacy. He
answered conclusive arguments with the objections of a child
questioning the power of the sun in summer. The Countess won

the day. The victory of sound sense over folly soothed her pain and she forgot her wounds. That day, she walked over to La Cassine and La Rhétorière for the purpose of deciding what construction work was to be done. The Count walked on ahead, the children were between us and we two followed behind, slowly, for she was speaking to me in that soft, low voice which made her phrases sound like wavelets murmured by the sea on to fine sand. She was sure of success, she said. There would shortly be competition for the present transport service from Tours to Chinon, set up by an enterprising man, a mail messenger, and a cousin of Manette's, who wanted a big farm on the main road. His was a large family: his eldest son would drive the coaches, the second would undertake the haulage. Installed in a central position on the main road, at La Rabelaye, one of the farms to be let, the father could run the coaching stage, and would cultivate the land well, with the manure provided by his stables. One of their four tenant-farmers, an honest, intelligent and active man who sensed the advantages of the new farming methods, was already offering to take a lease on La Baude, the second farm, the one situated a stone's throw from Clochegourde. As for La Cassine and La Rhétorière, they were the best farming lands in the county. Once the farmhouses were built and the land was fully tilled, it would merely be necessary to advertise them in Tours. In two years, Clochegourde would consequently be worth about twenty-four thousand francs in rents; La Gravelotte, the farm in the county of Maine belonging to Monsieur de Mortsauf which he had found on his return from exile, had just been let for nine years at an annual rent of seven thousand francs; the pension of *maréchal du camp* was worth four thousand; if this income did not yet constitute a fortune, it made for circumstances of considerable ease. Later on, further improvements might perhaps allow her to go to Paris and supervise Jacques' education, in two years' time, when the health of the heir presumptive was consolidated.

How tremblingly she pronounced the word "Paris"! I was at the root of this project. She wanted to stay as close as possible to the beloved friend.

At this, I grew impassioned. I told her that she did not know me; without mentioning it, I said, I had planned to work day and night to complete my education, so that I could be Jacques' tutor, for I could not bear the thought of her having a young man in her house. At these words she grew serious. "No, Felix," said she, "that will not be, any more than your idea of taking Holy Orders. You have, by that one remark, stirred a mother's innermost heart, but the woman in me loves you too sincerely to let you fall a victim to your attachment. The price of this devotion would be hopeless discredit in the world's eyes and I could do nothing to remedy that. Oh no, let me not be harmful to you in any way whatever! You, the Vicomte de Vandenesse, a tutor! You, whose proud device is 'No man buys me!' Were you a Richelieu, you would have debarred yourself from life for good. You would cause your family endless grief. My dear, you do not know how much insolence a woman like my mother can put into a patronising look, how much abasement in a word, how much scorn in a greeting."

"And if you love me, what do I care for the world?"

She pretended not to have heard me and went on:

"Although my father is the best of men and is usually prepared to grant me what I ask, he would never forgive you for having put yourself in a bad position in life and he would refuse you his protection. I should not want to see you as tutor to the Dauphin! Take society as it is. Commit no errors in life. My friend, this senseless proposal, inspired by —"

"Love," said I quietly.

"No, charity," she said, fighting back her tears. "This mad notion gives me an insight into your character. Your heart will be your undoing. I claim, from now on, the right to teach you certain things. Leave to my woman's eye the task of seeing for you sometimes. Yes, from the depths of my Clochegourde, I want to watch, in mute delight, the spectacle of your success. As for the tutor, do not worry, we will find a nice old abbé, some former Jesuit scholar, and my father will gladly part with a sum of money for the education of the child who is to bear his name. Jacques is my pride. He is eleven years old," she added after a pause, "but the same applies to him as applies to you; when I first saw you, I thought you were thirteen."

We had reached La Cassine where Jacques, Madeleine and I followed her about, the way tiny children follow their mother. But

96

we were in the way. I left her for a while and went into the orchard where Martineau the elder, her forester, in company with Martineau the younger, the overseer, was examining the trees, to see whether or not they should be cut down. They were debating the point as if they were discussing their own property. I saw then how much the Countess was loved. I voiced my thoughts to a poor day labourer who, one foot on his spade, an elbow resting on the handle, was listening to the two professors of pomology. "Oh, yes, sir," he replied, "she's a good woman and not proud like all those ugly great peahens over at Azay, who'd see you die like a dog sooner than allow you a 'sou' for digging an extra yard of ditch! The day that woman leaves the district, the Holy Virgin will weep and so will we. She knows what's due to her, but she knows our troubles and takes thought for them."

How gladly did I give all the money I had on me to that man!

A few days later, a pony arrived for Jacques. His father, an excellent rider, wanted to train him gradually to the rigours of horsemanship. The child was provided with a handsome little riding habit, from the proceeds of the walnuts. The morning he took his first lesson, escorted by his father, to Madeleine's astonished cries as she skipped about on the lawn around which Jacques was riding, was, for the Countess, the first great heyday of her maternity. Jacques was wearing a collar embroidered by his mother, a little jacket in sky blue broadcloth with a black patent leather belt, white breeches and a tartan cap from under which his ashblond hair escaped in thick curls; he was an enchanting sight. All the household staff gathered round to share in this domestic felicity. The young heir smiled at his mother as he passed, sitting fearlessly up on his mount. How delightful a reward for her, to see this first manly act in a child whose death had so often seemed near at hand, and to know the hope of a fine future for him, confirmed now as he rode by, looking so handsome, so attractive and so fresh! The father's joy, as the years fell from him and he smiled for the first time for many a day, the happiness reflected in the eyes of all the servants, the exclamation of an old Lenoncourt groom, on his way back from Tours, who, seeing the way the child held the reins, said to him, "Well done, Monsieur le Vicomte!" It was all too much. Madame de Mortsauf burst into tears. She, so calm in distress, was suddenly too weak to bear the joy she felt at the sight of her child riding over that sandy path where she had so often prematurely mourned him, as she took him for short walks in the sunshine. Now, she leaned on my arm without misgivings and said "I feel that I have never been unhappy. Don't leave us for the rest of to-day."

The lesson over, Jacques threw himself into his mother's arms. She caught him up and held him to her with the strength lent by an excess of pleasure and there were kisses and caresses without end. I went with Madeleine to gather two magnificent bouquets with which to decorate the table in honour of the horseman. When we returned to the drawing-room the Countess said to me "The 15th of October will be a great day to remember. Jacques had his first riding lesson and I have just sewn the last stitch of my chair cover."

"In that case, Blanche," said the Count, laughing, "I must reward you for it."

He gave her his arm and led her out to the forecourt, where she saw a carriage, a gift from her father, for which the Count had bought two English horses, brought over with those of the Duc de Lenoncourt. The old groom had got everything ready in the forecourt during the riding lesson. We started the carriage, and went to see the lay-out of the driveway which was to lead in a straight line from Clochegourde to the Chinon road and which, owing to the recent acquisitions, could now be built across the new estates. On the way back, the Countess said to me, with an air of intense melancholy, "I am too happy. For me happiness is like an illness. It overwhelms me and I am afraid lest it should fade like a dream."

I was too passionately in love not to be jealous—and I could give her nothing! In my rage, I searched my mind for some way of dying for her. She asked me what thoughts were shrouding my gaze. I told her, ingenuously. She was more touched by them than by all her presents and she poured balm on my heart when, having led me on to the porch, she whispered "To love me as my aunt loved me; is that not tantamount to giving me your life? And if I take it, as I do, does that not make me beholden to you every second of the day? It was high time I finished my tapestry," she added, as we went back into the drawing-room, where I kissed her hand as if to renew my vows.

"You may not know why I set myself that lengthy task, Felix. Men find resources against sorrow in their work. The busy round helps to take their mind off things. But we women have no prop within ourselves to help us bear our heartache. To enable me to smile at my husband and children when sad thoughts obsessed my mind, I felt the need to keep a rein on suffering by some sort of physical movement. I avoided, in this way, the nervelessness that follows great expenditure of strength, as well as any periodical flashes of elation. The action of raising the arm at regular intervals gently rocked my mind and communicated to my soul, where the storm raged, the ebb and flow of peace, by thus regulating its emotions. Each stitch was the confidant of my secrets. Do you see? Well, while I was making my last chair, I thought too often of you, yes, far too often, my dear. What you put into your flower arrangements I said in my embroidery designs."

The dinner was a gay one. Jacques, like all children when one makes a fuss of them, threw his arms round my neck on seeing the flowers I had picked for him by way of a victor's wreath. His mother pretended to sulk over this piece of faithlessness. I leave you to guess how gracefully the dear child offered her that coveted bouquet! That evening, the three of us played a game of backgammon, myself against Monsieur and Madame de Mortsauf, and the Count was charming. And then, at nightfall, they accompanied me as far as the Frapesle path, on one of those calm, harmonious evenings when the sensibility gains in depth what it loses in vivacity.

It was an unique day in the life of this poor woman, a shining dot where her memory often lingered on difficult days. Indeed, the riding lessons soon became a source of discord. The Countess feared, with good reason, the father's harsh scolding of his son. Jacques was losing weight already and his fine blue eyes had dark circles round them. Rather than cause his mother any grief, he suffered in silence. I hit on a cure for his ills by advising him to tell his father he was tired whenever the Count lost his temper: but these palliatives were not enough; it was found necessary to substitute the old groom for the father, who did not allow his pupil

99

out of his clutches without a struggle. The arguments and the shouting began again; the Count found chapter and verse for his eternal complaints in the paltry gratitude of the female sex. He threw the carriage and the horses and the liveries in her face twenty times a day. Finally there occurred one of those events which natures of that type and illnesses of that sort love to seize upon. Expenses exceeded by half the estimated sum at La Cassine and La Rhétorière, where the walls and rotten flooring collapsed. A workman tactlessly broke this news to Monsieur de Mortsauf, instead of telling the Countess. It gave rise to a quarrel, quietly begun, but which grew progressively more venomous and where the Count's hypochondria, dormant for some days, clamoured for its arrears from poor Henriette.

I had left Frapesle at ten-thirty that day, directly after lunch, in order to arrange a bouquet with Madeleine at Clochegourde. The child had brought the two vases out on to the balustrade of the terrace for me, and I went through the gardens and the nearby fields in search of autumn flowers, so lovely but so rare. As I returned from my last trip, my little lieutenant in her pink belt and lace trimmed cape was no longer to be seen and I heard shouts issuing from Clochegourde.

"The general," Madeleine told me, in tears—and for her the term was one of hatred for her father, "the general is scolding my mother. Oh, do go and defend her!"

I flew up the steps and entered the drawing-room unnoticed and ungreeted, either by the Count or by his wife. On hearing the madman's high-pitched cries I went to shut all the doors, but turned back; I had seen Henriette, her face as white as her dress.

"Felix, never get married!" said the Count. "Women are prompted by the Devil. The most virtuous of them would invent evil if it did not exist, and all the others are brutish idiots."

I was treated forthwith to a string of arguments without head or tail to them. Harking back to the negative stand he had taken in the past, Monsieur de Mortsauf repeated the witless nonsense of the peasants who resisted the new methods. Had he run Clochegourde, he maintained, he would be twice as rich as he was now. As he uttered his violent and abusive blasphemies, he cursed, sprang from one piece of furniture to the next, struck them and pushed them out of place. Then, he would break off in the middle of a sentence to say his marrow was burning, or that his brain was gushing away in waves just like his money. His wife was ruining him. Wretched man, of the income of thirty odd thousand "livres" which he possessed, his wife had already brought him in more than twenty. The duke's property and that of the duchess represented an income of over fifty thousand francs which was reserved for Jacques. The Countess gave a superb smile and raised her eyes to heaven.

"Yes, Blanche," he cried, "you are my executioner, you are kill-ing me, I am a burden to you! You want to be rid of me! You are a monster of hypocrisy! And she laughs! Do you know why she is laughing, Felix?"

I stared at my feet, and said nothing.

"This woman," he went on, answering his own question, "de-prives me of all happiness. She is as much yours as she is mine and she makes out she is my wife! She bears my name and she fulfils none of the duties ordained by divine and human law! She is lying to God and man alike! She loads me with errands and tires me out so that I'll leave her alone. I disgust her, she hates me, and devotes all her skill to remaining a virgin! She is driving me insane with the privations she inflicts on me, for then it all rushes up to my poor head! She is killing me by inches and she takes herself for a saint! She goes to communion every month, if you please!"

The Countess was weeping bitterly now, humiliated to see this man sink so low, and all she could say in answer to him was "Monsieur ... Monsieur ... Monsieur ..."

Although the Count's words made me blush for him as well as for Henriette, they stirred me violently too, for they echoed the feelings of chastity and delicacy which are, so to speak, the very stuff of one's first love.

"She is a virgin at my expense," said the Count. At this the Countess cried "Monsieur!"

"What do you mean," he said, "by your imperious 'Monsieur'? Am I not the master? Must I teach you that at last?"

He bore down upon her, thrusting out his white wolfish head, hideous now, for there was an expression in his yellow eyes which made him look like a ravenous beast emerging from a wood.

Henriette slipped from her chair on to the floor to receive the blow which never came: she lay stretched on the floor, unconscious, utterly broken. The Count looked suddenly like a murderer who feels his victim's blood spurt in his face. He stood there, quite dazed. I took the poor woman in my arms; the Count let me do so as if he thought himself unworthy to carry her, but he went ahead to open the door of the room adjoining the drawing-room, sanctum into which I had never set foot. I stood the Countess on her feet and held her with one arm, putting the other round her waist, while Monsieur de Mortsauf removed the bedspread, quilt and other bed clothes. Then we lifted her and laid her down fully dressed. When she came to, Henriette begged us, with a gesture, to loosen her belt; Monsieur de Mortsauf found some scissors and cut through everything. I gave her some smelling salts and she opened her eyes. The Count left the room, more shamefaced than repentant. Two hours passed in deep silence. Henriette's hand was in mine and she pressed it, unable to speak. From time to time she raised her eyes to tell me by a look that she wanted to stay quietly as she was, with no noise. Then she broke the silence for a second, raised herself on one elbow and said in my ear, "The poor wretch! If you only knew!"

She laid her head back on the pillow. The memory of her past suffering, allied to her present grief, renewed the nervous convulsions which I had only soothed by the magnetism of love, a power unknown to me then, but which I used instinctively. I steadied her with a strength tempered with gentleness and during this last attack, she threw me glances which brought tears to my eyes. When the spasms ceased, I smoothed her dishevelled hair, touching it for the first and last time in my life; than I took her hand again and gazed intently at that brown and grey room, the simple bed with its chintz curtains, the dressing table trimmed in the old style, the little day bed with its studded mattress. What poetry there was in that place, what scorn for personal luxury! Her luxury was the most exquisite cleanliness. Noble cell for a married nun, full of saintly resignation, its only ornament the crucifix by the bed, above which could be seen the portrait of her aunt. Then, on either side of the holy water font, her own pencil sketches of her children and locks of their baby hair. What a retreat for a woman whose appearance in society would have made the greatest beauties pale! Such was the bower where the daughter of an illustrious family always shed her tears and where now, flooded with bitterness, she refused to yield to the love that would have comforted her. Secret, irreparable woe! And tears in the victim for the murderer, and tears in the murderer for the victim! The chambermaid came in with the children and I left the room.

The Count was waiting for me. He acknowledged me already as a mediating power between himself and his wife, and he seized my hands and cried, "Don't go, Felix, don't go!"

"Unfortunately," said I, "Monsieur de Chessel has company; it would not do for the guests to enquire into the possible reasons for my absence. But I shall come back after dinner."

He came out with me and saw me to the bottom gate without uttering a word. Then, not realising what he was doing, he accompanied me all the way to Frapesle. At last, when we got there, I said to him, "In Heaven's name, Monsieur le Comte, let her run your estate for you if she pleases and don't torment her so!"

"I have not long to live," he said seriously. "She will not suffer much longer on my account. My head is throbbing fit to burst."

And he left me in a fit of unconscious egoism. After dinner, I returned to enquire after Madame de Mortsauf and found her much better already. If these were the joys of marriage for her, if such scenes repeated themselves often, how could she go on living? What a slow, unpunished assassination was this! I came to understand, in the course of that evening, with what unspeakable torments the Count plagued his wife. Before what tribunal could she bring such griefs? These thoughts blunted my wits, I could think of nothing to say to Henriette. But I spent the whole night writing to her. Of the three or four letters I drafted, there remains this one, unfinished, which did not satisfy me. But although I considered that it expressed nothing, or that I said too much about myself, instead of concerning myself, as I should, exclusively with her, it will give you some insight into my state of mind.

To Madame de Mortsauf:

How much did I not have to tell you when I arrived, things which I thought of on the way and which I forget whenever I see you! Yes, as soon as I see you, dear Henriette, my words no longer seem in harmony with those reflections of your spirit which so enhance your beauty; and I experience such infinite happiness when I am with you that the present feeling obliterates the things I felt before. I am reborn each time into a wider sphere of living. I am like a traveller climbing some mighty rock and discovering at every step a new horizon. Each time I talk to you, do I not add to my immense treasures a newer treasure still? There, I think, lies the secret of long and inexhaustible attachments. Consequently, I can only talk to you about yourself when I am away from you. In your presence I am too dazzled to see, too happy to question my happiness, too full of you to be myself, too eloquent through you to speak, too burningly anxious to seize the present moment to recall the past. Remember this constant state of rapture and forgive me for its errors. Near you, I can only feel. Nevertheless, I will dare to tell you, my dear Henriette, that never among all the numerous joys you have created, have I felt anything comparable to the delights that filled me yesterday, when, after that appalling tempest, when you fought against evil with superhuman courage, you came back to me, and only me, in the half light of your room, where that miserable scene had led me. I alone knew how a woman glows when she comes from the gates of death to the gates of life, and the dawn of rebirth tints her brow. How harmonious was your voice! How small words, even your words, seemed, when in the sound of your adored voice there reappeared the dim sensations of past pain, mingled with the divine consolation with which you finally reassured me, by giving me, as you did, your very first thoughts. I already knew you as a creature radiant with every human splendour. But yesterday, I caught a glimpse of a new Henriette, who would be mine if God wished it so; a glimpse of some indefinable being freed from those bodily fetters which prevent us from stirring the soul's fires. How beautiful you were, darling, in your prostration and how majestic in your weakness! Yesterday, I discovered something lovelier than your loveliness, something sweeter than your voice, lights more sparkling than the light in your eyes, perfumes for which there are no words; yesterday your soul became visible and tangible.

Ah, how I suffered at not being able to open my heart to you, and coax you back to life in it! Yesterday, at long last, I shed that respectful terror you inspire in me; had not your faint brought us closer to each other? I found out, then, what breathing meant when I drew breath with you, as soon the fainting fit allowed you to breathe our air again. How many were the prayers that rose to Heaven in that one moment! If I did not expire on the way through the expanses I crossed in order to ask God to leave you to me, then one does not die of joy or grief. That moment left me with memories embedded in my soul and never will they reappear on the surface without my eyes moistening with tears; each joy will intensify them, each sorrow will deepen the imprint they have left. Yes, the fears that racked my soul yesterday will be my yardstick for all the pain to come, just as the joy that you have given me so liberally, dear eternal thought of my life, will tower above all the joys which the hand of God will deign to give me. You have helped me to understand Divine Love, that unwavering love, which, sure of its strength and permanence, knows neither jealousy nor suspicion.

A deep gloom gnawed at my soul. The spectacle of that inner life was deeply distressing to a young heart unversed in human emotions. To meet this abyss at my first step into the world, a bottomless abyss, a dead sea! This dreadful concert of misfortunes started an infinite train of thoughts in me and I had, on my first step into social life, an immense measure beside which other scenes could not now be anything but small. Monsieur and Madame de Chessel assumed from my sadness, that my love must be unrequited and I had the joy of knowing that my passion was in no way detrimental to my noble Henriette.

The following day, when I came into the drawing-room, she was alone. She looked at me for a second as she held out her hand and then said, "Will the friend always be too loving, then?"

Her eyes misted, she rose and said in a tone of imploring desperation: "Do not write to me like that again."

Monsieur de Mortsauf was attentive. The Countess was once more cheerful and serene of brow, but her pallor betrayed the previous day's sufferings, which had abated, but were smouldering still. That evening, as we strolled among the dead autumn leaves crackling beneath our feet, she said "Pain is infinite, joy has its limits", a remark which revealed the extent of her suffering, when set against her fleeting joys.

"Do not speak ill of life," said I. "You have never been in love, and the senses can know a bliss whose radiance reaches to the stars."

"Be quiet," said she. "I want no part of it. Greenlanders would die in Italy! I am happy and at peace when I am with you, I can tell you all my thoughts. Do not destroy my trust in you. Why should you not have the virtuousness of the priest and the appeal of the unattached man?"

"You could make a man drink whole cups of hemlock," said I, laying her hand on my fast-beating heart.

"Again!" she cried, withdrawing her hand as if she had felt some stabbing pain. "Do you want to rob me of the mournful pleasure of having my wounds staunched by a friendly hand? Do not add to my sufferings, you do not know them all! The most secret of them are the hardest of all to bear. If you were a woman you would understand into what despondency mixed with disgust a proud soul can sink when it finds herself the object of attentions which mend nothing, and which are fondly expected to make amends for everything. For a few days I shall be courted, my forgiveness will be sought for the wrong that *one* has brought upon *oneself*. At such times I could obtain consent to the most unreasonable demands. I am humiliated by this self-abasement, by those caresses which stop the moment it is thought that I have forgotten everything. To owe the good graces of one's lord and master only to his faults—"

"To his crimes!" I said quickly.

"Is this not a dreadful way to live?" she said, giving me a wan smile. "Besides, I do not know how to use this temporary power. Just now, I am like the knights who would not strike their fallen adversaries. To see the man one should revere prostrate on the ground, to help him to his feet only to receive fresh blows, to suffer from his fall more than he does himself, and to think oneself dis-honoured if one takes advantage of a momentary influence, even in a useful cause; to spend one's strength, to exhaust the treasures of the spirit in these ignoble struggles, to reign only at the moment when one sustains mortal wounds! Better death. If I had no children I should let myself drift on the current of this existence, but without my hidden courage, what would become of them? I must live for their sakes, however painful life may be. You spoke of love. Why, my dear, just think into what hell I should fall were I to give that pitiless creature—pitiless like all weak souls, the right to despise me? I could not bear the faintest breath of suspicion. The purity of my conduct is my strength. Virtue, dear child, has holy waters where one can bathe and emerge renewed in the love of God!"

"Listen to me, dear Henriette. I have only one more week here and I want —"

"Oh, are you leaving us?" she broke in.

"I must find out what plans my father has made for me. It is nearly three months since —"

"I did not count the days," she replied, with the abandon bred of deep emotion.

She regained her composure and said "Come, let us walk to Frapesle." She called the Count and the children and sent for her shawl. Then, when everyone was ready to go, she, so slow, so calm, became suddenly as brisk as a Parisian woman and we left in a body for Frapesle, to pay a call which the Countess did not owe.

She made a noble effort to converse with Madame de Chessel, who was fortunately extremely talkative. The Count and Monsieur de Chessel talked about their business affairs. I was afraid that Monsieur de Mortsauf would boast of his carriage and horses, but he behaved with impeccable taste. His neighbour asked him about the work he was undertaking at La Cassine and La Rhétorière. On hearing the question, I looked at the Count, thinking he would refrain from discussing a subject so fraught with memories and so cruelly bitter for him, but he proceeded to expound how urgent it was to improve the standard of agriculture in the district and to build fine farms with clean and salubrious living quarters; in short, he vaingloriously attributed his wife's ideas to himself. I looked at the Countess and flushed. This lack of delicacy in a man who in some circumstances had so much, this ability to forget that fatal scene, this adoption of ideas he had so violently opposed, this belief in himself, left me transfixed. When Monsieur de Chessel asked if he thought he could get back what he had spent, he replied, "That and more," with an affirmative gesture. Such aberrations could only be explained by the word "lunacy".

Henriette, celestial creature, was radiant. Did not the Count show up as a man of sense, a good administrator, an excellent agronomist? Delightedly she stroked Jacques' hair, happy for herself, happy for her son. Oh, the horrible farce, the derisive drama of it! I was appalled. Later, when the social stage raised its curtain for me, how many Mortsaufs did I not see, minus this man's flashes of honesty, minus his religion! What strange and mordant power is it that perpetually throws the angel to the lunatic, the evil woman to the man sincere and poetic in his love, the queenly to the stunted and a sublime and lovely creature to this ape; to the noble Juana a Captain Diard, whose story was related to you in Bordeaux; to Madame de Beauséant a d'Ajuda; to Madame d'Aiglemont her husband; to the Marquis d'Espard his wife. I have, I confess, long sought the key to this enigma. I have investigated many a mystery, I have discovered the principle of several natural laws, the meaning of one or two divine hieroglyphics, but about this I know nothing. I study it still, like the face on an Indian war-club, whose symbolic construction the Brahmins have kept to themselves. Here the genius of evil is all too visibly the master and I dare not accuse God. Woes without remedy, whose idle hand is it that spins you? Were Henriette and her Unknown Philosopher right after all? Could their mysticism contain a general truth about humanity?

The last days I spent in the district were those of leaf-scattered autumn, days darkened by clouds which at times obscured the Touraine sky, always so clear and warm at this lovely time of year. The eve of my departure, before dinner, Madame de Mortsauf took me out on to the terrace. "My dear Felix," she said, after we had taken a turn in silence under the leafless trees, "you are about to go into the world and I want to accompany you in thought. Those who have suffered intensely have lived intensely too. Do not think that solitary souls know nothing of this world. They judge it. If I am to live through my friend, I do not want to feel ill at ease in his heart or in his conscience. In the heat of the fight, it is very difficult to remember all the rules. Will you let me give you a little motherly advice?"

"The day of your departure, dearest child, I shall give you a long letter, where you will find my woman's thoughts on society, on the world of men and on the way to tackle difficulties in this great maelstrom of conflicting interests. Will you promise me not to read it until you get to Paris? My request springs from one of those whims of sentiment which we women like to keep secret; it is not, I think, impossible to understand it, but we might, perhaps, be sorry to see it understood. Leave me those little paths where a woman likes to wander on her own."

"I promise," said I, kissing both her hands.

"Ah," said she, "I have another promise to extract from you. But you must promise before I tell you what it is."

"Oh, yes!" said I, thinking it was to be a question of fidelity.

"It has nothing to do with me," she went on, with a bitter smile. "Felix, never gamble, no matter in whose house. I except nobody's."

"I shall never gamble," I answered.

"Good," said she. "I have thought of a better use for the time you would dissipate at the gaming table. You will see that where others are bound to lose sooner or later, you will always win."

"How?"

"The letter will tell you," she answered, with a gaiety of manner that robbed her injunctions of the solemnity which attends the cautionary sermons of one's grandparents.

The Countess talked to me for about an hour and proved the depth of her affection for me by revealing how carefully she had studied me during these last three months. She penetrated to the innermost recesses of my heart and tried to imprint her own there. Her accents were varied and convincing, her words fell from maternal lips and they showed, by their tone as well as by their content, how many bonds already held us together.

"If you only knew," she concluded, "how anxiously I shall follow you on your road, how joyful I shall be if you go straight ahead, how many tears I shall shed if you crash into sharp corners! Believe me, my affection for you is unequalled; it is both involuntary and deliberate. Oh, I should like to see you happy, powerful, highly thought of, you who will be a sort of animated dream for me!"

She brought tears to my eyes. She was both gentle and terrible. Her feeling for me was too fearlessly laid bare, too pure to allow the faintest hope to the pleasure-starved young man that I was.

In return for my flesh, left lying in pieces in her heart, she lavished the ceaseless, incorruptible beams of that love which satisfies the soul alone. She rose to heights where the speckled wings of the passion that had thrown me ravenously on to her shoulders could not carry me. To reach her, a man would need to win the white wings of the seraphim.

"In all things," I said, "I shall ask myself, what would my Henriette say to this?"

"I'm glad. I want to be the sanctuary and the star," she said, referring to the daydreams of my childhood, and trying to offer me their realisation as a substitute for my desires.

"You will be my religion and my light, you will be everything!" I cried.

"No," she replied, "I cannot be the source of pleasure to you."

She sighed and gave me the smile of the secret sorrows, the smile of the slave in a fleeting moment of rebellion. From that day she was not the dearly loved but the most beloved; she lived in my heart, not as the woman who demands a place there, and carves out her niche in it by devotion or excess of pleasure; no, she had all of my heart, she was somehow necessary to the play of its muscles; she became what the Florentine poet's Beatrice was, the Venetian's immaculate Laura, the mother of great thoughts, the unknown cause of resolutions that can save a man, the mainstay of the future, the light that shines in the gloom like the lily in the dusky foliage. Yes, she prompted that high resolve that takes no heed of fire, that shoulders the imperilled cause. She gave me the Coligny-like steadfastness that conquers conquerors, that rises anew after defeat, that outfights the strongest fighters.

The next day, after lunching at Frapesle and bidding goodbye to my hosts, who had been so tolerant of me in the egoism of my love, I made my way to Clochegourde. Monsieur and Madame de Mortsauf had suggested accompanying me as far as Tours, whence I was to travel overnight to Paris. On the way, the Countess was affectionately silent. She pretended at first to have the migraine, then blushed at the falsehood and softened it by saying that she was sorry to see me go. The Count invited me to stay at his house, should I feel a desire to revisit the Indre valley when the de Chessels were away. We parted heroically, without visible tears, although Jacques, like some children whose health is poor, had a surge of emotion which caused him to weep a little, while Madeleine, a woman already, squeezed her mother's hand.

"Dear child," said the Countess, giving Jacques an impassioned kiss.

When I found myself alone in Tours, after dinner, there swept over me one of those unaccountable fits of frenzy which one only experiences in youth. I hired a horse and covered in an hour and a quarter the distance between Tours and Pont-de-Ruan. There, ashamed of showing my folly, I ran on foot along the path and reached the terrace on tiptoe, like a spy. The Countess was not there. It occurred to me that she might not be well. I still had the key to the little gate and I went in. She was coming down the verandah steps with her two children, sad and slow-footed, to breathe the gentle melancholy imprinted on that landscape in the setting sun.

"Mother! Here's Felix," said Madeleine.

"Yes, it is I," I whispered in her ear. "I asked myself what I was doing in Tours when it was still so easy for me to see you. Why should I not gratify a wish which in a week's time I shall no longer be able to fulfil?"

"Mother, he's not going away after all!" cried Jacques, jumping up and down.

"Be quiet," said Madeleine, "you'll bring the general here."

"This was not sensible of you," murmured Henriette, "what a senseless thing to do!"

What ample payment of love's exorbitant account were those tear-muted harmonies in her voice!

"I forgot to give you back this key," I said with a smile.

"Will you not be coming back again then?" said she.

"Are we parting at all?" I asked, giving her a look which made her drop her eyelids to veil her mute reply.

I left, after a few moments spent in that euphoric stupour known to souls who have reached the point where exaltation ends and wild ecstasy begins. I walked away with slow steps, looking repeatedly over my shoulder. When, at the top of the plateau I gazed on the valley yet once more, I was struck by the contrast it offered with the way it had looked when I first came to it; was it not green-growing then, was it not ablaze, just as my desires blazed and my hopes grew green?

Initiated now in the sombre and melancholy mysteries of a family, sharing the anguish of a Christian Niobe, sad like her, and sobered in soul, I found the valley in tune, now, with my thoughts. The fields were shorn now, the poplars were losing their leaves, and those that remained were the colour of rust; the vine shoots were burned, the tree tops wore the sombre hues of that tan colour which the kings of old used to adopt for their dress and which hid the purple of power beneath the brown of sorrows. Still in harmony with my thoughts, the valley, where faded the yellow rays of a lukewarm sun, showed me yet another vivid image of my state of mind. To leave a woman one loves is a situation horrible or simple, depending on one's nature; in my case, I found myself, suddenly, stranded as it were, in a strange land, whose language I did not know. There was nothing I could cling to, as I saw things to which I no longer felt my soul was linked. And so, my love was unfurled in all its length, and my dear Henriette rose to her full height in that desert where her memory was my sole reason for living. She became a figure so fervently worshipped, that I resolved to stay without blemish in the presence of my secret divinity and I donned, in imagination, the white robe of the cleric, thus imitating Petrach, who never appeared before Laura de Novera unless clad from head to foot in white. How impatiently I awaited the first night under my father's roof, when I could read that letter! I touched it during the journey the way a miser fingers a sheaf of banknotes which he is forced to carry on his person. During the night, I kissed the paper on which Henriette had made her wishes known; from which I was to gather the mysterious emanations released by her hand and from where the intonations of her voice would leap into my receptive understanding. I have never read her letters in any other way than as I read her first, in bed, in the midst of an unbroken silence. I do not know how one can read the letters from a loved one in any other way. Yet, there are men, unworthy of a woman's love, who mix the reading of these letters with daily preoccupations, who lay them aside and pick them up again with odious imperturbability. Here Natalie, is the adorable voice which rang out suddenly in the silence of the night; here is the sublime figure that arose to point the way at the crossroads where I now stood.

"What happiness it gives me, my dear, to have to gather the scattered elements of my experience in order to pass them on to you and arm you against the dangers of the world in which you must soon skilfully make your way! I have tasted the lawful joys of maternal love, in devoting my time to you as I have done these last few nights. While I wrote this, sentence by sentence, transporting myself beforehand into the life that you will lead, I went from time to time to my window. And as I saw the moonlit turrets of Frapesle, I said to myself, 'He is asleep and I am keeping watch for him.' Sweet sensations that recalled the first happy days of my life, when I watched Jacques sleeping in his cradle and waited for him to wake in order to give him my milk. Are you not a child, man though you are, who needs the spiritual comfort of one or two precepts which you were not given in those dreadful schools where you were so unhappy, precepts which we women are privileged to give you? These trivial details influence your success, they pave the way for and consolidate it. What is this establishment of the set of values to which a man must refer all the actions of his life, but a spiritual mother-love, one the child is fully old enough to grasp?

"Dear Felix, allow me, even though some of the things I say might well be wrong, to set the sanctifying seal of disinterestedness upon our friendship. Is not handing you over to the world tantamount to giving you up? But I love you enough to sacrifice my delight in you to your fine future. For nearly four months now, you have caused me to ponder strangely on the laws and customs which govern this age of ours. The talks I had with my aunt, talks whose inner content belongs to you since you have taken her place; the things Monsieur de Mortsauf told me about his own life; the words of my father, who knew the Court so well; events both great and small in my own experience; all this rose up in my memory for the benefit of my adopted son whom I see now, about to leap into the world of men, virtually alone; about to find his way without advice in a land where many perish through the ill-considered use of their good qualities, where some succeed through judicious use of their bad ones.

"Before anything else, think carefully about my overall views on society; I have condensed them, but with you few words suffice. I do not know if social communities are of divine origin or if they are of man's invention. Nor do I know in what direction they tend. But one thing, to my mind, is certain: they exist. The moment you accept them instead of standing outside them, you must regard the basic conditions of their structure as valid. To-morrow you will sign a kind of contract between yourself and them. Does present-day society use man more than it benefits him? I think so, but whether man encounters more responsibilities than he does gain, or whether he pays too dearly for what advantages he does obtain, are questions which concern the legislator and not the individual. In my opinion then, you must bow to the universal law in all things, whether it harms or woos your interests. Simple though this principle may seem, it is difficult to apply. There is a sort of sap which must spread along the tiniest capillaries in order to give life to the tree, help it keep its foliage, develop its blossom and improve its fruit so magnificently that it excites general admiration. Dear one, laws are not all written in a book, human behaviour creates laws too, and the most important of them are the least well known; there are neither teachers, nor treatises, nor schools for this law, which governs your deeds, your speech, the outward circumstances of your life and the way you show yourself to the world or set about making your fortune. To break these hidden laws is to remain at the bottom of the social order instead of towering above it. Even though this letter may tell you things you already know, let me give you my own attitude to life, as a woman sees it. To explain society in terms of personal happiness, cleverly grasped at the expense of everybody else is a fatal doctrine, the grim deductions of which lead man to believe that everything he can obtain, on the quiet, without the law, society or the individual being aware of any felony, is well and rightfully won. According to this charter, the nimble thief is blameless, the woman who fails in her wifely duty unbeknownst to anyone is virtuous and happy. Kill a man without the law's having one single shred of proof of it, and if by so doing you win some diadem, Macbeth-fashion, you have acted well. Self-interest becomes the supreme law; the whole problem becomes a mere matter of turning aside, without witnesses or evidence, the hurdles which law and custom set between you and your gratification. For a man who views society like this, my dear, the problem of making a fortune reduces itself to a gamble in which the stakes are a million or a prison sentence, political eminence or dishonour. Then again, the green baize will not accommodate all those who want to play and it takes the forcefulness of genius to plan a winning throw. I am not speaking of sentiments or religious beliefs. It is a question here of the wheels of a machine of gold and iron and of the immediate results with which men are concerned. Dear child of my heart, if you share my horror of this criminal theory, society can only be explained in your eyes as it explains itself to all sane minds, by the concept of duty. Yes, you owe a duty to one another in a hundred different ways. In my opinion a peer of the realm owes a greater duty to the poor man or the artisan than does the artisan or the poor man to the peer. Obligations increase in proportion to the benefits which society bestows on man, following the principle, as true in politics as it is in business, that the weight of care is always proportionate to the size of the profit. Each discharges his debt in his own way. When our poor labourer at La Rhétorière comes home to bed, weary from his toil, do you think he has not fulfilled his obligations? He has most certainly met them better than many highly placed people have theirs. If you take this view of the community in which you will want a position commensurate with your intelligence and capabilities, you must set yourself, as a fundamental principle, the following maxim: never to take liberties with one's own or with the public conscience. Although you may think it superfluous of me to stress this so, I implore you—yes, your Henriette implores you to weigh these words very carefully. They seem simple, but they signify, dear one, that uprightness, honour, integrity, and courtesy are the surest and speediest instruments of your success. In this selfish world, a host of people will tell you that one does not get to the top through fine feelings, that too much regard for ethical considerations are a handicap in a career. You will see men, ill-bred, ill-educated or incapable of sizing up the future, snubbing someone of small account, behaving discourteously to an old woman, refusing to spend a moment's boredom with some kindly old man, on the pretext that such folk cannot be of any use to them. Later on, you will see these men caught by thorns which they omitted to blunt and missing success on account of a trifle; whereas the man broken in at an early age to this concept of social obligation will meet with no obstacles. He may get there less quickly but his success will be stable and will endure when that of others crumbles.

"When I tell you that the application of this doctrine demands above all the science of good manners, you may think that my jurisprudence smacks a little of the Court and the training I received in the house of Lenoncourt. Oh, my dear, I attach the greatest importance to this training, outwardly trivial though it may be. The ways of high society are as necessary to you as the extensive and varied knowledge which you possess. They have often made up for it. Certain men, comparatively ignorant but endowed with a native wit, and used to co-ordinating their ideas, have achieved a greatness which eluded worthier men than they. I have studied you closely, Felix, in an attempt to find out whether your education, communally acquired as it was in your schools, had not spoilt anything in you. Only God will know the joy I felt when I saw that you could acquire what little you now lack. With many people reared in these traditions politeness is purely superficial, for exquisite courtesy and fine manners spring from the heart and from a deep sense of individual dignity. That is why, despite their education, some aristocrats have an air of vulgarity, while certain persons of middle-class extraction have natural good taste and need only a few lessons to acquire, without any hint of awkward imitation, quite excellent manners. Believe a poor woman who will never stir out of her valley, this noble good breeding, the stamp of this graceful simplicity upon one's speech, bearing, dress and even on one's house constitute a sort of physical poetry whose charm is irresistible, so imagine its power when it springs from the heart! Good manners, dear child, consist in appearing to forget oneself for others' sake. With many people they are a social grimace which is belied as soon as self-interest, too thwarted, peeps out from behind it. The rich and powerful become ignoble then. But—and

this is the way I want you to be, Felix—true courtesy implies a
Christian mind. It is like the flower of charity and consists in *true*
forgetfulness of self.

"In memory of Henriette, do not be a fountain without water;
have the spirit as well as the outward form. Do not be afraid that
you will often be the dupe of this social virtue; sooner or later you
will reap the fruits of so many seeds seemingly scattered to the
winds. My father observed long ago that one of the most wounding
aspects of politeness, as it is commonly misunderstood, is the
abuse of promises. When someone asks you a favour you know you
cannot perform, refuse at once and do not arouse false hopes. Any
favours you intend to do, do at once. You will thus acquire both
the grace that comes of being able to say no and the grace of doing
a good deed, a twofold sign of integrity which adds immense zest
to a man's character. I do not know if one incurs more ill-feeling
over dashed hopes than gratitude for favours done. Above all, my
dear—these minor matters are well within my scope, and I think
I may stress the things I can be said to know about—be neither
trivial, nor over-zealous, nor trusting—three great pitfalls! Too
many confidences diminish respect, triviality earns us contempt,
zealousness makes us excellent targets for exploitation. Besides,
dear child, you will not have more than two or three friends in the
course of your life, your entire trust is your gift to them. Are you
not betraying them if you give it to all and sundry? Should you
form one or two relatively closer relationships, do be discreet about
yourself. Always be as reserved as if you expected, some day, to
have those men as competitors, opponents or enemies; the hazards
of life make this so. So always behave in a way which is neither
cold nor effusive; learn to steer that middle course which a man can
maintain without committing himself to his detriment. Yes, believe
me, the true gentleman is as far removed from the spineless sycophancy of a Philinte as he is from the acrid virtuousness of an
Alceste. The genius of the great comic poet is at its most brilliant
in the indication of the true middle way, which the noblest of his
readers will readily adopt. True, they are all more likely to veer
towards the absurdities of virtue than towards the overweening
contempt that lurks behind the easy charm of egoism, but they will
know how to save themselves from both. As for triviality, although

117

it may make a few fops call you a charming man, those whose habit it is to plumb and to assess human capabilities will gauge your defects and you will fall forthwith, in their estimation, for triviality is the standby of the weak. Now, weak folk are unfortunately despised by a society which sees each of its members as no more nor less than organic parts—and perhaps rightly so, for nature condemns imperfect creatures to death. Perhaps too, the touching protectiveness of women springs from the delight they take in battling against this blind force, in making the heart's intelligence triumph over the brutality of matter. But society, more stepdam than mother, adores the children who flatter her vanity. As for zeal, that first and sublime error of youth, which finds genuine satisfaction in testing its own strength and so begins by being its own dupe before becoming that of others, keep it for the feelings you will share, keep it for women and for God. Do not bring to the world's bazaar, or to the speculations of political life, treasures in exchange for which they will give you worthless glass. Please believe the voice that bids you have nobility in all things, while begging you not to squander yourself to no purpose. For unfortunately, men will value you in proportion to your usefulness, without giving a thought to your true worth. To use a metaphor that will stamp itself on your poetic turn of mind; be the cypher of an exaggerated size, traced in gold or written in pencil, it will never be other than a cypher. As a man of our epoch has said, 'Never be zealous!' Zeal invites trickery, it makes for errors of judgement; you will never find, in those above you, an answering warmth that tallies with your own. Kings, like women, claim everything as their rightful due. Sad thought this principle may be, it is a true one. But it need not deflower the soul. Set your pure feelings in inaccessible places where their flowers will win impassioned admiration, where the artist will dream, lovingly almost, of the masterpiece.

"Duties, my dear, are not feelings. Doing what one must is not the same as doing what one likes. A man must die coldly for his country. He can give his life gladly, to a woman.

"One of the most important rules in the science of good manners is an almost total silence about oneself. Treat yourself to the pastime, some day, of talking about yourself to people of slight acquaintance; hold forth to them about your woes, your pleasures or your business affairs; you will see indifference follow hard upon feigned interest, then, once boredom has set in, if the hostess does not politely interrupt you, every man will seize on an ingenious excuse to slip away. But if you want to command all their sympathies, to pass for a likeable man, lively of wit and consistently pleasant of manner, talk to them about themselves, do your utmost to make them the centre of attention, even by bringing up a subject seemingly unconnected with the individuals concerned. Brows will come to life, lips will smile for you and when you have left, everyone will sing your praises. The voice of heart and conscience will tell you where contemptible flattery begins and graceful conversation ends. One word more, about airing your opinions in public. My dear, young people are always prone to a certain swiftness of judgement which is to their credit, but not to their advantage. Whence the silence that the upbringing of bygone days imposed upon the young, who spent a period of probation with the eminent, during which time they studied life; for in days of old, Nobility, like Art, had its apprentices, pages who owed allegiance to the masters who fed and clothed them. To-day, youth has a hot-house knowledge, hence predominantly acid, which induces it to judge actions, ideas and writings with severity; it cuts with the edge of a blade which has not yet been used. Avoid this failing. Your judgements would be strictures which would wound many of those around you and they may all forgive a secret injury less readily than any wrong you might do them in public. Young men are without indulgence because they know nothing of life or its difficulties. The old critic is gentle and good-natured. The young one is implacable. The latter knows nothing, the former everything. Besides, there is, at the root of all human actions, a labyrinth of determining reasons, on which God has reserved the final judgement. Be hard only on yourself. Your fortune is before you, but nobody on earth can make his own unaided. So frequent my father's house; you have the entrée to it now. The connections you will form there will be of use to you on countless occasions. But do not yield an inch of ground to my mother; she tramples underfoot anyone who lets her walk over him and admires the pride of the man who can stand up to her. She is like iron; beaten, it can amalgamate with iron, but anything less hard than itself it breaks on contact.

"Cultivate my mother, then. If she is well disposed towards you she will introduce you to fashionable hostesses, in whose drawing-rooms you will acquire that crucial knowledge of the world, the art of conversing, of listening, of answering questions, of introducing yourself and of taking your leave; you will learn precision of speech, that indefinable something which is not the sum total of superiority any more than tailoring is of genius, but without which the fairest talents will never find recognition. I know you well enough to be certain that I am cherishing no fond illusions in visualising you, beforehand, as I want you to be, simple in your ways, gentle of manner, proud without fatuousness, respectful towards the old, obliging without servility and above all, discreet. Show your wit but do not serve as entertainment to others—for remember that if you make a dull man feel inferior he will keep quiet and say when you have gone 'He is most amusing'—which is a term of contempt. Let your superiority be always leonine. And do not strive to please your fellow men. In your dealing with them, I would recommend a certain coolness, which can go as far as insolence without giving them cause to resent you. Everyone looks up to the man who looks down on them and this disdain will win you the good favours of all women, who will esteem you for the scant respect you have for men. Never keep company with people of disrepute, even when they do not deserve their reputation, for the world calls us to account as much for our friendships as for our enmities. Where these are concerned, let your judgement be long and maturely weighed, but let it be irrevocable. When men you spurn have justified your spurning of them, your good opinion will be sought after and you will inspire that tacit respect which increases a man's stature in the world of men. So there you are, armed with the youth that pleases, the grace that charms, the wisdom that keeps what it has won. Everything I have told you can be summed up in an old maxim: *Noblesse oblige.*

"Now, apply these precepts to the strategy of business affairs. You will hear some people say that shrewdness is the secret of success; that the way to break through the crowd is to divide men so that they will make room for you. My friend, those principles held good in the Middle Ages when there were rival powers that princes could set one against the other and so destroy. But to-day, nothing can be done under cover, and this method would do you great disservice. Indeed, you will find in your path, now a true and honest man, now a treacherous enemy, one who will proceed by calumny, backbiting and deceit. Well, remember that you have no more powerful ally than the latter, for this man is his own worst enemy. You can fight him with honest weapons; sooner or later he will be despised. As for the former, your frankness will win his esteem and once your interests are reconciled (these things can always be worked out) he will be useful to you. Do not be afraid of making enemies; woe to him who has none in the world you are about to enter. But try not to lay yourself open to ridicule or discredit. I say try, for in Paris a man is not always master of his fate, he is subject to circumstances beyond his control; you cannot escape the mud from the gutter or the danger of the falling tile. Morality has its streams whence dishonoured folk try to splash the noblest individuals with the mud in which they are about to drown. But you can always command respect by showing yourself, in all spheres, implacable when you have once made up your mind. In this conflict of ambitions, in the midst of this web of difficulties, always make straight for the fact, tackle the problem resolutely and never fight save on a point of honour, and then with all your might. You know how much Monsieur de Mortsauf hated Napoleon. He pursued him with his curse, he watched him as the law watches a criminal; nightly he called him to account for the Duc d'Enghien, the only misfortune, the only death that ever drew a tear from him. Well, my dear, he admired him as the boldest of captains; he often explained his tactics to me. Cannot that strategy then, be applied to the war of conflicting interests? It would save time, as the other saved men and space. Think this over; a woman can often be mistaken in matters of this sort, which we judge by instinct and sentiment. One point I can stress; all cunning, all double-dealing gets found out and harms the doer in the end; whereas any situation is less risky, to my mind, when a man takes his stand on the terrain of candour. If I could quote my own case, I would tell you that at Clochegourde, forced as I was by Monsieur de Mortsauf's character to avoid all litigation and to settle out of court, immediately, any impending lawsuits, which would otherwise have affected him rather like a disease that he would enjoy even as he succumbed to it, I invariably settled everything myself by going straight to the knot and saying to the opponent 'Let us untie it or else cut it through!' You will often find yourself in a position to be of use to others, to do them a favour, and you will get scant reward for it. But do not imitate those who complain of men and boast of meeting nothing but ingratitude. Is that not putting one-self on a pedestal? Then again, is it not rather foolish to admit how little one knows of the world? But will you do good the way a usurer lends his money? Will you not do it for its own sake? *Noblesse oblige!* Nevertheless, do not render such great services that you force people to be ungrateful, for they will become your irreconcilable enemies; there is such a thing as the despair of being beholden just as there is the despair of ruin, and it lends incalculable strength. As for you, accept as little as you can from others. Do not be anybody's vassal; stand on your own feet. I am giving you ad-vice, my dear, only in the little things of life. In the world of politics, everything takes a different aspect; the rules which govern the individual bend before great interests. But if you should reach the sphere where great men move, you would be like God, the sole judge of your decisions. You would not then be a man, you would be living law; you would no longer be an individual, but the in-carnation of the nation. Later, you will appear before the centuries and you know enough of history to appreciate the sentiments and the actions which give birth to true greatness.

"I come now to the grave question of your behaviour towards women. In the drawing-rooms to which you will go, make it a rule not to waste your energies by indulging in the petty game of flirtation. One of the most successful men of the last century made it a habit never to devote himself to more than one lady in an evening and to attach himself to those women who appeared to be neglected. This man, dear child, dominated his era. He had wisely calculated that, in time, everyone would obstinately sing his praises. The majority of young men waste their most precious asset, the time needed to make good connections, which are the half of social life: as they are liked themselves there is little they need do for people to espouse their interests. But this springtime is a short one, learn how to use it well. Cultivate influential women. The women with influence are the old women. They will tell you the marriage connections and the secrets of every family and the short cuts which can lead you speedily to your goal. They will be yours, heart and soul. Patronage is their last love, when they are not piously inclined. They will serve you wonderfully well; they will plead your cause and make you sought after. Shun young women! Do not think there is the slightest personal interest in what I am saying. The woman of fifty will do everything for you. The woman of twenty nothing. The latter wants your entire life, the other will only ask a moment of your time, a small mark of attention. Laugh at young women, treat whatever they say as a joke, they are incapable of a serious thought. Young women, my dear, are self-centred, small-minded, incapable of real affection. They love none but themselves; they would sacrifice you for the sake of a conquest. Besides, they all demand complete devotion and in your position it will be essential that others devote themselves to you, two irreconcilable claims. Not one of them will have any understanding of your interests; they will all think of themselves and not of you, they will all do you more harm by their vanity than good service by their attachment. They will devour your time without a qualm, make you miss your chance of success and destroy you with the best will in the world. If you complain, the silliest of them will prove to you that the world is well lost for her glove; that nothing is more glorious than serving her. All of them will tell you that they bring true happiness and they will make you forget your fine destinies. Their happiness is prone to change; your greatness is a certainty. You do not know with what perfidious an art they set about gratifying their whims and converting a passing fancy into a love which begins in this world and ostensibly continues in the next. The day they leave you, they will tell you that the words, 'I do not love you any more' justify the leaving, just as the words, 'I love you' excused their passion, and that love is beyond our control. An absurd doctrine, dear one! Believe me, real love is eternal, infinite, always true to itself. It is steadfast and pure and without exaggeration outward show; it sees itself with white hair and still young in heart. You will find none of these things in society women. They are all acting a part. This one will arouse your interest by her misfortunes; she will appear to be the gentlest and least demanding of women. But when she has made herself indispensable, she will dominate you, bit by bit, and make you do her bidding. You want to be a diplomat, to go where you will, to study men, interests, foreign lands? No, you will stay in Paris or on her estates. She will sew you with malicious glee to her skirts, and the more devoted you are, the less grateful she will be. Another one will try to gain your interest by her submissiveness; she will turn herself into your page, follow you romantically to the ends of the earth, compromise herself in order to keep you; and she will be a millstone round your neck. One day you will drown, and the woman will stay afloat. The least artful of women has infinite wiles, the most witless triumphs through the scant suspicion she arouses. The least dangerous would be an easy lady who would love you without knowing why, who would leave you for no reason, and take you back again out of vanity. But every one of them will do you harm, either at the time or later on. Every young woman who moves in society, who lives for pleasure and the satisfactions of vanity is half corrupted and will corrupt you. Not there will you find the chaste and withdrawn creature in whose soul you will reign for always. Ah, she will be a solitary soul, the one who loves you! Her loveliest feast days will be the looks you give her, and she will live for the things you say. Let this woman be the world to you, for you will be everything to her. Love her, give her neither grief nor rivals, do not arouse her jealousy. To be loved, dear one, to be understood, is the greatest happiness there is. I hope that you will taste it, but do not compromise the flower of your soul; be really sure of the heart in which you place your affections. That woman will never be her own self; she must never think of herself but of you. She will claim nothing from you, she will never consider her own interests and she will know how to sense danger for you where you will see none, and be oblivious of her own. And if she is unhappy, she will suffer uncomplainingly; she will be without personal vanity but will have a kind of reverence for what you love in her. Respond to this love by surpassing it. If you are lucky enough to find what your poor friend must forever do without, a love as deeply inspired as it is felt, remember, whatever the completeness of that love, that there lives for you, somewhere in a valley, a mother whose heart is so deepened by the feeling with which you have filled it that you will never plumb its depths. Yes, I feel for you an affection the extent of which you will never know; for it to show itself as it really is, you would have to lose that fine intelligence you have, and then you would not have the wit to see just how far my devotion could go. Am I suspect in telling you to avoid young women, all of them more or less guileful, mocking, vain, futile, extravagant—and to attach yourself to influential women, those imposing dowagers, full of good sense as was my aunt, who will serve your interests so well, who will defend you against secret allegations by destroying them, who will say of you what you could not say yourself? Is it not generous of me to order you to reserve your adoration for the angel with the pure heart? If the phrase *Noblesse oblige* holds a large part of my first recommendations, my advice on your dealings with women is also summed up in this phrase, motto from the age of chivalry: 'Serve them all, love but one.'

"Your learning is immense; your heart, preserved by suffering, has remained untarnished; all is fine, all is good in you: now, *forge ahead*! Your future rests now on that one phrase, the phrase of great men. Say, dear child, that you will obey your Henriette, that you will allow her to go on telling you what she thinks of you and of your dealings with the world? I have an eye in my soul which sees the future for you, as it does for my children. Let me then, give you the benefit of that faculty, mysterious gift which has created my life's peace and which, far from waning, thrives in solitude and silence. I ask you in return to give me a great happiness. I want to see you grow in stature among men, without one of your successes bringing a pucker to my brow: I want you to put your fortune with all speed on a level with your name, so that I can tell myself that I have contributed more than would fulfilled desire to your greatness.

"This secret co-operation is the only pleasure I can allow myself. I shall wait. I will not say goodbye to you. We are apart; you cannot have my hand under your lips, but you must have guessed the place you occupy in the heart of
Your Henriette."

When I had finished this letter, I could feel under my fingers the warm pulsing of a mother's heart, chilled as I was by my mother's heartless reception. I guessed why the Countess had forbidden me to read the letter while I was in Touraine. No doubt she was afraid lest I fall at her feet and bathe them with my tears.

I made, at long last, the acquaintance of my brother Charles, who had been hitherto practically a stranger to me; but there was, even in his slightest dealings with me, an arrogance which set too great a distance between us for brotherly love. All gentle feeling depends upon kinship of mind and there was no point of contact between us. He was forever instructing me in those small matters which can be grasped intuitively by the mind or the heart; at every turn, he seemed to be attacking me; had I not had my love to lean on, he would have reduced me to blundering stupidity by his pretence that I knew nothing. He did, however, introduce me into society, where no doubt my fatuity was intended to show off his talents to advantage. Had it not been for the misfortunes of my childhood, I might have mistaken his conceited patronage for brotherly affection. But isolation of the mind produces the same effects as isolation of the body: silence allows us to catch the faintest echo and the habit of retiring into oneself breeds a sensibility whose delicate balance records every fine distinction in our relations with each other.

Before knowing Madame de Mortsauf, a hard glance would wound me, a harsh word would strike me to the heart. I would suffer agonies, whilst knowing nothing yet of endearments and tenderness; whereas on my return from Clochegourde I was able to make comparisons which perfected my precocious knowledge. Observation based on suffering is incomplete; happiness is illuminating too. Now that Charles no longer fooled me, I was all the more willing to submit to the crushing weight of his elder-brother superiority.

I went alone to visit the Duchesse de Lenoncourt, where Henriette was not discussed, and where no one except the good old Duke himself, the soul of simplicity, ever so much as mentioned her. But from the way in which he received me, I had an inkling of some secret recommendation from his daughter. Just as I was beginning to lose the air of gaping astonishment with which any newcomer views the great world, just as I had caught a glimpse of its pleasures, and begun to understand the rewards it offers to those with ambition; just as I was putting into practice the maxims of Henriette, and marvelling at the profound truth they contained, the events of the 20th March took place. My brother followed the Court to Ghent; I accompanied the Duc de Lenoncourt, on the advice of the Countess, with whom I was conducting an active correspondence, albeit on my side only. The Duke's benevolence developed into a genuine protectiveness once he saw that I was devoted to the Bourbons, head, heart and limb; he presented me personally to His Majesty. There are few who pay court to misfortune; youth has its naïve admirations, its spontaneous loyalties. The King was a good judge of men; what would have escaped notice at the Tuileries was therefore much remarked at Ghent, and I was fortunate enough to find favour with Louis XVIII. A letter from Madame de Mortsauf to her father, delivered along with dispatches by an envoy of the Vendée party, and in which there was a note for me, informed me that Jacques was ill. Monsieur de Mortsauf, in despair as much at the ill health of his son as at seeing a second emigration about to begin without him, had added a few words from which I was able to judge the predicament of my beloved. Tormented no doubt by him for spending every moment by her son's bedside, taking no rest by day or by night, above petty irritation, but lacking the strength to overcome it when she was devoting all of herself to nursing her child, Henriette must surely be longing for the support of a friendship which had made her life less burdensome, if only to make use of it for the purpose of entertaining Monsieur de Mortsauf. Several times already, I had taken the Count out of the house when he threatened to torment her, an innocent ruse the success of which had earned me now and then a few of those looks expressive of a passionate gratitude, which love interprets as a promise. Impatient as I was to follow in Charles's footsteps (he had recently been sent to the Congress of Vienna) and to fulfil, at the risk of my life, the prophecies of Henriette and shake myself free from my brother's vassalage, my ambition; my desire for independence; the interest I had in remaining with the King; all this paled before the sorrowful image of Madame de Mortsauf; and I made up my mind to leave the Court of Ghent to go and serve my true sovereign. God rewarded me. The envoy of the Vendée party was unable to return to France, and the King needed a man who would undertake the task of carrying his despatches. The Duc de Lenoncourt, knowing that whoever undertook this perilous enterprise would not be forgotten by the King, proposed me for the post without consulting me. I accepted, glad to be able to return to Clochegourde whilst still serving the good cause.

After having, at the early age of twenty-one, an audience with the King, I returned to France where, either in Paris or in the Vendée, I had the good fortune to accomplish His Majesty's intentions. Towards the end of May, pursued by the Bonaparte authorities, who had my description, I was obliged to take to flight. Travelling as a county squire returning to his manor, I proceeded on foot from estate to estate, from wood to wood, across the *haute Vendée*, Bocage and Poitou, altering course as occasion demanded. I reached Saumur, from Saumur I got to Chinon, and from Chinon, in the space of a single night, I reached the forest of Nueil, where I met the Count riding over a stretch of waste land; he took me on the crupper and back home with him, without our meeting anyone who might have recognised me.

"Jacques is recovering," was the first thing he said.

I told him of my rôle as foot-slogging diplomat, hounded like a wild animal, and the Count, battling old royalist that he was, vied with Monsieur de Chessel for the danger of giving me hospitality. When we came in sight of Clochegourde, it seemed to me that the eight months which had just passed were no more than a dream. The Count went into the house ahead of me.

"Guess whom I've brought you—Felix!" he said to his wife.

"Can it be true?" she asked, her arms hanging limply by her sides, amazement written on her face.

I showed myself, and the two of us remained stock-still, she pinned to her chair and I in the doorway, gazing at each other with the avid intentness of two lovers bent on recouping, with a single look, all the time they have lost; but embarrassed by a surprise which thus laid bare her heart, she rose. I went towards her.

"I prayed for you," she said, when she had held out her hand for me to kiss.

She asked for news of her father; then, guessing that I was tired, she went to make arrangements for my night's rest, whilst the Count had food brought for me, for I was dying of hunger. I was given the room above her own, her aunt's room; she asked the Count to show me up to it, after having set her foot on the first stair, deliberating no doubt, as to whether she would accompany me herself: I turned; she blushed, bade me good-night and hurriedly withdrew. When I came down to dinner, I learned of the disasters of Waterloo, Napoleon's flight, the armies' march on Paris and the probable return of the Bourbons. These events were everything to the Count; they meant nothing to us. Do you know the biggest piece of news, after the children had been kissed and fondled?—for I will not speak of my fears when I saw the Countess looking so pale and thin; I knew what damage could be done by a gesture of surprise and was careful to express nothing but delight at seeing her again. No, the great news was: "You are to have some ice!" She had often been vexed, the previous year, because she could never give me water that was cold enough, for, as I drank nothing else, I liked it iced. Heaven knows what inconvenience it must have cost her to have an ice-chest built. You know better than anyone how love can thrive on a word, a look, a tone of voice, a seemingly trivial attention; its highest privilege is to be its own proof. And so her words, her pleasure and the look in her eyes, showed me the depth of her feelings, just as I had told her mine by the way I behaved at the backgammon table. But she gave me innumerable artless tokens of her affection. Seven days after my arrival she had regained her freshness; she sparkled with health, happiness and youth; I found my beloved lily again, lovelier than ever, and in full flower, just as I found the treasures of my heart increased. Is it not in small minds or vulgar hearts only that absence lessens feelings, effaces the features of the soul and diminishes the loveliness of the beloved? For ardent imaginations, for those whose enthusiasm runs into the bloodstream and dyes it a new scarlet, and whose passion takes the form of constancy, has not absence the same effect as the tortures which served to strengthen the faith of the early Christians, and made God visible to them? Is there not, in a heart filled with love, those ceaseless longings which give a greater worth to the forms desired by letting one glimpse them through the multicoloured flame of dreams? Do not one's fevered passions lend an ideal beauty to the features of the adored by loading them with thoughts? The past, recaptured memory by memory, grows greater, the future is a treasure-house of hopes. Between two hearts so charged with these electric clouds, a first meeting is like a soothing storm which revives the earth and fecundates it with the sudden flash of lightning. How many sweet delights did I not taste when I saw that these thoughts and these sensations were reciprocal? With how charmed an eye did I follow the growth of happiness in Henriette! A woman who revives beneath the beloved's very eyes gives perhaps a greater proof of feeling than one who dies murdered by a doubt or withered on the stem for want of sap. I do not know which of the two is the more touching. The re-birth of Madame de Mortsauf was as natural as the effect of the month of May upon the meadows or of the sun and rain on drooping flowers.

Like our valley of love, Henriette had had her winter, and like it she sprang to life again in spring. Before dinner we went down on to our beloved terrace. There, while she stroked the head of her poor child, frailer now than I had ever seen him, as he walked by his mother's side, silent as though still sickening for some illness, she told me of the nights she had spent at his bedside. During those three months, she had lived, she told me, utterly withdrawn into herself. She had dwelt, as it were, in some sombre palace, afraid to enter sumptuous state rooms, ablaze with light, gay with festivities she was forbidden to share, at the doors of which she would stand, one eye on her child, the other on a face she could but dimly see, one ear listening for moans of pain, the other waiting for a voice. She spoke a kind of poetry inspired by solitude, such as no poet ever wrote before; but all this ingenuously, without realising that there was the faintest trace of love or hint of sensuous thoughts or honeyed oriental poesy sweet as a rose from Frangistan, in what she said to me. When the Count joined us, she continued in the same vein, like a woman who can be proud of herself, who can look proudly at her husband and kiss her child's brow without a blush of shame.

She had prayed a great deal, she had held Jacques beneath her clasped hands through many a long night, willing him not to die.

"I went," she said, "to the very doors of the Sanctuary, to beg God for his life."

She had had visions; she began to tell me about them, but when, in her angelic voice, she spoke the marvellous words "While I slept my heart kept watch!" her husband cut in with "In other words you were half out of your mind." She said nothing. She was cut to the quick, as if this was the first wound she had received; as though she had forgotten that, for thirteen years, this man had never failed to drive his arrows into her heart. Sublime bird hit in mid flight by this crude leaden pellet, she fell into a dazed and downcast silence.

"Why, monsieur," she continued, after a pause, "will no remark of mine ever find clemency at the tribunal of your mind? Will you never be indulgent to my weakness, nor understanding of my woman's ideas?"

She stopped. Already this angel was repenting of having murmured, and measuring at a glance both her past and her future; could she hope to be understood? Would she not provoke a virulent apostrophe? Blue veins throbbed violently at her temples. She did not cry, but her green eyes turned pale; then she lowered them so as not to see in my own her pain increased, her feelings guessed, her soul caressed in my soul and above all, the angry compassion of young love, ready like a faithful dog, to tear to pieces the man who hurts his mistress, without a thought for the strength or quality of the attacker. At such cruel moments the Count's superior air was a sight to see. He imagined that he was getting the better of his wife and would then proceed to batter her with a hail of words that repeated the same idea over and over again, like the blows of an axe producing the same ring.

"Is he the same as ever, then?" I asked her, when the Count, summoned by his gamekeeper, was forced to leave us.

"Just the same!" replied Jacques.

"Just as fine, my son," she said to Jacques, trying to rescue Monsieur de Mortsauf from the criticism of his children. "You see only the present, you know nothing of the past. It would be unfair of you to criticise your father. And even if you were so unfortunate as to see faults in him, family honour demands that you bury such secrets in the deepest possible silence."

"How are the alterations going at La Cassine and La Rhétorière?" I asked her, to draw her out of her bitter thoughts.

"Beyond my hopes," she said. "The buildings are finished and we have found two excellent farmers to take them over, one at four thousand five hundred francs, taxes paid, and the other at five thousand; and the leases have been drawn up for fifteen years. We have already planted three thousand saplings on the two new farms. Manette's cousin is delighted to have La Rabelaye. Martineau has La Baude. The property of our four farmers consists of meadows and woodland, and they do not, like some of our less scrupulous farmers, help themselves to the manure reserved for our fields. So *our* efforts have been crowned with the most wonderful success. Clochegourde, without the reserve fields which we call the home farm, and not counting the woodland and the vineyards, brings in nineteen thousand francs, and the trees we have planted have secured us a handsome income for the future. I am fighting to have our home farm handed over to Martineau, our gamekeeper, who can now be replaced by his son. He is offering three thousand francs for it if Monsieur de Mortsauf will build him a farmhouse at La Commanderie. We could then clear the approaches to Clochegourde, complete the avenue we planned right up to the Chinon road, and have only our vines and woods to look after. If the King returns, *our* pension will return too; *we* shall agree to everything after a few days' of battling against our wife's commonsense. Jacques' fortune will thus be indestructible. Once these last results are obtained, I shall leave Monsieur de Mortsauf to save a sum of money for Madeleine, for whom the King will incidentally, provide a dowry, as is the custom. My conscience is clear; my task is nearly finished ... And you?" she asked.

I explained my mission, and pointed out how fruitful and wise her advice had been. Was she gifted with second sight, that she could so foresee events?

"Did I not say as much, when I wrote to you?" she said. "For you alone I am able to exercise this amazing faculty. I have spoken of it to no one save Monsieur de la Berge, my confessor; he attributes it to divine intervention. Often, after some deep meditation, inspired by my fears for my children's health, my eyes would close to earthly things and see into another sphere. When I saw Jacques and Madeleine radiant with light, they would be in good health for a certain time. If I saw them wrapped in mist, they soon fell ill. As for you, not only do I always see you shining bright, but I hear a soft voice, telling me, wordlessly, by a sort of mental communication, exactly what you must do. What law is it that only lets me use this marvellous gift for my children and for you?" she asked pensively. "Can it be that God wants to be a father to them?" she mused, after a pause.

"Let me believe," said I, "that I obey nobody but you!"

She threw me one of those wholly gracious smiles which so enthralled my heart that I would not have felt a mortal blow.

"As soon as the King is in Paris," she went on, "leave Clochegourde and go there. Degrading as it may be to solicit favours and positions, it is equally foolish not to be at hand to accept them. There will be great changes. The King will need capable and trustworthy men. Do not fail him. You will be embarking early on your career, and this will stand you in good stead; for statesmen, as for actors, there are certain tricks of the trade that native talent cannot give; they must be learnt. The Duc de Choiseul told my father a little of the King's plans. Think of me," she said, after a pause. "Let me taste the pleasures of eminence in a soul that is entirely mine. Are you not my son?"

"Your son?" I retorted, with a sulky air.

"Nothing but my son," she said, mockingly. "Is that not a high enough place to hold in my heart?"

The bell sounded for dinner. She took my arm and leaned contentedly on it.

"You have grown," she said, as we went up the steps.

When we reached the verandah, she shook my arm as though to divert my penetrating gaze, for although she was looking downwards, she knew that I had eyes for nobody but her. Then, in that mock-impatient tone, so gracious, so winning, she said, "Come, spare a glance for our dear valley!" She turned, and clasping Jacques to her, she covered our heads with her white silk parasol; and the nod of her head as she indicated the Indre, the little boat, the meadows, proved that, ever since my first visit and our walks, she had come to a secret understanding with those hazy horizons and their blurred and sinuous outlines. Nature was the cloak beneath which her thoughts took shelter. She knew now what the nightingale sighs in the darkness and what the songbird of the marshes chants as he reiterates his single plaintive note.

At eight o'clock that evening, I witnessed a scene which stirred me deeply. It was one I had never had a chance to see, for I always remained with Monsieur de Mortsauf, playing backgammon while it was taking place in the dining-room, before the children went to bed. The bell sounded twice, and all the household assembled.

"You are our guest, you must obey the convent rules!" she said, drawing me by the hand, with that air of innocent mockery which distinguishes truly religious women. The Count followed us. Master and mistress, children, servants, all knelt, bareheaded, in their usual places. It was Madeleine's turn to say prayers: the sweet little girl pronounced them in her childish voice, whose artless tones rang clearly in the harmonious rural silence and gave the words the saintly candour of innocence, that gift of the angels. It was the most moving prayer I have heard. Nature answered the child's words with the thousand rustling sounds of evening, like the light touch of an accompanying organ. Madeleine was on the Countess's right and Jacques on her left. The grace of their two tufted heads, between which rose the mother's carefully braided one, and higher still, the completely white hair and yellowed scalp of the Count, made a picture whose colours repeated in some way to the mind the thoughts aroused by the melodies of the prayer: finally, as if to satisfy the conditions of unity which are the hall-mark of the sublime, the whole devout gathering was bathed in the subdued light of sunset, the red tints of which coloured the room, inducing in poetic or superstitious souls the belief that the fires of Heaven were visiting these faithful servants of God as they knelt there, without distinctions of rank, in the equality the Church decrees. Thinking back to patriarchal days, my thoughts enhanced the scene, already so great in its simplicity, into something greater still. The children said good-night to their father, the servants bowed, the Countess left, taking each child by the hand, and I went back with the Count to the drawing-room.

"We shall lead you to salvation that way and damnation this," he said, pointing to the backgammon board.

The Countess joined us half an hour later and brought her tapestry loom near to our table.

"This is for you," she said, unrolling the canvas; "but during these past three months the work went very slowly. Between this red carnation and this rose, my poor child suffered."

"Come, come," said Monsieur de Mortsauf, "let us not talk about that. Six-five, Monsieur envoy!"

When I went up to bed, I listened for her step as she walked up and down in her room. If she remained calm and pure, I was racked with insane ideas inspired by intolerable desires. "Why should she not be mine?" I asked myself. "Perhaps she too is caught up in this whirling turmoil of the senses?" At one o'clock, I crept noiselessly downstairs, reached her door and lay down beside it, my ear close to the crack. I could hear her breathing, gently and evenly like a child. When I began to feel cold, I went up to my room again, got into bed and slept peacefully until morning. I do not know to what predestination, to what natural instinct I should attribute the delight I take in stepping to the very edge of precipices, in plumbing the abyss of evil, testing its bed, feeling the chill of it and drawing back, white and shaken. That midnight hour, spent outside her door, where I wept with rage, without her even knowing next day that she had trodden on my tears and kisses—on her own virtue by turns ravished and respected, cursed and adored; that hour, absurd in the eyes of some, was inspired by that same nameless urge which drives soldiers (some have told me that they did indeed gamble with their lives like this) to hurl themselves before a gun battery to see whether they will escape the rain of bullets; whether they will know happiness by riding full tilt into the abyss of probabilities, like Jean Bart, smoking on a keg of gunpowder.

The next day I picked some flowers and made two bouquets. The Count admired them, he whom nothing of the kind usually touched, and for whom Champcenetz' remark, "*il fait des cachots en Espagne*" might have been invented.

I spent several days at Clochegourde, making only short visits to Frapesle, where I did, nevertheless, dine three times. The French Army came to occupy Tours. Although I was obviously life and health to Madame de Mortsauf, she urged me to make for

Châteauroux and thence to go with all speed to Paris by way of Issoudun and Orléans. I started to protest but she insisted; the household genius had spoken, she said. I obeyed. This time our farewells were washed with tears. She feared for my sake the temptations of the world I was now entering. Should I not be obliged to take a serious part in the hurly-burly of self-interest, passions and pleasures which makes Paris as dangerous to unsullied love as it is to the unclouded conscience? I promised to write to her every evening about the events and thoughts of the day, even the most trivial. At this promise, she leaned her languid head upon my shoulder and said, "Remember to tell me everything: I shall be interested in every detail." She gave me letters for the Duke and Duchess, whom I went to see the second day after my arrival.

"You are in luck," said the Duke. "Dine with us here and then come with me to-night to the palace. Your fortune is made. The King mentioned you this morning and said 'He is young, capable and loyal!' And His Majesty was sorry that he did not know whether you were alive or dead, or where events had taken you after you had so successfully carried out your mission."

That evening, I was allotted the post of recorder in the Council of State and was given employment of a confidential nature in the service of King Louis XVIII, which was to last as long as he was on the throne; it was a post of trust, without conspicuous favours, but without risk of disgrace, and it set me at the hub of Government affairs and became the mainspring of my prosperity. Madame de Mortsauf had seen true; I therefore owed everything to her: power and wealth, happiness and knowledge. She guided and encouraged me, kept my heart pure and gave my will that unity without which the forces of youth are dissipated uselessly. Later on, I was given a colleague. Each of us served for six months, and could each take the other's place in case of need. We had a room in the palace, our own carriage, and ample allowances for expenses when we had to travel. Strange position! To be the secret disciples of a King, whose policy his enemies have since resoundingly acclaimed; to hear him at first hand, to have inside knowledge of all matters both at home and abroad, to be without overt influence and to be consulted sometimes as Laforêt was by Molière; to feel the hesitations of a ripe experience seeking confirmation from the sincerity of youth. Our future, moreover, was provided for in a way guaranteed to satisfy the most ambitious. Apart from my appointment as recorder, paid for out of the funds of the Council of State, the King gave me a thousand francs a month on his own privy purse and often added some personal gratuity. Although the King felt that a young man of twenty-three would not stand up for long to the burden of work he laid on me, my colleague, now a Peer of France, was not appointed until about August, 1817. This choice was so difficult, our functions demanded so many special qualities, that the King took a long time to make up his mind. He did me the honour of asking me which of the young men he had singled out would be most congenial for me to work with. Among them was one of my schoolmates from the hated *pension Lepître*. I mentioned him. His Majesty asked me why.

"The King," I replied, "has chosen men of equal loyalty but of varying degrees of ability; I have named the one whom I believe to be the ablest; I am sure that we shall get on most amicably together."

My judgement tallied with that of the King, who was always grateful to me for the sacrifice I made on that occasion.

"You will be Number One," he said.

He took care to inform my colleague of my recommendation, and in return for this service, the latter gave me his loyal friendship. The consideration shown me by the Duc de Lenoncourt was a yardstick for that accorded to me by everyone. The words: "The King is taking a keen interest in this young man; this young man has a future; the King has a liking for him" would have stood me in stead of talent, but they lent to the gracious reception usually afforded to young men, that indescribable something which is the privilege of power. Whether at the Duke's house or at my sister's, (she had just married her cousin the Marquis de Listomère, son of the old relative I used to visit in the Ile Saint-Louis) I began, little by little, to make the acquaintance of the most influential people in the Faubourg Saint-Germain.

Henriette soon launched me into the heart of that circle known as the *Petit-Château* Society, through the good offices of the Princesse de Blamont-Chauvry, who was her great-aunt by marriage; Henriette wrote so warmly about me to her, that the Princess invited me forthwith to visit her. I cultivated her acquaintance, she grew to like me and she became, not my patroness, but a friend whose feelings towards me were in some sort maternal. The old Princess introduced me to her daughter, Madame d'Espard, to the Duchesse de Langeais, to the Vicomtesse de Beauséant and the Duchesse de Maufrigneuse, women who held the sceptre of fashion by turns and who were all the more gracious towards me for my unpretentious behaviour and my readiness to be agreeable to them. My brother Charles, far from disowning me, began from that time on to lean on me; but my speedy success inspired in him a secret jealousy which later on caused me a good deal of unhappiness. My father and mother, surprised at this unexpected good fortune, felt their vanity flattered and adopted me at last as their son, but as their feeling for me was in some measure artificial, not to say assumed, this return to grace had little influence on my embittered heart. Besides, affection that is tainted with self-interest inspires little fellow-feeling: the heart abhors ulterior motives and all greed for gain.

I wrote faithfully to my dear Henriette, who wrote back once or twice a month. And so her spirit hovered over me, her thoughts bridged the distance between us, and purified the atmosphere around me. No woman was able to ensnare me. The King knew of my abstinence; (in this sphere of activity, he was of the school of Louis XV) and laughingly dubbed me "Mademoiselle de Vandenesse", but my irreproachable conduct pleased him greatly. I am convinced that the patience I had practised as a child, and above all at Clochegourde, did much to win me the good graces of the King, who was always extremely kind to me. No doubt the fancy took him to read my letters, for he was not long deceived by my monk-like way of life. One day, the Duke was on duty; I was writing at the King's dictation. His Majesty turned a mischievous eye upon us both as the Duke came into the room.

"Does that old devil of a Mortsauf insist on staying alive, then?" he said, in that fine, silvery voice which he could lace, at will, with the biting spice of epigram.

"He does indeed," returned the Duke.

"The Comtesse de Mortsauf is an angel," continued the King,

"and I should be most glad to have her here. But if I can do nothing about that, my chancellor here will be more fortunate. You have six months to yourself," he said, turning to me. "I have decided to give you the young man we spoke of yesterday for a colleague. Enjoy yourself at Clochegourde, Monsieur Cato!" And he had himself wheeled out of his study, smiling as he went.

I flew like a swallow to Touraine. For the first time, I was about to show myself to the woman I loved, not only a little less of a simpleton, but furthermore attired like a young man of fashion whose manners had been shaped by the most elegant *salons*, whose education had been completed by the most gracious women, a young man who had at last recouped the price of his sufferings and put to good use the experience of the fairest angel to whose care Heaven ever entrusted any child.

You know how I was attired during the three months of my first stay at Frapesle. When I returned to Clochegourde at the time of my mission to the Vendée, I was dressed as a hunter. I wore a green jacket with rusty metal buttons, striped breeches, leather gaiters and thick shoes. The long journey on foot in the underbush had so torn my clothing that the Count had been obliged to lend me some linen. This time, two years' stay in Paris; the habit of the King's company; the manners that come with affluence, coupled with the fact that I was fully grown now; a young face inexpressibly aglow with the serenity of a soul magnetically at one with that pure spirit that shone on me from Clochegourde; all this had transformed me. I had assurance without fatuousness; I had an inner contentment at finding myself, despite my youth, at the apex of affairs; I was aware that I was the secret stay and unvoiced hope of the most adorable woman on this earth. Perhaps I felt a little stab of vanity when the postilion's whip cracked in the new avenue which now led from Chinon to Clochegourde and a gate I had not seen before opened into a circular walled enclosure that had recently been built. I had not written to tell the Countess I was coming, as I wanted to give her a surprise. I was doubly wrong to do this. To begin with, she underwent the shock that comes from a pleasure long awaited and deemed impossible; furthermore, she showed me that all planned surprises are in bad taste.

When Henriette saw a young man where before she had only

ever seen a child, her gaze fell in a slow tragic sweep to the ground; she let me take her hand and kiss it without evincing any of that intimate pleasure which I could always sense by the sensitive quiver that ran through her; and when she raised her eyes again to look at me, I saw that she was pale.

"You haven't forgotten old friends, I see," said Monsieur de Mortsauf, who had neither aged nor altered.

The children flung their arms around my neck. I caught sight of the grave face of the Abbé de Dominis, Jacques' tutor, framed in the doorway.

"No," I said to the Count, "from now on I shall have six months' freedom every year and they will always belong to you. Why, what is the matter?" I said to the Countess, slipping my arm round her waist to steady her, in full view of her family.

"Let me be, please!" she said, darting away from me. "It is nothing."

I could see into her heart, and I answered her secret thoughts when I said: "Do you not recognise your faithful slave?"

She took my arm, left the Count, her children, the Abbé and all the servants who had come running up, led me away from everyone and walked me round the lawn, although we remained within sight of the others. Then, when she felt she could not be overheard, she said, "Felix, my dear, forgive me for my fears. I have only one thread to guide me through an underground labyrinth and I tremble in case it should snap. Tell me again that I am as much your Henriette as I ever was, say that you will never leave me, that nothing will ever take my place, that you will always be a loyal friend to me. I have suddenly seen into the future, and you were not there, as you always are, with your face shining and your eyes on me. You were turning your back on me."

"Henriette, idol whom I worship more than God, my lily, flower of my life, how can you have forgotten, you who are my very being, that I am so incarnate in your heart that my soul is here while my body is in Paris? Must I tell you that it took me only seventeen hours to get here? That every turn of the wheel brought with it a world of thoughts and longings which burst like a hurricane the moment I set eyes on you?"

"Tell me, tell me! I am quite sure of myself, I can listen to you without doing wrong. God does not want me to die. He has sent you to me the way He breathes life into His creatures, the way He sends rain from His clouds on to parched earth. Tell me, tell me! Do you love me chastely?"

"Yes, chastely."

"For always?"

"For always."

"As you would a Virgin Mary, who must always hide beneath her veil and her white crown?"

"Like a visible Virgin Mary."

"Like a sister?"

"Like a sister too well loved."

"Like a mother?"

"Like a mother secretly desired."

"Chivalrously, without hope?"

"Chivalrously, but with hope."

"Yes, but as if you were still no more than twenty years of age and dressed in that horrid little blue suit you had on at the ball?"

"Oh! more than that! I love you like that and ... I love you the way —"

She watched me with lively apprehension.

"—— the way your aunt loved you."

"I am glad. You have dispelled my fears," she said, walking back towards the family, who were all astonished at our secret conclave. "But be a child here! For you are still a child. If it is your policy to be a man when you are with the King, kindly remember, Monsieur, that here you will be well advised to remain a child. As a child, you will be loved. I shall always fight against the strength of a man, but what can I refuse a child? Nothing: there is nothing he might wish for that I could not give him. We have told each other our secrets," she said, looking at the Count with a mischievous air that gave one a glimpse of her original nature and of the young girl she had been.

Never, in three years, had I heard such full happiness in her voice. For the first time I heard those winsome swallow-calls, those child-like notes which I have already described to you. I had brought a hunting habit for Jacques and a workbasket for Madeleine, which her mother ever after used. At last, I was able to repair the niggardliness to which my mother's meanness had condemned me in the past. The delight of the two children as they showed each other their presents seemed to irk the Count, who was always put out when he was not the centre of attention. I gave Madeleine a knowing wink and followed the Count, who wanted to talk to me about himself. He led me towards the terrace; but we stopped on the way up the steps at each grave fact that he imparted to me.

"My poor Felix," he said, "you see them all well and happy: I am the skeleton at the feast; I have taken their ills upon myself, and I thank God for having laid them on my shoulders. Before, I did not notice what was wrong with me; but now I know. I have a defective pylorus. I can no longer digest a single thing."

"How is it that you have grown as learned as a professor of the School of Medicine?" I asked with a smile. "Is your doctor so indiscreet as to tell you such —?"

"Heaven preserve me from consulting doctors!" he exlaimed, manifesting the repulsion that most imaginary invalids feel for the medical profession. I was then subjected to a crazy monologue, during which he told me quite ridiculous things about himself, complained of his wife, his servants, his children and life in general, taking an obvious delight in repeating his daily assertions to a friend who, not having heard them before, could show surprise at them, and who was forced for politeness' sake, to listen with interest. He must have been pleased with me, for I gave him my undivided attention in an endeavour to penetrate his incredible nature and to discover what new torments he had been inflicting on his wife of which she had not told me. Henriette put a stop to our conversation by appearing on the verandah: the Count saw her and shook his head. "*You* have the grace to listen to me, Felix, but no one else here has any sympathy for me!"

And off he went, as though aware of the cloud he was casting over my encounter with Henriette, or as though, out of a chivalrous consideration for her, he realised that it would please her if he left us together. There were some really inexplicable quirks in his nature, for he was jealous like all weak people, and yet his confidence in his wife's saintliness was boundless; perhaps it was the very pain done to his wounded pride by the superiority of this high-minded virtue, which gave rise to his constant opposition to the wishes of the Countess, whom he defied as children defy their teacher or their mother. Jacques was at his lessons and Madeleine was dressing, so I was able to walk alone with the Countess on the terrace for about an hour.

"Well, dear Angel," I said, "so the chains have grown heavier, the sands are fiery hot, the thorns grow thicker?"

"Hush," she replied, guessing the thoughts that my conversation with the Count had suggested to me. "You are here, all is forgotten! I am not unhappy. I have never been unhappy!" She took a few light steps as though to air her white dress and surrender to the breeze her snowy folds of tulle, floating sleeves, crisp ribbons, her pelerine and the soft curls of her Sévigné coiffure; and I saw her for the first time looking like a young girl, gay with her natural gaiety and playful as a child. I knew then the tears of joy and the happiness a man feels when he gives pleasure to another.

"My lovely living flower, who has my soul's kisses and my thought's caress—o my lily!" I cried, "still pure and upright on its stem; still white, proud, fragrant and alone!"

"Enough, Monsieur," she said, smiling. "Talk to me about yourself, be sure to tell me everything."

And so, under that mobile vault of quivering foliage, we talked at length, our conversation full of interminable asides, digressing, losing the thread, taking it up again, in which I told her all about my life and what I had been doing; I described my Paris apartment, for she wanted to know everything; and—a joy I did not then appreciate, I had nothing to hide from her.

When she learned my state of mind, and knew all the details of an existence burdened with overwork, when she realised the full extent of those functions, in which without a rigid honesty, one could so easily cheat and feather one's own nest, but which I performed so stringently that the King, I told her, had nicknamed me "Mademoiselle de Vandenesse", she caught my hand and kissed it, dropping on to it a tear of joy. This sudden transposition of rôles, this paeon of praise, this thought, so swiftly expressed and even more swiftly understood: "Here is the master I should like to have had! Here is my dream!"; the wealth of avowals implicit in that gesture, where humility attained the heights of grandeur, and where love revealed itself in a sphere forbidden to the senses, this tornado of heavenly things broke over my heart and quite overwhelmed me. I felt dwarfed; I would have liked to die at her feet.

"Ah," said I, "you will always surpass us in everything! How could you doubt me? For there was a doubt just now, Henriette."

"Not about the present," she replied, looking at me with an ineffable sweetness which veiled, for me alone, the brightness of her eyes, "but when I saw you looking so handsome, I said to myself: 'Our plans for Madeleine will be ruined by some woman who will divine the treasure hidden in your heart, who will worship you and steal our Felix and destroy our little world.' "

"Always Madeleine!" said I, expressing a surprise which only partially distressed her. "Is it to Madeleine I owe fidelity?"

We lapsed into a silence which was untowardly broken by Monsieur de Mortsauf. My heart full, I was obliged to keep up a conversation bristling with difficulties, in the course of which my sincere replies as to the policy then being followed by the King came into conflict with the ideas of the Count, who forced me to explain His Majesty's intentions. Despite my enquiries about his horses, the state of his agricultural activities, whether he was satisfied with his five farms, whether he intended cutting down an old avenue of trees, he turned the conversation back to politics with the teasing obstinacy of an old maid and the persistence of a child; for minds of this sort love to go charging into the nearest source of light. They come back to it again and again, buzzing away without finding an entry and wearying the spirit the way bluebottles weary the ear when they buzz along the window panes. Henriette said nothing. To damp this conversation before the hotheadedness of youth made it burst into flame, I replied in approving monosyllables, thus avoiding pointless arguments; but Monsieur de Mortsauf was far too sharp-witted not to see how insulting my politeness was. Finally, annoyed by winning every point, he stiffened, his eyebrows and the wrinkles on his brow began to work, his yellow eyes popped, and his red nose turned a deeper purple, just as on the day when I witnessed for the first time one of his fits of demented fury.

Henriette threw me imploring looks, giving me to understand that she could not exert in my favour the authority she used to justify or to defend her children. I proceeded to answer the Count's remarks, taking him seriously and handling his stormy temperament with as much skill as I could muster.

"Poor sweet, poor sweet!" she murmured from time to time, and these two words touched my ears like a breeze.

Then, when she thought it safe to intervene, she stopped and said: "Do you know, gentlemen, that you are being extremely tedious?" Reminded by this remark of the chivalrous obedience due to women, the Count stopped talking politics; we in our turn bored him with small-talk, and he left us to continue our stroll alone, saying that it made him giddy to keep pacing up and down on the same spot.

My sad conjectures were true. The gentle landscape, the warm air, the clear sky, the intoxicating poetry of this valley which for fifteen years had soothed the throbbing fantasies of this sick man, were now of no avail. At a time of life when, in other men, the corners are blunted and the sharp edges are rubbed smooth, the character of the old nobleman had become even more aggressive than before. Over the past few months he had taken to contradicting for the sake of contradiction, for no reason, without justifying his opinions; asking the why's and wherefore's of everything; fretting over every little delay or omission; meddling in all the domestic arrangements and demanding an account of the smallest household items, thus wearing out his wife and servants and giving them no freedom to make their own decisions. Before, he had never flared up without some superficially plausible reason; now he was in a constant state of irritation. Perhaps his financial troubles, the hazards of agriculture and his daily activities had deflected his acrimonious temper by giving his anxious nature something to feed on and his restless brain something to think about. Now perhaps, his relative idleness had brought his illness to grips with itself; robbed of its outlet, it asserted itself by fixed ideas; the mental self had taken hold of the physical self. He had become his own physician; he probed into medical books, fancied he was suffering from diseases of which he had read a description, and would then take unbelievable precautions for his health, precautions that changed from minute to minute, were impossible to anticipate, and hence impossible to satisfy. At one moment, he wanted no noise, and when the Countess had established absolute silence around him, he would suddenly complain that he might as well be in a tomb; there was a middle way, he said, between not making a noise and the void of a Trappist monastery. At other times he would affect complete indifference to earthly things; the whole house would breathe again, the children played, the household tasks were done without criticism, and then, suddenly, his voice would come wailing out above the noise.

"You're trying to kill me! If it were your children, my dear, you would soon find out what was ailing them," he would say to his wife, aggravating the unfairness of these words by the sour, icy way he said them.

He was forever putting extra clothing on and taking it off again, studied the slightest variations in the temperature and did nothing without first consulting the barometer. Notwithstanding the maternal attentions of his wife, he found no food to his taste, and claimed that his ruined digestion caused him such pains that he scarcely ever got a wink of sleep; yet he ate, drank, digested and slept so perfectly that the most learned doctor would have marvelled at it. His erratic whims wearied his household staff who, bound by routine like all domestic servants, simply could not cope with orders that were forever being countermanded. If the Count gave orders for all windows to be kept wide open, on the pretext that fresh air was necessary to his health, then a few days later fresh air would become unbearable, because it was too humid or too warm; he would then scold, start a quarrel and, to prove himself right, would frequently deny his previous orders. Defective memory or bad faith would win him his case in any discussion where his wife attempted to confront him with something he himself had said.

Life at Clochegourde had become so intolerable that the Abbé de Dominis, a profoundly learned man, had seized on the device of retreating into a feigned absent-mindedness, ostensibly absorbed in solving certain knotty intellectual problems. The Countess had given up the hope she once had of being able to keep these outbursts of insane rage within the immediate family circle. The servants had already witnessed scenes where the groundless exasperation of the prematurely old man passed all bounds; they were so devoted to the Countess, that no word of it penetrated beyond the house, but she lived in daily dread of a public outburst of these ravings, which normal respect for other people no longer held in check. I learnt, later, some frightful details of the Count's behaviour towards his wife. Instead of comforting her, he would bombard her with dire prophecies, and hold her responsible for all ills to come because she refused to give her children the insane treatments he wanted to prescribe for them. If the Countess took a walk with Jacques and Madeleine, the Count would predict a storm, despite the cloudlessness of the sky; if, by chance, events bore out his forecast, his self-satisfaction rendered him insensible to his children's ills; if one or other of them was unwell, the Count would use all his ingenuity to root out the cause of the indisposition in the methods of treatment adopted by his wife. He would cavil at the minutest details, concluding always with the murderous remark: "If your children fall ill again, you'll have no one to blame but yourself." He behaved in the same way over the slightest detail of household management, where he only ever saw the worst side of things and acted, to quote his old coachman, "the devil's advocate" at every turn. The Countess had arranged for Jacques and Madeleine to have their meals at a different time from their parents, thus shielding them from the terrible effects of the Count's malady and thereby attracting all the storms on to herself. Madeleine and Jacques rarely saw their father. With the sort of hallucination particular to egoists, the Count had not the slightest inkling of the harm he was doing. In the confidential conversation we had had, he had chiefly complained of being far too good to his family. So he brandished the whip, beat down and smashed everything he could see just like a gorilla; then, when he had wounded his victim, he denied ever having touched her. I understood then what had brought those lines, etched as if by some razor's edge, which I had noticed on the Countess' brow when I first arrived. There is a modesty in noble spirits which deters them from expressing their unhappiness; they proudly hide the extent of it from those they love, out of a kind of voluptuous charity. Indeed, despite my entreaties, I did not at first succeed in drawing all of these confidences out of Henriette. She was afraid of grieving me; she would begin to tell me things and then stop suddenly and flush.

But I soon guessed how much the Count's enforced idleness had aggravated the household troubles at Clochegourde.

"Henriette," I said to her a day or so later, showing her that I had plumbed the depths of her latest wretchedness, "was it not a mistake to organise your estate so well that the Count can find nothing to do there now?"

"Dear one," she said, smiling, "my dilemma is critical enough to warrant all the thought I can give it. Believe me, I have studied all possible alternatives, and they are all exhausted. And my worries have indeed gone from bad to worse. But as Monsieur de Mortsauf and I are always together, there is little point in my reducing one worry merely to increase another; I did think of trying to give my husband a new interest by advising him to breed silk-worms at Clochegourde. There are already a few mulberry trees here, relics of the old Touraine industry; but I realised that he would be just as tyrannical at home and that I should have the countless worries of the new enterprise besides. I will tell you something, you student of human nature! In youth, people's bad qualities are held in check by society, diverted by the interplay of the emotions, hampered by public opinion. But later on, with age and solitude, small failings emerge, all the more terrible for having been long repressed. Human weaknesses are essentially shabby: they give one neither peace nor respite; what you granted them yesterday they will demand to-day, to-morrow and always: they establish themselves firmly on the ground you yield them and continue to grab more. Power is essentially merciful; it bows to circumstance, it is just and peaceable. But the passions born of weakness know no pity. They are happiest when they can behave like children, who prefer stolen apples to those they can eat at table. Monsieur de Mortsauf takes a positive delight in catching me out; and he, who would not deceive a soul, deceives me with the greatest glee, so long as his wiles are not discovered."

About a month after my arrival, one morning, after lunch, the Countess took my arm, darted through a gate that gave on to the orchard and pulled me after her into the vineyard.

"He will kill me!" she cried, "Yet I want to live, if only for my children! Will there never be one day's respite from it all? Must one always struggle through the undergrowth, miss one's footing at every step and perpetually have to muster all one's strength so as to keep one's balance? No creature living is equal to such expense of energy. If I really knew the ground on which I am supposed to toil, if I knew just what I have to fight against, my spirit could adapt itself. But no, the nature of the attack changes from day to day; it takes me unawares. My unhappiness is not one but multifold. Oh, Felix, Felix, you cannot imagine the hateful form his tyranny has taken, what savage demands his medical books have suggested to him! Oh, my dear!" she said, leaning her head on my shoulder, without continuing the confidence she had begun. "What will become of me? What am I to do?" she went on, fighting off the thoughts that she had not expressed. "How can I survive this? He will kill me. No, I shall kill myself, sin though it is! Should I run away?—what about my children? A legal separation, then?—but after fifteen years of marriage how could I tell my father that I cannot live with Monsieur de Mortsauf, when, if my father or mother were to come here, he would be composed, well behaved, courteous and entertaining? Besides, has a married woman a father—has she a mother? She belongs, body, soul and worldly goods to her husband. My life was at least peaceful, if not happy; I did, I admit, draw a little strength from my chaste solitude; but if I am deprived of this negative happiness, I shall go mad myself. My continued resistance is based on powerful reasons, and they are not personal ones. Is it not a crime to bring poor creatures into the world and condemn them beforehand to a life of unremitting pain? However, any step I might take would raise such grave questions, that I cannot decide them alone; I am both judge and accused. I shall go to Tours to-morrow to consult the Abbé Birotteau, my new confessor—for my dear, saintly Abbé de la Berge is dead," she added, interrupting herself. "Although he was severe, I shall always miss his spiritual strength. His successor is an angel of sweetness, who is moved to sympathy instead of reprimand; nevertheless, whose courage would not emerge refreshed from the waters of religion? Where is the mind that would not gain new strength at the voice of the Holy Ghost? My God," she went on, drying her tears and raising her eyes to Heaven, "what are you punishing me for? We must believe," she said, pressing my arm with her fingers, "yes, Felix, we must—that there is a red crucible we must pass through before we arrive, saintly and perfect, into the higher spheres. Is it wrong to talk like this? Do you forbid me, O Lord, to weep on a friend's breast? Do I love him too dearly?"

She held me to her heart, as if she were afraid to lose me.

"Who will solve these doubts for me? My conscience has nothing to reproach me for. The stars shine on us from above; why should not the soul, that human star, wrap a friend in its light, when only the pure thoughts are allowed to shine on him?"

I listened in silence to this terrible outcry, holding her damp hand in my own damper one; I held her to me with a strength to which Henriette responded with a strength equal to mine.

"Where on earth are you?" shouted the Count, coming towards us, bareheaded. Ever since my return he had persistently intruded on our talks, either because he hoped they might amuse him, or else because he thought the Countess was confiding her sorrows to me and weeping on my shoulder, or again because he was jealous of any pleasure which he did not share.

"See how he follows me!" she said, despairingly. "Let us go and look at the vineyards, we can avoid him that way. Let's bend down behind the hedges, then he will not see us." Using an overgrown hedge as a rampart, we ran to the vineyards, and soon found ourselves at some distance from the Count, in an avenue of almond trees.

"Dear Henriette," I said at last, pressing her arm to my heart and stopping to look at her stricken face, "not so long ago you steered me skilfully through the perilous highways of the great wide world. Let me now, give you a few hints to help you finish this duel you are fighting without seconds and which you are bound to lose, for you are not fighting it with equal weapons. Do not waste your time battling against a madman —"

"Hush," she said, holding back the tears that welled up into her eyes.

"Listen to me, dearest! After an hour of his conversation, which I am forced to endure out of my love for you, my thoughts are all awry, my head is heavy; the Count makes me doubt my own intelligence; despite myself, the ideas he repeats over and over again engrave themselves upon my brain. Self-evident monomania is not contagious. But when madness lies in a man's way of looking at things, when it hides behind perpetual argumentativeness, it can wreak havoc on those that live in its neighbourhood. Your patience is sublime, but is it not stultifying you? For your sake, for your children's sake, change your tactics with the Count. Your wonderful tolerance has fed his egotism; you have treated him as a mother treats a spoilt child; but now, if you want to live—and," I said, looking at her, "you do!—then make full use of the power you have over him. You know he loves you, and is afraid of you. Make him fear you even more. Meet his diffused whims with your own concentrated will. Extend your power, just as he cleverly extended the concessions you made *him*, and confine his mania in a mental cage, the way they shut lunatics up in a cell."

"Dear child," she said, with a bitter smile, "it takes a heartless woman to play a part like that. I am a mother, I should make a bad executioner. Oh, I know how to suffer, but—to make others suffer! Never," she said, "not even in a great or honourable cause. Besides, would I not have to belie my heart, disguise my voice, mask my face, pervert my every gesture? ... Do not ask such lies of me. I can stand between Monsieur de Mortsauf and his children; I will take his blows, so that they will not touch others here. That is the most I can do to reconcile so many warring interests."

"Let me adore you, my saint, my threefold saint!" I cried, falling on one knee, kissing her dress and wiping on it the tears that came to my eyes. "But what if he kills you?"

She turned pale and said, raising her eyes to Heaven, "God's will be done!"

"Do you know what the King said to your father about you? 'Is that old devil Mortsauf still living?'!"

"A joke on the King's lips," she said, "is a sin here." Despite our precautions, the Count had followed our tracks. He came up to us, bathed in sweat, as we stood under a walnut tree where the Countess had stopped as she made her last grave remark. Seeing him, I began to talk about the harvest. Was he harbouring some unfounded suspicion? I do not know, but he stood there, looking at us, without saying a word, heedless of the cold air that emanates from walnut trees. After one or two insignificant remarks, interspersed with highly significant pauses, the Count said he had a headache and felt sick; he complained quietly, without sueing for sympathy and without describing his aches and pains with highly coloured imagery. We paid no attention to him. When we got back, he felt worse, talked of going to bed and did so without ceremony and with an absence of fuss which was unusual for him. We took advantage of the truce afforded by his hyponchondriac mood and went down to our beloved terrace, accompanied by Madeleine.

"Let us go out in the boat," said the Countess after we had taken a short turn on the lawn. "We will go and watch the game-keeper catch the fish he promised us to-day."

We went through the little gate and down to the boat, we jumped in and there we were, sailing slowly up the Indre. Like true children amused at the least thing, we looked at the grasses on the banks and the blue and green dragon flies; and the Countess was astonished at being able to enjoy such peaceful pleasures in the midst of her poignant sorrows; but does not the calm of nature, going her way careless of our struggles, cast a comforting spell upon us all? The turmoil of a love full of contained desire harmonises with the whirl of water; flowers unsullied by the hand of man express its most secret dreams, the languorous rocking of a boat vaguely imitates the thoughts that float in the mind. We felt the numbing influence of this dual poetry. Words, attuned to the diapason of nature, displayed a mysterious grace, and our eyes shone all the more brilliantly as they shared in the light which the sun poured so generously over the blazing fields. The river was like a path over which we were flying, and, undistracted by the necessary motion of walking, our minds gave themselves over entirely to the wonder of creation. And was not the tumultous joy of a little girl at play, so graceful in her movements, so irritating in her prattle, a living expression of two free spirits who took a delight in fashioning, in their imagination, that wondrous creature dreamed of by Plato and known to all whose youth was fulfilled by happy love? To convey this hour, not in its indescribable details but in its entirety, I will tell you that we loved each other through all the things, all the creatures that surrounded us; we felt, outside of ourselves, the happiness each of us was longing for; it penetrated us so vividly that the Countess took off her gloves and let her lovely hands trail in the water as if to cool a secret ardour. Her eyes spoke, but her mouth, lips slightly parted like a rose unfolding to the air, would have closed at the first sign of desire. You know the harmony of low notes blending perfectly with higher ones? It has always reminded me of the harmony of our two souls at that moment, a harmony that can never come again!

"Where is your fishing done," I asked, "if you can only fish on the banks that belong to you?"

"Near Pont-de-Ruan," she said. "The river belongs to us from Pont-de-Ruan, right up to Clochegourde now. Monsieur de Mortsauf has just bought forty acres of meadowland with two years savings and the arrears of his pension. Does that surprise you?"

"I would like the whole valley to belong to you!" I cried.

She answered with a smile. We arrived at a point below Pont-de-Ruan, where the Indre is wide. Some men were fishing there.

"Well, Martineau?" she said to one of them.

"Ah, Madame la Comtesse, we are out of luck! Three hours we have been at it, working upstream from the mill and not a single catch."

We landed alongside, to watch the last nets being cast, and the three of us took a seat in the shade of a *bouillard*, a sort of poplar, with a white bark, which is found on the Danube, on the Loire, and probably on all great rivers, and which sheds a silky white fluff that protects its blossom. The Countess had regained her dignified serenity. She almost regretted having revealed her sorrows and cried out like Job instead of weeping like Magdalen—a Magdalen without lovers, without carousal or dissipation, though not without fragrance or loveliness. The net drawn up at her feet was full of fish: tench, mullet, pike, perch and a huge carp flapped on the grass.

"You'd think the fish knew!" said the gamekeeper. The fishermen stared in admiration at this woman, who looked like a fairy whose magic wand had tipped the nets. At that moment, the groom appeared, riding across the meadow at full gallop. A shudder of apprehension shook her entire frame. Jacques was not with us and a mother's first thought, as Virgil said in verse, is to clasp her children to her breast at the slightest mishap.

"Jacques," she cried. "Where's Jacques? What has happened to my son?"

She did not love me! Had she really loved me, she would have uttered that anguished lioness cry for *my* sufferings too!

"Madame la Comtesse, Monsieur le Comte is feeling worse."

She breathed again. She and I ran side by side followed by Madeleine.

"Stay with Madeleine and don't hurry," she said. "That darling child must not get too hot. You see! Monsieur de Mortsauf's haste in this hot weather made him sweat and his lingering under that walnut tree may have brought about some disaster."

That word, spoken in the throes of her agitation, gave proof of her purity of soul. The death of the Count—a disaster! She hurried back to Clochegourde, passing through a gap in the wall and across the vineyards. I "took my time", right enough.

Henriette's remark had enlightened me, but the way lightning lights up the barn as it destroys the stored-up hay. While we were on the river, I had thought I was her favourite. I reflected bitterly that she had meant what she said. A lover has everything or nothing at all. So I loved alone, with the desires of a love that knows what it wants, that feeds on the promise of hoped-for caresses, and makes do with spiritual delights because it mingles with them those that the future holds in store. If Henriette was in love, she knew nothing of the tempests or the delights of love. She lived on the sentiment itself, like a saint with God. I was the object on which she had pinned her half-understood thoughts and feelings, just as a swarm of bees attaches itself to the branch of a flowering tree; but I was not the mainspring of her life, merely an off-shoot of it. I was not the whole of life to her. Like a king dethroned, I wandered this way and that, wondering who would give me back my kingdom. In my mad jealousy I blamed myself for not having dared to make a move, for not having strengthened the bonds of affection, which now seemed to me more tenuous than real, with the chains of that positive right which comes from possession.

The Count's indisposition, brought on perhaps by the cold air round the walnut tree, grew serious within a few hours. I went into Tours to fetch a well-known doctor, a Monsieur Origet. I was unable to bring him back until the evening; but he spent all night and the whole of the following day at Clochegourde. He had sent the groom for a large supply of leeches, as he deemed it urgent to bleed his patient, but then found he had no lancet with him. In less time than it takes to tell, I had dashed over to Azay, in appalling weather, woken up the surgeon there, Monsieur Deslandes and forced him to come back with me. Ten minutes later, the Count would have succumbed, but the bleeding saved him. Despite this initial success, the physician gave warning of an impending fever of the most pernicious kind, such as attack people who have enjoyed perfect health for twenty years. The Countess, utterly stricken, believed herself to be the cause of this fatal attack. Too nerveless to thank me for what I had done, she threw me one or two smiles, whose sweetness equalled the kiss she had laid upon my hand; I would have liked to read in them remorse for an illicit love, but I saw the act of contrition of a penitent, painful to see in a soul so pure; I saw an admiring tenderness for the man she regarded as noble, and self-accusation for an imaginary crime. Yes, she loved as Laura loved Petrarch; not as Francesca da Rimini loved Paolo: appalling discovery to one who dreamed that these two kinds of love could be united! The Countess lay, slumped, her arms hanging limp, in a shabby chair in that pigsty of a room. The next evening, as he was leaving, the doctor told the Countess, who had been up all night, that she must engage a nurse, for the illness would be a long one.

"A nurse?" she said. "No, no. We will nurse him," she cried, looking at me; "we owe it to ourselves to save him!"

At her cry, the doctor threw us a curious and questioning glance. The expression in her voice led him to conjecture that we had failed in some secret obligation. He promised to come back twice a week, told Monsieur Deslandes what treatment to follow and indicated the symptoms which might render it necessary to send for him from Tours.

So as to give the Countess at least one night's rest in two, I asked her to let me stay up with the Count on alternate nights. And so I persuaded her, not without difficulty, to go to bed on the third night. When all was quiet in the house, at a moment when the Count was dozing, I heard a painful moan issuing from Henriette's room. My anxiety grew so acute that I went in to her; she was on her knees before her *prie-Dieu*, weeping and beating her breast.

"O Lord, if this is the price of a murmur, I will never complain again. Why, you have left him alone!" she cried, when she saw me.

"I heard you weeping and moaning and I was afraid for you."

"Oh, I!" she said. "There is nothing wrong with me!" She wanted to make sure that her husband was asleep, and we went downstairs together, and by the light of a lamp, we stood and looked at him. He was not asleep so much as weak from the severe blood letting. His hands plucked nervously at the bedclothes as he tried to draw them over him.

"They say that dying people do that," she said. "Oh, if he dies of this illness which we brought on him, I shall never marry again, I swear it!" And she laid her hand on the Count's brow in a gesture of solemnity.

"I did all I could to save him," I said.

"Yes, you have been very kind," she replied, "but I—I am the real culprit!"

She bent over that ravaged brow, brushed away the sweat on it with her hair, and kissed it reverently; but I saw, not without a secret joy, that she performed the caress as a kind of expiation.

"Blanche ... water!" said the Count in a faint voice.

"You see? He does not recognize anyone but me," she said, as she brought him a glass. And, by her tone, by her affectionate manner, she attempted to violate the sentiments that bound us by sacrificing them to the sick man.

"Henriette," I said, "go and get some rest, I beg of you."

"Not Henriette—not ever again!" she cut in, with imperious abruptness.

"Go to bed, or you will make yourself ill. Your children, *he himself*, demand that you should look after yourself: there are times when selfishness becomes a sublime virtue."

"Yes," she said.

She went, commending her husband to my care with gestures which might have betokened impending hysteria, had they not mingled child-like grace with the beseeching emphasis of a penitent at prayer.

This scene, so terrible when one compared it with the usual state of mind of this pure soul, alarmed me considerably. I feared the hypersensitivity of her fevered conscience. When the doctor came again, I told him about the pangs of guilt that were tormenting my snow-white Henriette. Although fairly revealing, this confidence dispelled Monsieur Origet's suspicions and he calmed the turmoil of that fine spirit by saying that the Count was bound in any case to have had this attack and that his standing under the tree had done more good than harm in the sense that it had served to bring his incipient illness to a head.

For fifty-two days the Count hovered between life and death. Taking it in turns, Henriette and I each stayed up for twenty-six nights. Monsieur de Mortsauf undoubtedly owed his recovery to our nursing and to the scrupulous accuracy with which we carried out Monsieur Origet's orders. Like those medical philosophers whose sagacious observations give them the right to call in question the sincerity of a fine action, when it is merely the covert fulfilment of a duty, this man, even while he witnessed the heroic struggle which was taking place between the Countess and me, could not resist throwing us furtive and speculative looks, so afraid was he of being misled in his admiration.

"With this sort of illness," he said to me, at his third visit, "death finds a willing ally in a patient's morale. When it is at such a low ebb as the Count's, doctor, nurse, all those who surround the patient, hold his life in their hands; a word, a sudden fear betrayed by an unguarded gesture, have the potency of poison."

As he spoke, Origet studied my face and bearing, but he saw in my eyes the clear expression of a candid mind. Indeed, during the course of that cruel illness there had not formed in my mind the faintest suggestion of those unbidden bad thoughts which sometimes streak the clearest consciences. To those who take an overall view of nature, everything tends to unity by assimilation. The world of the spirit must be governed by some such similar principle. In a pure sphere, all is pure. Near Henriette, the air had a scent of Heaven about it; one had the impression that a hint of reprehensible desire would separate her from you for ever. And so not only was she happiness, but she was virtue, too. Seeing us always equally attentive and solicitous, the doctor was indefinably respectful and compassionate in his manner and in the things he said, as if he were saying to himself, "Those are the real patients; but they hide their wounds and forget them!" In contrast to his normal nature—a phenomenon, so this kindly man told us, quite

157

usual in men as broken down as he—Monsieur de Mortsauf was patient, obedient, uncomplaining and marvellously docile; he, who when in good health, did not do the simplest little thing without endless protest. The secret behind this submission to medicine, so denigrated not so long ago, was the lurking fear of death, yet another contrast in a man of unchallengeable bravery. This fear might well account for various odd quirks in a character which his misfortunes had so altered.

Shall I confess to you, Natalie, and will you believe me, that those fifty days and the month that followed were the happiest time of my life? Does not love flow through the infinite expanses of the soul like a great river in some lovely valley, collecting the showers, the streams, the waterfalls, the trees and flowers that fall, the loose gravel of the banks and the high rocks tumbling down the hillside? It swells with storms and with the slow trickle of limpid fountains too. Yes, when one is in love, love's tide sweeps all before it.

After the initial danger was over, the Countess and I grew accustomed to the Count's illness. Despite the constant untidiness which the various treatments the Count required brought with them, his room, which we had found in such a chaotic state, became clean and attractive. Soon we were like two people stranded on a desert island; for not only does misfortune isolate one, but it silences the petty conventions of society. Furthermore, in the invalid's interests, we were forced to come into contact with each other in a way that no other event would have sanctioned. How many times did our hands, so shy before, not meet as they performed some service for the Count! For did I not have to help Henriette and steady her sometimes too? Often, absorbed, like a soldier on duty, in some essential task, she would forget to eat; and then I would serve her, on her lap sometimes, a meal eaten in haste that necessitated a host of small attentions. It was a childhood scene, played beside a half-open grave. She would order me briefly to perform certain extra attentions that might help to ease the Count's discomfort and kept me busy with a thousand little tasks.

During the early days, when the intensity of the danger stifled, as it does in battle, the fine distinctions that characterise the events of ordinary life, she shed the decorum which every woman, even the most natural, preserves in her speech, her eyes, her bearing when she is in company or with her family, and which is out of place in casual attire. Did she not come and relieve me, as the first birds began to sing, dressed in her morning robe, which sometimes allowed me to glimpse once more the dazzling treasures which in my wild imaginings, I thought of as mine? While still remaining stately and proud, how could she help then but be on familiar terms with me? Besides, during those early days, danger so successfully removed all passionate significance from our intimacy that she saw no harm in it. Then, as soon as she had a little time to think, she may have concluded that it would be insulting, for her as for me, if she were to change her manner now. We found ourselves imperceptibly growing used to each other, married in a certain sense. She trusted me nobly, as certain of me as she was of herself. And so I came to have a more important place in her heart. The Countess became my Henriette once more, a Henriette more than ever constrained to love the man who strove to be her second self. Soon I no longer had to crave her hand, now always unresistingly surrendered at the first pleading look; I could, without her attempting to avoid my gaze, run my eyes with rapture along the outline of her lovely form during the long hours we spent listening to the sick man's breathing as he slept. The meagre pleasures we allowed ourselves, those melting looks, those words spoken in whispers so as not to wake the Count, the fears, the hopes told and retold—in a word, the countless events in that complete fusion of two hearts long kept apart; all this stood out vividly against the dark and painful background of the present scene.

We grew to know each other through and through in this testing time when the strongest affection frequently goes under, unable to survive the close contact at all hours and that constant cohesion which makes life either lighter or heavier to bear. You know what havoc the illness of the master of the house brings in its train; what disruption in household affairs. There is no time for anything; the hiatus in his life upsets the smooth running of his home and the day to day existence of his family. Although Madame de Mortsauf carried all the burdens, the Count was still quite useful out of doors. He talked to the farmers, called on business people, collected moneys; if she was the spirit, he was the body. I appointed myself her steward, so that she could take care of the Count without jeopardising anything in the external affairs of the estate. She accepted it all without demur and without thanks. These household duties shared, these orders given on her behalf were but one more sweet sweet sign of our intimacy. I spent many an evening with her in her room, talking about her children and her plans. These talks lent yet another semblance of reality to our ephemeral marriage. How gladly Henriette let me play the part of husband to her; sat me in his chair at table; sent me out to speak to the gamekeeper; all this with a total innocence, though not without that secret pleasure that the most virtuous woman in the world will feel at finding a way to combine strict obedience to the rules with the satisfaction of her unavowed desires.

Removed by his illness, the Count ceased to weigh upon his wife or his household; and so the Countess could be herself. She had the right to fuss over me and make me the object of a host of small attentions. What a joy it was to divine in her the determination, dimly conceived perhaps, but enchantingly expressed, to display the full value of her qualities and personal worth to me, to let me see how different she could be if she were understood! This flower, perpetually closed in the chilly atmosphere of her household, unfolded beneath my gaze, and to my eyes alone. She took as much delight in opening her petals as I did in casting into them the searching gaze of love. She proved to me in countless little ways how ever-present I was in her thoughts. On the days when, after having spent the night at the sick man's bedside, I slept late, Henriette rose early, before anyone else was afoot and saw to it that I had absolute silence. Without being told, Jacques and Madeleine would go out of earshot to play; she would use all the stratagems at her command to secure the right to lay my place at table; finally, she would serve me herself, and then what sparkling joy there was in all her movements, what wild, swallow-like grace! How rosy were her cheeks, how quivering her voice, how lynx-like the darting penetration of her eyes!

Can one describe these effusions of the spirit? She was often quite numbed with fatigue; but if, in those moments of lassitude, I should happen to need her, for me, as for her children, she would call up new reserves of strength, and she would spring to life, agile, gay and vital. How she loved to cast the rays of her tenderness about her! Ah, Natalie, there are indeed some women who share, here below, the privileges of seraphic spirits, and who, like them, spread that radiance which Saint-Martin, the Unknown Philosopher, called "intelligent, melodious and fragrant light!" Sure of my discretion, Henriette took a delight in raising for me the heavy drapes that hid the future and letting me see the two women in her; the fettered creature who had won my heart despite her lack of blandishments, and the free woman whose sweetness was to secure my love for ever.

What a difference there was between the two! Madame de Mortsauf was like the Bengal lark transported into chilly Europe, perched sadly on its wooden swing, dumb and dying in some naturalist's cage; Henriette was the bird warbling its oriental poems in some wooded grove beside the Ganges, fluttering like a live gem from branch to branch, among the roses of an immense volkameria in perpetual bloom. Her beauty grew more beautiful, her liveliness of mind returned. This never-ending festive blaze was a secret between our two minds, for the eye of the Abbé de Dominis, that representative of society, was more formidable to Henriette than was Monsieur de Mortsauf's. But she took, as I did, a great delight in giving an ingenuous turn to her thoughts; she would hide her contentment beneath the cloak of persiflage and covered the emblems of her love with the eye-catching panoply of gratitude.

"We have put your friendship to a severe test, Felix! We can allow him the same liberties as we do Jacques, can't we, Monsieur l'Abbé?" she would say at table. The stern Abbé would answer with the pleasant smile of the pious man who looks into a heart and finds it pure. Besides, he showed, for the Countess, that blend of respect and adoration which the angels inspire. Twice, in those fifty days, the Countess may have overstepped the limits which she had set to our affection; but even these two occasions were wrapped in a veil which was not to lift until the day of the supreme avowals.

One morning, in the early days of the Count's illness, round about the time when she repented of having treated me so harshly and withdrawn the innocent privileges granted to my chaste tenderness for her, I was waiting for her to take my place at the bedside. Overtired, I leaned my head against the wall and fell asleep. I awoke with a start as something touched my brow, something cool which gave me the same sensation as if someone had gently pressed a rose on it. I saw the Countess standing three paces away from me.

"Here I am," she said.

I left the room; but as I wished her good-morning, I took her hand. It was damp and trembling.

"Are you ill?" I asked her.

"Why do you ask me that?" she said.

I looked at her, blushing and confused.

"I had a dream," I said.

One evening, during one of the last visits from Monsieur Origet, who had definitely declared that the Count was virtually convalescent, I found myself with Jacques and Madeleine out on the veranda. The three of us were sprawled on the steps, engrossed in a game we were playing with straws and pin-hooks. Monsieur de Mortsauf was asleep. While they were harnessing his carriage, the doctor and the Countess were talking in low voices in the drawing-room. Monsieur Origet left without my noticing his departure. After seeing him out, Henriette leaned against the open window, where she must have been looking at us for some time without our noticing her. It was one of those warm evenings when the sky has coppery tints in it, and the countryside echoes with a thousand intermingling sounds. The sun's last rays glowed pale on the turrets of the house, the scent of flowers came wafting from the gardens, the cowbells tinkled in the distance as the herds were driven back into the sheds. We conformed to the quietness of this mild hour and kept our voices down in case we woke the Count. Suddenly, despite the rustle of a dress, I heard the choking sound of a sigh violently bitten back. I dashed into the drawing-room. The Countess was sitting in the window seat, a handkerchief pressed to her face. She recognised my step and waved me imperiously away, indicating that she wished to be alone. I came closer, filled with apprehension, and tried to pull away her handkerchief. Her face was bathed in tears. She fled to her room and did not come out again until it was time for prayers. For the first time for fifty days I took her out on to the terrace and asked her the cause of her distress; but she affected the most unbridled gaiety and gave Origet's good news as the cause of it.

"Henriette, Henriette," I said, "you already knew that when I saw you crying. A lie is a monstrosity between us two. Why would you not let me dry your tears? Were you crying over me?"

"I was thinking," she said, "that this illness had been a kind of interim in my anguish. Now that I no longer tremble for Monsieur de Mortsauf, I must tremble for myself."

She was right. The Count's recovery was heralded by the return of his capricious moods; he began to declare that neither his wife nor myself nor the doctors were capable of looking after him; we none of us knew anything about his illness, his temperament, the pain he suffered or the way to treat it: Origet, obsessed with his own cranky notions, had diagnosed his complaint as a deterioration of the body fluids, when he should have concentrated on the pylorus. One day he looked at us maliciously, as if to convey that he had been watching us and that we had not fooled him and said to his wife, with a smile: "Well now, my dear, if I had died, you would have been sorry, I'm sure. But you'd have resigned yourself to it, I'll wager!"

"I would have worn Court mourning—pink and black," she replied with a laugh, so as to silence her husband. But there were, especially on the subject of food, scenes and tantrums incomparably more violent than anything that had happened in the past, for the Count's disposition showed itself all the more terrifying for having, as it were, lain dormant. The doctor prescribed his diet and strongly urged that, while convalescing, the patient should not eat his fill. Fortified by the doctor's instructions and the obedience of her servants; egged on by myself, who saw in the present struggle a way of training her to exert her power over her husband, the Countess grew bolder in her resistance. She learnt to meet his insane yelling with a calm brow. She took him for what he was, a child, and inured herself to his insulting epithets. I saw with satisfaction that she was at last assuming control over that diseased mentality. The Count would shout and scream, but he obeyed, and the louder the protest the more docilely he subsequently did what he was told. Despite the evident results, Henriette would weep sometimes to see the weak, wasted old man, his brow yellower than a falling leaf, with his colourless eyes and shaking hands. She blamed herself for her harshness and could not often resist the joy in the Count's eyes when, as she measured out his portion at meals, she overstepped the limits prescribed by the doctor. She showed herself, moreover, even more gentle and gracious with him than she had been with me; but there were, nevertheless, certain differences that filled my heart with infinite joy. She was not indefatigable; she knew when to call the servants and tell them to wait on the Count when his whims followed a bit too closely on one another and he complained of not being understood.

The Countess wanted to give thanks to God for Monsieur de Mortsauf's recovery; she had a Mass said and asked me to accompany her to church. I gave her my arm as far as the door, but while she was at Mass I went to see Monsieur and Madame de Chessel. On our way home, she started to reproach me.

"Henriette," I said, "I cannot pretend what I do not feel. I can jump into the river to save my enemy if he is drowning, I can give him my cloak to keep him warm; I can even forgive him, but I cannot forget the injury he does me."

She said no more, and pressed my arm to her heart.

"You are an angel. I am sure you were sincere in your thanksgiving," I went on. "The mother of the Prince de la Paix was rescued from a howling mob that wanted to kill her and when the Queen asked her afterwards what she did at the time, she answered 'I prayed for them!' Women are like that. I am a man, and of necessity imperfect."

"Do not malign yourself," she replied, vehemently shaking my arm. "You are perhaps a better person than I."

"Yes," I said, "for I would give all eternity for one day of happiness—while you ..."

"While I?" she said, with a proud look.

I said nothing and dropped my eyes to avoid the lightning that flashed from her eyes.

"I?" she went on. "Which of the many 'I's' do you mean? I am conscious of so many selves in me. Those children," she added, pointing to Jacques and Madeleine, "are two of my selves. Felix," she cried with a heart-rending note in her voice, "Do you think me as selfish as that? Do you think I could sacrifice eternity to reward a man who has sacrificed his life to me? The thought is horrible; it goes against every religious sentiment I have. If a woman falls so low, can she ever rise again? Can her happiness absolve her sin? I can soon give you the answer to these questions! Why, yes, I will tell you one of the secrets of my conscience: that idea has often crossed my heart and I have often atoned for it by severe penances. It was the cause of those tears which you asked me to explain the other day."

"Are you not attaching too much importance to things which low-born women rate highly and which you should —"

"Oh!" she broke in, "do you rate them less highly then?" This piece of logic put an end to all argument.

"Very well," she went on, "I will tell you. Yes, I could be base enough to leave this poor old man whose whole life I am! But, my friend, these two helpless little creatures in front of us there, Madeleine and Jacques, would they not remain with their father? Now, answer me, do you think they would survive three months under the insane domination of this man? If I failed in my duty as a wife, and had only myself to think of —" She smiled a superb smile. "But would I not be killing my own children? It would mean certain death for them. Dear God!" she exclaimed, "why are we talking about such things? Get married do, and let me die!"

She said these words in so bitter and heartfelt a tone that she stifled the upsurge of my passion.

"You cried out up there under the walnut tree; I have just cried out myself, under these alders, that's all. I shall not mention it again."

"Your generosity tears at my heart," she said, raising her eyes to Heaven. We had reached the terrace and the Count was sitting in an easy chair in the sun. The sight of that disintegrated face, scarcely animated by a feeble smile, extinguished the flame which had sprung from the ashes: I leaned on the balustrade, contemplating the picture this moribund figure made, as he sat between his two still sickly children and his wife, pale from her sleepless nights; thin with the overwork, the fears and perhaps the joys of those two terrible months, her face unusually flushed now with the emotion of the scene which had just taken place. At sight of this stricken family, framed by the quivering foliage through which filtered the grey light of a cloudy autumn sky, I felt the bonds that unite mind and body loosen within me. For the first time

I experienced that spiritual depression which they say the most robust of fighters knows in the heat of combat; a sort of icy panic which makes a coward of the bravest man, a firm believer of a sceptic and renders one indifferent to everything, even the most vital sentiments—those of honour, those of love; for doubt drains away our knowledge of ourselves and our zest for living. Poor highly strung creatures, whom the richness of your make-up delivers, defenceless, to some baleful genius, where are your peers and judges? I saw now how the daring youth, one hand already on the baton of the Marshals of France, able negotiator and intrepid soldier, had turned into the innocent murderer I saw before me. Could my ambitions, crowned with roses now, end in the way that his had done? Appalled by the cause as well as the effect; asking, like the blasphemer, where was the hand of Providence in this, I could not hold back the tear that started from my eyes.

"What's the matter, Felix dear?" piped Madeleine, in her childish voice.

Henriette finally dispelled these murky clouds with a look of tender solicitude that pierced my soul like rays of sunlight. At that moment the old groom handed me a letter he had brought from Tours, the sight of which drew from me such a sharp cry of surprise that the Countess started to tremble. I had seen the Royal seal: the King was recalling me. I handed her the letter. She read it at one glance.

"He is going away!" said the Count.

"What will become of me?" she said to me, seeing for the first time the sunless desert that stretched ahead of her. We sat there in a stupor which lay heavy on each one of us, for we had never felt so vividly how necessary we all were to each other. Whenever she spoke to me, even of unimportant things, the Countess had a new note to her voice, as if the instrument had lost some of its strings and the remainder had grown slack. Her gestures became lifeless and her eyes lacked lustre. I begged her to tell me what she was thinking.

"Am I thinking, even?" she said.

She took me to her room, sat me on the couch, looked in the drawer of her dressing-table, knelt down beside me and said: "Here is the hair I have lost in the past year. Take it, it belongs to you. You will know why one day." I brought my face slowly towards her brow; she did not lower it to avoid my lips and I pressed them there chastely, without guilty rapture, or thrill of sensual joy, but with tender solemnity. Was she on the verge of sacrificing everything? Or was she merely stepping, as I had done, to the extreme edge of the precipice? If love had prompted her to yield to me, she would not have had this profound calm, this saintly look, she would not have said, in that pure voice:

"You are not angry with me now, are you?"

I left at night-fall. She insisted on coming some of the way along the Frapesle road, and we halted at the walnut tree; I showed her it and told her how I had glimpsed her from there, four years ago now.

"How beautiful the valley was then!" I cried.

"And now?" she said quickly.

"You are under the walnut tree," I said, "and the valley is ours."

She bowed her head, and we said our goodbyes. She got back into her carriage with Madeleine, and I into mine, alone. Back in Paris, I was fortunately immersed in urgent work which utterly absorbed my mind and forced me to retire from society, which forgot me forthwith. I corresponded with Madame de Mortsauf, to whom I sent my daily account of events at the end of every week. She answered twice a month. An obscure, full life, similar to those lush, flower-strewn glades, screened from the human eye which I had again admired, not so long ago, when I composed some more of my poems in flowers, during the last two weeks of my stay at Clochegourde.

O you who are in love!—set yourselves fine tasks like these, aim to fulfil a set of rules such as the Church gives Christians to fulfil each day! There is an inspired idea behind the strict observances created by the Church of Rome. They deepen the channels of duty in the soul, through a repetition of the actions which keep hope and fear alive. Feelings flow swift and clear along these watercourses, that purify the streams they carry, constantly refresh the heart and fertilize life with the abundant treasures of a hidden faith—that divine spring which multiplies the single seed of a one and only love.

My passion, which recalled the chivalrous ideal of the Middle

Ages, somehow became common knowledge. Perhaps the King and the Duc de Lenoncourt talked about it. From this exalted circle, the simple and romantic tale of a young man's reverent adoration for a beautiful, uncourted woman, noble in her solitude, faithful without the mainstay of social duty, must have percolated into the heart of the Faubourg Saint-Germain. In fashionable drawing-rooms, I found myself the object of irksome attention. A modest way of life has advantages which, once tasted, make the glare of perpetual lime-light intolerable. Just as eyes accustomed to soft colours are hurt by the brilliant light of day, so there are certain minds which dislike violent contrasts. I was like that in those days. You may find it surprising to-day; but be patient, the oddities of the present de Vandenesse will soon explain themselves. To resume, I found the women charmingly disposed towards me and society everything that one could wish. The wedding of the Duc de Berri marked the return of pomp and splendour to the Court. The traditional festivities of France came into their own again. The foreign occupation was over, prosperity was beginning to reappear, people could enjoy themselves again. Personages illustrious by their rank or esteemed for their great wealth flocked from all over Europe to the capital of cultural life, where the virtues and vices of other countries are to be found, magnified and sharpened by French wit.

I had left Clochegourde in the middle of winter. Five months later, my good angel wrote me a desperate letter telling me that her son had been seriously ill. He was out of danger now, but it had left her with considerable fears for his future. The doctor had said that he must take precautions for his chest—dread word which, uttered by medical men, darkens every hour of a mother's life. Hardly had Henriette begun to breathe again, hardly was Jacques convalescent, than his sister gave cause for anxiety. Madeleine, that pretty little plant that responded so well to maternal care, had a bout of serious ill-health, which although not unexpected, was gravely alarming in so frail a constitution. Already exhausted by the fatigue of Jacques' long illness, the Countess could summon no strength to bear this new blow and the spectacle of those two beloved little creatures rendered her insensible to the redoubled torments of her husband's temper. And so, increasingly violent stormwaves, heavy with lashing shingle, tore up the hopes most deeply rooted in her heart. She had moreover given in, for the sake of peace, to the tyranny of the Count, who promptly took back all the ground he had lost.

"When all my strength went to my children," she wrote, "how could I use it against Monsieur de Mortsauf; how could I defend myself against his attacks and fight off death at the same time? As I walk to-day, alone and weakened, with the two young melancholy souls who keep me company, I am overwhelmed by an unconquerable distaste for life. What blow can I feel, to what affection can I respond, when I see Jacques on the terrace, motionless, with nothing to show that he is alive save his two lovely eyes, huge in his thin face, and sunken like those of an old man; with his intelligence—a fatal sign!—so far outstripping his frail body? I look at my pretty Madeleine, so lively, so affectionate, so colourful, now pale as death; and her hair and her eyes seem to me to have faded; she looks languishingly at me, as though she were about to say goodbye. No dish will tempt her, and when she does ask for food, she frightens one by the strangeness of her tastes; the candid creature, who never had secrets from me before, blushes when she confesses them to me. Try as I may, I cannot amuse my children; they smile at me, but those smiles are coaxed from them by my cajolery; they are not spontaneous. They weep at not being able to respond to my caresses. Suffering has slackened everything in them, even the ties that hold us together. So you can imagine what a sad place Clochegourde is now. Monsieur de Mortsauf reigns uncontested. Oh, my friend, my life's glory," she wrote further on, "you must love me very much if you can love me now, lifeless, thankless and petrified as I am with grief!!"

It was then, at a time when I felt possessed as never before, when my whole life was lived in that spirit to whom I strove to send the luminous breeze of my mornings and my golden hopes at evening, that I met, in the drawing-rooms of the *Elysée-Bourbon*, one of those illustrious English ladies who are little short of queens. Immense wealth, a lineage free, since the Conquest, of any misalliance; a marriage with one of the most distinguished old peers of the English aristocracy—all these assets were but trimmings that enhanced this woman's wit and that indefinable, diamond-like brilliance which dazzled and held one in thrall. She was the idol of the day and she reigned all the more surely over Paris society for having qualities essential to success, the iron hand beneath the velvet glove that Bernadotte used to speak of. You know that singular personality common to the English—the proud, impassable Channel, the chilly Saint George waterway they set between themselves and those who have not been presented to them. They give one the impression that mankind is an ant-hill over which they walk. They know no one of their own species save those they admit to their circle. As for the others, they do not even understand their language; they see lips that move and eyes that see, but neither sound nor look so much as reaches them; as far as they are concerned, those folk might as well not exist. The English are consequently a sort of microcosm of their island, where law governs everything, where all conforms to its particular sphere, where the exercise of virtue seems to be something they do by clockwork at certain unalterable times of day. The fortifications of polished steel built around an Englishwoman, trapped as she is in the golden cage of her household, but where her food, her drinking trough, her seed tray and her perch are marvels of workmanship—all this gives her an irresistible attraction.

No other race has more carefully paved the way for the hypocrisy of the married woman. She is confronted at every turn with the choice of social survival or social suicide. For her, there is no stepping stone between honour and shame. Either the fall from grace is total or there has been none. It is "all or nothing", Hamlet's "to be or not to be". This alternative, coupled with the constant disdain bred in her by the habits of social life, makes the Englishwoman a being apart. She is a pathetic creature, coerced into virtue and easily tempted to depravity; condemned to live in a perpetual web of lies, but outwardly delightful, for this race has sacrificed everything to outward form. Hence the beauty particular to the women of that country; the tendency to passionate friendship, which can be the whole of life to them; the exaggerated care they take of their appearance; the delicacy of their love, so gracefully depicted in the famous scene from *Romeo and Juliet*, where Shakespeare's genius has, with one stroke, expressed the essence of the Englishwoman. To you who envy them so much and who know them so well, what can I say about those milk-white sirens, seemingly impenetrable yet so easy to know, who believe that love is sufficient unto itself, and who bring melancholy to its delights because they never vary them; whose souls have but one note, whose voices but one syllable—ocean of love where he who has not swum will forever miss something of the poetry of the senses, just as he who has never seen the sea will have some strings the fewer to his lyre?

You know what is behind all this. My affair with the Marchioness of Dudley acquired a disastrous notoriety. At an age when the senses have so much sway over the things we do, and for a young man whose passions had been so violently suppressed, the image of the saint enduring her long martyrdom at Clochegourde shone out so strongly that I was able to resist any woman's blandishments. This fidelity was the beacon that earned me the attention of Lady Arabelle. My resistance whetted her passion. What she wanted, as do many Englishwomen, was the flamboyant, the extraordinary. She wanted spice, pepper for her heart's appetites, in the same way that the English need hot condiments to awaken their sense of taste. The dullness that the ideal of material perfection makes for in these women's lives, the methodical regularity of their habits, leads them to worship the romantic and the difficult. I proved unable to assess this sort of character. The more I withdrew behind a cold disdain, the keener was Lady Dudley's interest. This struggle, which became a matter of personal honour to her, excited the curiosity of one or two *salons*; this initial gratification made her feel that she must, in honour bound, go on to victory. Ah, I should have been saved if only some friend had repeated to me the atrocious remark she made about Madame de Mortsauf and me.

"I am bored," she said, "with the sighs of those two turtle doves!"

While in no way trying to justify my crime, I must point out, Natalie, that a man has fewer means of resisting a woman than your sex has of escaping our pursuit. Custom forbids a man that brutal repression of the instincts which, in you, serves as a bait to prospective lovers and which, moreover, convention imposes upon you. For us, on the contrary, there is a kind of fatuous masculine law which ridicules reserve in us; we leave to you the monopoly of modesty, so that you may have the privilege of granting the favours; but reverse the roles and man is showered with derision. Although protected by my passion, mine was not the age when one remains insensible to the triple seduction of pride, beauty and devotion. When Lady Arabelle laid at my feet, at some ball where she was undisputed queen, the homage that was being paid to her, and watched my face to see whether her dress was to my taste; when she shivered with pleasure at any sign that I found her attractive; I was stirred by her excitement. She was, moreover, on a ground where I could not possibly escape her. It was difficult for me to refuse certain invitations from the diplomatic circle; her rank opened all doors to her, and with that skill that women display when they are set on something, she saw to it that the hostess placed her next to me at table; where she then proceeded to talk to me in whispers.

"If I were loved as Madame de Mortsauf is," she would say, "I would sacrifice everything for you." She would laughingly stipulate the most modest of conditions, she swore the most complete discretion, or else she asked me merely to allow her to love me. One day, she said something which satisfied all the cowardice of a capitulating conscience and all the unbridled desires of a young man.

"Your friend for always," she said, "and your mistress when you will."

Finally, she devised a scheme to make my very sense of honour my downfall. She bribed my valet, and after a reception, at which she had appeared looking so beautiful that she was sure of having aroused my desire, I found her in my room. The noise of this resounded in England, and its aristocracy were as dismayed as very Heaven at the fall of its brightest angel. Lady Dudley left her cloud in the Imperial British firmament, made do with her own private fortune, and did her best to eclipse by her sacrifices HER whose virtue was the cause of this ill-famed catastrophe. Lady Arabelle took a delight, like the Devil on the high summit of the Temple, in showing me the richest domains of her ardent kingdom.

Read this, I beg you, with indulgence. I deal now, with one of the most absorbing problems of human life: a crisis undergone by the majority of men, and one which I would like to go into, if only to light a warning beacon on that perilous reef. This fine English lady, so willowy, so fragile; this milky woman, so broken, so breakable, so sweet; with her caressing brow crowned with such fine tawny coloured hair; this creature whose brilliance seems luminous and evanescent, is an edifice of steel. No horse, whatever his mettle, can fight against her nervous wrist, her soft hand that nothing in the world can tire. She has the feet of a doe, small, dry and muscular beneath an indescribably graceful sheath of skin. She has a physical strength which makes her fearless in any combat; no man can keep pace with her on horseback; she would carry off the prize in a steeplechase with centaurs; she can shoot deer and hart without reining her horse. Her body is innocent of sweat; it breathes in fire from the atmosphere and is at home in water. Her passion is all African; her desire rises like a whirlwind in the desert, that desert whose burning immensity is painted in her eyes, desert full of azure and love, with its unchanging sky and its cool, starry nights. What a contrast to Clochegourde! The Orient and the Occident; one of them drawing to her the slightest drop of moisture for her nourishment, the other exuding her very soul, swathing her devotees in an aura of light; this one vital and slender, the other slow-moving and plump. Have you ever reflected on the general meaning of the English way of life? Is it not the deification of matter, a specific, calculated Epicureanism, scientifically applied? Whatever she may say or do, England is a materialistic nation, unbeknownst to herself perhaps. She has religious and ethical pretensions, from which divine spirituality and the Catholic soul is absent, the fruitful grace of which no amount of hypocrisy, however well simulated, can ever replace. She possesses in the highest degree that science of comfortable living which gives a relish to the smallest details of material existence; which makes your slipper the most exquisite slipper in the world, gives your linen an ineffable freshness, lines your chest of drawers with scented cedar; pours, at a given hour, a fragrant tea, expertly served; banishes dust, nails carpeting from the lowest stair to the remotest corners of the house; scrubs the walls of cellars, polishes

the door-knocker, oils the carriage-springs; makes out of surrounding matter a nourishing, downy pulp, bright and spotlessly
clean, where the soul dies smothered by delights; produces the
ghastly monotony of well-being; offers a life without setbacks,
stripped of spontaneity and which, in a word, turns you into a
machine.

And so I suddenly came to know, in the heart of this English
luxury, a woman, perhaps unique of her sex, who caught me in the
toils of a desire which had almost died in me, and to the lavishness
of which I brought an uncompromising continence; it was the kind
of love which has moments of heartbreaking beauty, an electricity
all its own, a love that admits you to paradise through the ivory
gates of semi-slumber, or snatches you up on its winged back and
flies there with you. A hideously thankless love, that bestrides the
corpses of its victims, laughing: a love that has no memory, a cruel
love, cruel like English foreign policy and to which nearly all men
succumb. You can already grasp the problem. Man is made up of
mind and matter; in him, the animal kingdom ends and the angel
begins. Hence the struggle we all feel between a far distant destiny
we can dimly foresee and the memory of our primeval instincts
from which we are not yet entirely free; a carnal love and a divine.
One man resolves the two into one; another abstains from both:
one explores the entire sex to find the satisfaction his atavistic
appetites crave for; another idealises it in one woman who is for
him the essence of the universe: some drift undecided between the
delights of matter and those of mind; others spiritualise the flesh
and ask of it what it cannot give. If, bearing in mind these general
aspects of love, you take into account the aversions and affinities
which spring from the diversity of temperaments and which break
the pacts made between those who have not put each other to the
test; if you add to these the mistakes arising from the hopes of those
who live preponderantly through the mind, through the heart or
through action, as the case may be—those in fact who think, or
feel, or act and whose inclinations have been forced out of true in
a relationship where *two* people are concerned, each of them dual
in their turn, then you will be excessively indulgent towards the
misfortunes for which society shows no pity. Well now, Lady
Arabelle satisfies the instincts, organs, appetites, vices and virtues

of that intricate matter of which we are made. She was the mistress of the flesh; Madame de Mortsauf was the wife of the spirit. The love which a mistress can satisfy has its limits; matter is finite; its properties have certain known powers; it inevitably reaches saturation point. I would often feel a kind of emptiness in Paris with Lady Dudley. Infinity is the domain of the heart; at Clochegourde, love had no limits.

I loved Lady Arabelle passionately, and indeed, if the animal in her was sublime, she was superior in intelligence too. The barbs of her witty conversation embraced everything. But it was Henriette whom I adored. At night I wept with happiness; in the morning I wept with remorse. There are certain women clever enough to hide their jealousy beneath the most angelic sweetness; like Lady Dudley, these are the women over thirty. These women are able to feel and to calculate, to savour the present to the full and to take thought for the future. They can stifle groans which are frequently legitimate with the energy of the huntsman who pays no heed to a wound as he gallops furiously on to the kill. Without ever mentioning Madame de Mortsauf, Arabelle was trying to kill her in my heart, where she was continually meeting her, and her passion would be fanned into flame by the breath of this unconquerable love. So as to triumph by comparisons which would be in her favour, she took care to be neither suspicious, irritating or inquisitive, the way most young women are. But like the lioness who seizes her prey in her maw and brings it back to her den to gnaw, she took care that nothing should disturb her happiness and she guarded me like an unsubdued conquest.

I would write to Henriette before her very eyes, but never once did she read a single line or try to discover the address I wrote on my letters. I was entirely free. It was as if she had said to herself: "If I lose him, I shall have only myself to blame." And she was proudly upheld by a love so devoted that she would have given her life for me unhesitatingly, if I had asked for it. Indeed, she had managed to make me believe that if I left her she would kill herself forthwith. You should have heard her on this subject, vaunting the practice of Indian widows who burn themselves upon their husband's funeral pyre.

"Although in India, this custom is restricted to the noblest caste," she would say, "and in this respect is little understood by Europeans, who are incapable of appreciating the haughty grandeur of this privilege; you must confess that in our flat, modern way of life, the aristocracy can no longer distinguish itself save by the conspicuous grandeur of its sentiments. How could I impress upon the middle classes that the blood in my veins is different from theirs, if not by dying a different death? Women without breeding can have the diamonds, the brocades, the horses, even the escutcheon which should be ours exclusively—for even a title can be bought! But to hold one's head high and love without regard for rules; to die for one's chosen idol and cut oneself a shroud out of his bed sheets; to subordinate heaven and earth to one man and filch from the Almighty the right to create a god; not to betray him to anything, not even virtue—for surely to refuse oneself to him in duty's name is tantamount to giving oneself to something which is not *him*! (whether it be a concept or another man, it is still betrayal!)—these are the heights to which lowborn women cannot aspire; they only know two common highways, the broad road of virtue and the muddy footpath of the courtesan!"

Her procedure, as you see, was directed at my pride; she flattered a man's every vanity by deifying it; she set me so high that she could live only at my feet. Moreover, all the blandishments her mind could conceive were expressed by her submissive slave-girl pose and by her total subjection. She could spend the entire day lying on the floor at my feet, without saying a word, looking at me, biding her time until the hour of pleasure like an houri in a seraglio and bringing it forward with artful coquetry, while giving every impression that she was patiently awaiting it. With what words can I describe those first six months during which I was a prey to the enervating joys of a love, fruitful in its delights and varying them with the ability born of experience, while hiding its learned skill behind the transports of passion? These pleasures, sudden revelation of the poetry of the senses, constitute the vigorous bond that fastens young men to women older than themselves; but this link is the convict's ball and chain; it leaves an indelible mark upon the soul; it gives it a distaste for fresh and candid loves, rich in flowers only, who do not know how to serve alcohol in curiously wrought cups of gold, studded with gems that flash with inexhaustible fires.

As I savoured the sensuous bliss I had dreamed of without knowing of it, and expressed, in my secret imaginings, the delights rendered a thousand times more ardent by the union of two souls, I found a wealth of paradoxes with which to justify to myself the unresisting ease with which I drank from that fine goblet. Often when, lost in the endless wastes of lassitude, my mind, freed from the body's leash, would hover far above the earth, I though of these pleasures as a means of annihilating matter and setting the spirit free for its sublime flight. Often, Lady Dudley, like so many women, would take advantage of the exaltation induced by an excess of happiness to bind me with promises and under the spur of desire would prompt me to blaspheme against the angel of Clochegourde. Once turned traitor, I became a cheat. I continued to write to Madame de Mortsauf, as though I were still the same child in the horrid little blue dress suit whom she so loved! But, I confess, her gift for second sight filled me with terror when I thought of the ravages some indiscretion might cause in the pretty castle of my hopes. Many a time, in the midst of my delight, a sudden cold pain would shoot through me as I heard Henriette's name spoken by some voice from above, like the "Cain, where is thy brother Abel?" in the Scriptures. My letters remained unanswered. I was seized with terrible anxiety and decided that I must go to Clochegourde. Arabelle made no objection, but talked quite naturally of accompanying me to Touraine. Her desire for me, whetted by my resistance; her presentiments of bliss borne out now by a happiness beyond her expectations; all this had bred in her a deep and genuine love which she wanted to render unique. Her woman's genius had seen in this trip a means of taking me away from Madame de Mortsauf for good; whereas I, blinded by fear and carried away by the naïveté of true passion, did not see the trap into which I was about to fall. Lady Dudley set the most undemanding conditions and forestalled any objections I might put forward. She agreed to stay in the neighbourhood of Tours, out in the country, incognito and in disguise, without stirring out of doors by day and meeting me only at a time of night when we could be sure that nobody would see us. I left Tours on horseback for Clochegourde. I had my reasons for this, as I needed a horse for my nocturnal excursions. Mine was an Arab which Lady Hester Stanhope had sent the Marchioness and which she exchanged with me for the famous Rembrandt she has in her drawing-room in London and which I came by in such a curious way.

I took the road I had taken on foot six years before, and came to a halt under the walnut tree. From there, I could see Madame de Mortsauf, on the edge of the terrace, wearing a white dress. I made towards her like a streak of lightning and reached the foot of the wall in a few minutes, having covered the distance in a straight line as if I were running a point to point race. She heard my prodigious leaps as I sped like a swallow across the desert, and when I stopped dead at the corner of the terrace, she said, "Oh, so it's you!" Those four words struck me like a thunderbolt. She knew of my affair. And who had told her? Her mother, whose loathsome letter she showed me later. The indifferent thinness of her voice, so full of life before, the flat pallidity of its tone, betrayed a ripened grief and gave off an indefinable scent of flowers forever broken on the stem. The hurricane of infidelity, like those floodwaters of the Loire that leave a permanent sand-deposit on whole areas of land, had swept over her soul and left a desert where lush green fields had flourished. I led my horse in through the little gate; it lay down on the ground at a word from me and the Countess, who had come slowly towards me, exclaimed, "What a beautiful animal!" She held her arms crossed, so that I should not take her hand, and I guessed her intention.

"I will tell Monsieur de Mortsauf you are here," she said and left me.

I stood there, dumbfounded, letting her go, watching her, still noble, leisurely, proud, and snowier than I had ever seen her, but bearing on her brow the yellow stamp of the bitterest depression, her head dropping like a lily overburdened with rain.

"Henriette!" I cried with the frenzy of a man who feels that he is dying.

She did not turn, she did not stop, she disdained to tell me that she had taken back my special name for her and that she no longer answered to it; she walked on. I may, in that dread vale where a million races long since turned to dust must throng, races whose spirit now moves over the surface of the globe—I may, I say, feel small in the midst of that multitude surging beneath the luminous vastness that shines on them with all its glory, but I will be less flattened than I was by that white figure, climbing, the way an inexorable flood climbs a city street by street—climbing with measured tread up to her château of Clochegourde, Clochegourde the pride and torment of that Christian Dido!

I cursed Arabelle with a single imprecation which would have killed her had she heard it—she who had left everything for me, as one gives up everything for God! I remained lost in a world of thoughts, perceiving on all sides the limitless expanses of sorrow. And then I saw them all coming down towards me. Jacques was running with the artless impetuosity of his years; like a gazelle with dying eyes, Madeleine walked beside her mother. I clasped Jacques to my heart, shedding on him the effusive heartfelt tears which his mother had spurned. Monsieur de Mortsauf came towards me with outstretched arms, pressed me to him, kissed me on both cheeks and said, "Felix, I found out that you saved my life!"

Madame de Mortsauf turned her back on us during this scene, seizing the pretext of showing the stupefied Madeleine my horse.

"Devil take it! Isn't that women all over?" cried the Count angrily. "They are examining your horse." Madeleine turned round and came towards me. I kissed her hand, looking as I did so at the Countess, who flushed.

"Madeleine looks much better," I said.

"Poor girlie," said the Countess, kissing her on the brow.

"Yes, at the moment, they are all well," put in the Count. "I alone, my dear Felix, am as dilapidated as a tumbledown old tower."

"It seems the general still has his melancholy moods?" I said, looking at Madame de Mortsauf.

"We all have our 'blue devils!' " she replied. "Isn't that the English expression?"

We climbed up the slope towards the enclosures, walking together, all of us feeling that some grave event had taken place. She had no desire to be alone with me. I was merely her guest.

"By Jove, what about your horse?" said the Count.

"You will see," said the Countess, "I shall be blamed if I mention it and equally blamed if I don't."

"Why, of course," he said, "everything has to be seen to at the right time."

"I'll go," I said, finding this chilly reception unbearable. "Nobody but me can make him come and settle him down properly. My groom is coming by the Chinon coach. He will rub him down."

"Does the groom come from England, too?" she asked.

"The only decent grooms do," said the Count, who cheered up when he saw his wife was sad. His wife's coldness gave him a chance to be contrary. He overwhelmed her with affectionate attention and I saw how burdensome a husband's fondness can be. Do not think that the moment when their attentions bludgeon noble spirits to death is the time when their wives are lavishing on others an affection which their men consider should by rights come to them. No, they are odious and intolerable the day when that love dies. Mutual understanding, an essential ingredient in attachments of this kind, shows itself then as a means; it is oppressive then and horrible as are all means whose end no longer justifies them.

"My dear Felix," said the Count, taking my hands and clasping them affectionately. "You must forgive Madame de Mortsauf. Women can't help being crotchety. Their weakness excuses them. They are incapable of the even temper which our strength of character gives us. She is devoted to you, I know; but ......"

While the Count was speaking, Madame de Mortsauf moved gradually away from us, and we found ourselves alone. "Felix," he went on in a low voice, gazing after his wife, who was making her way back to the house with her two children, "I do not know what is going on in Madame de Mortsauf's mind, but her character has completely changed over the past six weeks. She, who has always been so gentle, so devoted, has suddenly become quite unbelievably sullen."

Manette told me later that the Countess had fallen into a state of depression which rendered her quite insensible to the Count's plaguing. No longer finding a soft target where he could plant his arrows, the man had grown uneasy, like a child who finds that the wretched insect he has been tormenting has suddenly stopped moving. At the present moment, he needed someone to confide in, in the same way that an executioner needs an assistant.

"Do try," he went on, after a pause, "to question Madame de Mortsauf. A woman always has secrets from her husband; but perhaps she will confide in you and tell you what is troubling her. Even if it cost me half my remaining days and half my fortune, I would sacrifice it all to make her happy. She is so necessary to my life! If in my old age I did not feel the constant presence of that angel by my side, I should be the unhappiest of men! I want to die in peace. So tell her she will not have to endure me for much longer. I am going, Felix, my poor friend, I know it. I am hiding the fatal truth from everyone. Why distress them before I need? Still the old pylorous, my friend! I have at last realised the causes of this illness; hypersensitivity has been the death of me. In fact, all our feelings affect the gastric organs—"

"So that," I said smiling, "people with soft hearts are carried off by their stomachs."

"Do not laugh, Felix, nothing could be more true. Too much sorrow overworks the sympathetic nerve, and this constant stimulation of the sensibility keeps the stomach lining in a perpertual state of irritation. If this state of affairs goes on, it causes disturbances, imperceptible at first, in the digestive system: the secretions dry up, the appetite falls off and the digestion becomes erratic. Soon sharp pains appear; they grow worse and more frequent day by day. Then the disorder comes to a head, as if some slow poison were mingling with the alimentary bolus; the stomach lining thickens, hardening of the pylorus sets in and a tumour forms which is bound to be fatal. Well, I have reached that stage, my dear fellow! The hardening has set in and nothing can stop it. Look at my straw-yellow skin, my dry, bright eyes, my abnormal thinness. I am drying up. What can you expect? I picked up the germ of this disease during my exile. I suffered terribly at the time! My marriage, which could have repaired the ills of emigration, far from soothing my ulcerated spirit, rubbed salt into the wound. What have I found here? Everlasting fears for my children, domestic woes, a fortune to be built up again, the need to economise, which meant imposing a thousand sacrifices on my wife and from which I was the first to suffer. Finally—and I can confide this to nobody but you—-this is what I find hardest of all to bear: Blanche is an angel, but she doesn't understand me: she has no idea of the pain I suffer and she exacerbates it. But there, I forgive her! Look, this is a dreadful thing to say, my dear fellow, but a less virtuous woman would have made me happier by lending herself to certain soothing little activities of which Blanche has no conception; she is as silly as a little girl. Added to this, my servants plague the life out of me; they are all blockheads who look at me as if I were talking Greek when I give them an order in simple ordinary French. By the time our finances were on their feet again, more or less, and I was beginning to have fewer worries, the harm was done. First my appetite deteriorated; then came my serious illness, that Origet treated so incompetently. In short, to-day, I give myself a bare six months to live ..."

I listened, terror-stricken, to what the Count was saying: when I saw the Countess, I had been struck by the dry brightness of her eyes and the straw-yellow colour of her brow. I drew the Count towards the house, pretending to listen to his tale of woe, interspersed with medical dissertations, but I could only think of Henriette. I wanted to have a good look at her. I found her in the drawing-room, where she sat listening to Jacques having a mathematics lesson with the Abbé de Dominis and showing Madeleine a tapestry stitch. In the past, she would have managed, on the day of my arrival, to postpone her occupations in order to devote herself to me; but so deeply sincere was my love that I stifled the grief I felt at this contrast between the present and the past, for I could see the fatal straw-yellow tinge, which on that celestial face resembled the divine glow that the Italian painters gave to the faces of their saints. I felt the icy wind of death sweep through me. Then when the fire of those eyes, denuded of the liquid in which her gaze used to float so limpidly, turned upon me, I shivered. I saw then certain changes brought about by grief which I had not noticed in the open air; lines, so fine when I last saw her that they left the merest imprint on her brow, had now made deep creases there; her bluish temples looked fiery and hollow; her eyes were sunken beneath their softly arching brows, and there were brown rings round them; she was wasting, like a fruit on which the dark bruises are starting to appear, its pith already blanched by the worm buried in its heart. And I—whose sole ambition was to pour happiness in waves on to her heart—had I not thrown gall into the spring that watered her existence and refreshed her courage? I took a seat beside her and said in a voice heavy with repentant tears:

"Are you happy about your health?"

"Yes," she replied, looking deep into my eyes. "There lies my health," she went on, pointing to Jacques and Madeleine.

Emerging victorious from her struggle against nature, Madeleine, at fifteen, was a woman. She had grown; her Indian rose colouring had reappeared in her dusky cheeks; she had lost the unreserve of the child who looks squarely at the world around it, and had begun to drop her eyes. Her movements were becoming infrequent and grave like her mother's; her waist was supple and her bosom was in flower already; already a feminine touch had preened her magnificent black hair, parted into two bands, Spanish fashion, on either side of her brow. She looked like one of those charming mediaeval statuettes, so delicate in outline, so slender of form that the eye is fearful lest they fall to pieces under its caress. But health, that fruit born of so much effort, had brought a peach bloom to her cheeks and to her neck the silky down, which like her mother's, caught the play of light. She would live! God had inscribed it—darling bud from the loveliest of human flowers—on the long lashes that fringed your eyelids, on the curve of your shoulders, which promised to develop richly like your mother's! This dark young girl, with her willowy figure, contrasted sharply with Jacques, a frail young lad of seventeen, whose head had grown in size, whose forehead was disquieteningly high, whose tired feverish eyes harmonised with his deeply sonorous voice: his throat produced too great a volume of sound, just as his eyes gave out too many thoughts. Here were the intelligence, the heart, the soul of Henriette consuming with their rapid flames a body without substance; for Jacques had that milky complexion enlivened by a vivid flush which distinguishes young English girls marked down by disease for an early death; deceiving bloom of health! Obedient to the sign whereby Henriette, after drawing my attention to Madeleine, pointed to Jacques, who was tracing geometrical figures and algebraic equations on a blackboard for the Abbé de

Dominis, I gave a start, appalled to see death lurking beneath the wreathing flowers, and I respected his poor mother's self-deception.

"When I see them looking so well, joy silences my own pain, just as it vanishes when I see them unwell. My friend," she said, her eyes shining with maternal pleasure, "if other loves betray us, the sentiments rewarded here, the duty done and crowned with success, compensate for the defeat suffered elsewhere. Jacques will be, like you, a highly educated man, full of virtuous learning; like you, he will bring honour to his country; he may even help to govern it, aided by you who will have reached a position of such eminence. But I shall do my best to ensure that he stays faithful to his first affections. Madeleine, the dear creature, is already sublime in heart. She is as pure as the topmost Alpine snows; she will have the devotion and gracious understanding of a true woman; and she is proud, she will be worthy of the de Lenoncourts! The mother who was once so torn is happy now, happy with a boundless, undiluted happiness; yes, my life is full, my life is rich. You see? God has made joy bloom at the heart of lawful affections, and stirs gall into those toward which a dangerous bent was drawing me."

"There now!" cried the Abbé gaily. "Monsieur le Vicomte knows as much as I do!" As he completed his mathematical problem, Jacques coughed slightly.

"That will do for to-day, my dear Abbé!" said the Countess, moved, "and certainly no chemistry lesson. Go for a ride now, Jacques," she went on, receiving her son's kiss with the caressing but dignified pleasure of a mother, her eyes turned to me, as though to insult my memories.

"Go along, dearest, and be careful."

"But," I said, as she followed Jacques with a long look, "you have not answered me. Do you feel any pain?"

"Sometimes yes, in the stomach. If I lived in Paris, I should have all the glory of a bout of gastritis, the fashionable complaint."

"Mother has a lot of pain, often," said Madeleine.

"Oh!" said she, "Does my health interest you, then?"

Madeleine, astonished at the profound irony behind these words, looked from one to the other of us. My eyes were counting the pink roses on the cushions of the grey and green sofa.

"This situation is intolerable," I whispered.

"Did I create it?" she asked. "Dear child," she continued aloud, affecting that cruel brightness of manner with which women enhance their revenge, "are you ignorant of modern history? Are not France and England eternal enemies? Madeleine knows that; she knows that a great sea divides them, a cold, a stormy sea."

The vases on the chimney piece had been replaced by candlesticks, no doubt in order to deprive me of the pleasure of filling them with flowers; I caught sight of them later in her room. When my servant arrived, I went out to give him his orders; he had brought me some things which I wanted to put in my room.

"Felix," said the Countess, "be sure you go to the right room. My aunt's old room is now Madeleine's; yours is above the Count's."

Although I was guilty, I had a heart, and these words were daggers thrust coldly into its most vulnerable spots, which she seemed to choose carefully before she dealt each blow.

Mental pain is not absolute, it is relative to the sensitivity of the soul and the Countess had trodden every bitter rung in pain's grim ladder; but for this very reason, the best of women will be all the more cruel, the greater has been her kindness. I looked at her, but she lowered her head. I went to my new room, a pretty one, all white and green. Once there, I burst into tears. She heard me and came in, carrying a bunch of flowers.

"Henriette," I said, "has it come to this? Can you not forgive this most excusable of human failings?"

"Never call me Henriette again," she replied, "she no longer exists, poor woman. But you will always find in Madame de Mortsauf a devoted friend who will listen to you and love you. Felix, we will talk later. If you still have any feeling for me, let me get used to seeing you again; and when words stab at my heart a little less, when I have won back a little courage, then, only then ... Look at the valley," she said, pointing to the Indre, "it hurts me, but I love it still."

"God perish England and all Englishwomen! I shall resign the King's service and die here forgiven."

"No, give that woman your love! Henriette no longer exists; this is not a game, you will soon see that."

She left me, revealing, by the tone of this last remark, how deeply she was hurt. I sprang after her, held her back and said: "Do you not love me any more, then?"

"You have done me more harm than all the others put together. Now, I suffer less, and so I love you less; but only in England does one say: 'Neither never nor forever'; here, we say 'Forever'! Be kind, do not add to my grief; and if you are unhappy, remember that *I* go on living!"

She withdrew her hand, which lay cold and nerveless, though moist, in my own and darted away along the passage, where this truly tragic scene had taken place. During dinner, the Count had an unsuspected ordeal in store for me.

"The Marchioness of Dudley is not in Paris, then?" he asked.

I blushed profusely and said no.

"Is she in Tours?" he persisted.

"She is not divorced; she can go back to England. Her husband would be most happy for her to go back to him," I said in my brightest social manner.

"Has she any children?" asked Madame de Mortsauf, in a strangled voice.

"Two sons," I said.

"Where are they?"

"In England, with their father."

"Come, Felix, be honest—is she as beautiful as they say?"

"How can you ask such a question! Is not the woman one loves always the most beautiful of all?" cried the Countess.

"Always," I said with pride, casting her a glance which she did not sustain.

"You are lucky," went on the Count, "yes, you're a lucky young spark. Ah! in my youth I would have been beside myself at such a conquest ..."

"That will do," said the Countess, drawing his attention to Madeleine with a glance.

"I am not a child," said the Count, who liked recapturing his youth.

When we left the table, the Countess led me out on to the terrace. When we had reached it, she exclaimed:

"Do you mean to say that there are women who can sacrifice

their children to a man? Money, society, that I can imagine—even eternity perhaps! But children! To give up one's children!"

"Yes, and such women would like to have even more to sacrifice; they give everything ..."

The Countess' world turned topsy-turvy, her ideas were thrown into confusion. Struck by this awe-inspiring notion, suspecting that happiness might justify such immolation, and hearing within herself the cries of the rebellious flesh, she stood there dazed in the face of her wasted life. Yes, she had a moment of hideous doubt; then she drew herself up again, tall and noble, holding her head high.

"Love this woman well then, Felix!" she said, with tears in her eyes. "She shall be my happy sister. I forgive her the harm she has done me if she gives you both what you were never to find here and what you can no longer have from me. You were right; I never told you that I loved you, and I never did love you the way people do love in this world. But, if she is no mother, how can she love at all?"

"Dearest saint," I replied, "I should need to be calmer than I am now to explain that you soar victoriously above her. She is an earthly woman, a child of the fallen races, and you are the daughter of heaven, the adored angel. You have all of my heart and she has only my body. She knows it; she is in despair, and she would gladly change places with you even though the most cruel martyrdom were the price of that exchange. But there is nothing to be done. My soul, my thoughts, my unsullied love, my youth and age are yours; she has only my desire and the pleasures of a fleeting passion; my memory is yours in all its compass; she will have nothing but the most profound oblivion."

"Tell me, tell me—oh tell me so then, my dear!" She sat down on a bench and dissolved in tears.

"So virtue, chastity, maternal love are not so many errors, Felix! Oh, pour that balm on my wounds! Repeat the words that will send me up to heaven, where I aimed to go with you in equal flight. Bless me with a look, with a sacred word and I will forgive you the pain I have suffered these two months."

"Henriette, there are mysteries in a man's life which you know nothing of. I met you at an age when sentiment can stifle the desires prompted by our nature; but many scenes, whose memory will warm me at the hour of death, must have shown you that that time was drawing to an end and your eternal triumph has been that you prolonged its unspoken delights. A love without possession is sustained by the very exacerbation of desire; then there comes a moment when we are one continuous ache, we who are so utterly unlike you. We have a potency from which we cannot abdicate, on pain of ceasing to be men. Deprived of the nourishment that should sustain it, the heart feeds on itself and experiences a drained lassitude which is a kind of forerunner of death. Nature cannot be thwarted for long: at the slightest accident it awakens with an energy akin to madness. No, I have not tasted true love, but I have thirsted in the middle of the desert."

"The desert!" she exclaimed bitterly, indicating the valley. "And how well he argues!" she added. "So many fine distinctions! Faithful souls are not so nimble witted."

"Henriette," I said, "let us not quarrel over a few random phrases. No, my soul never wavered, but I was not master of my senses. This woman knows that it is you alone I love. She takes second place in my life, she knows that and she is resigned to it; I have the right to leave her, as one leaves a courtesan ..."

"And what then?"

"She told me she would kill herself," I answered, thinking that this resolution would surprise Henriette. But on hearing it, she let slip one of those disdainful smiles that convey even more than the thoughts they express.

"Dear conscience of mine," I persisted, "If you took into account how hard I resisted and the wiles that planned my downfall, you would have some idea of the fatal ..."

"Fatal indeed!" she said. "I had too much faith in you! I thought you would not lack the virtue practised by the priest and ... native to Monsieur de Mortsauf," she added, with an edge to her voice at the epigram. "It is all over," she added after a pause. "I owe you a great deal, my friend. You have extinguished the flames of bodily passion in me. The hardest part of the road is over; old age is approaching and I am a sick woman. I could never be the radiant enchantress who showers you with favours. Be faithful to Lady Arabelle. Madeleine, whom I brought up so well for you—whose wife will she be? Poor Madeleine! Poor Madeleine!" she repeated in a painful refrain. "If you could have heard her say to me: 'Mother, you are not kind to Felix!' The dear creature!"

She looked at me as we stood beneath the soft rays of the setting sun filtering through the leaves and, seized with a kind of compassion for our ruin, she plunged into our unsullied past, losing herself in thoughts that we both shared. We lived our memories again; our eyes ranged from the valley to the vineyard, from the Clochegourde windows to Frapesle, thronging the dream with our perfume-laden bouquets, with the romantic saga of our desire. It was her last taste of pleasure, savoured with the candour of the Christian. This scene, so meaningful to us, had plunged us into a common melancholy. She believed what I had said and saw herself where I was placing her—in the heavens.

"My dear," she said, "I shall obey God, for his hand is in all this."

It was not until later that I realised the depth of this observation. We went slowly up along the terraces. She took my arm and leaned on it, resigned, her wounds bleeding, but bandaged now.

"Life is like this," she said. "What has Monsieur de Mortsauf done to deserve his fate? All this serves to prove that there exists a better world than this one. Woe to those who complain then, at having taken the virtuous road!"

She began then, to evaluate life so well, to consider it so minutely in all its different aspects, that her cold calculations showed me the consuming disgust she now felt for all things here below. When we reached the verandah steps, she let go my arm and concluded with this observation:

"If God has given us the sense of and taste for happiness, must he not look after innocent souls who have found nothing but affliction here below? This must be so, or else there is no God. And in that case, life would seem to be a bitter mockery."

At these last words, she went abruptly back into the house, and I found her lying on her couch, supine as though struck down by the same voice that felled Saint Paul.

"What is it?" I asked her.

"I no longer know what virtue is," she said, "and I am not conscious of my own!"

We remained there transfixed, listening to the sound of these words echoing in space like a stone hurled into an abyss.

"If I have been wrong in the way I lived my life, it is *she* who is right, *she!*" continued Madame de Mortsauf.

And so her last battle followed her last delight. When the Count came in, she complained of being unwell, she who never complained; I begged her to be more precise, but she refused to explain and retired to bed, leaving me a prey to recurring pangs of remorse. Madeleine went with her mother; she told me, the next day, that the Countess had been seized with fits of vomiting caused, she said, by the violent upsets of the previous day. And so I, who yearned to give my life for her, was killing her.

"My dear Count," I said to Monsieur de Mortsauf, who insisted on our playing backgammon, "I believe the Countess is seriously ill. There is still time to save her; send for Origet, and beg her to follow his advice ..."

"Origet? The man who killed me?" he interrupted. "No, no, I shall consult Carbonneau."

The whole of that week, and particularly the first few days, everything in me turned to pain; incipient atrophy of the heart, wound to the vanity, wound to the spirit. One must have been the centre of things, the focal point of looks and sighs, the principle of life, the hearth from which each draws his light, in order to know the horror of the void. The same things were there, but the spirit that gave them life had died, like a snuffed flame. I understood then, the frightful necessity for lovers not to see each other after love has flown. To be nothing where once one reigned supreme! To meet the chill silence of death where the joyous rays of life once shone!—these comparisons leave one crushed. Soon I reached the point when I longed for that painful ignorance of happiness which had cast a shadow on my early youth. And my despair grew so deep that the Countess was, I think, moved by it. One day, after dinner, as we were all walking by the water's edge, I made a last attempt to win forgiveness. I asked Jacques to take his sister on ahead and, letting the Count walk on alone, I led Madame de Mortsauf towards the little ferry boat.

"Henriette," I said to her, "just one word, I entreat you, or I shall throw myself into the river! I failed you, I know, but am I not dog-like in my sublime devotion? Like him, I come to heel, as full of shame as he; if he does wrong he is punished, but he worships the hand that strikes him. Rain blows upon me, but give me back your heart ..."

"Poor child," she said, "are you not still my son?"

She took my arm and caught up with Jacques and Madeleine in silence, returning to Clochegourde with them by way of the vineyard and leaving me with the Count, who began to discuss his neighbours' politics.

"Let us go indoors," I said, "you are not wearing a hat and the evening dew might give you a chill."

"*You* are always sympathetic about my health, my dear Felix," he replied, misunderstanding my intention. "My wife has never given me any comfort—intentionally, perhaps."

Never before would she have left me alone with her husband. Now I had to make up excuses to go and join her. She was with her children, busy explaining the rules of backgammon to Jacques.

"There you are," said the Count, always jealous of the affection she bore her children, "there are the ones for whom I am always deserted. Husbands, dear Felix, always have the worst of it. The most virtuous of women will yet find a way of satisfying her needs and stealing marital affection."

She continued to caress the children and did not answer him.

"Jacques," said he, "come here". Jacques hung back and protested a little.

"Your father wants you, my son. Go along," said his mother, giving him a little push.

"They love me upon instructions," continued the old man, who was at times quite clear-sighted about his position.

"Monsieur," she replied, stroking Madeleine's hair, which was dressed in the *belle Ferronnière* style, "do not be unfair to women; poor things, life is not always easy for them, and perhaps children are a mother's virtues."

"My dear," replied the Count, taking it into his head to be logical for once, "that means that, without children, women would have no virtue and would leave their husbands on the spot."

The Countess rose abruptly and took Madeleine out on to the veranda.

"There's marriage for you, my dear fellow," said the Count. "Are you trying to suggest, by going out like that, that I am talking nonsense?" he shouted, catching hold of his son's hand and joining his wife outside, his eyes blazing with fury as he glared at her.

"On the contrary, Monsieur, you frightened me," she said in a hollow voice, throwing me a guilt-ridden look. "If virtue does not consist in sacrificing oneself for one's husband and children, what is virtue then?"

"*Sacrificing oneself!*" shouted the Count, bringing each syllable down like a crowbar on his victim's heart. "What are you sacrificing for your children, pray? What are you sacrificing for me? What? Whom? Answer me! Answer me this instant! What exactly is going on here? What are you driving at?"

"Why, Monsieur," she replied, "would it satisfy you to be loved for the love of God, or to know that your wife was only virtuous for virtue's sake?"

"Madame is right," I broke in, in a voice faltering with emotion that vibrated in those two hearts, as I flung into them all my lost hopes and soothed them both by accents of the deepest anguish, whose smothered cry put a stop to their quarrel, just as, when the lion roars, everything falls silent. The greatest privilege that reason has conferred on us is the ability to bring our strength to the aid of those whose happiness is our handiwork and whom we make happy, not calculatingly, nor out of duty, but from a boundless and willing affection.

A tear shone in Henriette's eyes.

"And, my dear Count, if a woman should happen to be enslaved against her will to some sentiment outside those ordained by society, you must admit that the more irresistible that feeling, the more virtuous she would be in stifling it, in *sacrificing* herself for her children and her husband! This theory does not as it happens, apply to me, since I offer, alas, an example to the contrary, nor to you, whom it will never concern."

A hand at the same time moist and burning hot laid itself on mine and quietly pressed it.

"You have a fine nature, Felix," said the Count, putting his hand not ungraciously round his wife's waist and drawing her gently to him.

"Forgive me, my dear," he said. "I am a poor sick man and I daresay I want to be loved more than I deserve."

"Some souls are generosity itself," she replied, resting her head on the Count's shoulder. He took her remark as meant for him and the misunderstanding sent a sort of shudder through the Countess. Her comb dropped out, her hair came loose, she turned pale. Her husband, who was steadying her, let out a kind of roar as he felt her sway. He picked her up as he would have his daughter and carried her to the couch in the drawing-room, where we all stood round her. Henriette held my hand in hers, as if to tell me that we alone knew the secret of this scene, outwardly so simple, yet so appalling in its heartbreak.

"I have wronged you," she whispered, when the Count had left us for a moment to fetch a glass of orange-flower water, "I have wronged you a thousand times over. I tried to make you desperate when I should have greeted you with gratitude. Dear one, you have an adorable kindness which only I can appreciate. Yes, I know, some kindness is inspired by passion. Men have several ways of being kind: they are kind out of disdain, habit, self-interest, lazy-mindedness. But you, my dear, have just shown unadulterated kindness."

"If that is so," I said, "let me tell you that anything fine I may have in me comes from you. Have you forgotten that you made me what I am?"

"Those words are enough for a woman's happiness," she said, just as the Count came back. "I feel better," she added, getting up. "I need some air."

We all went down on to the terrace, which was fragrant with the scent of acacias still in flower. She had taken my right arm and she pressed it against her heart, conveying a world of painful thoughts: but from the look on her face, it was the kind of pain she loved. She wanted no doubt to be alone with me, but her imagination, unversed in feminine wiles, suggested no excuse for sending her husband and children away; and we chatted about unimportant things while she racked her brains for a way to snatch a moment in which to pour out her heart to me at last.

"It is a long time since I went for a drive," she said finally, seeing how fine an evening it was. "Monsieur, do please order the carriage, so that I may take a ride."

She knew that before prayers it would be impossible for us to talk and she was afraid that the Count might want to play back-gammon. She could, of course, join me out on that warm, fragrant terrace when her husband had gone to bed; but she was perhaps afraid to linger beneath these shady trees through which filtered such a voluptuous glow, or to stroll along the balustrade, from where our eyes would span the curve of the Indre through the meadows. Just as a cathedral with its sombre, silent vaulting beckons one to prayer, so do leafy, moonlit trees laden with pungent scents and alive with the muffled sounds of spring, stir the instincts and weaken the will. The countryside, which soothes the passions of the old, excites those of young hearts; well we knew it! Two rings of the bell announced the time for prayers, and the Countess gave a start.

"My dear Henriette, what is the matter?"

"Henriette is no more," she replied. "Do not bring her to life again. She was exacting and capricious. Now you have a placid friend, whose virtue has been strengthened by the words which heaven dictated to you. We will speak of all this later. Let us not be late for prayers. It is my turn to say them to-day."

When the Countess spoke the words asking God's help against life's adversities, her tone of voice was such that others besides myself were struck by it. She seemed to have used her gift of second sight to glimpse the terrible emotion to which a blunder, caused by my forgetfulness of what I had arranged with Arabelle, was to subject her.

"We have time for three rubbers before the horses are ready," said the Count, dragging me into the drawing-room. "You go for a drive with my wife. I shall go to bed."

Like all our games, it was a stormy one. From her room, or from Madeleine's, the Countess could hear her husband's voice.

"You have a strange way of treating guests," she said to the Count, as she came back into the drawing-room. I looked at her in amazement; I could not get used to her sharpness; she would never have attempted to rescue me from the Count in the old days.

She was happy, then, to see me sharing her sufferings and bearing them patiently for love of her.

"I would give my life," I whispered, "to hear you murmur 'poor sweet, poor sweet' again."

She lowered her eyes, as she recalled the time to which I was alluding; her gaze, though veiled, flowed out to me and it expressed the joy of a woman who sees the most fleeting utterances of her heart preferred to the deep delights of some other love. And so, as always, when I was subjected to such insults, I forgave the Count and felt that she understood. The Count was losing and said he felt tired as an excuse for breaking up the game, and we went for a walk round the lawn while waiting for the carriage. As soon as he had left us, pleasure shone so brightly in my face that the Countess questioned me with a curious and astonished glance.

"Henriette *does* exist," I said, "she still loves me! You hurt me with the obvious intention of breaking my heart; I can still be happy!"

"There was only one shred of her left," she said in terror, "and you have just taken it away. Praise be to God who gives me courage to endure my deserved martyrdom. Yes, I love you too much still; I was on the point of weakening, but the Englishwoman lit up the abyss for me."

We got into the carriage and the coachman asked for orders.

"Go along the new drive to the Chinon road and bring us back by the Charlemagne heath and the Saché road."

"What day is it to-day?" I asked, rather too quickly.

"Saturday."

"Do not go that way, Madame; on Saturday evenings the road is full of tradesmen going to Tours; we would run into their carts."

"Do as I say," she insisted, looking at the coachman. We were both too sensitive to the inflexions of the other's voice, to keep the faintest traces of emotion from each other. Henriette had understood everything.

"You were not thinking of the tradesmen when you picked this night," she said, with a tinge of irony. "Lady Dudley is in Tours. Do not lie; she is waiting for you nearby. *What day is it? Tradesmen! Carts!*" she went on. "Did you ever make remarks like that when we went out before?"

"They prove that I forget everything when I am at Cloche-gourde," I said simply.

"She is waiting for you?"

"Yes."

"At what time?"

"Between eleven and midnight."

"Where?"

"On the heath."

"Do not deceive me, is she not waiting under the walnut tree?"

"On the heath."

"We will go there," she said. "I shall see her."

At these words, I felt that my life had finally come to a halt. I formed a sudden resolve to put an end, by a formal marriage with Lady Dudley, to the agonising struggle which threatened to drain my sensibilities and to destroy their sensuous subtleties, so like a fruit-tree's blossom, by so many repeated shocks. My savage silence hurt the Countess. I did not yet know how high-minded she could be.

"Do not be angry with me," she said, in her golden voice; "this, dearest, is my punishment. You will never be so loved as you are here," she added, putting her hand to her heart. "Have I not confessed as much? The Marchioness of Dudley has saved me. Let her love be soiled, I do not envy it. Mine is the glorious love of angels! I have covered immense distances since you came back. I have come to a certain conclusion about life. Let the soul soar and you rend it; the higher you go, the less fellow-feeling you will meet; instead of suffering in the valley, you suffer in the open sky, like the eagle that hovers overhead, carrying in its heart an arrow that some vulgar shepherd has let fly. I see now that earth and sky are incompatible. Yes, for those who can live in the heavenly heights, God alone is possible. Our soul must then be loosed from all earthly things. We must love our friends as we love our children, for their sakes and not for our own. The self is the cause of sorrows and misfortunes. My heart will reach greater heights than does the eagle; there I will find a love that will not deceive me. As for earthly life, it debases us and lets the selfish senses hold sway over the spirituality of the angel who is in us. The pleasures that passion gives are horribly tempestuous: their price is the disquiet that breaks the mainsprings of the soul. I have come very close to the sea where such storms rage and I have had too close a view of them. They have often cast their clouds over me and their waves have not always broken before they reached my feet; I have felt their rough embrace send its chill through my heart. I must go up on to the heights. I should die by that vast expanse of sea. I see in you, as in all those who have hurt me, the keeper of my virtue. My life has been shot with anguish, anguish in keeping, fortunately, with my strength, and so I have remained untainted by bad passions, free of beguiling rest and always ready for God. Our relationship was the senseless bid, the wild striving of two sincere children to satisfy their hearts, their fellow men and God ... How mad we were, Felix!"

She paused. "What name does this woman call you by, Felix?"

"Amédée," I replied. "Felix is a man apart. He will never belong to anyone but you."

"Henriette is a long time a-dying," she said, with a gentle smile. "But," she went on, "she will perish at the first effort of the humble Christian, the proud mother, the woman whose virtue wavered yesterday but is firm again to-day. How can I explain? Why, yes, my life has followed the same pattern, in large issues as in small. The heart where I ought to have planted the first roots of tenderness, my mother's, closed against me, despite my persistent search for one small corner there into which I might slip. A mere girl, coming after three dead boys, I strove in vain to fill their place in my parents' affection; I could not heal the wound done to the family pride. When, after this sombre childhood, I made the acquaintance of my adorable aunt, death immediately took her away. Monsieur de Mortsauf, to whom I pledged myself, struck at me constantly, unremittingly, unknowingly, poor man! His love has the same naïve selfishness our children have for us. He does not share the secret of the unhappiness he causes me, for he is always forgiven! My children, those dear children who are linked to my flesh by all their illnesses, to my soul by all their good qualities and to my nature by their innocent joys, were they not given me to show how much strength and patience there is in a mother's breast? Oh, my children are indeed my virtues! You know yourself how I am scourged by them, for them, in spite of them. For me, becoming a mother meant purchasing the right to suffer all the time. When Hagar cried out in the desert, an angel made a fresh spring well forth for this too dearly beloved slave; but for me, when the clear stream to which (do you remember?) you wished to guide my steps, came to flow about Clochegourde, it offered me none but bitter waters. Oh, you caused me untold suffering! God will no doubt forgive him who came to know affection only through pain. But if the sharpest sorrows I have felt were caused by you, it may be that I deserved them. God is not unjust. Ah, yes, Felix, a kiss furtively planted on a brow implies a crime perhaps! Perhaps one must atone, harshly, for the steps one took ahead of one's husband and children, as one wandered away, in the evening, in order to be alone with thoughts and memories which did not belong to them—the soul wedded to another, as one walked alone! When one's innermost being draws itself together and makes itself small enough to occupy the space allotted to embraces, perhaps that is the worst of crimes! When a woman stoops to receive her husband's kiss upon her hair, so as to compose her brow into a semblance of serenity, that is a crime! It is a crime to forge oneself a future based on someone's death, a crime to imagine the future as a motherhood without anxieties, with handsome children playing in the evening with a father adored by all his family, beneath the tender gaze of a happy wife. Yes, I have sinned, I have sinned greatly! I acquired a taste for the penances imposed by the Church, penances that in no way atoned for the faults which the priest doubtless viewed too indulgently. God set the punishment at the very heart of all those errors, by making him for whom they were committed the instrument of His avenging wrath. When I gave you my hair, was I not promising myself? Why did I love wearing a white dress? It made me feel more like your lily. Did you not catch your first glimpse of me, here, dressed in white? Alas, I loved my children that much less, for all strong affection is borrowed from that due by rights to others. You see, Felix, how all suffering has its own significance? Strike me, strike me harder than did my husband or my children! This woman is an instrument of God's wrath; I shall approach her without hatred, I shall smile at her: on pain of failing as a Christian, wife and mother, I must love her. If, as you say, I have helped to preserve your heart from all associations that would have blighted it, then this Englishwoman cannot hate me. A woman must love the mother of the one she loves, and I am your mother. What did I want from your heart? Simply the place left unfilled by Madame de Vandenesse. Oh, yes! You have always complained of my coldness! I am indeed no more than your mother. Forgive me, then, for the unconsciously harsh things I said on your arrival; a mother should rejoice to see her son so well beloved." She laid her head on my breast, and repeated "Forgive me! Forgive me!" I had never heard her speak in those tones before. This was not her young girl's voice, with its joyous ring, nor her woman's voice with its authoritative finality, nor the sighing of the sorrowful mother; it was a heart-rending voice, a new voice for a new pain.

"And you, Felix," she went on in a more lively tone, "are the friend who can do no wrong. You have lost no ground in my heart; do not reproach yourself; you need feel no remorse. Was it not the height of selfishness to ask you to sacrifice to an impossible future the most intense delights, since, to savour them, a woman has left her children, given up her rank and renounced eternity? How many times have I not thought you superior to me! You were great and noble; I was small and sinful! There, now I have said it; I can be nothing to you but a gleam of light above your head, glittering and cold, but unchangeable. But Felix, do not leave me to love my chosen brother all alone! Cherish me! A sister's love has no uneasy aftermath, no difficult moments. You will not need to lie to the indulgent soul who will thrive on your good fortune, will never fail to grieve at your distress, to be cheered by your joys, to love the women who make you happy and to be indignant against those who betray you. I never had a brother I could love like this. Be generous enough to shed all vanity and to seal our attachment to each other, hitherto so storm-tossed and uncertain, by this gentle and blest affection. I can still live in this way. I will make the first move by clasping Lady Dudley's hand."

She did not weep as she spoke those words, so full of bitter wisdom, which, by tearing off the last veil that hid her suffering spirit, showed me with how many links she had bound herself to me and how many strong chains I had sawn through. So distraught were we that we did not notice it was pouring with rain.

"Would not your ladyship care to shelter here a moment?" asked the coachman, indicating the main inn in Ballan.

She consented with a nod and we stood for about half an hour beneath the porch, to the great astonishment of the serving people at the inn, who were wondering what Madame de Mortsauf was doing on the roads at eleven o'clock at night. Was she going to Tours? Or coming back perhaps? When the storm was over and rain dwindled into what they call in Tours a *brouée*, which allowed the moon to shine through the upper mists as they swiftly scattered in the wind, the coachman emerged and to my great joy, turned the carriage back in the direction we had come.

"Follow my orders," called the Countess gently. And so we took the road through the Charlemagne heath, where it began to rain again. Halfway across the heath, I heard the barking of Arabelle's favourite dog; a horse sprang suddenly from behind an oak; cleared the path at one leap; jumped the ditch dug by the owners to separate their respective areas of ground, in those stretches where it was thought that the land was capable of cultivation; and Lady Dudley rode on to the heath to see the carriage go by.

"What joy to wait for one's child like this, when to do so is no crime!" said Henriette.

The barking of the dog had told Lady Dudley that I was in the carriage; no doubt she thought I had come to fetch her thus because of the bad weather: when we reached the spot where the Marchioness stood, she flew along the edge of the path with that equestrian skill so typical of her, and at which Henriette marvelled as at some prodigy. Out of winsomeness, Arabelle only ever said the last syllable of my name, pronounced in the English way, a form of address that on her lips held a fairy-like charm. She thought that nobody but me would hear her when she cried:

"My Dee!"

"Here he is, Madame," said the Countess, gazing in the clear light of a moonbeam at this strange creature, with her impatient face weirdly framed by the long locks of her wet, uncurling hair.

You know how speedily two women look each other over. The Englishwoman recognised her rival and was gloriously English. She swept us with a glance full of her English disdain and vanished like an arrow into the heather.

"Back to Clochegourde, quickly!" cried the Countess, for whom this scathing glance had been a knifethrust in her heart.

The coachman turned back and took the Chinon road, which was better than the Saché one. As the carriage drove alongside the heath again, we heard the mad hoofbeats of Arabelle's horse and her dog running beside it. All three were skirting the edge of the woods on the other side of the heath.

"She has gone; you have lost her forever," said Henriette.

"Let her go, then," said I, "I'll not pine for her!"

"Oh, wretched women that we are!" cried the Countess, in compassionate horror. "But where is she going?"

"To La Grenadière, a little house near Saint-Cyr," I said.

"Away she goes, alone," said Henriette, in a tone which proved to me that women are solidly with their sex in matters of love and will always stand by one another.

Just as we were entering the Clochegourde avenue, Arabelle's dog ran out in front of the carriage, yapping joyfully.

"She has got here before us!" cried the Countess. She paused and went on: "I have never seen a more beautiful woman. What hands, and what a figure! Her skin puts the lily to shame, and her eyes are bright as diamonds! But she is too good a horsewoman, she must love to exercise her strength. I think she must be violent and energetic; and she seems to set herself too boldly about convention; a woman who knows no laws comes very near to heeding naught but her own whims. Those who so love to shine and make a stir have not the gift of constancy. Love, to my mind, requires more serenity. I see it as a vast lake whose depths cannot be plumbed; where the storms can be violent, though rare and held in by insuperable barriers; where two beings live on a flower decked island, far from the world, whose luxury and flamboyance would offend them. But love must take the imprint of individual natures, so perhaps I am wrong. If the laws of nature bend to the patterns laid down by climate, why should it not be so with feelings in different individuals? No doubt, human feelings, which in essence obey the general law, differ only in the way they are expressed. Each loves in his own fashion. Lady Dudley is the strong woman who conquers distance and acts with the strength of a man; who would free her lover from captivity, kill gaolers, guards, and executioners: whereas certain creatures can only love with all their heart; in danger, they kneel down, pray and die. Which of these two women pleases you the most? That is the whole point. Yes, Lady Dudley loves you; she has sacrificed so much for you! Perhaps she is the one who will go on loving you, when you have fallen out of love with her!"

"May I, dear angel, ask you what you once asked me? How do you know these things?"

"Every sorrow has its lesson, and I have suffered in so many ways that my knowledge is vast."

My servant had heard her giving her instructions to the coachman and thought we would come back by way of the terraces. He held my horse ready saddled in the avenue; Arabelle's dog had scented the horse, and his mistress, led by understandable curiosity, had followed him through the woods, where no doubt she was now hiding.

"Go and make your peace," said Henriette, smiling, and without a sign of melancholy. "Tell her how wrong she is about my motives; I wanted to show her the full worth of the treasure she has won. My heart holds none but friendly feelings for her; there is certainly no hatred or contempt in it. Tell her that I am her sister, not her rival."

"I shall not go!" I cried.

"Has it ever struck you," she said, with the martyr's flashing pride, "that to be over careful not to hurt someone's feelings can sometimes be downright insulting? Now, go!"

And so I ran to Lady Dudley to find out what mood she was in.

"If only she would fly into a rage and leave me!" I thought. "I would go straight back to Clochegourde then!"

The dog led me to an oak tree, and the Marchioness leapt out and cried, "Away! Away!"

There was nothing I could do but follow her to Saint-Cyr, where we arrived at midnight.

"That lady is in perfect health," said Arabelle, as she dismounted.

Only those who have known her can imagine the wealth of sarcasm in this remark, thrown out drily as if to say:

"Had it been I, I should be dead!"

"I forbid you to venture a single one of your two-edged taunts at Madame de Mortsauf," I retorted.

"Am I displeasing Your Grace by commenting on the perfect health enjoyed by one dear to your precious heart? They say that Frenchwomen hate even their lover's dog. In England, we love everything our sovereign lords love, we hate all that they hate, because we live as one with our lords and masters. Allow me then to love this lady as much as you love her yourself. But, dear child," she said, putting her arms, damp with rain, around me, "if you were to betray me, I would not be on my feet; nor lying on my back; nor in a carriage flanked by lackeys nor taking an airing on Charlemagne's heath, nor on any other heath in any other country in the world, nor in my bed, nor in my father's house! I should no longer be alive. I was born in Lancashire, where women die for love. To have known you and then to let you go! I would not give you up to any power on earth—not even death, for I would go with you!"

She led me to her room, where comfort had already spread out its delights.

"Love her, my dear," I said heatedly, "she loves you, not ironically but sincerely."

"Sincerely, little one?" she said, unlacing her riding habit.

With a lover's vanity, I wanted to show this conceited creature the sublimity of Henriette's nature. While her maid, who knew not a word of French, was doing her hair, I tried to describe Madame de Mortsauf by sketching her life: I repeated to her the lofty thoughts that had inspired her in a situation where all other women are spiteful and small-minded. Although Arabelle seemed to be paying not the slightest attention, not one of my words was lost to her.

"I am delighted," she said, when we were alone, "to know that you enjoy this kind of Christian conversation. In one of my estates there is a vicar who composes sermons better than anyone I know. Even our farm labourers understand them, so well does he suit his style to his listeners. I will write to my father to-morrow and ask him to send the good man over by channel boat; you can meet him in Paris; once you have heard him, you will not want to listen to anybody else—all the more so since he, too, enjoys perfect health. His moralising will cause you no upsetting tears; it flows gently along like a clear spring and makes you feel deliciously sleepy. If you like you can satisfy your passion for sermons every evening as you digest your dinner. English moralising, dear child, is as superior to that of Touraine as is English cutlery, silver and horseflesh to your knives and your animals. Promise me you will do me the honour of listening to my vicar! I am only a woman, my love, I can love you, I can die for you if you wish; but I did not go to Eton or Oxford or Edinburgh; I am neither a professor nor a clergyman; so I should not know how to serve you a moral lesson. I am quite unfitted to do so. I should be unspeakably bad at it if I were to try. I am not criticising your tastes; were they twice as depraved, I would do my best to fit in with them, for I want you to find, with me, everything that you enjoy: pleasures of love, pleasures of the table, pleasures of religion, good claret and Christian virtues. Would you like me to wear a hair-shirt this evening? She is very fortunate, this woman, to be able to provide you with morals! In what university do Frenchwomen graduate? Poor me! I can only give myself; I am only your slave ..."

"Then why did you run away when I wanted you both to meet?"

"Are you mad, my Dee? I would go from Paris to Rome disguised as a lackey, I would do the most outrageous things for you; but how can I talk in the street to a woman to whom I have not been introduced and who was about to embark on a three-point sermon? I will speak to a farm labourer, I will ask a workman to share his bread with me if I am hungry, I'll give him a guinea or two and all will be quite in order: but stop a carriage, as do the gentlemen of the highway in England—that is not in my code. Is loving all you know, my poor boy? Don't you know how to behave? Besides, I am not entirely like you yet, my angel! I do not care for sermons. However, in order to please you, I am capable of the greatest efforts. So quiet now! I'll do my best for you! I'll try to turn preacher. Jeremiah will be a buffoon beside me. I shall venture no more caresses unless larded with verses from the Bible."

She made use of her power, nay, abused it, as soon as she saw in my eyes that ardent expression which came into them as soon as her witchery began. She carried all before her, and I complaisantly belittled the refinements of Catholic thought, compared with the grandeur of a woman who surrenders to perdition, who renounces the future and makes her entire virtue out of love.

"Does she love herself more than she loves you, then?" she said. "She puts something other than yourself before you? How is it possible to attach more importance to what is one's own than to what is one's beloved's? No woman, however great a moralist, can be equal to a man. Walk over us, kill us, never encumber your existence with us. It is for us to die, for you to live proud and great. For us, the dagger thrust: for you, love and forgiveness. Does the sun bother about the flies that hover in its rays and draw life from it? They stay there as long as they can, and when the sun goes down, they die ..."

"Or fly away," I cut in.

"Or fly away," she said, with an indifference which would have deflated the man most determined to use the singular power with which she invested him.

"Do you think it befits a woman to make a man swallow the buttered bread of virtue and to persuade him that religion is incompatible with love? Am I an impious heathen, then? One gives oneself or one withholds oneself, but to withhold oneself and sermonise too, that is a double penalty, and foreign to any country's laws. Here, you will have none but the excellent sandwiches prepared by the hand of your servant Arabelle, whose entire moral code will be to devise caresses never before enjoyed by any man—and in that the angels will inspire me!"

I know of nothing more corrosive than an Englishwoman's wit: she brings to it the grave eloquence and the air of pompous conviction beneath which the English hide the high idiocies of their prejudice-ridden life. French wit is like lace; with it women enhance the joys they give and the quarrels they provoke; it is a spiritual ornament, as graceful as their dress. But English wit is an acid which so corrodes the persons on which it falls that it turns them into cleanly polished skeletons. The tongue of a witty Englishwoman is like a tiger's, who tears the flesh to the bone with a playful stroke of its paw. All-powerful weapon of the devilish imp who says, with a sneer: "What a fuss about nothing!"—mockery leaves a mortal poison in the wounds which it opens for fun. During that night, Arabelle was anxious to show her power, just as a sultan, to prove his skill, amuses himself by beheading innocent victims.

"My angel," she said to me, when she had plunged me into that dozing state where one forgets everything save happiness, "I have been moralising to myself too: I have been wondering if I was not committing a crime by loving you, if I was not transgressing divine laws; and I have come to the conclusion that nothing could be more religious or more natural. Why should God make some of his creatures more beautiful than others, if not to show us that we should adore them? The crime would be *not* to love you; are you not an angel? This woman insults you by rating you with other men: the rules of morality do not apply to you; God has placed you above all that. Does not loving you bring me a little nearer to you? Can He blame a poor woman for having an appetite for divine things? Your vast, luminous heart is so like the sky that I am taken in, like moths that burn their wings on festive candles! Will they be punished for their error? Besides, is it an error? Is it not a lofty adoration of the light? They die of an excess of worship, if one can call it dying to fall upon the neck of the man one loves. I have the weakness to love you; this woman has the strength to sit in her Catholic chapel. Don't scowl like that. Do you think I resent her? No, little one! I adore her moral code; it prompted her to let you remain free and allowed me to win you and keep you for always—you will always be mine, will you not?"

"Yes."

"For always?"

"Yes."

"Am I reprieved then, Sultan? I alone guessed your full worth! She knows how to cultivate land, you say? I'll leave that knowledge to farmers; I would rather cultivate your heart."

I am trying to recall this intoxicating chatter, in order to give you a clear picture of this woman, to bear out what I told you about her and to give you an insight into the reasons for what was to happen later. But how can I describe what accompanied those sweet nothings? They were comparable to the most extravagant fancies in our dreams; now creations like my bouquets, grace fused with strength, tenderness and its languid softness, offset by volcanic eruptions of passion; now the most expert musical modulations applied to the orchestra of sensuous bliss; then, playful sport like that of serpents intertwined; in a word, the most caressing turns of speech spiced with the gayest notions, all that the mind can add by way of poetry to the senses' delight. She wanted to annihilate with the lightning of her impetuous love the mark left on my heart by Henriette's chaste and withdrawn spirit. Lady Dudley had observed the Countess as well as she herself had been observed. Each had accurately summed up the other. The strength of the attack launched by Arabelle showed me the extent of her fear and the secret admiration she felt for her rival. In the morning, I found her in tears. She had not slept.

"What is wrong?" I asked her.

"I am afraid that my great love for you will do me harm," she said. "I have given everything. This woman is cleverer than I. She has something in her that you find desirable. If you prefer her, forget me: I will not plague you with my grief or my regrets or my heartache. I will go and die far, far away, like a plant without its lifegiving sunshine."

She succeeded in tearing protestations of love out of me, to her great joy. What can one say, after all, to a woman who weeps the morning after? An unfeeling word seems to me monstrous then. If we did not resist her the night before, we are obliged to lie next day; the male code makes it our duty to lie, for sweet gallantry's sake.

"Well, I shall be generous," she said, drying her tears. "Go back to her; I do not want to owe you to the strength of my love, but to your own free will. If you come back to me, I shall believe that you love me as much as I love you, a thing I had never imagined possible."

She managed to persuade me to return to Clochegourde. The falseness of the position in which I was about to place myself did not strike me, gorged as I was with happiness. If I refused to go back to Clochegourde I should be acknowledging Lady Dudley's victory over Henriette. Arabelle would then take me with her to Paris. But would not going there be an insult to Madame de Mortsauf? And would that not throw me all the more surely back to Arabelle? Has any woman ever forgiven such crimes against love? Unless she is an angel descended from heaven and not the rarified spirit that soars thither, a woman in love would see her lover draw his last painful breath sooner than see him happy with another woman: the more she loves him, the more will she be hurt. And so, viewed in these two aspects, my position, the moment I left Clochegourde for La Grenadière, was as fatal to my chosen love as it was profitable to my casual amours. The Marchioness had calculated everything with studied thoroughness. She confessed to me later that, had Madame de Mortsauf not come to meet her on the heath, she had planned to compromise me by lurking round about Clochegourde.

When I approached the Countess, who looked pale and exhausted, like someone who has spent a long and sleepless night, something arose in me, something which is not tact, but a sort of hypersensitivity native to all hearts that are still young and generous, a flair which makes them sense the implications of certain deeds —deeds without significance in the eyes of the crowd, criminal in the judgement of higher minds. And at once, like a child who finds to his anguished dismay, that whilst picking flowers and playing, he has gone down into a chasm out of which he cannot hope to climb again; can only see safe ground an unscaleable distance away and feels utterly alone in the darkness with wild beasts howling round him, I realised that a whole world separated me from her. A great cry rang out in our hearts, a kind of echo of that lugubrious *consummatum est!* they call in Church on Good Friday at the hour of our Saviour's passing—terrible scene, chilling to those young spirits for whom religion is a first love. All Henriette's illusions died at one stroke; her heart had suffered its Passion. She, so far above pleasure, which had never dared entwine her in its numbing folds—did she sense now, the heady bliss of happy love, that she should so avert her eyes?—for she withdrew from me the light that had shone upon my life for six whole years. Did she, then, know that the source of the beams that stream out of our eyes is in our souls; that they are the road by which kindred spirits enter into each other, meet and fuse, part again and play like two women who trust each other and tell each other their heart's secrets? I was made bitterly aware of the error of bringing under this roof, so innocent of love's caresses, a countenance where pleasure's wings had scattered their bright dust.

If, the previous day, I had let Lady Dudley go her way alone; if I had come straight back to Clochegourde, where Henriette might even have been waiting for me; perhaps—yes, perhaps Madame de Mortsauf would not have offered so cruelly to be a sister to me. Now, to all the kind attentions she showed me, she lent a ceremonious exaggeration; she threw herself violently into her part, so as to ensure that she would not step out of it again. During luncheon, she was extraordinarily attentive, humiliatingly attentive, for she looked after me like some invalid whom she felt sorry for.

"You were out walking very early," said the Count. "You must have a splendid appetite—you haven't had your stomach ruined like me!"

This remark, which drew from the Countess no smile of sisterly conspiracy, was the final, crushing proof of the absurdity of my position. It was impossible to be at Clochegourde by day and at Saint-Cyr by night. Arabelle had counted on my delicacy and the generosity of Madame de Mortsauf. During the whole of that long day, I was made to feel how difficult it is to become friends with a woman one has long desired. The transition, so simple when the years have paved the way, is an illness in youth. I was ashamed; I cursed the treacherous senses. I would have liked Madame de Mortsauf to demand my blood. I could not tear her rival to pieces, for she avoided all mention of her, and had she spoken ill of Arabelle, I would have despised Henriette, she so magnificent, noble to the innermost core of her being. After five years of delightful intimacy, we could think of nothing to say; our words did not tally with our thoughts; we were each concealing our gnawing unhappiness—we for whom unhappiness had always been a faithful go-between. Henriette affected a cheerful air, both for her own sake and for mine; but she was sad. Although claiming at every turn to be my sister, and in spite of being a woman, she could find no way of keeping up the conversation, and we sat for the most part in a strained silence. She added to my inward torment by feigning the belief that she was Lady Dudley's only victim.

"My suffering is greater than yours," I said, at a moment when the sister had let slip a wholly feminine taunt.

"I beg your pardon?" said she, in the haughty tone of voice women adopt when one attempts to cap their feelings.

"Why, all the blame is mine!"

For a moment the Countess treated me with an air of cold indifference that quite broke my heart. I made up my mind to leave. That evening, out on the terrace, I said my farewells to the assembled family. They all followed me on to the lawn where my horse was pawing the ground and stood at a safe distance. As I seized the reins, she came up to me.

"Let us go along the avenue, on foot, just we two," she said. I gave her my arm and we walked out through the courtyards, slowly, as though savouring the unison of our movements, until we came to a clump of trees shadowing a corner of the outer wall.

"Goodbye, my friend," she said, laying her head on my breast and putting her arms around my neck. "Goodbye, we shall not meet again! God has given me the sorry power of seeing into the future. Do you not remember the terror that seized me once, when you came back so handsome, so young: how I seemed to see you turn your back on me, as you are doing now that you are leaving Clochegourde to go to La Grenadière? Well, once again, last night, I was able to cast a glance over our destinies. My dear, we are talking now for the last time. I shall scarce be able to say more than a few words, for it will no longer be the whole of me that speaks to you. Death has already struck a blow at part of me. You will have taken my children's mother from them. Take her place! You can! Jacques and Madeleine love you as dearly as if you had always made them suffer."

"Death!" I cried in terror, looking at her and seeing the dry brightness of her eyes, which one cannot convey to those who have never seen a loved one in the throes of that terrible malady, save by comparing them to two globes of burnished silver.

"Death! Henriette, I order you to live. You have asked me for promises in the past; well, now I insist on one from you. Swear to me that you will consult Origet and do all he says ..."

"Do you want to oppose the clemency of God?" she broke in, with the cry of despair outraged at being misunderstood.

"Do you not love me enough, then, to obey me blindly in all things, like that wretched Lady Dudley? ..."

"Yes, darling, anything you wish," she said, spurred on by a jealousy which in an instant made her span the distance she had hitherto taken such care to keep between us.

"I shall stay here," I said to her, kissing her eyes. Alarmed by her lack of resistance, she slipped out of my arms, and went to lean against a tree; then she walked quickly back towards the house, without turning round. I followed her; she was weeping and muttering a prayer. When we reached the lawn, I took her hand and kissed it respectfully. This unexpected submissiveness touched her.

"I am still yours!" I said, "for I love you as your aunt loved you."

She gave a start and gripped my hand.

"One look!" I begged, "look at me once more the way we used to look at one another. The woman who gives herself body and soul," I cried, my soul lit to its depths by the look she threw me, "gives me less life and spirit than I have just received. Henriette, you are the most beloved, the only love!"

"I will live!" she told me, "but you must get well too."

That one look had effaced the impression of Arabelle's sarcasm. So there was I, plaything of the two irreconcilable passions I have described, each of which held me in turn under its sway. I loved an angel and a demon; two women, equally beautiful, one of them adorned with all the virtues which hatred of our imperfections induces us to hurt, the other with all the vices which our selfishness prompts us to deify. As I walked back along the avenue, turning every few moments to look at Madame de Mortsauf as she leaned against a tree, surrounded by her children waving their handkerchiefs, I felt a surge of pride at knowing myself to be the arbiter of two such handsome destinies; at being the glory, in such different ways, of two such superior women and at having inspired such intense passions that in each case death would follow if I failed them. This passing fatuousness has been doubly punished, believe me! Some fiend in me was telling me to stay with Arabelle and wait until a fit of despair, or the Count's death, made Henriette mine, for Henriette loved me still: her harshness, her tears, her remorse, her Christian resignation were eloquent signs of a sentiment which could no more shut itself out of her heart than out of mine. As I rode at a walking pace along that lovely avenue, thinking these thoughts, I was no longer twenty-five years old but fifty. Is it not a young man, even more than a woman, who steps overnight from thirty years to sixty? Although I dismissed these black thoughts with a breath, I must confess that they obsessed me. Perhaps their underlying principle was to be found in the Tuileries, beneath the panelled ceiling of the royal study: who could resist the deflowering mind of Louis XVIII, who used to say that men only know true passion in their riper middle years, since passion is only fine and furious when impotence plays a part in it, and when one meets each pleasure like a gambler placing his last bet? At the end of the avenue, I turned and glanced back, to find that Henriette was still there, alone! I went back to say a last farewell, bathed with atoning tears whose cause was hidden from her. Genuine tears, devoted unknowingly to those fair hours of love forever lost, to those virgin emotions, those flowers of life that never bud again: for later on, man no longer gives, he receives; he loves himself in his mistress: while in youth he loves his mistress in himself. Later, we inject our tastes, our vices too, perhaps, into the woman we love; whereas at the beginning of life the one we love gives us her virtues and her tender conscience. She beckons us to the good life with a smile and teaches us devotion by her example. Woe to the man who never had his Henriette! Woe to him who has not known some Lady Dudley! If he marries, the one will not keep his wife, the other will perhaps be deserted by his mistress; but happy the man who can find both in one; happy Natalie, the man whom you love!

Back in Paris, Arabelle and I became more intimate than in the past. Soon we came to abandon by degrees the conventions I had imposed upon myself, the strict observance of which often leads society to forgive the falseness of the position in which Lady Dudley had placed herself. Society, so fond of looking beyond outward appearances, will acknowledge them as genuine once it has probed the secret underlying them. Lovers forced to live in high society will always be wrong to overturn the barriers decreed by the world of fashionable drawing-rooms; wrong not to obey scrupulously all conventions imposed by custom; not so much for

others' sake as for their own. The distances to overcome, the outward respectability to be preserved, the parts to be played, the
secrets to be hidden, all this strategy of happy love fills one's life,
renews desire and protects the heart against the apathy of habit.
But, essentially wasteful, first passions, like young men, cut their
forests bare instead of trimming them. Arabelle did not believe in
these bourgeois notions, she had accepted them to please me. Like
an executioner branding his victim in advance in order to lay claim
to him, she wanted to compromise me in the eyes of all Paris and
so make me her *sposo*. What is more, she used all her wiles to have
me live in her house, for she was not content with her elegant
scandal, which, for want of proof, gave rise to little more than
whisperings behind the fan. Seeing her so glad to commit an indiscretion which so frankly underlined her position, how could I fail
to believe she loved me? Once submerged in the soft delights of an
illicit marriage, despair swept over me, for I saw myself trapped
into a way of life that ran counter to accepted opinion and the
recommendations of Henriette. And so I lived with that kind of
fury which seizes a consumptive when, sensing that his end is near,
he refuses to let a doctor sound his chest. There was a corner of
my heart into which I could not withdraw without pain; an
avenging spirit would incessantly confront me with thoughts I
dared not entertain. My letters to Henriette described this spiritual
illness and caused her infinite distress. At the price of so many lost
treasures, she would at least have wished me to be happy, she said
in one letter I received from her. And I was not happy! Dear
Natalie, happiness is absolute, it does not admit comparisons. My
first ardour past, I was bound to compare these two women; it was
a contrast I had not yet had a chance to study. Indeed, all great
passions weigh so heavily upon our character that they suppress, at
first, all its rough edges and cover the tracks of the habits that
constitute our qualities or our defects; but later, when two lovers
have grown used to each other, the features of the spiritual physi-
ognomy reappear; both pass mutual judgement and there often
arise in the course of this reaction of character upon passion, antipathies that pave the way for that disunion which superficial people
pounce on in order to accuse the human heart of instability. And
so this later period set in. Less blinded by her seductiveness, and

taking, as it were, an inventory of my pleasure, I embarked, perhaps unwittingly, on a scrutiny of Lady Dudley which was not to her advantage.

I found her, first of all, wanting in that wit that distinguishes the Frenchwoman from all others and makes her the most delightful of all to love—according to the reports of those whom circumstances have put in the way of experiencing how women of other countries behave when they are in love. When a Frenchwoman is in love, she undergoes a complete change; her much vaunted stylishness of dress she uses to adorn her love, her dangerous vanity she nobly sacrifices and devotes all her energies to the ideal of loving as deeply as she can. She espouses the interests, the enmities, the friendships of her lover; she acquires in a day the experienced shrewdness of the business man; she studies law, she understands the intricacies of finance, she charms open the coffers of a banker; extravagant and irresponsible, she will not put a foot wrong nor waste a louis; she becomes mother, housekeeper, and doctor all rolled into one and brings to all these transformations a happy grace which reveals in every smallest detail an unbounded love; she combines the special qualities that commend women of every country and blends these diverse elements into a whole by means of wit, that French yeast that enlivens, sanctions, justifies and gives variety to everything and destroys the monotony of a sentiment based on the first person singular of a single verb.

The Frenchwoman loves you all the time, tirelessly and unremittingly, in public and in private; in public she speaks in tones which have meaning for one ear alone; she speaks by her very silence, and can look at you when her eyes are looking down; if circumstances forbid both word and glance, she will use the sand under her foot and trace a thought in it: alone, she expresses her passion even while she sleeps; in a word, she moulds the whole world to her love.

The Englishwoman, on the other hand, moulds her love to the world. Accustomed by education to preserve that icy manner, that self-satisfied British bearing I have already described, she opens and shuts her heart with the ease of an English machine. She has an impenetrable mask which she takes on and off with phlegmatic ease. Passionate as an Italian woman when no eye can see her, she

becomes coldly dignified when the guests arrive. The most passionately loved man will doubt his power then, when he sees the total
immobility of face, the calm voice and perfect composure which
distinguishes an Englishwoman, once out of the boudoir. At that
moment, hypocrisy goes as far as indifference; the Englishwoman
has forgotten everything. Indeed, the woman who can throw off
her love like an article of clothing invites the supposition that she
can also change it for another. What stormy waves rise in the heart
when the tide of feeling is stirred by the wounded pride of seeing
a woman taking up, laying aside and returning to love like a piece
of embroidery! Such women are far too much mistress of themselves
to belong to us completely; they pay too much respect to the world
for our dominion to be complete. Where the Frenchwoman will
comfort the patient with a glance, betray her annoyance with visitors by a few elegant witticisms, the silence of the Englishwoman
is absolute; it irritates the feelings and exasperates the mind. These
women lord it so incessantly at every opportunity that for most of
them the omnipotence of fashion must dictate their pleasures too.
Whoever exaggerates prudery must also exaggerate love. Englishwomen are like this: they put everything into the outward form,
without their love of form producing any sense of artistry: whatever any of them may say, Protestantism and Catholicism explain
the differences which render the spirit of the Frenchwoman so
superior to the reasoned, calculating love of her English counterpart. Protestantism doubts, examines and kills belief. It therefore
spells death to art and to love. Where Society commands, society
people must obey: but the passionate flee it instantly, for to them
it is intolerable. So you can understand what a blow it was to my
pride to discover that Lady Dudley could not do without Society
and that she was used to this British habit of switching from it to
love and back again. It was not a sacrifice imposed upon her by
Society; no, she showed herself quite naturally in two forms, each
hostile to the other: when she loved, she loved ecstatically; no
woman of any other country could compare with her; she was
worth an entire harem; but once the curtain had fallen on this en-
chanted scene, she wiped out all memory of it. She would respond
neither to a look nor to a smile; she was neither mistress nor slave,
but like an ambassadress, obliged to round her phrases and her

elbows; she would irk one by her calm, and outrage the heart by her decorum; she reduced love to a physical need, instead of elevating it to an ideal with her ardour. She expressed neither fear, nor regret, nor desire; but at a given time, her tenderness flared up like a fire suddenly lit and seemed to spit in the face of her reserve. Which of these two women was I to believe in? A million little pin-pricks made me aware of the immeasurable difference between Henriette and Arabelle. When Madame de Mortsauf left me for a moment, she seemed to tell the air to talk to me about her; the folds of her dress as she left a room spoke to my eyes, just as their billowing sound delighted my ear on her return; there would be infinite tenderness in the way she unfolded her eyelids when she looked down; her voice, that musical voice, was a perpetual caress; her conversation bore witness to unremitting thoughtfulness and she would always be herself; she did not split her spirit into two—one half ardent and the other icy; in short, Madame de Mortsauf kept her wit and the flower of her thought to express her feelings; she practised the coquetry of ideas with her children and with me.

But Arabelle did not use her wit to make life pleasant; nor did she use it for my benefit; it existed only by and for Society. She was purely mocking; she loved to bite and tear apart, not for any amusement, but to satisfy a whim. Madame de Mortsauf would have hidden her happiness from all eyes: Arabelle wished to show hers to all Paris and, by a hideous contortion, she remained within the boundaries of convention, even while parading with me in the Bois. This mixture of dignity and ostentation, of indifference and love, was a perpetual wound to my heart, which was both passionate and virginal, and as I could not pass from one temperature to another like this, my moods were affected. I would be throbbing with love just when she was resuming her conventional reserve. When I complained, not without great circumspection, she turned her triple-darted tongue on me, lacing the flamboyance of her passion with that barbed English wit I have endeavoured to describe to you. The moment she disagreed with me, she would take a delight in hurting my feelings and humiliating me. She handled me like putty. To remarks about the necessity to steer a middle course in all things, she would respond by caricaturing my ideas and pushing them to the ultimate extreme. When I reproved her for her attitude towards me, she would ask if I wanted her to kiss me before the whole of Paris, in the Boulevard des Italiens: she became so caught up with this notion that, knowing her taste for getting herself talked about I trembled lest she carry out her threat. Despite her genuine passion, I never sensed anything contemplative, saintly, or profound, as with Henriette; she was insatiable, like a stretch of sandy soil. Madame de Mortsauf was always composed, and could sense my mood from an inflexion or a glance, whereas the Marchioness was never moved by a look, a handclasp or a softly spoken word. There is more to come!—the happiness of the night before was of no account next day; no token of love ever gave her pause. She had such a great need of movement, noise and brilliance, that nothing, I imagine, could come up to her dreams in this respect, hence her furious efforts in love; in her exaggerated fancy, it was she who mattered, not I. That letter from Madame de Mortsauf—that light which still shone on my life, and which proved how the most virtuous of women can obey the moving genius of the Frenchwoman, by her perpetual vigilance, her ceaseless understanding of my fortunes—that letter must have shown you how closely Henriette followed my material interests, my political associations, my moral victories; with what ardour she embraced all the aspects of my life that were permitted to her. On all these points, Lady Dudley affected the reserve of a mere acquaintance. At no time did she enquire into my affairs, my fortune, my work, personal problems, friendships or enmities. Lavish with herself, without being generous, she did, when all's said, separate business and pleasure a little bit too much. Without having put it to the test, I knew that to spare me a moment's distress, Henriette would have gone to all lengths to get me something which she would not have lifted a finger to obtain for herself. In one of those misfortunes which are liable to attack the richest and most high-ranking man—and there is evidence enough of them in history!—I would have gone to Henriette for advice, but I would let them drag me to prison without saying a word to Lady Dudley.

So far, the contrast has been confined to sentiment, but the same was true of material things. In France, luxury is man's way of expressing himself, it is the manifestation of his ideas, of his special poetry; it reflects character and gives value to the most trivial attentions between lovers by spreading around us the radiance of the loved one's ever-present thoughtfulness. But this English luxury, whose subtleties I had found so seductive, was mechanical as well! Lady Dudley put nothing of herself into it. Merchants called, things were purchased. The countless, soothing attentions of Clochegourde were, in Lady Dudley's eyes, a matter for the domestic staff, each of whom had his own special duties. It was the task of the major-domo to choose the best footmen, the way one might choose horses. She had no feeling for her servants. The death of her most prized one would not have affected her: money would buy an equally skilled replacement for any one of them. As for her fellow-men, I never detected a tear of sympathy in her eyes for others' misfortune; in fact the naïveté of her egoism was positively funny. The crimson brocades of the great lady concealed a heart of bronze. The delicious alma who rolled on the carpets in the evenings, soon reconciled the young man to the hard, insensitive Englishwoman; and it was only by degrees that I discovered the stony soil on which I was wasting my seeds, and which would never yield a harvest. Madame de Mortsauf had immediately seen into her nature, on that one brief encounter: I remembered her ·prophetic words. Henriette had been right in everything: Arabelle's love was becoming intolerable to me. I have since noticed that most women who ride well have little tenderness. Like Amazons, they are one breast short and some corner of their heart, I do not know which, has grown hard.

At the moment when I was beginning to feel the weight of this yoke; when weariness was creeping over mind and body: when I realised how much blessedness true feeling can bring to physical love; when my heart was heavy with memories of Clochegourde as I breathed, despite the distance, the scent of its roses, the warmth of its terrace, and the song of its nightingales; at the hideous moment when I saw the torrent's stony bed through its now shallower waters; then it was that I was dealt a blow which I still feel even now, for at every hour it finds an echo. I was working in the King's apartments. His Majesty was due to leave at four o'clock. The Duc de Lenoncourt was on duty; as he came in, the King asked him for news of the Countess. I raised my head with a jerk that was altogether too revealing. The King, shocked by the gesture, threw me the look that always preceded the harsh reprimands he knew so well how to deliver.

"Sire, my poor daughter is dying," replied the Duke.

"Would His Majesty graciously grant me leave?" said I, with tears in my eyes, braving the storm which threatened to break.

"Fly, milord!" he answered, smiling at the epigram and sparing me a reprimand in favour of his wit.

More courtier than father, the Duke did not ask for leave, and got up into the royal carriage to accompany the King. I left without saying goodbye to Lady Dudley who by good luck was out. I wrote her a note saying I had been sent on a mission for the King. At La Croix-de-Berny I met His Majesty returning from Verrières. As he accepted a passing bouquet, which he let fall at his feet, the King threw me a look charged with that royal irony so shattering in its penetration, as if to say, "If you wish to make a name for yourself in politics, come back! Don't amuse yourself holding court with the dead!" The Duke gave me a mournful wave of the hand. The two stately carriages with their eight horses apiece, the gold braided colonels, the escort with its whirling dust passed rapidly by to the cry of "Long live the King". I had the impression that the Court had trampled on Madame de Mortsauf's body with the indifference nature shows for our catastrophes. Although an excellent man, the Duke would doubtless play a game of whist when the King had retired. As for the Duchess, she had long ago dealt her daughter the first blow. She was the first and only one to tell her about Lady Dudley.

My journey sped by like a dream, but it was the dream of a ruined gambler; I was in despair at having had no news. Had her Confessor stretched severity so far as to forbid me access to Clochegourde? I accused Madeleine, Jacques, the Abbé de Dominis, everyone, even Monsieur de Mortsauf. Beyond Tours, as I came out of the city by the Saint-Saveur bridges to join the poplar-lined road leading to Poncher, which I had so admired as I ran in search of my unknown lady long ago, I met Monsieur Origet. He guessed that I was going to Clochegourde; I guessed that he had just left there: we each stopped our carriage and alighted, I to ask for news, he to impart it.

"How is Madame de Mortsauf?" I asked.

"I doubt if you will see her alive," he replied. "She is dying a terrible death; she is dying of starvation. When she called me in last June, it was no longer in the power of medicine to combat the disease; she had the terrible symptoms which I daresay Monsieur de Mortsauf must have described to you, since he used to fancy he felt them. When I saw her, Madame de Mortsauf was not suffering from the temporary effects of a disturbance brought on by some inner conflict—a disturbance which a doctor can use to bring about an improved state of health: nor was it a sudden attack; that too can be cured. No, her illness had reached the point where skill is of no avail; it was the incurable outcome of grief, as surely as a mortal wound is the result of a dagger thrust. This state is brought about by the inactivity of an organ whose function is as necessary to life as that of the heart. Grief has done the dagger's work. Make no mistake! Madame de Mortsauf is dying of some unknown sorrow."

"Unknown!" I cried. "Are you sure her children have not been ill?"

"No," he said, with a meaning look, "and since she has been seriously ill, her husband has ceased to torment her. I can be of no further use. Monsieur Deslandes, at Azay, will suffice. There is no cure, and the pain is terrible. Imagine her, rich, young, beautiful, dying, wasted and aged with hunger—for she will die of hunger! For forty days, her stomach, which is as it were closed up, has rejected all food, however it is prepared."

Monsieur Origet pressed the hand I held out to him; he had begged for it almost, as he respectfully held out his own.

"Courage, Monsieur!" he said, raising his eyes to heaven. The phrase expressed compassion for the distress he thought we shared in equal measure. He little knew that his words were envenomed darts which pierced me to the heart. I climbed hurriedly back into my carriage, promising the coachman a substantial tip if I arrived in time.

Despite my impatience, I had the impression that we had covered the ground in no time at all, so absorbed was I in the bitter thoughts that came crowding in on my mind. Dying of grief, and her children in good health! So she was dying because of me! My threatening conscience pronounced one of those indictments which echo throughout all one's life, and sometimes beyond it. Oh, the weakness and impotence of human justice! It avenges only overt actions. Why shame and death for the murderer who kills with one blow, who comes upon you generously in your sleep and sends you to sleep for always, or who strikes unexpectedly and spares you a long death agony? Why happiness, why esteem for the murderer who pours gall, drop by drop into the soul, and saps the body's strength till it succumbs? So many murderers unpunished! So much indulgence for elegant vice! Such an acquittal for the death caused by mental torture! What avenging hand, I wonder, suddenly lifted the painted curtain that conceals Society? I had a vision of some of those victims, whom you know as well as I: Madame de Beauséant going away to Normandy to die, only a day or so before my departure! The Duchesse de Langeais compromised! Lady Brandon arriving in Touraine to die in that modest little house where Lady Dudley had spent two weeks, and killed in those terrible circumstances which you know only too well! Our age abounds in events like these. Who does not remember that poor girl who poisoned herself, overcome by the jealousy which was perhaps killing Madame de Mortsauf? Who has not shuddered at the fate of that enchanting girl who, like a flower stung by a gadfly, withered away after two years of marriage, victim of her own chaste ignorance, victim of the wretch whom Rouquerolles, Montriveau, de Marsay, shake by the hand because he falls in with their political plans? Who has not thrilled to the account of the last moments of that woman whom no entreaties could move and who refused ever to see her husband again, after she had so nobly paid his debts? Did not Madame d'Aiglemont come very near the grave, and but for my brother's care, would she be living now? Medical Science and Society are accomplices in these crimes, for which there are no Courts of Justice. Nobody, it seems, dies of grief; or despair; or love; or secret misery; or barren hopes, incessantly replanted and uprooted. The new nomenclature has ingenious terms to explain it all: gastritis; pericarditis; the countless ailments of women, whose names are spoken in whispers; all these serve as passport for the hearses escorted by hypocritical tears, which the lawyer's hand soon wipes away.

Is there, at the heart of this woe, some law of which we are unaware? Must the centenarian pitilessly strew the ground with dead and scorch the earth around him in order to survive, just as the millionaire assimilates the efforts of a host of little industries? Is there some strong, poisonous life force that feeds on sweet and gentle creatures? Oh God!—Did I belong to the tiger's breed? Remorse gripped my heart with its burning fingers and my cheeks were streaked with tears when I entered the avenue at Clochegourde, on a damp October morning when dead leaves were falling from the poplars planted under Henriette's orders, this avenue where not so long ago, she had waved her handkerchief as if to call me back! Was she still alive? Should I feel her two white hands on my bowed head? In a single moment I paid for all the pleasures Arabelle had given me and I found them costly indeed! I swore that I would never see her again, and I found myself hating England. Although Lady Dudley was but a variety of the species, I wrapped all Englishwomen in the mourning veils of my own condemnation. On entering Clochegourde, I received a further blow. I found Jacques, Madeleine and the Abbé de Dominis all kneeling at the foot of a wooden cross planted in the corner of a patch of land which had been fenced in with the property at the time when the gate was built and which neither the Count nor the Countess had wanted to do away with. I leapt from my carriage and went towards them, the tears streaming down my face, my heart stricken at the sight of those two children and that grave personage beseeching God. The old gamekeeper was there, too, standing a step or two away, bare-headed.

"Well, sir?" I said to the Abbé de Dominis, as I kissed Jacques and Madeleine on the brow. They glanced at me coldly and continued their prayers.

The Abbé stood up, and I took his arm and leaned on it.

"Is she still alive?" I asked.

He gave a sad, gentle nod of the head.

"Tell me, I implore you, in the name of Our Lord's Passion! Why are you praying at the foot of this cross? Why are you here and not with her? Why are the children out here on such a cold morning? Tell me everything, so I'll not do something unfortunate by not knowing."

"For some days now, Madame la Comtesse will only see her children at certain hours. Monsieur," he went on, after a pause, "perhaps you should wait an hour or so before seeing Madame de Mortsauf; she is greatly changed! But it would be as well to prepare her for your visit; you might cause her added suffering. As for death, it would be a blessing."

I clasped the hand of this holy man, whose voice and eyes caressed the wounds of others without chafing them.

"We are all praying for her," he continued, "for she, who is so saintly, so resigned, so ready for death, has for some days had a secret horror of it. She looks at those who are full of life with an expression tinged for the first time with the shadow of envy. Her terrors are aroused, I think, less by the horror of death than by some inner fever, by the faded flowers of her youth, which are fermenting as they wither. Yes, Satan is vying with Heaven for her pure soul. Madame de Mortsauf is fighting *her* battle on the Mount of Olives: she weeps at the falling of the white roses that crowned her as a bride. Wait a while. Do not show yourself immediately; you would bring the dazzle of the Court with you; she would see on your face the glow of worldly festivities and it would give renewed force to her griefs. Have pity on a weakness which God himself pardoned in the Son who became Man. Besides, what merit is there in conquering without an adversary? Let her confessor and myself, two old men whose ruins are not offensive to her sight, prepare her for this unhoped-for visit, and for the emotions which the Abbé Birotteau had insisted she renounce. But there is, in the things of this world, an invisible web of celestial causes, perceptible to the religious eye and, since you have come, perhaps you were led here by one of those celestial Stars that shine in the world of the spirit, and that point the way to the grave as well as to the Cradle."

And then he told me, with that unctuous eloquence which falls like dew upon the heart, that for six months the Countess had suffered more and more each day, despite Monsieur Origet's care. The doctor had been coming to Clochegourde every evening for two months in the hope of robbing death of its prey, for the Countess had cried to him to save her. "But to cure the body, we should have had to cure the heart!" cried the old doctor one day.

"With the progress of her illness, the words of this woman, once so gentle, have grown bitter," said the Abbé de Dominis. "She cries out to the earth to keep her here, instead of calling upon God to take her: then she repents of having murmured against the decrees of Heaven. This conflict is tearing her heart in two and the struggle between body and soul is horrible to see. Often, it is the body that triumphs. 'You are costing me dear!' she said to Madeleine and Jacques one day, as she pushed them away from her bedside. But a moment later, recalled to God when she saw me, she said these angelic words to Mademoiselle Madeleine: 'The happiness of others,' she said, 'becomes the joy of those who can no longer be happy.' And her tone was so heart-rending that I felt my eyes grow moist. She stumbles, it is true, but after each fall she raises herself higher towards heaven."

Smitten by the series of despatches which chance was sending me and which, in this great concert of misfortune, were heralding, with painful modulation, the solemn dead march, the great cry of expiring love, I cried:

"Do you believe this lovely broken lily will bloom again in Heaven?"

"When you left, she was still a flower," he replied, "but you will find her consumed and purified in the fire of pain, and untarnished as a diamond still hidden in the ashes. Yes, this shining spirit, this angelic star, will emerge in splendour from the clouds and enter the kingdom of light."

As I shook hands with this holy man, my heart heavy with gratitude, the Count's head, entirely white now, appeared in the doorway of the house. He hastened towards me, with a gesture of surprise.

"She was right! Here he is! 'Felix, Felix! Felix is coming!' That is what Madame de Mortsauf has just cried. My friend," he went on, with a look of wild terror, "death is here! Why could it not take an old fool like me, whom it has already half consumed?"

I walked towards the château, summoning my courage; but on the threshold of the long ante-chamber which led across the house from the veranda to the lawn, the Abbé Birotteau stopped me.

"Madame la Comtesse begs you not to go in yet," he said.

Glancing in, I saw servants running busily to and fro, dazed with grief and no doubt astonished at the orders Manette was passing on to them.

"What is going on?" asked the Count, in a panic at this sudden activity, as much through fear of the dread event, as from his innately anxious nature.

"A sick woman's whim," replied the Abbé. "Madame la Comtesse does not want to receive Monsieur le Vicomte in her present state. She is talking of dressing; why cross her?"

Manette went to fetch Madeleine and we saw her come out a moment or so after entering her mother's room. Then the five of us, Jacques and his father, the two abbés and myself, walked in silence over the lawn alongside the house and beyond it. I gazed at Montbazon and Azay, looking into the yellowing valley, whose mourning echoed as always, the feelings that stirred in me. Suddenly, I caught sight of the darling girl running hither and thither and picking the autumn flowers, doubtless to make posies of them. As I thought of all that this replica of my own love tokens signified, I felt a strange stirring in my entrails, my vision blurred, and I staggered. The two abbés, between whom I had been walking, carried me to the edge of a terrace where I remained for a while, quite broken, although I did not completely lose consciousness.

"Poor Felix," said the Count, "she forbade us to write and tell you; she knows how much you care for her!"

Although I was prepared to suffer, I had suddenly found myself defenceless against a mark of solicitude which summed up all my memories of happiness.

"Here it is," I mused, "here is that heath, all dried up like a skeleton, lit by a grey day, and graced by a solitary flowering shrub, that I never looked at, long ago, without a sinister and awestruck shudder, and which is a reflection of this lugubrious hour!"

Everything in this little château, once so animated, so alive, was desolate. Everything seemed to weep, everything spelt despair and neglect. Here half-raked avenues, work begun and abandoned; there, workmen standing about watching the house. Although they were harvesting in the vineyard, there was not a sound, not a voice to be heard. The vines seemed to be deserted, so deep was the silence. We walked like people whose pain rejects commonplace chatter, and listened to the Count, the only one of us who said anything. After the automatic phrases prompted by the unthinking love he felt for his wife, the Count was led, by his particular turn of mind, into complaining about the Countess. His wife, he said, had perpetually refused to look after herself or listen to his good advice; he had been the first to notice the signs of her illness, for he had studied them in himself, fought against them and cured himself unaided, without the help of anything but diet and the avoidance of all excitement. He could well have cured the Countess, too; but no husband could take on such a responsibility, especially when he has the misfortune to see his experience scorned at every turn. Despite his objections, the Countess had chosen Origet as her doctor. Origet, who had looked after him so incompetently in the past, was now killing his wife. If this illness was caused by an excess of grief, he had certainly had every reason to suffer from it himself, but what possible sorrows could his wife have? The Countess was happy; she had no troubles or difficulties! Their fortunes, thanks to his efforts and his good ideas, were flourishing; he allowed Madame de Mortsauf to rule Clochegourde; her children, well-behaved and in good health, gave her no reason for anxiety now; so what possible reason had she to grieve? And he began to argue and intersperse his outbursts of despair with insane accusations. Then, soon reminded, by some memory, of the admiration due to this noble creature, a few tears started from his eyes, that had so long been dry.

Madeleine came to tell me that her mother was ready to see me. The Abbé Birotteau followed me. The grave young girl stayed with her father, saying that the Countess wished to be alone with me; the presence of several people, she said, would be too tiring. The solemnity of that moment produced in me that sensation of inner warmth and outward chill which overcomes us in the great events of life. The Abbé Birotteau, one of those men whom God has marked out as his own, by investing them with simplicity and gentleness and granting them the gifts of patience and compassion, led me aside.

"Monsieur," he said, "I would like you to know that I have done all that is humanly possible to prevent this reunion. The salvation of this saintly woman made it necessary. I was thinking of her, not of you. Now that you are about to see again one to whose presence the angels should have barred your way, let me tell you now, that I shall be there too, to protect her against you and perhaps against herself. Respect her weakness. I am pleading for her, not as a priest, but as a humble friend whom you did not know you had and who wants to spare you remorse. Our beloved patient is literally dying of hunger and thirst. Since this morning, she has been in the throes of the feverish irritation which precedes that horrible death, and I cannot conceal from you how much she yearns for life. The shrieks of her rebellious flesh sink, unheard by others, into my heart, where they strike all too tender echoes; but we have undertaken this pious task, Monsieur de Dominis and I, in order to conceal the sight of such a spiritual death-agony from this noble family, who no longer recognise their morning and their evening star. Her husband, her children, her servants, all ask 'Where is she?', so greatly has she changed. When she sees you, her lamentations will spring to life again. Shed your worldly thoughts, forget the heart's vanities, be Heaven's messenger, not the earth's. Let this saint not die doubting, with words of despair on her lips."

I did not answer. My silence dismayed the poor confessor. I saw, heard, walked, and yet was no longer on the earth. The thought: "What has happened? In what state shall I find her, then, for them to take such precautions?" gave rise to fears all the more cruel for being ill defined; it was the sum total of all grief. We arrived at the door of her room, which the anxious confessor opened for me. And then I saw Henriette, in a white dress, seated on her little couch before the chimney-piece where our two vases stood, filled with flowers; and more flowers on the pedestal table by the window. From the look of stupefaction on the Abbé Birotteau's face at the sight of such improvised festivity and at the change in this room, so suddenly restored to its former state, I guessed that the dying woman had banished the unsightly paraphernalia that surrounds a sick-bed. She had spent her last feverish spurts of strength in decorating her disordered room, in order to receive in a manner deserving of the occasion the one she now loved more than anything in the world. Beneath a froth of lace, her emaciated face, greenish pale like budding magnolias, appeared like the first outlines of a beloved head, drawn in chalk on light brown canvas; but, to appreciate how deeply the vulture's claws sank into my heart, imagine the eyes in this sketch fully drawn and bright with life—hollow eyes, that shone with uncommon brilliance in a dead face. She no longer had that calm majesty which constant victory over suffering used to give her. Her brow, the only part of her countenance which might have kept its fine proportions, expressed the aggressive boldness of desire and smothered threats. Despite the waxen tones of her elongated face, inner fires glowed through like the liquid shimmer that blazes over the fields on a hot day. Her hollow temples, her sunken cheeks revealed the underlying structure of her face and the smile on her white lips had a vague resemblance to the grin of death. Her dress, folded across her breast, bore witness to the thinness of her once lovely bosom. The expression on her face was proof enough that she knew she had changed and was in despair at it. This was not my enchanting Henriette, nor the sublime and saintly Madame de Mortsauf: here was Bossuet's 'thing without a name', struggling against the void, propelled by hunger and thwarted desire in life's selfish struggle against death. I sat beside her, and took her hand to kiss it. It was dry and burning to the touch. She sensed my painful surprise from the very effort I made to conceal it. Her bloodless lips stretched over her famished teeth in one of those forced smiles beneath which we hide the irony of vengeance, the eagerness for pleasure, the soul's ecstasy and the rage of disappointment.

"Ah, this is death, my poor Felix," she said, "and you don't care for death! Hateful death, that every living creature, even the most intrepid lover, shudders at! This is where love ends. I knew it. Lady Dudley will never see you look amazed at the change in *her*! Oh, why did I so long for you, Felix? You have come at last and I am rewarding your devotion with the same hideous spectacle that drove the Comte de Rance into a monastery, long ago—I who wanted to stay tall and beautiful in your memory, to live there like an eternal lily! I am taking away all your illusions. True love never calculates. But don't run away. Stay with me. Monsieur Origet said I was much better this morning. I shall come back to life, I shall be born again each time you look at me. And when I have gained a little strength, when I can start to take a little nourishment, I shall be beautiful again. I am barely thirty-five, I have many fine years ahead of me. Happiness makes one younger, and I want to know happiness. I have enchanting plans, we shall leave *them* at Clochegourde and go to Italy together."

My eyes grew moist with tears and I turned towards the window as if to look at the flowers. The abbé Birotteau came hurriedly towards me and, leaning over the flowers, whispered in my ear:

"No tears!"

"Henriette, don't you love our dear valley any more?" I said, as an excuse for my abrupt move.

"Yes," she said, bringing her brow to my lips caressingly, "but without you it is fatal to me ... *without you darling*", she repeated, brushing my ear with her hot lips and dropping those three words, like three sighs, into it.

I was horrified by this wild caress, which enhanced the dread pronouncements of the two Abbés. My initial surprise was fading now: but although I was able to use my reason, my will was not strong enough to repress the nervous twitching that seized me during this scene. I listened without answering, or rather answered with a fixed smile and gestures of assent, so as to humour her, the way a mother does her child. Struck at first by the physical change, I saw now that this woman, once so sublimely stately, showed in her behaviour, her voice, her manner, her ideas and the look in her eyes, the naïve ignorance of a child, the artless grace, the restlessness, the profound indifference to anything but itself or what it wants, in fact all the weaknesses which make one want to protect a child. Is it so with all dying people? Do they all strip off social disguises, just as a child has not yet put them on? Or, now that she was on the brink of eternity, was the Countess, by spurning all human sentiments save love, proclaiming like Chloe, its sweet innocence?

"You are going to give me back my health, Felix, the way you did in the old days," she said, "and my valley will do me good again. How could I fail to eat what you put before me? You are such a good nurse! And you are so rich in strength and health that life is contagious when one is near you. My dear, prove to me that I cannot die, that I cannot die deceived! They think that thirst is my greatest torment. Oh, yes, I am thirsty, my dear! The sight of the Indre waters hurt me very much, but my heart feels a thirst more raging still. I was thirsty for you, darling," she went on in a stifled voice, taking my hands in her hot ones and drawing me to her to pour these words into my ear:

"My death struggle was not seeing you! Did you not tell me to live? I want to live. *I* want to go out riding, too! I want to know it all—Paris, gaiety, pleasure!" Oh, Natalie, this dreadful clamouring, this materialism of the cheated senses, which sounds flat at a distance, rang shrill in the ears of the old priest and myself. The accents of that magnificent voice described the conflicts of a lifetime, the anguish of true love deluded. The Countess rose with a gesture of impatience, like a child who wants a toy. When the Confessor saw his penitent thus, he fell to his knees, folded his hands and began to pray aloud.

"Yes, to live!" she said, pulling me to my feet and leaning against me. "To live by realities and not by lies! Everything in my life has been a lie; I have been adding them up these last few days—all those impostures! Can I be dying—I who have never lived, I who never went to meet my sweetheart on a heath?"

She stopped and listened a moment, as if she smelt something through the walls.

"Felix! The grape pickers are going to dinner, and I," she said, in a childish voice, "I am the mistress and *I* go hungry. It is the same with love; *those* girls are happy!"

"*Kyrie eleison!*" said the poor Abbé, who, hands folded, eyes turned to Heaven, was chanting litanies.

She threw her arms about my neck, kissed me wildly and held me close.

"You will never escape me again!" she said. "I want to be loved. I shall run wild, like Lady Dudley! I'll learn English, so I can call you 'My Dee'."

She gave a slight nod, as she used to do, long ago, when she left the room, to tell me that she would be back directly.

"We will dine together," she said, "I will go and tell Manette ..."

She was halted by sudden faintness, and I laid her, fully dressed, on her bed.

"You carried me like that once before," she said, opening her eyes.

She was very light, and extremely feverish. As I picked her up,

I felt her whole body burning hot. Monsieur Deslandes came in, and was surprised to see the room decked out in this way. But he understood everything when he saw me there.

"It is painful to die, Monsieur," she said, in a hoarse voice.

He sat down, felt his patient's pulse, rose abruptly, whispered something to the priest, and left the room. I followed him.

"What are you going to do?" I asked.

"Spare her a terrible death agony," he said. "Who would have believed she could muster so much strength? We cannot understand how she can stay alive, save by remembering the way she always lived. This is the forty-second day the Countess has not eaten, nor drunk nor slept."

Monsieur Deslandes sent for Manette. The Abbé Birotteau led me out into the gardens.

"Leave her to the doctor," he said to me. "With Manette's help, he will surround her bed with opium smoke. Well, you saw for yourself. Let us hope she is not conscious of these fits of insane frenzy!"

"No," said I, "she is no longer herself."

I tried to free myself from the force that kept me alive, a torment comparable to the one by which the Tartars punished adultery, by trapping one of the culprit's limbs in a vice, and leaving him a knife to cut it off with, if he did not want to starve to death; a terrible lesson for my soul, compelled as I was to cut off the finest part of it! My life had been a failure too! Despair aroused the strangest thoughts in me. At times I wanted to die with her, at others to shut myself up in la Meilleraye, where the Trappists had just established themselves. My dimmed eyes no longer saw the outside world. I gazed at the windows of Henriette's room where she lay suffering, and thought I glimpsed the light that shone there the night I pledged myself to her. Should I not have obeyed the simple life she had devised for me, and kept myself for her in my work? Had she not commanded me to become a great man, so as to keep me free from the base and unworthy passions to which, like all men, I had yielded? Was not chastity a sublime distinction I had been unable to hold? Love, as Arabelle conceived it, suddenly filled me with disgust. Just as I lifted my bent head, wondering where light and hope would spring from now on, and what point there would be

231

in living, the air was stirred by a faint sound. I turned to look at the terrace and saw Madeleine walking slowly up and down it, alone. While I was walking back towards the terrace, to ask the dear child the reason for that cold look she had given me at the foot of the little cross, she had taken a seat on the bench. She caught sight of me halfway, rose and made as though she had not seen me, so as not to be alone with me. She hurried pointedly away. She hated me. She was fleeing from her mother's murderer.

As I climbed up the steps to Clochegourde, I saw Madeleine, erect and motionless as a statue, listening to the sound of my footsteps. Jacques was sitting on a step, his attitude expressive of that same insensibility which had struck me when we were all walking together and which had given rise to thoughts that I stored, the way one does, in a corner of my mind, in order to take them up again at leisure and probe into them. I have noticed that all young people who carry death within them are insensitive to funerals. I tried to question this melancholy soul. Had Madeleine kept her thoughts to herself, or had she passed her hatred of me on to Jacques?

"You know," I said to him, to open the conversation, "that you have in me the most devoted brother."

"Your friendship is useless to me: I shall go the same way as my mother," he replied with a savage look of pain.

"Jacques," I cried, "you too?"

He coughed, and moved away. When he came back, he gave me a quick glimpse of his blood-stained handkerchief.

"Now do you see?" he said.

So each of them had his fatal secret. As I saw later, the brother and sister were running away from each other. With Henriette struck down, everything at Clochegourde was in ruins.

"Madame is sleeping," Manette came to tell us, happy in the knowledge that the Countess was not in pain.

At such dreadful moments, although each is aware of the inevitable end, true affections become frenzied and cling to trivial joys. Every minute is a century that one would like to fill with good deeds. One would like to lay the sufferers on a bed of roses; to take their pain upon oneself; one would like them not to know which breath is to be their last.

"Monsieur Deslandes made me remove the flowers; they were upsetting Madame's nerves," said Manette.

So the flowers had caused her delirium; she was not responsible: earthly loves, the rites of fertility, the caresses of plants had intoxicated her with their perfume and no doubt awakened thoughts of happy love which had been slumbering since youth.

"Come, Monsieur Felix," she said, "Come and see Madame; she is as beautiful as an angel."

I went back into the dying woman's room just as the setting sun was touching with gold the lacy turrets of Azay. All was serene and pure. A gentle light shone on the bed where Henriette lay, bathed in opium. The body was, as it were, annulled now; only the spirit reigned on that face, serene like a clear sky after the storm. Blanche and Henriette, those two sublime aspects of the same woman, appeared again, all the more beautiful as my memory, my thoughts, my imagination, lending their aid to nature, repaired the changes in each feature, where the triumphant spirit shone, in waves of light that mingled with those of her breathing. The two abbés were sitting by the bed. The Count remained standing, thunderstruck, as he saw death's banners flying over this adored creature. I sat where she had sat, on the couch, and we all four exchanged glances in which admiration for that celestial beauty mingled with tears of regret. The lights of thought announced God's return to one of His loveliest tabernacles. The Abbé de Dominis and I talked to each other in signs, exchanging thoughts that we both shared. Yes, the angels were watching over Henriette! Their swords were gleaming above that noble brow, revisited now by those august signs of virtue which had once created, as it were, a visible soul, with which other spirits in its sphere communed. The lines of her face were becoming purer; everything about her grew and became queenly beneath the invisible censers of her guardian seraphim. The green tinge of bodily pain gave place to the total whiteness, the cold, flat pallor of approaching death. Jacques and Madeleine came in; Madeleine sent a shiver through us all by the impulsive adoration with which she flung herself down beside the bed, folded her hands and uttered the sublime exclamation:

"At last, here is my mother!"

233

Jacques was smiling; he was sure that he would soon be following his mother.

"She is entering harbour," said the Abbé Birotteau.

The Abbé de Dominis looked at me as if to say:

"Did I not tell you that the star would rise again shining?"

Madeleine stayed with her eyes fixed upon her mother, breathing when she breathed, imitating her light breath, that last thread that linked her with life and which we followed, in terror, fearing with each new pull to see it break. Like an angel at the portals of the sanctuary, the young girl was calm and avid, prostrate and strong. The angelus sounded from the town belfry. The waves of soft air sent out the rippling chimes which told us that at this hour the whole Christian world was repeating the words the angel said to the woman who redeemed the sins of her sex. This evening the *Ave Maria* seemed like a salutation from Heaven. The prophecy was so clear and the event so close at hand that we burst into tears. The murmur of evening, the music of the breeze among the leaves, the last twitterings of the birds, the humming drone of insects, the chatter of water, the plaintive cry of the tree frog—the whole countryside was bidding farewell to the fairest lily of the valley and to her simple, pastoral life. This religious poetry, allied to all the poetry of nature, was so apt an expression of her swan-song that our sobs redoubled. Although the door of the room was open, so immersed were we in this awesome contemplation, aiming, as it were, to imprint the memory of it forever on our hearts, that we had not noticed the servants kneeling in a group outside, fervently praying. All these poor people, accustomed to hoping, believed that they could still save their mistress, and this all too clear omen had overwhelmed them. At a gesture from the Abbé Birotteau, the old gamekeeper went to fetch the curé of Saché. The doctor, standing beside the bed, calm as science as he held his patient's sleeping hand, had made a sign to the Confessor to tell him that this sleep was the last painless hour that remained to this redeemed angel. The moment had come to administer the last sacrament. At nine o'clock she awoke gently, looked at us with a wondering, but gentle eye, and we saw our idol again in all the beauty of her finest days.

"Mother, you are too beautiful to die! Life and health are coming back to you!" cried Madeleine.

"Dear child," she replied, smiling, "I shall live, I shall live in you."

The mother and children exchanged heart-rending embraces. Monsieur de Mortsauf kissed his wife reverently on the brow. The Countess saw me and flushed.

"Dear Felix," she said, "I believe this is the only grief I ever caused you. But forget anything I may have said to you, poor crazed thing that I was!"

She held out her hand. I took it and kissed it. Then, with her pure and gracious smile, she said:

"The way it used to be, Felix?"

We all went out and gathered in the drawing-room until the sick woman had made her last confession. I stood beside Madeleine. Good manners forbade her to shun me publicly; but, like her mother, she looked at no one, kept silent and never once glanced in my direction.

"Dear Madeleine," I whispered to her, "why are you angry with me? Why should there be hard feelings now? Everyone should forget their differences in the presence of death."

"I can almost hear what my mother must be saying now," she replied, with the expression on her face which Ingres found for his *Mère de Dieu*, that Virgin already sorrowing and preparing to protect the world where her Son is to perish.

"And you condemn me just when your Mother is absolving me—if indeed I am guilty?"

"*You*, always *you*!"

Her tone betrayed a hatred as calculated as a Corsican's, implacable as are the judgements of those who have not studied life and admit no excuse for errors committed against the laws of the heart. An hour went by in a deep silence.

The Abbé Birotteau returned after having heard the Countess' confession and we all went back into the room. Prompted by one of those ideas that occur to noble spirits, all sisters in intention, Henriette had had herself dressed in a long garment, which was to serve as a shroud. We found her sitting up, beautiful in her expiation and beautiful in her hopes: I saw in the hearth the black ashes of my letters, which had just been burned, a sacrifice she had not wanted to make, her Confessor told me, until the hour of her death. She smiled at us all with her old smile. Her eyes, moist with tears, announced a supreme enlightenment; she already glimpsed the celestial joys of the promised land.

"Dear Felix," she said, holding out her hand and pressing mine, "stay here. You must witness one of the last scenes of my life. It will not be the least painful of them, but you have an important part to play in it."

She made a sign; the door closed. At her invitation, the Count sat down; the Abbé Birotteau and I remained standing. Aided by Manette, the Countess rose, knelt before the Count and remained at his feet, quelling his protest. Then, when Manette had withdrawn, she lifted her head, which she laid on the knees of the astonished Count.

"Although I was a faithful wife to you," she said in a halting voice, "I may have failed in my duty sometimes. I have just prayed to God to give me the strength to ask your forgiveness for my faults. I may have brought to a friendship outside the family circle attentions more loving even, than those I owed you. It may have angered you to compare those attentions and those thoughts with the ones I devoted to you. I have felt a strong affection," she went on, in a low voice, "which no one, not even he who was the object of it, has ever fully known. Although I remained virtuous according to human laws, although I have always been a blameless wife to you, thoughts, voluntary or involuntary, have often crossed my heart and I am afraid, now, that I may have welcomed them too warmly. But as I have loved you very dearly; as I have always been your dutiful wife: as the clouds that passed beneath the sky did not affect its purity, you see me now, asking for your blessing with an unstained brow. I shall die without one bitter thought if I hear from your lips a gentle word for your Blanche, for the mother of your children—and if you forgive her all those things which she did not forgive herself until after the assurances of that tribunal which governs us all."

"Blanche, Blanche," cried the old man, tears starting from his eyes and falling on his wife's head, "do you want to see me die?"

He lifted her up to him with unaccustomed strength, kissed her chastely on the brow, and held her to him.

"Must I not ask *your* forgiveness?" he went on. "Have *I* not often been harsh? Are you not magnifying childish scruples?"

"Perhaps," she replied. "But, my dear, be indulgent to the weaknesses of the dying; set my mind at rest. When your time comes, you will remember that I left you with a blessing. Will you allow me to leave our friend here this token of a deep and sincere feeling?"

She pointed to a letter lying on the chimney-piece.

"He is my adopted son now, that is all. The heart, my dear Count, has its testaments to make. My last wishes give our dear Felix certain sacred tasks to do. I do not think I have asked too much of him. Show me that I have not asked too much of you either, by allowing me to bequeath him a few thoughts. I am still a woman," she said, bowing her head in gentle melancholy. "When I am forgiven, I shall ask you one last favour. Read this, but only after my death," she said, handing me the mysterious epistle.

The Count saw his wife turn pale. He picked her up and carried her to bed. We gathered round her.

"Felix," she said, "I may have done you some wrong too. I may often have caused you pain by allowing you to hope for joys before which I shrank; but is it not my steadfastness as a wife and mother that permits me to die reconciled with everyone, to-day? So you must forgive me too, you who so often accused me, and whose unjust reproaches warmed my heart!"

The Abbé Birotteau laid a finger on her lips. At this, the dying woman bent her head; weakness overcame her and she motioned with her hands for the priest and her children and servants to be shown in; then, she pointed, with an imperious finger, at the prostrate Count and the children who had just come in. The sight of that father, of whose secret insanity we alone knew, guardian now of those frail creatures, prompted her to a mute entreaty which fell on my heart like sacred fire.

Before receiving extreme unction, she asked forgiveness of her servants for having sometimes been short with them: she begged them for their prayers and commended each one personally to the Count; she generously admitted having, during this last month, voiced unchristian complaints which might have shocked her servants; she had repulsed her children and uttered unseemly sentiments, but she blamed her failure to submit to the will of God on her intolerable pain. Finally, she publicly thanked the Abbé Birotteau, with touching warmth, for having shown her the nothingness of worldly things. When she had finished speaking, the prayers began. Then the curé from Saché administered the last Sacrament. A few moments later, her breathing became difficult and a veil spread over her eyes. Then, she opened them wide, gave me one last look and died before our eyes, hearing perhaps the chorus of our sobs. As she drew her last breath, her last stab of pain in a life that had been one long pain, I felt a blow inside me that stunned all my faculties. The Count and I stayed by the deathbed all through the night, with the two abbés and the curé, keeping watch, by the light of the candles, over the dead woman as she lay on the mattress of her bed; calm now, there where she had suffered so much.

It was my first experience of death. I remained there the whole of that night with my eyes fastened on Henriette, spellbound by the pure expression which the abatement of all storms brings with it; by the whiteness of that face which I still endowed with its innumerable affections, but which no longer responded to my love. What majesty there was in that silence, in that coldness! How many thoughts did it not express! And what beauty in that absolute repose, what despotism in that immobility!—all the past is in it still, and the future is beginning to grow there. Oh, I loved her in death as much as I had loved her in life! At dawn, the Count went to bed; the three priests, tired out, fell asleep at that heavy hour so well known to those who keep watch. And so I was able, unseen by anyone, to kiss her brow with all the love she had never allowed me to express.

Two days later, on a fresh autumn morning, we accompanied the Countess to her last resting-place. She was carried by the old gamekeeper, the two Martineaus and Manette's husband. We went down by the path I had climbed so joyously the day I had found her again; we crossed the Indre valley and came to the little Saché graveyard, a humble village cemetery, situated behind the church, on the brow of a hill. In her Christian humility she had asked to be buried with a plain black wooden cross—like a poor peasant woman, she had said. When, halfway across the valley, I caught sight of the village church and the cemetery, I was seized with a convulsive shudder. Alas, we all have our Golgotha, where we leave our first thirty-three years, as the lance pierces our heart and the crown of thorns replaces the rosewreath on our head. That hill was to be my mount of expiation. We were followed by a huge crowd come to voice their regrets on behalf of that valley, where she had buried a host of good deeds beneath a cloak of silence. Manette, her confidante, had told how she would keep herself short of dresses in order to help the poor when her savings had run out. Naked children clothed, layettes sent, mothers helped, sacks of corn paid for at the millers' in winter for helpless old people, a cow given to some penniless family; in a word, the good deeds of the Christian, the mother and the chatelaine: then, dowries given when needed, to unite young lovers; compensation paid to young men fallen on hard times; the touching offerings of a loving woman who said "the happiness of others is the consolation of those who can no longer be happy". Such things, related during those three long nights of watching, had brought a multitude of people to the spot. I was walking with Jacques and the two abbés behind the coffin. According to local custom, neither Madeleine nor the Count was with us; they stayed at Clochegourde alone. Manette insisted upon coming.

"Poor Madame," I heard her say, through her sobs. "Poor Madame! She is happy at last!"

When the cortège left the mill road, there was a chorus of groans, mixed with the sound of weeping; one would almost have believed that the valley was mourning for its soul. The church was full of people. After the service, we went to the cemetery where she was to be buried beside the cross. When I heard the earth and the pebbles drop on to the coffin my courage left me, and I staggered. I asked the two Martineaus to steady me and they led me, half-dead, to the castle at Saché; the hosts courteously offered me hospitality, which I accepted. I confess I did not want to go back to Clochegourde and I shrank from going to Frapesle, from where I could see Henriette's house. Here, I was close to her. I stayed for several days in a room whose windows gave on to the peaceful, lonely vale I have described to you. It is a vast fold of land, bordered by oaks two centuries old, and after heavy rainfall, a torrent tumbles through it. The sight of it was conducive to the stern and solemn meditation to which I intended to devote myself. I had realised, during the day that followed that fateful night, how importunate my presence at Clochegourde would be. The Count had been violently shaken by Henriette's death, but he had been expecting that terrible event, and there was, at the back of his mind, an attitude very similar to indifference. I had noticed it on several occasions and, when the dying Countess had handed me that letter which I dared not open, when she spoke of her affection for me, this sombre man had not cast me the thunderous look I had expected from him.

He had attributed Henriette's words to the extreme delicacy of that conscience he knew to be so pure. This egotistical insensitiveness was natural to him. The minds of these two people were no more married than their bodies; they had never known that constant communication which keeps feeling alive; they had never exchanged either sorrows or delights, those strong bonds which leave countless raw spots when they are broken, because they touch every fibre of our being, because they have taken root deep in our hearts and caressed the soul that sanctioned all these clinging tendrils. Madeleine's hostility had closed Clochegourde to me. This hard young girl was not disposed to call a truce with hatred over her mother's coffin; and I should have been horribly ill at ease between the Count, who would have talked about himself, and the mistress of the house, who would have shown me invincible repugnance. To be there in such circumstances, in a place where once the very flowers caressed me, where the terrace steps were eloquent, where all my memories clothed the balconies, borders, balustrades and terraces, the trees and views with poetry; to be hated there, where everything had once loved me: it was a thought I could not bear. And so my mind was made up from the start. Alas! This was the epilogue to the most ardent love that ever blazed in a man's heart. In the eyes of strangers, my conduct would be condemned, but my conscience condoned it. This is how the finest feelings, the highest dramas of youth, come to an end. Nearly all of us set out in the morning as I did from Tours on my way to Clochegourde, grasping at the world, the heart craving for love. Then when our riches have been put through the crucible, when we have mingled with men and events, everything dwindles by imperceptible degrees; we find a very little gold among a lot of ashes. That is life, life as it really is: great hopes, and small realities. I meditated long and deeply about myself, wondering what I was going to do, now that the scythe had cut down all my flowers. I decided to fling myself into politics and science, on to the tortuous paths of ambition, to remove women from my life and to become a man of state, cold and without passions and remain faithful to the saint whom I had loved. My thoughts wandered on into the distance while my eyes stayed fixed on the magnificent tapestry of golden oaks, with their stark tips and roots of bronze; I asked myself whether Henriette's virtue had not been ignorance, whether I really was to blame for her death. I struggled with the encroaching tide of remorse. And finally, on a mild autumn afternoon, one of those last smiles from heaven, so lovely in Touraine, I read her letter, which, following her instructions, I was not to open until after her death. I leave you to imagine my feelings when I read it.

LETTER FROM MADAME DE MORTSAUF
TO THE
VICOMTE FELIX DE VANDENESSE:

Felix, friend whom I loved too well, I must now open my heart to you, less to show how much I love you, than to make you see how great are your obligations, by showing you the depth and the gravity of the wounds you have inflicted. Fortunately, just as I am falling, overcome by the hardships of the journey, exhausted by the blows received during the fight, the woman in me is dead; only the mother lives on. You will see, dear one, how you have been the prime cause of my ills. If earlier, I took a weak pleasure in offering myself to your blows, to-day I am dying, stricken by a final wound from you; but there is excessive bliss in feeling oneself broken by the man one loves. Soon pain will no doubt rob me of my strength; and so I must make use of the last glimmers of my intelligence to beg you once again to replace the heart you took away from my children. I would impose this burden on you as a command if I loved you less; but I prefer to let you take it of your own accord as a sign of your saintly repentance and also as a continuation of your love: was not our love always mixed with bouts of repentant thought and expiatory fears? And we love each other still, I know it. It was not your transgression in itself that proved so fatal, but the way I allowed it to re-echo deep inside of me. Did I not tell you that I was jealous, so jealous I could die of it? Well, I am dying. But console yourself: we have obeyed human laws. The Church, by one of its purest mouthpieces, told me that God would be indulgent to those who had immolated their natural inclinations to His commandments. Beloved, let me tell you it all, for I want you to know every one of my thoughts. What I shall confide to God in my last moments, you too must know—you the King of my heart, as He is King of Heaven. Until that ball given for the Duc d'Angoulême, the only one I ever attended, marriage had kept me in that ignorance which gives an angel's beauty to a maiden's soul. True, I was a mother, but love had crowned me with none of its lawful joys. How had I stayed like this? I do not know: nor do I know by what law everything in me changed in the space of a second. Do you still remember your kisses? They have dominated my life; ploughed furrows in my soul. The ardour of your blood awoke the ardour of my own; your youth penetrated into mine; your desires drove straight into my heart. When I rose so proudly, I was experiencing a sensation for which I know no terms in any language, for children have never yet found a word to express the marriage of their eyes with the light, nor the kiss of life upon their lips. Yes, it was sound filling its echo, light flung on to the shadows, movement given to the Universe; it was at least as swift as all those things; but far more beautiful, for it was the life of the soul! I realised that there existed in the world something unknown to me, a force lovelier than thought. It was all thoughts, all forces, a whole future of shared emotion. I no longer felt more than half a mother. As it fell on my heart, this lightning flash lit up desires that slumbered there unknown to me; I suddenly guessed what my aunt meant when she kissed me on the brow and cried "*Poor* Henriette!" When I returned to Clochegourde, the springtime, the first leaves, the scent of flowers, the pretty white clouds, the Indre, the sky, everything spoke a language I had never before understood, and it stirred in my soul something of the emotion you had quickened in my senses. If you have forgotten those terrible kisses, I myself have never been able to wipe them from my memory: I am dying of them! Yes, each time I saw you, you deepened the impression they had made; I was moved from head to foot at sight of you, at the very presentiment of your arrival. Neither time nor my firm will could master that imperious delight.

I found myself wondering "what must the *reality* of pleasure be?" The looks we exchanged, the respectful kisses you planted on my hands, my arm resting on yours, the loving accents in your voice, the slightest things stirred me so violently that nearly always a mist would float across my eyes, and the din of the rebellious senses filled my ears. Ah, if at those moments when I was doubly cold towards you, you had taken me in your arms, I should have died of happiness! There were times when I longed for you to make some violent move, but prayer speedily banished that evil thought. Your name on my children's lips filled my heart with warmer blood that straightway gave colour to my face and I would set traps for my poor Madeleine so as to make her say it, so fond was I of the bubbling turmoil of this sensation. How can I put it?—your very handwriting breathed a spell, I would gaze at your letters the way one studies a portrait. Yes, that very first day, you acquired a sort of fatal power over me, so you see, my dear, how infinite it became when I was able to see into your soul. What bliss flooded me then, at finding you so pure, so utterly true, gifted with such fine qualities, capable of such great things and already so tested by life! Man and child, so timid and so brave! What joy to find you consecrated, with me, by sufferings we had both shared! Ever since that evening when we confided in each other, losing you would have meant death; and it was pure selfishness that made me want you near. Monsieur de la Berge's realisation that I would die if you went away touched him deeply, for he could see into my heart. He esteemed that I was necessary to my children and the Count: he did not order me to forbid you my house, for I promised to remain pure in deed and pure in thought. "Thought is involuntary," he said,

243

"but once in the mind torture will not wring it from you."

"If I think," I told him, "all is lost. Save me from myself. Let him stay with me, and help me to stay pure!" The good-hearted old man, although most severe, was indulgent to so much good faith. "You can love him as one loves a son," he said, "by thinking of him as a husband for your daughter." I bravely accepted a lifetime of unhappiness in order not to lose you; and I welcomed my suffering with love when I saw that we were harnessed to the same yoke. Dear God, I stayed neutral and faithful to my husband, and did not let you take a single step into your rightful kingdom, Felix. The greatness of my passion reacted on my faculties; I regarded the torments Monsieur de Mortsauf inflicted on me as a sort of expiation and I bore them proudly as a way of violating my guilty inclinations.

In the early days, I was inclined to murmur; but when you came to me, I recovered some of my old gaiety again and Monsieur de Mortsauf reaped the benefit of it. Without that strength which you lent me, I should have succumbed long ago to the secret unhappiness of which I told you. If you played a large part in my wrongdoing, you were also largely responsible for the fact that I did my wifely duty. The same was true with regard to my children. I believed I had deprived them of something and I was afraid that I would never be able to do enough for them. My life, from that time on, became one continual pain which I grew to love. Feeling less of a mother, less of a virtuous woman, remorse came to lodge in my heart; and fearing lest I fail in my obligations, I grew ever more anxious to outdo them. And so, in order not to weaken, I put Madeleine between myself and you and I destined you for each other, erecting, by so doing, a barrier between us two. Flimsy barrier!—nothing could stifle the tremors you caused in me! Present or absent, you had the same power. I put Madeleine before Jacques because Madeleine was to be yours. But I did not yield you to my daughter without many struggles. I told myself that I was only twenty-eight when I met you, that you were nearly twenty-two. I bridged the gap between us, indulged in groundless hopes. Oh, Felix, I am confessing all this to you so as to spare you any remorse and perhaps too, to let you know that I was not insensible, that our love pangs were indeed cruelly equal and that Arabelle was in no way superior to me. I too was one of the daughters of that fallen race whom men love so. There was a moment when the struggle was so terrible, that I would weep all night long. My hair fell out. That very hair I gave to you! Do you remember Monsieur de Mortsauf's illness? Your generosity of soul then, far from ennobling mine, diminished me. Alas, all during that time, I wanted to give myself to you as a reward for so much heroism; but that fit of madness was shortlived. I laid it at God's feet during the Mass which you refused to attend. Jacques' illness and Madeleine's sufferings appeared to me as threats from God, who was powerfully drawing the lost sheep back into His fold. Then your quite natural love for this Englishwoman revealed to me secrets of which I was myself unaware. I loved you even more than I thought. Madeleine vanished. The constant emotions of my storm-tossed life, the efforts I made to master myself with no help other than that of religion, all this paved the way for the illness of which I am now dying. That terrible blow caused nervous attacks, which I kept strictly to myself. Death was the only solution I could see to this secret tragedy. There followed two months of uncontrolled jealousy and rage, between the news my mother gave me of your affair with Lady Dudley and your arrival here. I wanted to go to Paris, I was athirst for murder, I wanted that woman to die, I was insensitive to my children's caresses. Prayer, hitherto such a balm to me, had now no effect on my soul. Jealousy made the wide breach through which death entered. I remained, nevertheless, serene of brow. Yes, that period of constant struggle was a secret between God and me. When I realised, beyond all doubt, that I was loved as much as I myself loved you and that I had been betrayed by nature only and not in your thoughts, I wanted to live ... and it was too late. God had taken me under His protection, out of pity, no doubt, for a creature who was true to herself and true to Him, and whom pain had so often led to the doors of His temple. My beloved, God has judged me, Monsieur de Mortsauf will doubtless forgive me, but you—will you be merciful? Will you heed the voice that rises now, out of my grave? Will you repair the harm for which we are both equally guilty—you less than I, perhaps? You know what I want to ask you. Be to Monsieur de Mortsauf what a Sister of Mercy is to a sick man; listen to him; love him; for no one else will love him. Stand between him and his children the way I did. Your task will not last long. Jacques will soon leave home and go to live with his grandfather in Paris, and you have promised me that you would steer him through the pitfalls of that world. As for Madeleine, she will marry. Oh, may she come to care for you one day! She is all of myself and what is more, she is strong, she has that will power which I lacked, that energy one needs to be the helpmeet of a man whose career destines him to the tempests of political life; she is clever and far seeing. If fate brings you together, she will be happier than was her mother. By acquiring, in this way, the right to continue my work at Clochegourde, you would wipe out wrongs which have not been sufficiently atoned for, forgiven though they are in Heaven—and on earth too, for *He* is generous and will forgive me. I am, you see, as selfish as ever; but is not that proof of overrriding love? I want to be loved by you through my nearest and dearest. As I could not be yours, I bequeath you my thoughts and my duties! If you love me too much to obey me, if you do not want to marry Madeleine, take thought at least for my soul's repose and make Monsieur de Mortsauf as happy as he is capable of being.

Farewell, dear child of my heart. This is a completely conscious farewell, full of life still, the farewell of a soul where you poured joys too great, my darling, for you to need feel the least remorse for the catastrophe which they engendered; I use this word in the knowledge that you love me, for *I* am nearing the resting place, immolated to duty and—(and this makes me tremble) not without regret! God will know better than I if I practised His holy laws in their true spirit. I stumbled no doubt, often, but I did not fall and the most powerful excuse for my faults is the very greatness of the temptations that surrounded me. The Lord will see me as tremulous as if I had indeed succumbed. Again, farewell, a farewell similar to the one I said yesterday to our beautiful valley, in whose bosom I shall soon be resting—and where you will often come, won't you?

Henriette.

I sank into an abyss of thoughts as I saw the unsuspected depths of that life, lit now by this last flame. The clouds of my egoism blew away. So she had suffered just as much as I, more than I, for she had died of it! She fondly imagined that others must be excellently disposed towards her friend; she had been so blinded by her love that she had not suspected her daughter's hostility. This last token of her tenderness hurt me deeply. Poor Henriette, who wanted to give me Clochegourde and her daughter!

Natalie, since that everlastingly terrible day when I went, for the first time, into a cemetery and accompanied the mortal remains of my noble Henriette, whom you now know, the sun has been less warm and less bright, the night darker, my movements less swift, my thoughts more ponderous. There are people whom we bury in the ground, but there are others, more dearly cherished, who have our hearts for a shroud, and whose memory mingles daily in our heartbeats. We think of them the way we breathe, they live inside of us by the sweet law of a transmigration of souls native to love. A soul lives in my soul. When some good deed is done by me, when some fine word is spoken, it is this soul that speaks and acts. Anything that is good in me emanates from that grave, like the fragrance of a lily that hangs heavy on the air. Mockery, wickedness, everything you condemn in me comes from myself. Now, when a cloud dims my eyes and they speed heavenwards after having long been fixed upon the ground, when my lips are silent to your words and your attentions, do not ask me again "What are you thinking about?"

Dear Natalie, I stopped writing for a while: these memories had moved me too much. Now I must give you an account of the events that followed this catastrophe, events which require few words. When life consists of nothing else but actions and activity all is soon told. But when it has been lived in the highest regions of the soul, its history becomes diffuse. Henriette's letter shone in my eyes with a kind of hope. In the midst of that great shipwreck, I glimpsed an island where I could drop anchor. To live at Clochegourde with Madeleine and devote my life to her was a destiny where all the thoughts that troubled my soul found peace, but I would have to find out what Madeleine's true feelings were. I had

247

to say my farewells to the Count, so I went to Clochegourde to see him. I met him on the terrace. We strolled together for a long time. At first, he talked of the Countess, as a man who knew the extent of his loss and the full havoc it had wrought in his inner life. But, after the first cry of pain, he showed himself more concerned with the future than the present. He was afraid of his daughter, who, he said, lacked her mother's gentleness. Madeleine's strong character, in which a certain heroic something mingled with the graceful qualities of her mother, terrified this old man, used as he was to Henriette's tender affection, and aware now, of a will which nothing could bend. But what consoled him for this irreparable loss was the certainty that he would soon join his wife; the turmoil and the grief of these last few days had worsened his already ailing state, and revived his old sufferings. The battle soon to be fought between his authority as a father and that of his daughter who was now mistress of the house, would cause him to end his days in bitterness, for where he had been able to fight against his wife, he was perpetually forced to give in to his child. Besides, his son would be leaving home, his daughter would get married and what sort of son-in-law would he have? For all his talk of an early death, he felt he would be alone and friendless for a long time yet.

In that hour, when he talked exclusively about himself and asked for my friendship in the name of his wife, he put the last touches to the great figure of the 'Emigré', one of the most impressive types of our epoch. Although he was weak and broken in appearance, life yet gave signs that it would struggle on in him, precisely because of his sober habits and rural occupations. He is still alive as I write this.

Although Madeleine must have seen us walking along the terrace, she did not come down: she stepped out on to the verandah and into the house again three or four times, in order to show her contempt for me. I seized the moment when she came out on to the steps and begged the Count to go back to the house as I had something to say to Madeleine. I made the excuse that the Countess had made known one last wish to me; for this was my last chance of seeing her. The Count went to fetch her and left us together on the terrace.

"Dear Madeleine," I said, "since I must talk to you, should it not be here where your mother used to listen to me when the circumstances of her life, rather than anything in my behaviour, drew a murmur from her? I know what you are thinking, but are you not condemning me without knowing the facts? My life and my happiness are bound up with this place, you know that, and yet you are banishing me with the coldness that has replaced the sisterly affection you used to have for me. Death has drawn us even closer now, with the bonds of a mutual grief. Dear Madeleine—for whom I would this instant give my life without hope of reward, without your knowing it even, so much do we love the children of those who have protected us in life—you do not know the plans your adorable mother cherished during these last seven years. They would surely alter your feelings towards me; but I will have none of those advantages. All I beg of you is that you do not take away from me the right to come and breathe the air of this terrace and to wait until time has changed your ideas about life and the world. I would take infinite pains not to challenge them just now. You are not yourself and I respect your grief, for my own too, deprives me of the ability to view sanely the circumstances in which I now find myself. The saint who watches over us at this moment will applaud my reticence, when I beg you merely to keep an open mind about your feelings towards me. I love you too dearly, despite the aversion you are showing for me, to tell the Count of a plan which he would welcome with open arms. I want you to be free. Later, think of me and remember that you will never know anyone in the world better than you know me, that no man's heart will ever hold more true devotion —"

Until now, Madeleine had stood listening with downcast eyes, but she stopped me with a gesture.

"Monsieur," she said in a voice trembling with emotion, "I know what is at the back of your mind, but my feelings toward you will not change. I would rather fling myself into the Indre than marry you. I will not speak of myself, but if my mother's name still has some power over you, it is in her name that I beg you never to return to Clochegourde so long as I am here. The very sight of you upsets me in a way I cannot explain and which I shall never be able to overcome."

She bowed in a gesture full of dignity and walked back to

Clochegourde, without turning round, impassive as her mother had been on that one day, but pitiless. The divining eye of this young girl had seen, though tardily, right into her mother's heart, and her hatred for a man whom she considered baleful was perhaps increased by a certain remorse at her own unwitting connivance. A great gulf yawned between us. Madeleine loathed me, and did not want to ask herself whether I was the cause or the victim of all these misfortunes; perhaps she would have hated both her mother and me had we been happy. And so the whole lovely edifice of my happiness was destroyed. I alone was to know the whole life-story of this great, unknown woman, I alone held the secret of her feelings, I alone had explored the far reaches of her soul; neither mother, father, husband nor children had known her. Strange thought! I search through this heap of ashes and take pleasure in spreading them out before you; we can all find something of our most cherished experience there. How many other families have their Henriette! How many noble creatures leave this earth without having met the understanding biographer who would have sounded their heart and measured its depth! This is human life in all its truth: a mother often knows as little about her children as her children do of her; so it is with husbands, lovers, brothers! Did I know that one day, over my father's very coffin, I would go to court against Charles de Vandenesse, my own brother, to whose advancement I had contributed so much? Dear God, how many lessons the simplest story can teach! When Madeleine had disappeared through the French windows, I went back, sick at heart, to say my farewells to my hosts, and left for Paris, following the right bank of the Indre, the way I had come on my first visit to the valley. Sadly I passed through the pretty village of Pont-de-Ruan. Yet I was rich now; the world of politics smiled on me; I was no longer the weary pedestrian I had been in 1814. Then, my heart had been full of desire; now, my eyes were full of tears. Before, I wanted to fulfil my life; now, I felt it empty as a desert. I was young enough, I was twenty-nine, but my heart was already withered. A few years had sufficed to strip that landscape of its first splendour, and me of my taste for living. You will readily understand now, the emotion I felt when, on turning round, I saw Madeleine on the terrace.

Overpowered by a consuming sadness, I had quite forgotten the purpose of my journey. Lady Dudley was far from my thoughts and it was without realising it that I found myself in the courtyard of her house. The folly once committed, I was obliged to see it through. I was in the habit of using her house with an almost conjugal informality, and I went up the stairs, ruefully, thinking of all the tedious worries that breaking off our relationship would entail. If you have fully grasped the character of Lady Dudley, you will readily imagine my discomfiture when her major-domo ushered me, clad as I was in my travelling clothes, into the drawing-room, where I found her, elaborately dressed and surrounded by five people. Lord Dudley, one of the most eminent elder English statesmen, was standing before the fireplace, stiff, arrogant, icy, with the air of sardonic superciliousness he no doubt wore in the House of Lords. He smiled when he heard my name. Arabelle's two children, both extraordinarily like de Marsay (one of the old man's natural sons, who was also present, sitting beside Lady Dudley), were standing near their mother. When Arabelle saw me, she immediately assumed a haughty air and glared at my travelling cap, as though about to ask what business I had in her house. She took stock of me as she might have some country squire who was being presented to her. As for our intimacy, as for that life-long passion, those vows to die if I stopped loving her, as for that Armida-like phantasmagoria—all that had vanished like a dream. I had never taken her hand, I was a stranger, she did not know me. Despite the diplomatic *sang-froid* I was fast learning to display, I was taken aback, and anyone else in my place would have been the same. De Marsay smiled down at his shoes, which he was examining with singular interest. I took a quick decision. From any other woman I would have modestly accepted defeat. But outraged at seeing, alive and in good health, the heroine who had sworn to die for love, and who had mocked the one who died, I decided to meet insolence with insolence. She knew of the tragedy of Lady Brandon: to remind her of it was to plunge a dagger in her heart, although the weapon would be blunted there.

"Madame," I said, "you will forgive me for calling on you so unceremoniously when I tell you that I have come from Touraine and that Lady Brandon has given me an urgent message for you. I feared you might have left for Lancashire; but as you are staying in Paris, I shall await your orders and an indication of the time when you will condescend to receive me."

She gave a slight bow and I left. From that day to this, I have not met her except socially, when we exchange a friendly greeting and an occasional witticism. I talk to her of the inconsolable women of Lancashire and she talks to me of the Frenchwomen who give their stomach disorders the noble name of broken heart. Thanks to her good offices I have a deadly enemy in de Marsay, to whom she is greatly attached: and I, in my turn, put it about that she is wife to two generations. The shambles of my life was thus complete. I followed the plan I had interrupted during my stay at Saché. I threw myself into my work, made a study of science, literature and politics; I entered the diplomatic service on the accession of Charles X who abolished the post I had occupied under the late King.

From then on, I resolved never to bother my head about any woman, however beautiful, witty or loving she might be. The decision served me wonderfully well; I acquired an unbelievable peace of mind and enormous capacity for work, and I realised how much these women sap our lives, while fondly imagining they have paid for it all with one or two pretty speeches. But all my resolutions came to nothing: you know how and why. Dear Natalie, by telling you the story of my life as unreservedly and sincerely as I would tell it to myself; by telling you about feelings in which you had no part, I may have bruised some corner of your jealous and sensitive heart; but what would anger a vulgar woman will, I am certain, be yet one more reason for you to love me. For stricken and ailing spirits, the superior woman has a sublime role to play—the role of a Sister of Mercy who staunches wounds, that of a mother who forgives the child. Artists and great poets are not the only sufferers: men who live for their country, for the future of nations, widening the circle of their thoughts and passions, often create for themselves a cruel solitude. They need to feel at their side a pure and devoted love: believe me, they understand the greatness and the worth of it. To-morrow, I shall know whether I was wrong to love you.

TO MONSIEUR LE COMTE FELIX DE VANDENESSE

Dear Count,

You once received a letter from that poor Madame de Mort-sauf, a letter which, you say, was not unhelpful in determining your behaviour in society; a letter to which you owe your conspicuous success. Allow me to put the finishing touches to your education. I do beg you to break yourself of one detestable habit; do not follow the example of those widows who never stop talking about their first husbands and who are forever throwing in the face of the second the virtues of the dear departed. I am French, dear Count; I should like to marry the whole of the man I love and really could not see my way to marrying Madame de Mortsauf. After reading your story with the attention it deserves—and you know how deeply I am interested in you—it struck me that you must have bored Lady Dudley considerably by confronting her with Madame de Mortsauf's perfection, and hurt the Countess a great deal by distressing her with tales of the ingenuity of English loving. You have shown a certain lack of tact towards myself, poor creature, whose only merit is that she finds favour with you; you gave me to understand that I loved you neither like Henriette nor like Arabelle. I admit my imperfections, I know them well; but why bring them home to me so brutally? Do you know who it is I feel most sorry for? The fourth woman with whom you fall in love. She will have to fight against three people. I must also, in your interests as well as her own, warn you against the dangers of your remarkable memory. I give up the laborious privilege of loving you; it requires too many Anglican or Catholic virtues and I am not interested in fighting ghosts. The virtues of the Virgin of Clochegourde would drive the most self-confident woman to despair, and your intrepid Amazon damps the boldest desires for bliss. Try as she may, a woman has no hope of ever giving you joys equal to her ambition. Neither heart nor senses will ever triumph over your memories. You forget that we often go riding together. I have not been clever enough to warm the sun that was cooled by the death of your saintly Henriette; you would start shivering at my side. My friend—for you will always be my friend—take care never to embark upon such confidences again. They lay bare your disenchantment, discourage love and force a woman to distrust herself. The woman who, before opening her mouth or climbing into the saddle, asks herself if some celestial Henriette did make nobler conversation, if a horsewoman like Arabelle did not display more grace, that woman, make no mistake, will be shaky of limb and trembling of tongue. You have made me long to receive one or two of your intoxicating bouquets; but you no longer make any. There are likewise a host of things you no longer dare to do—thoughts and delights which can never come to life again. No woman, believe me, will care to rub elbows in your heart with the dead lady you keep locked inside it. You ask me to love you out of Christian charity. There are, I confess, an infinite number of things I can do out of charity, everything, in fact, save making love.

You are sometimes bored—and boring, and you term your sadness melancholy. Good! But you are insufferable and you cause cruel distress to the one who loves you. The saint's grave has too often stood between us. I have looked into my own nature, I know myself and I should not care to die as she did. If you wearied Lady Dudley, who is an extremely distinguished woman, I, who have not her furious desires, would, I am very much afraid, cool sooner even than she. Let us forgo love between us two, since you can no longer taste its joys save with the dead and let us remain friends, I insist on it. My dear Count! You had, for your first love, an adorable woman, a perfect mistress who gave thought to your future, who raised you to the peerage, who loved you ecstatically and who merely asked you to be faithful—and you made her die of grief! Why, I never heard of anything more monstrous! Of all the ardent and unhappy young men who hawk their ambitions through the Paris streets, where is the one who would not behave himself for ten years in order to win the half of the favours which you had not the wit to recognise? When one is loved as much as that, what more can one ask?

Poor woman, she had more than her share of suffering; and when you have mouthed a few sentimental phrases you think you have paid your debt to her coffin. That, no doubt, is the price that awaits my tenderness for you. No thank you, dear Count, I want no rivals on this side of the grave or beyond it. When one has crimes of this sort on one's conscience, the least one can do is keep quiet about it. I made a rash request. I acted in the essence of my role as woman, as daughter of Eve. Yours consisted in estimating the repercussions of your answer. You should have lied to me; I would have thanked you later on. Have you never understood the real strength of philanderers? Can you not see how generous it is of them to swear that they have never been in love before and that we are their first love?

Your project is unrealisable. To be both Madame de Mortsauf and Lady Dudley, why, my friend, is that not fusing fire and water? Do you know anything about women at all? They are what they are, they have the defects of their qualities. You met Lady Dudley too soon to be able to appreciate her; and the way you malign her strikes me as a kind of revenge for your wounded vanity. You understood Madame de Mortsauf too late and you punished the one for not being the other. So what will happen to me who am neither one nor t'other? I love you enough to have given a great deal of thought to your future, for I really am extremely fond of you. Your "Knight of the Woeful Countenance" look has always interested me deeply. I believed in the constancy of melancholy men; but I did not know that you had killed the loveliest and the most virtuous of women at your first step into the world. I then asked myself what course was open to you now. I have given a great deal of thought to this. I think, my friend, that you must marry some Mrs Shandy who will know nothing of love nor its passions, who will not bother her head about Lady Dudley or Madame de Mortsauf; who will be highly indifferent to those moments of boredom you call melancholy, during which you are as entertaining as a rainy Sunday, and who will be the excellent Sister of Mercy whom you demand. As for loving; trembling at a word; knowing how to wait for happiness; how to give it and receive it; how to feel the thousand and one storms of passion; how to espouse the little vanities of the woman whom you love; my dear Count, give up all hope of *that*. You have followed your good angel's advice about young women too well; you have avoided them so successfully that you know nothing about them at all. Madame de Mortsauf was right to set you at the top of the ladder straight away; every woman would have been against you and you would not have achieved anything at all. It is too late now to begin your studies, to learn to tell us the things we love to hear, to be great when occasion demands, to adore our triviality when we like to be trivial. We are not so shallow-witted as you think; when we are in love, we put the man of our choice before all else. Whatever shakes our faith in our superiority shakes the foundations of our love. By flattering us, you flatter yourselves. If you are anxious to remain in Society and to enjoy the company of women, take care to hide from them all that you have told me. They care neither to sow the blossoms of their love on rocks nor to waste their caresses in bandaging an ailing heart. Every woman would notice the drought in your heart and you would always be unhappy. Very few of them would be candid enough to tell you what I am telling you, or generous enough to leave you without rancour, while offering you their friendship, as is doing to-day the one who calls herself your devoted friend.

Natalie De Manerville.

Paris. October, 1835.

THE END.